The Brotherhood

Book One in the Eirensgarth Chronicles

Philip M. Smith

THE BROTHERHOOD
Copyright © 2018 by Philip Smith

For information contact :

1:5 Media Publishing Group
1150 Anderson Dr.
Paris, TN 38242
United States of America

Cover Design by Tom McGrath, http://www.spikedmcgrath.com/
Cover Graphic Design: Phil Smith
Contributing Editors: Rachel Speer, Morgan Crain, and Marissa Grammol
Copy Editor: Karin Salisbury

ISBN: 978-1-7335890-0-0

First Edition Paperback: Fed 9th, 2019

10 9 8 7 6 5 4 3 2 1

DEDICATION

I'd like to dedicate this book to Robert and Rachel Speer, without whose help and support, this book would have forever merely sucked up space on my Google Drive.

We are privileged in this life to have many friends, but truly blessed to have even half a dozen we can call family.

-P. Smith

PROLOGUE

*T*he sound of steel-heeled boots clicking on polished stone echoed down the corridor as the prince strode towards the throne room. Twenty-four guards stood steadfast at each of the twenty-four stone pillars lining the hallway. Each of the men snapped to attention as he passed, their chainmail jingling like the bells hung out at Winter Solstice. The prince scowled as an unkempt soldier tried to adjust his poorly wrapped turban mid-salute. Had he been in less of a hurry, Feridar might have had the guard flogged for this, but he had no time to waste. He marched towards the large set of doors at the end of the hallway. The massive beams of oak were riddled with iron studs in intricate designs and were held to the castle's stone walls with iron hinges nearly as long as a horse. The prince surged forward, his leather gloves creaking as he flexed and unflexed his hands in anxious annoyance.

The two guards standing on either side of the doorway straightened uncomfortably; one of them grasped the thick iron ring bolted to one of the doors. He heaved against the weight of the oak beams, and the prince strode into the throne room without breaking his pace. The door slammed shut with a cavernous boom echoing down the hallway behind him.

"Father!" he shouted, marching into the circular room with vaulted ceilings of carved granite. He made his way to the steps of the black-marble dais, his spurs continuing to jingle and echo through the room with each step. The stone gave the hall an almost dungeon-like appearance, save where the fast-fading light of sunset crept through the stained glass windows. When the Sharadhen Court was in session, this room would be filled with nearly three hundred governors of the various provinces ruled in the kingdom, but now it sat barren and brooding.

Feridar took the steps of the dais two at a time to join his father, the king, emperor, and Great Shahir of the Shauds. His father turned from his place at the table that stood beside his gilded throne. On the opposite side of the table from his father stood three middle-aged men dressed in the white robes and wearing brass helmets of the Shaud's mighty army.

"Feridar, welcome," the Shahir muttered, his tone as dry as desert sand. "We've been expecting you."

He returned his attention to the table as Feridar reached the top of the staircase. The Shahir wore robes of silk bound by a golden sash. His russet eyes surveyed the prince with contempt from beneath his scarlet turban, but he motioned for him to approach the table, his many gold rings clicking against each other.

"What is this about?" the prince snapped, ripping off the leather gloves and slapping them on the table. "I was in the middle of prepping for the tournament when your monkeys pulled me off the training field."

"So sorry to interrupt, Your Highness, but there is men's work to be done," one of the officers snipped. The Shahir turned his glare from the prince to the aide-de-camp.

"General Valhaura, you are not addressing your stable hand in this room. That is my son, and Prince Feridar will be granted every honor and courtesy you would owe me. Am I clear?"

"Apologies, Your Eminence, for my subordinate's misguided words," the second general, General Ducast, said smoothly, giving a sly, knowing look at Valhaura. "After all these months, the good general seems to have left his courtesy in the Wild."

The Shahir ignored him, choosing to look instead at the many parchments spread in front of him. Feridar looked down at the table to see a large map of the continent of Eirensgarth. It was a sorry looking collection of scribbled rivers, mountains, and cities. The only real details showed the Shauden Empire as it currently stood, stretching from their coastal capital of Telesan to the five outpost castles on their western borders. Beyond that, there were only a few scrawled territory names along the tributaries of the Great River. The nearly impregnable Ohlmar mountains bordered the northwest quadrant of the map, and within those mountains, a vast pocket of forest was labeled, simply, "The Wild."

"A trip well worth the time and insolence, Your Majesty, I assure you," the third officer, General Haife, piped up. The stocky man's jet black beard quivered with the tremble in his voice. "As I'm sure you'll agree."

"What of it, General? All you did was cut a road from Aschin to Franghal. Or do you need me to win that campaign for you too?" The prince smirked, looking to the farthest western outpost on the map. The small black dot represented six years of hard frontier fighting, but it was the shining achievement in the young prince's short military career. Aschin was his crown jewel, among over a dozen forts that dotted the empire's borderland holdings. A similar small dot to the northwest of the fortress was scribbled in iron gall ink, marking the latest acquisition, thanks to a long six-month campaign. On the outside, Franghall was only a simple mining village at the rim of the Ohlmars. Although Feridar knew his father's interests in the mines lay deeper than diamonds, Franghal did give the empire another source of revenue to fund further campaigns across the continent.

"Not at all, My Prince," Ducast muttered. "There is now a clear road to the northlands cut through the mountain forests."

"Wonderful," the prince said dryly. "And you couldn't send me a written report for that?"

"My son, it is not significant because of what they did," the Shahir said coyly. "It is significant because of what they found."

The king pulled something small and metallic out of the pocket of his royal robes and tossed it onto the table. The prince felt a sudden prick in his chest, like a hot knife had been slipped between his ribs and was searing the bottom of his heart. Feridar stared down at a large gold signet ring that landed in the middle of the map and an image of a face flashed through his mind; a face he hadn't seen in almost twenty years. The circlet was carved to look like a coiled serpent, with the head resting atop Feridar's own heraldic crest. An anger he had been caging for almost two decades came rushing back, coursing through his veins like liquid fire. His temples throbbed like the echoing drumbeat of his now racing pulse. His knuckles cracked against the table where he'd been leaning on them; an identical ring on his own finger pressed deep into his skin. Feridar snapped his gaze to General Valhaura, his cold brown eyes flashing.

"Where did you get this?" he demanded, maintaining his composure with great effort.

"We took it off a travelling merchant our pickets detained four months ago," General Valhaura said, annoyance seeping into his words. "As soon we finished construction on the road, we pulled three divisions out and headed straight back to Telesan."

"You fools!" the prince screamed, sweeping his arms across the table and scattering maps towards the three generals in a shower of parchment. The Shahir didn't move, his sly expression betraying what might have been perceived as a hint of amusement. The generals were shocked at this venomous detonation of rage.

"One thousand apologies, Your Highness," the bearded general blubbered. "We came as soon as it was prudent to do so!"

"Your prudence is a poor excuse for incompetence, General Haife!" the prince bellowed, the thunder of his voice echoing off the smooth marble arches that made up the massive throne room. "Now, by the gods, he could be anywhere, and you lost what could have been a warm trail!"

"He has been gone for over seventeen years, my lord," General Valhaura snapped, indignant. "No trail would have been hot or even warm had we dropped everything and left our post to chase after some no-account bastard who made off with your-"

He looked like he was about to say more, but General Valhaura's face quite suddenly went from red to a sickly shade of white. He stuttered, trying to speak, but the words were failing to come together comprehensibly. He grasped the table for support as he choked on his own tongue, straining to get breath into his lungs. The other generals leaped back from the table, expressions of confusion and horror on their faces. Feridar's eyes whipped back to his father; a cruel sneer curled the emperor's thin lip. His left hand rested on his side while his wrist twisted in a circular motion, fingers clenching and relaxing in a smooth rhythm. General Valhaura turned a deep shade of purple; his eyes were bloodshot and panicked.

"General Valhaura," the Shahir hissed through clenched teeth. "How dare you address my heir in such a manner. It would appear the Wild has made a wild dog of you." He clicked his tongue with mocking disapproval, then shoved his hand high with a quick thrust. General Valhaura shot backwards and upwards as if moved by an invisible puppeteer. The Shahir bent his ringed fingers like talons gripping prey. Valhaura kicked and thrashed, gasping for breath and trying to scream.

"I thought I had been quite clear, General," the Shahir bellowed, his eyes flashing as he raised Valhaura even higher, almost to the top of the vaulted ceiling, "and unfortunately, I hate repeating myself!"

General Valhaura forced out a violent scream as the Shahir clenched his fist. The other men could hear the sounds of bone cracking as the general crumpled like he was being crushed in a vise. His helmet slid off his grey-streaked hair and fell to the floor below with a deafening clang. The Shahir ripped his fist back and thrust it forward, sending the general's broken body hurling towards one of the windows to the far left of the throne room. The old soldier shouted in agony as his body went smashing through the glass and fell a hundred feet to the ground below.

Generals Haife and Ducast cringed as the sound of an armor hitting the stone courtyard echoed into the room seconds later. They stared in disbelief at the Shahir, wide-eyed with pure terror. Feridar smirked. It was no secret to the prince that his father disdained the very sight of him, but these men were still less than noblemen, let alone equals to the royal family. The Shahir was not one to let such blatant disregard for status go by unchecked.

"Now," the Shahir heaved, straightening his crimson turban and stooping to pick up the signet ring from where it had landed during Feridar's outburst. "Does anyone have anything constructive to add to the discussion?"

Both generals gulped.

"I do hope that isn't a no, gentlemen."

"With your permission, Sire," Ducast said in a quivering voice, picking up the map off the floor with shaking hands. He spread it out on the table before them, the parchment sticking slightly to his now sweaty palms. "We picked up the trader here."

Ducast pointed to a spot not too far west of Franghal, in the dense forest lands labeled "the Wild." Feridar snarled.

"You found him on the edge of the Wild and somehow that is helpful? There's hundreds of miles in that barbaric forest. Surely that isn't all you're bring us to work with?"

"H-h-he said a chieftain traded him for a supply of linen and parchment for his wife," Haife stammered, glancing a fearful look at his king. "The merchant said th-th-that was about a year ago, but he swore he got it while visiting a village in the northlands o-o-of the Wild!"

"Did you happen to find out what this chieftain looked like?"

"Eh...well, not exactly...no, Your Highness," Haife muttered. The Shahir raised an eyebrow at the commander.

"Wait! My lord, he didn't say what the chieftain looked like but he did say he was missing a finger!" Ducast assured.

The Shahir's other eyebrow went up. "A missing finger, you say?"

"Indeed."

"How interesting," the Shahir muttered, fidgeting with the signet ring on his own hand with his thumb. "And did you think to fulfill the other part of your mission, general?"

"Yes, Great Shahir."

Haife looked to Ducast, who took a small bag from a clip on his belt, handing it to Feridar. The prince opened the pouch and pulled out a small glass vial. He held it up to the last remaining light of the sun fast sinking in the eastern sky over the edge of the Great Sea. Small clumps of brown, heavy earth jittered about inside as he shook the vial. The word "Franghal" was scribbled on a brown paper label glued to the glass.

"Well done, General," the Shahir praised, rubbing his hands together in delight. "I think we have what we need now to proceed with an effective strategy."

"Yes, my Shahir," both generals said in unison, bowing.

"Well, we have quite a bit of work to do, then," the king said, ascending the marble steps to his throne. The ruler's chair sat tall and wide, its stone seat carved from black marble and covered from top to bottom in flowing arabesque palmettes inlaid with gold. A pile of elegant purple pillows embroidered with gold and silver threads cushioned the cold stone. The old king sat down, poised like one of his queen's cats. "Go. Assemble your divisions and prepare General Valhaura's former command. Be ready to move out in three days."

"Yes, my Shahir," they both said again in chorus. The pair snapped to attention, bowed, and exited the throne room without another word. As soon as the door shut, Feridar whirled to face his father's throne.

"His wife?" Feridar bellowed. "So they did both escape alive!"

"It would appear so, my son," the Shahir said, eyeing the signet ring the generals had brought him.

"Then what are we waiting for!? Let me go drive him to his knees and bring him back!"

"The divisions must be rested and re-equipped," the Shahir sighed, waving his hand.

"But we're wasting—"

"We waste nothing, you impulsive little urchin," the Shahir snapped, taking the prince aback momentarily. Feridar glared at his father, knowing full well there was no love lost between them.

"A chieftain is not a lifestyle indicative of a man still on the run," the king said, stroking his beard. "Ala'haran must feel quite untouchable if he's settled down in the Wild. And if he's missing his finger..."

The Shahir held the ring in his palm and pondered over it. He closed his eyes and concentrated, his forehead furrowed in deep meditation. Slowly, the ring lifted out of his palm, spinning in midair as the Shahir summoned all his energy into mumbling unintelligible incantations.

As he spoke, the wind kicked up through the shattered window, blowing out the torches. The blue twilight darkness enveloped them as the ring began to glow bright red, hovering inches from the Shahir's hand. The ring sprang down the dais and hit the floor of the throne room without a single bounce. Wisps of red smoke shot out of the signet and swirled around the room, beginning to take shapes. The fog formed a tall, broad-shouldered man with long braided hair. A wild beard under high cheekbones defined his jawline. Feridar balled his fists at his sides when he recognized the man he hated more than any other being on this earth.

A second shape began to form beside him, and another till an entire scene was laid out before them in crimson smoke. The Shahir continued muttering incantations as he surveyed the scene, taking in every detail, including the three female forms that took shape beside the man. The taller of the three held his hand; the other two stood beside the first. A village made of the crimson mist surrounded them. Behind the entire scene stood two peaks of a mountain range, the two moons of the world fast rising from between them.

"So, Ala'haran. A family? Isn't that sweet." The Shahir looked intently on the scene and stroked his narrow beard.

Feridar glared at the figures with a hatred burning hot as a dragon's blood. "He's got to still have it," he hissed.

The Shahir laughed sharply, and the entire scene fell to the floor, dissipating in a fog of smoky red mist that left them standing in the cold blue of an unlit throne room.

"Indeed. So the only question left is: are you ready to take your revenge?"

Feridar could have cracked a walnut in his jaw.

"Don't patronize me, Father," the prince growled. "This isn't about me. It's never been about me. The moment you have the final page of the book back in your hands, you will have forgotten all about me and Ala'haran."

"And yet you'll march Valhaura's former division into the Wild without hesitation," the Shahir said with a wicked smile.

"Ala'haran is in a village in the southern edge of the Ohlmar mountains. Look for where the moons rise from between two tall peaks. There you will find your revenge waiting for you."

"Then I'm off to win you yet another victory, my lord," Feridar muttered, bowing slightly. Without another word, the prince turned and stomped back out of the throne room. He strode past a line of newly-adjusted turbans as he marched down the hallway and made for his chambers.

The path to the east wing of the palace took him down winding corridors and through open chambers where members of court stood about discussing the politics and gossip of the empire. As he passed, they ceased their whisperings and bent low to the ground, muttering platitudes. He paid them no mind; as he stomped towards the staircase that led to his chambers, a swelling of triumph began to bloom in his chest. Not even his father's enduring disdain for his existence and his accomplishments could weigh him down. At last, after over eighteen years of fruitless searching, he had Ala'haran within his grasp.

The prince took the winding tower steps two at a time, his heels scuffing in the dust as he leapt up the granite staircase. He burst through the gilded door and into the domed chamber he occasionally called his home when he wasn't campaigning or taking residence in his castle at Aschin. Feridar now had an excuse to leave behind a king who had no use for him and a father who held no love for him.

Feridar opened his campaign chest and threw in maps, charts, and other such things from his writing desk. A collection of servants scuttled in behind him, their bald and tattooed heads bowed as they entered.

"How may we serve you, Prince?" a mousy female voice chirped. Feridar gestured to the giant closet where ranks of armor, clothes, and boots stood at attention.

"Gather my belongings and have them put in a royal wagon."

"Shall we pack the blue or yellow marquee for the tournament?" the young woman peeped.

"Neither. Pack my campaign armor. Not the tournament set."

"You're not attending the tournament, sire?" another slave asked. This man was old enough to be Feridar's grandfather; his white mustache trailed towards the ground.

"No, Malacath," the prince smiled. "I'm heading back to Aschin. I know where Ala'haran is now."

The slave's eyes widened as he ushered the other servants to continue packing the prince's valuables. He scuttled over to Freidar's side and bent his head low as his voice became a whisper.

"My lord, can it be so? And does...the creature...does she still live? How can this be?"

"Ala'haran appears to have cut off his brand, so until now we had no idea where to begin tracking him," the prince growled. "But both he and the creature still live. And now that I know where, I will make them both suffer for their crimes against the empire."

"Their crimes against the empire? Or against you, my lord?"

The prince snarled at the old man, who kept his eyes downcast.

"If you had not bounced me on your knee as a boy, Malacath, I would have you thrown from that balcony," the prince growled. Malacath nodded his head.

"Understood, sire," the old slave muttered, backing away in submission. Feridar snatched up his sword belt and clipped the scimitar to the embossed leather. He crossed over to the veranda on the far side of the room.

The cool breeze of the sea swept through the balcony overlooking the great harbor of Telhesan. The sun had already disappeared beyond the eastern sky. The two moons, Tavian and Suntra, rose high in the west and cast two shimmering orbs across the surface of the vast ocean. The tower faced northeast, the circular city sprawling out before him. The desert sands to the north glowed a creamy blue in the light from the moons.

Most of the Shauden people took great pride in their city; the Jewel of the Empire. But Feridar chose instead to cross the balcony and gaze down at the palace courtyard. He could see the men scurrying about the barracks and stables, packing the carts and loading up the horses for the long journey ahead. Feridar relished in that sight more than a thousand moons casting light upon the sea. The frontier was where he belonged; the battlefield was his home, not Telesan.

If he had believed the gods had any real power, now would have been an ideal time to pray. Feridar believed in one thing: the might of his own saber, limited only by his own ambition. He smirked as he saw the columns of men being formed and set before the quartermaster's from each battalion for roll-call and equipment checks. The pagans in the Wild wouldn't stand a chance, even if the "Creator" they worshipped was real. No deity could stand up against such an army; the last two hundred years of Shauden dominance were a testament to that.

"Fool," Feridar muttered, twisting his own signet ring around the smallest finger on his left hand. He pulled it off and glanced at the scarred tissue beneath where the ring sat. Ala'haran had been smart to cut off his brand. Luckily the renegade hadn't known the ring did more than brand its wearer; it could also recall scenes from where it had been. It was a lucky break for the prince, and he trusted it would be a fatal one for his adversary.

The prince returned his ring to his finger and passed through his room to head downstairs once again. His long strides carried him to the kitchens which led out to the royal stables in the rear palace courtyard. As he exited the kitchen doors, he almost ran into a young man only a few years younger than himself, who was dragging an even younger male back into the castle by the collar of a beautifully tailored shirt.

"Watch it!" Feridar barked as the first young man bumped into his chest.

"Feridar, where you off to? It's late!" The offender laughed, taking a giant bite out of an apple as he leaned against the doorway, blocking Feridar's path. He was only a few inches shorter than Feridar, dressed in a simple linen shirt and buff breeches tucked into a pair of immaculate riding boots, which were now speckled with dust. His tousled black hair and close cut beard gave an interesting contrast to the youthful nature of his face. His brown eyes searched Feridar's face.

"Move, Tybahaz," Feridar growled. "Don't you have better things to do like charm another milkmaid?"

"She was a scullery maid, big brother," Tybahaz corrected. "And if you had seen the princess Father tried to pass off on me with that envoy from the Carellian Islands, you would have run for the scullery as well!"

"Quite," Feridar muttered. He glanced from Tybahaz to the boy his half-brother was dragging by the collar, and his glare deepened.

"What is wrong with Jaiden?"

"Just caught him doodling behind the livery," Tybahaz laughed, giving the teenager a ruffle of the hair. "Skipped out on his fencing lessons this evening again, so Master Alsaibeh sent me looking for him."

Feridar grabbed the teenager by the scruff of his neck and pushed him back outside and against the palace's coral-colored granite wall. The lad kept his eyes shut tight, refusing to look at his older half-brother.

"You call yourself the son of the Shahir!?" Feridar snapped, throwing the younger prince to the ground. Jaiden stumbled backwards, a notebook he'd been carrying hit the dusty ground and papers scattered everywhere. Feridar picked up a few of the charcoal sketches depicting horses and soldiers. Though he could not deny the sketches were accomplished, his anger and frustration at his youngest half-brother would not let him consider complementing the seventeen-year-old.

"You are a Prince of the Shauds!" he spat, crumpling the papers in his fist. "You were born to ride horses into battle, not sit on your shanks and draw them!"

"I was just—"

"You were just ignoring your obligations and playing like a little school girl!" Feridar shouted, throwing the wad of crumpled papers into the dirt. They blew away like tumbleweeds in the desert. The younger prince looked up at his brother with fear in his blue eyes.

"Get up," Feridar commanded. The boy scrambled to his feet, his gaze downcast and hidden in a shaggy mess of light brown hair.

"Get to the armory and maybe give some heed to the teachings of Master Alsaibeh. How can I trust you to carry a sword for me in battle one day if I can't even trust that you'll be where you're supposed to be?"

He held up the charcoal pencil that had fallen out of the notebook and pushed it against Jaiden's nose.

"You can't win a battle with one of these."

Feridar drew his scimitar and placed it to the boy prince's throat.

"You have to know how to use one of these."

The crown prince shoved Jaiden back through the door into Tybahaz's arms. Tybahaz looked annoyed but said nothing as he brushed the dirt off Jaiden's back and pushed him into the kitchen.

"Where is Ghaze?" Feridar demanded. Tybahaz shrugged.

"Probably in the library like he always is."

"Send him to the livery," Feridar demanded. Tybahaz rolled his eyes at being ordered about like a house slave, but nodded as he stepped back inside the palace kitchens. Feridar sniffed indignantly and made his way past the far side of the courtyard to the livery. He dismissed the two stable boys with a gruff wave of his hand as he entered the columned archway that led into the stables built into the courtyard wall.

The livery had over fifty large stalls and three separate tack rooms for use by the royal family. In his youth, this was one of the few places Feridar genuinely loved to be in Telesan. The smell of the beasts mingled with the scent of sweet, freshly-cut hay the slaves hauled in daily. The leather in the tack rooms reminded him of the countless tournaments he'd fought in his brief twenty-eight years. With each victory, his glory and ego grew, yet for all his trophies and victory banners, his father still looked at him like a second-choice son and heir.

Feridar walked over to the stall of his favorite war horse. The beast stood eighteen hands high, with a silky charcoal-grey coat fading into black feathering on large, heavy hooves. His mane was the same dark ebony color as his feathering, braided the full length of his hefty neck. He was a barbarian breed. The southern horses were one of the few things the prince did not despise about the lesser peasant kingdoms they had conquered over the last decade.

"What say you, Calif?" the prince said softly, offering the great war horse a sack of oats. The horses in the next two stalls whinnied in jealousy, but Calif paid them no mind as he buried his bulbous muzzle into the treat. The prince smiled for a moment. He began brushing his steed with deft strokes along the back of his high withers and down past the creature's loin. The minutes rolled by, and Feridar lost himself in the smooth, uncomplicated motions of the task at hand, the flickering lantern light teasing the shadows in the marble stall.

The sound of a throat being cleared pulled Feridar from his meditation. He looked up to see another young man closer to his age standing in the doorway of the stables. He had a shaved head tattooed with snakes and dragons intertwining in knotted patterns, his dark eyebrows hiding deep set brown eyes. The man was wearing the loose-fitting robes of a cleric with a pair of expensive magnified reading spectacles perched atop his thin nose. He was shorter than Feridar by almost a full hand's width, but he had a sharp, keen look about him that was enough to intimidate the brawniest of officers in the Army, regular and irregular alike.

"You asked to see me?" the young man queried in a higher-pitched voice than one might expect, yet every word was measured and precise.

"Yes, Ghaze. I need to ask you about the Branding Spells," Feridar grunted, pulling the loose hair from Calif's brush and tossing it on the floor.

"A favor for information." Ghaze demanded. Feridar almost smiled as he tossed a thick wool blanket on Calif's back. Out of all four of his brothers, Ghaze was his only full brother and the only one he did not loathe. As the second eldest of the Shahir's palace-born princes, Ghaze was as intellectual as Feridar was militant. He had studied the dark arts and barbarian's magic almost as well as his father, and had read almost every book in the vast library of the palace.

"Name it," Feridar said, pulling his travel saddle out of the tack room and setting it atop the saddle blanket.

"To be determined. But don't worry, it won't be above your mental faculties."

The crowned prince snorted in disgust.

"Fine. A favor. When I get back."

"Back?"

"We're leaving tomorrow for the Wild."

"So soon? I hadn't heard of any impending campaigns at court."

"It just came up," Feridar muttered.

"Has our father calculated the cost of a second campaign in the season? Fall is already underway, the troops will be needing to settle into winter quarters and the treasury can only handle—"

"We've got Ala'haran," blurted out Feridar, cinching the saddle belt tight. Calif stomped, irritated, and Ghaze's jaw dropped.

"Ala'haran is alive?"

"For the moment."

"I see. And your question about Branding Spells?"

"Yes. I need to know if it's possible to rid yourself of one."

Ghaze leaned against the stable wall and folded his arms, rubbing his stubbled chin thoughtfully.

"In theory. It would take some strong concealment magic most likely."

"What about removing the actual physical brand?"

"You mean like a surgery?"

"I mean, if I cut off this finger," Feridar snapped, pulling the signet ring off his little finger and showing the scarred tissue the ring had branded him with all those years ago. "Will father still be able to see visions of me?"

"Probably not," Ghaze speculated. "Why?"

"I think Ala'haran cut off his finger to avoid being tracked," Feridar muttered.

"That would definitely help. Too bad Father didn't brand him somewhere he couldn't cut off."

"Is there any other way of tracking him through the ring now that it is in our possession? Father was able to get vague placement with some sort of 'Last Sight' spell, but I need to be more precise than that."

"Not that I know of. Without the brand he's still a ghost in the Wild," Ghaze said, face contorted in concentration.

"No. Not a ghost," Feridar said, mounting Calif and wheeling the war horse around in the stable's hallway twice. It felt good to be back in the saddle. "Ghosts can't bleed. And I fully intend to make that a priority."

"Well then, best of luck to you, my Prince," the younger prince said, nodding courteously to Feridar. "Try not to make too much of a mess?"

Fereidar laughed cruelly and spurred Calif into a full gallop out of the livery. He charged through the courtyard on his way to meet with his generals, the two moons lighting his pathway from their perch the night sky. He had a hunt to conduct, and the sly fox would not slip past him. Not this time. It would be a long night, but for Feridar, the fun had just begun.

THE
BROTHERHOOD

CHAPTER I

UP TOP

"Nice and steady, now. That's a good girl."

Paige held her breath, sighting the shaft of her arrow as she pulled back on the braided sinew bowstring. She drew back until her right thumb grazed her smooth white cheek just above her jawline. The deer that stood twenty yards ahead of them slowly raised his head. His jaw rolled as he chewed on the lush green grass of the meadow. The buck turned and glanced in their direction while Paige exhaled slowly. His ear flicked when he caught a whiff of something on the wind. Paige tightened her grip on her polished yew bow, then released.

The arrow slid off the notch with a sharp schick, and the white goose feathers flashed as the arrow wobbled and righted itself through the air. The buck tensed his slender legs. Before he could spring away, the arrow thudded into the deer's side, down through the middle of his ribcage. The beast bleated in alarm and staggered before bounding into the thicket.

"Aw, come on!" Paige spat, wrinkling her face in frustration and disgust. She huffed, sending blonde bangs flying up. A deep, soft chuckle emanated from behind her. Paige turned to scowl at her father.

"You got him, that's all that matters," he encouraged, his sapphire eyes twinkling with mischief. "Of course, now you've scared off our dinner, which means that much more walking once we get him carved up."

Paige rolled her steel blue eyes and headed for where the deer had stood before he bolted. Her moccasins brushed the leaves of the forest floor with a deft whisper. Her father sauntered along behind her, chuckling. His boots kicked up sticks and twigs without a care in the world.

"How far do you think he would have gotten with that shot?" Paige asked.

"A lot farther than if I had shot him."

"Well, it's a new bow," she countered, scrunching up her face.

"Excuses, excuses."

Paige picked up a pinecone and chucked it at her father's head. He ducked and scooped up a handful of leaves, dumping them in her hair.

"You really need to improve your aim all around, it looks like," he teased.

"You're the absolute worst!" She lightly hit his shoulder. He leapt back to avoid her second swipe and tripped over a root, crashing into a pile of crimson maple leaves.

"Serves you right!" Paige quipped, pulling leaves out of her braid. Her papa snickered, shaking the leaves out of his hair and tossing more handfuls at his daughter.

"What can I say, I've got to get all my mischief out while I can!" He smiled at her. "In the next year or two, some young fella is gonna whisk you and your sister off your feet, and I'll be left all alone with no one to mess with!"

"Oh, whatever," Paige said, eyes rolling. "You know you'd love to spend all day, every day with just Mother."

"Well, you're not wrong!" he said with a grin. "Now, we'd better get that buck so we can get back before the Burgess's meet and decide their chief is too tardy to keep around!"

They shook themselves free of the myriad of colored leaves, the first the season had to offer. Paige stooped and tucked her trousers back into the top of her moccasin, tying the leather laces tight. She snatched up all the arrows that had fallen out of her belt quiver, taking the time to nock one to her bow. Then, quiet as a mouse, she jogged into the trees.

Because the leaves were still mostly on the trees, it wasn't hard to find the blood trail down into a deep gully. Paige darted around the mossy trunks and boulders as she descended into the hollow. Her father kept up easily behind her.

The forest she'd grown up calling home, commonly referred to as "the Wild," was beautiful this time of year. From the time the sun rose in the west every morning till the two moons danced in the sky together at night, the forest was alive with the chatter of all manner of creatures. Paige loved taking walks in cool, early autumn with both her father and mother. The crisp air she would breathe in every dawn would fill her lungs with a sense of vigor that no other season could match.

"Here!" her father called, touching blood on a rock at the bottom of the gully. "He can't be far now."

Paige ran up beside him and looked at the trail. It wound around the bottom of the ravine and over a small rise. They jogged to the top of the incline and looked down into a gully filled with fallen leaves, remnants of green poking up from patches in the earth where the blades of sweet grass seemed to be begging for one more day of spring.

The buck lay on one such patch of grass, heaving for air. Paige felt a pang of guilt. She enjoyed hunting, even if most in the village would have considered it a chore. But there was nothing sporting about a wounded animal.

"Finish him quick, darling," her father said softly, placing a reassuring hand on her shoulder. "End his suffering."

Paige nodded and knelt down beside the wounded buck. It didn't even try to rise. She drew her knife from its sheath on her belt and covered the deer's eyes with her hand.

"I'm sorry," she whispered.

A quick movement and a moment later, the buck's eyes closed for good. Paige laid his majestic head down in the damp, dewy grass where he had spent his final moments. She started to brush away a tear before it could escape her eye, but her father caught her hand.

"Let it fall," her father encouraged. "There is no shame."

His eyes were filled with love and kindness, and though she felt some sorrow in her heart, she couldn't help but notice a warmth spread inside her chest.

"I should have been a better shot," she said mournfully. "I don't feel bad about taking his life. Just in making him suffer."

"And that, my brave, little Alwasu," her father said, using her elvish name, "is the difference between the hunter and the butcher."

Paige nodded as her papa placed his gloved hand reassuringly on her face, his palm warm against her cold cheek. She cleared her throat, put a hand on the deer and whispered a prayer to the Creator. She thanked Him for the success of the hunt and asked His blessings on the life they could now sustain, thanks to life sacrificed. She grabbed one antler while her father grabbed the other, and together they pulled the deer over to a tree at the far end of the gully.

"Let's get the nasty part over with," her papa said, dropping his pack on the ground and unclasping the leather buckles to open the top flap. He removed several different-sized knives from the pack and placed them on the ground, tossing Paige a small hand shovel and a length of rope. She secured the latter around the buck's neck while her father began laying out large pieces of linen cheesecloth.

Paige had done this enough times to know what was expected of her. While her father strung up the kill using the tree as a gallows, she took the shovel off a few paces and dug a forearm-deep hole in the earth. As soon as she had a sizeable hole dug, her father came over with a linen bag which now contained all the inner parts of the deer. Paige wrinkled her nose at the smell but helped her father bury them without complaint.

"Well, that was painless," Papa said, grinning as he wiped his blade off on his doublet.

"Mother's going to murder you if you get any more bloodstains on your shirts," Paige scolded.

Her father shrugged. "Being the chief means I can negotiate a trade deal with the weavers in the Kinnebrek for a new shipment of linen, right?" He winked.

Paige rolled her eyes. Papa didn't have time for such nonsense, even if he had been serious. Luckily for Paige, though, demand on the chief's time had lessened as the harvest drew to a close, so they got to spend more moments in the woods than they normally did.

The princess took out her knife and began helping her father skin their prize, peeling the hide off the carcass, moving her blade with deft strokes. Her fingertips slid between the animal's fat and the smooth, pearly membrane of his hide. She spread her fingers and loosened the shaggy coat, inch by inch, until it lay in a pile on the forest floor.

With both of them working, it didn't take long to get the hide off, folded, and wrapped in a piece of linen. Paige's father wasted no time getting the backstrap cut from along the spine, then reaching inside the ribcage and pulling the tenderloins out by hand.

"We'll give the rest to the market, I think," he said, tossing the second tenderloin to Paige, who began wrapping them in cloth. "But I'm afraid I love your mother's backstrap and butterfly steaks too much to let these go!"

The chieftain carved up the flanks into shanks and hams, each wrapped in the clean cloth and placed in his pack. With most of the meat carved, Paige's papa dropped the carcass from the tree and dragged it over by the filled-in waste pile. He took the head from the beast to bring with the hide to the tanner in the village. Stepping back from the remainder of the skeleton, he said one more prayer to the Creator as he began slipping his pack on.

"That will make a fine meal for a few of our forest folk," he said. He wiped his last knife clean on his shirt, despite Paige's scolding look.

She unstrung her bow and slipped it into a special loop on her quiver belt. She adjusted the belt to sling the whole lot over her shoulder, grabbed the buck's head from her father and carried it back up the gully by the antler. Her father trekked behind her, hefting the heavy pack effortlessly along with him.

The walk back to their village was an easy stroll, all things considered. One of the benefits of being this deep into the Wild was the plentiful game within an hour's hike from their house in Kapernaum.

"You pick out what you're wearing to the feast tomorrow?" Papa asked, falling into step with her.

"I think mother made Olivian and me dresses. She's just been trying to keep them a surprise."

"That sounds like her. What gave it away?"

"The smile."

"Ah, yes. Gets her every time."

"You think maybe it's an elf thing? It's like she has so much excitement when she's planning a surprise, it leaks all over her face when she tries to hide it. Which makes it even worse!"

"You've no idea. I knew we were going to have you three weeks before she told me!"

"Ha! Sounds about right. I still will never understand how you ended up getting so lucky on that one," Paige teased.

Her father's expression was amused. "It's a long story." He chuckled softly. Paige leaned over and pushed against him playfully, knocking him slightly off balance. She knew all about their beautiful woodland wedding they'd had in the mists of the Wild, their arrival in Kapernaum, and the stories of how they helped build it into the village it was today. But the one story she had yet to hear was how her father and her mother met. It was a story every person in the village had tried to pry out of them at some point, considering that it was unheard of for a human to marry an elf. But Papa always winked and said, "It's a long story," and left it at that.

Paige tucked away a strand of hair and felt the noticeable taper of her ear. She hadn't given it much thought when she was younger, but the older she got, the more curious she became about that untold story. By the time she'd been born, everyone in Kapernaum had just gotten used to the fact that their chieftain was married to an elf. Apparently it had caused quite a stir at first, not only in Kapernaum, but in the villages in the surrounding forest as well. An elf hadn't been seen in the Wild for nearly two hundred years, according to the elderly citizens. News of one not only appearing but marrying a human had spread through the mountains faster than a lightning-strike forest fire.

"Try and act surprised for her sake, okay?" her father encouraged, moving along with the conversation. "I know she's worked hard on both those dresses for the last two weeks."

"Oh, I will. Don't worry," Paige assured as they came out of the forest and onto a well-worn path heading southeast.

The jagged pathway lay covered in a mosaic of fallen leaves. They plodded downhill with the trail as they moved into an area of the forest that became thinner with larger trees spaced farther apart from one another. Birds called as they darted in and out of the canopy, their chipper songs tempered only by the muffled stillness of the forest around them until they heard the faint sound of steel ringing when, somewhere around the next bend in the road, a hammer struck an anvil. She smelled the woodsmoke of a hundred fires going. Her heart warmed as they rounded the last turn of the pathway.

"Smells like the baker hasn't been wasting his morning." Papa grinned, inhaling deeply as he quickened their pace.

Kapernaum's market bustled ahead. It was an area of tents and smaller shelters set up underneath the village for commerce and bartering among themselves and any neighboring traders that happened to be traveling through. Bright colored canvases and hand-painted signs swayed in the whispering breeze. The smell of baking breads and fresh candies wafted over Paige in the sharp early autumn air. She inhaled deeply, memorizing every note of sweetness.

Above the makeshift tent city, the village's two-hundred or so buildings sat nestled in the high canopy overhead--a small city of treehouses, platforms and rope bridges that the locals referred to as "Up Top." Most of the buildings encircled the living tree's trunk, not unlike a mud wasps' nest on a blade of grass. The siding and roof shingles were almost entirely cut from cedar, due to its rot resistance and natural red-toned beauty.

Initially, the Alatarians had chosen the area for the very presence of the giant, red-wooded Elder Trees; their fifteen- to twenty-foot wide trunks and monstrous branches provided both ample protection from the elements as well as a solid base to construct their platforms and dwellings. The trees were said to have been as old as Eirensgarth itself, having stood the test of time from the last two ages into this, the third age, strong and unmoving as time itself seemed to be in the Wild.

No matter how many times she walked the village, Paige still marveled at its beauty and unique charm that none of the surrounding villages had. It was the Wild's best kept secret from the outside world, her Papa always said, and Paige was glad of it.

"Alaire!"

Paige turned to see a tall man with broad shoulders stride towards them, heavy fur boots thudding against the ground like the hooves of a draft horse plowing the field. The man's bald head glistened in the sun, but his thick beard was almost long enough to tuck into his belt. He wore a coat made of sheepskin with the sleeves ripped off to reveal his bulging biceps, rippled and riddled with zoomorphic tattoos. A wide, upturned collar barely covered his large, cherry-red ears from the frosty morning. His linen trousers were carelessly tucked into his thick, black fur-lined boots. An elegant bow nearly twice as long as Paige's own was strung and slung over his barrel chest, a quiver of oak arrows dangling by his side. He smiled warmly at Paige's papa, bright blue eyes sparkling under dark, thick eyebrows.

"Gerik, the mighty Rabbit Slayer returns! It's good to see you, old friend! I don't recall gazing on that beautiful beard of yours in this village for at least a week!" Papa extended both arms in an embrace. Gerik grasped her papa by the shoulders and smacked his arm good-naturedly, a large, toothy grin poking out from his unkempt facial hair.

"You old fox, how have you been!?" The men touched their foreheads together, one hand grasping the back of the other's neck in the traditional embrace of the Alatarian warriors. Paige smiled. Gerik was one of her father's oldest friends and as close to an uncle as Paige had ever known. He was a hunter by trade, specializing in trapping the Longbottom Hares that roamed the depths of the Wild and the mountains beyond it. Papa always teased Uncle Gerik for being "the Bane of Bunnies," but hunting a thirty-two pound hare that could outrun a horse was no small feat.

"I've been fortunate, you ol' rapscallion!" Papa responded, dropping his pack to the ground and opening the top flap to show off their morning kill. "This was Paige's first kill this season."

"Only her first?" the giant hunter said, feigning surprise and scrunching up his wild eyebrows at Paige. "Losing your touch?"

"This coming from the man I outshot fair and square at our last hunt together," she said, jutting her chin out in similar mockery. "If I remember correctly, I'm the one who downed that Longbottom in Culver's gulley last spring, not you!"

"Oh, you're living in the past, kid!" Uncle Gerik poked the bridge of Paige's small, slightly upturned nose she'd inherited from her father. She crossed her wide blue eyes to humor him, then laughed and swung a playful upper cut at his long bearded jaw. He caught her fist in one of his massive hands, powerful tattooed fingers curling around like an iron cage. He pulled her in and spun her around into a bear hug.

"It is good to see you, Alwasu."

"It's good to see you too, Uncle Gerik!" Paige grinned and gave him a quick kiss on the cheek. He spun her round, affectionately patting her rosy, frost-nipped cheek.

"Ah, Alaire, how are you keeping the young lads away from the fine filly you've raised?"

"Ha! More like an ornery bobcat, I'd say!" Papa teased, earning him an eye-roll from his youngest daughter.

"Aye, hunts like one too, it would seem!"

"Speaking of, where are your hares, Gerik? Haven't lost your touch, have you?"

Uncle Gerik frowned, a hundred crinkles etched into his bald forehead. "Not a lick of luck all week, mate."

"No! Truly?"

"Not even a trail." Gerik spat. "I went up and down the eastern forest and couldn't find anything. Ran into old Hob. You remember ol' Hob, don't you? That beefy guy with the stained beard, always smelled like sour cheese? Anyways, he told me he hasn't seen any Longys in nearly two weeks. Said three weeks ago they were all over the place, and then they vanished!"

"That doesn't sound normal, does it? You think they all migrated?"

"It isn't. They're hibernators—they should be out fattening up for at least two more full moons before catching a long nap over the winter months!"

Papa stroked his scruffy chin thoughtfully. "Only thing I can think of is if those miners from the northeast had strayed into the Wild for hunting again. They usually honor the treaty, but if meat is getting scarce in the Ohlmars, they may be wandering down from the mountains now."

"I haven't seen a miner in nearly five years, myself. I didn't even know they still ran mines anymore," Gerik said, poking into Papa's rucksack.

"Neither have I," Papa remarked. "I wonder how that town fared after the last two blizzards. I can't even remember what they called that village, can you?"

"Don't know, don't care." Gerik shrugged. "All I know is something's got my Longys spooked and that's bad for business."

"Ger, I'm sorry," Papa said. "Swing by and eat with us tonight?"

"Is Elennas cooking that backstrap of hers?" Gerik asked.

"Best in town!"

"If she lets me back in the house, I'll be there," the hunter said with a polite bow, unexpected from a man wearing such ignoble garb.

"We'll see you at sunset, then." Papa smiled, returning the slight bow. "Till then, old friend!"

"Till then!" Gerik said, heading for the center of the market, waving over his shoulder. Paige and her father waved back, then Papa hefted the pack once more.

"Right," he said. "Where were we?"

They made their way through the hum of the crowd to their favorite butcher's tent.

"No, no, I said it was three Cops for the rib rack, nine for the hams!" a fat butcher wheezed at a disgruntled old woman.

"Finneas Hideborrow, don't you take that tone with me! I spanked you when you were a wee lad, and so help me, I'll do it again right here in front of the whole town!"

"Mrs. Peddledew, please," the butcher insisted in an urgent, hushed tone. "Not in front of the other customers! Talk like that will make me the laughingstock of the town!"

"You're already the laughingstock of the town, ya halfwit!" She grabbed the ham off the butcher's block, dropped three copper-stamped coins on the table, and huffed away. The butcher looked perplexed but said nothing in protest as he pocketed the three coins.

"You drive an unbeatable bargain, Fin!" Papa teased, plopping the backpack on to the butcher's chewed-up block. The butcher looked distraught as he wiped off a smudge from the block.

"She used to watch me when I was a wee tot. Spanked me every day. Dreadful woman."

"What say I make your day a little more enjoyable?" Papa said, removing some of the wrapped meat. The butcher inspected the hunt with the eye of a jeweler. Paige always laughed at how meticulous Fin was with his business for only being a butcher in a small village market. A small table in the middle of the tent held a beautiful assortment of gleaming, polished knives bereft of a single stain or nick in the edge. His petite wife stood on the other side of the shop, wrapping some smaller orders for other customers. Even with such a mousy disposition, Paige was willing to bet there wasn't a man in the Wild who could hold a candle to Harla Hideborrow's ability with a butcher knife. She was downright terrifying with serrated steel clutched in that tiny, balled-up fist of hers.

"These cuts are quite good, Alaire," the butcher said, pinching a ham between his pudgy fingers. "You're getting better."

"I learn from the best."

The butcher scrutinized a flank steak in the streaming sunlight.

"Well, you'll have to come back for another lesson one afternoon and I'll teach you how to butterfly steaks better; these are a sorry sight compared to your hams."

"I guess we all have our flaws." Papa chuckled.

"I'll give you fifteen Cops for it," the butcher offered, sizing up Paige's papa with a stern look.

"My wife might whip me if I come home with anything less than twenty-five!" Papa laughed.

"A fine hunter you may be, Chief, but your meat isn't speckled with gold dust."

"I could go twenty-three."

"Eighteen."

"Twenty. And," Alaire said, taking the deer's head and slapping it on the block, "I'll give you the hide to sell to the tanners for a profit."

The butcher thought for a moment, then spat in his hand and extended it for Papa to shake. The chief shook it heartily. Fin laughed and took out a handkerchief to wipe his red, round nose as he summoned his wife over to begin displaying the meat for the customers. Paige's father unloaded the remainder of the venison from his pack and collected the copper coins in return. He handed three to Paige before pocketing the rest, winking at her with his soft hazel eyes.

"What is this for?" Paige asked, staring down at the three Cops. The chief chuckled, slinging the empty pack over one shoulder.

"I thought you might want to get something for the feast tomorrow. You know, to accent those lovely dresses your mother has been working on," Papa said, admiring a rack of scarves as they passed by a nomadic milliner's shop.

Paige thought hard about what she might get. She'd never really put much stock in the frills and brightly colored fabrics her older sister, Olivian, did. She gazed at several shops as they walked through the northern side of market, mulling over in her mind what it was she could wear to the festival.

"Wait here and do a little shopping around," her father encouraged as they came to a cluster of traders showing off various forms of jewelry and sashes woven in brightly colored patterns. "I need to double check with Xandla on the water tanks for tomorrow night."

Paige would have much rather gone with Papa but realized he probably had some official business to discuss with the Keeper of the Water.

The Waterhouse that stood tall above Paige now was a large building built directly above the main village well. Paige was so caught up in gazing at the waterworks she failed to watch where she meandered. As she turned, she was promptly knocked off her feet with a thud.

"Hey!" she spat, rolling up and shaking the leaves out of her braid for the second time today. "Watch where you're going!"

She was addressing two large men clad in crimson cloaks. They were both two heads taller than Paige, with heavy boots tramping through the thin layer of early autumn leaves. They wore what appeared to be brigandine. These covered their torsos beneath the red cloaks, and they wore dirks strapped to their thighs. Ivory scarves wound around their heads and necks. Their waists were covered by baggy, black pants tucked into well-crafted boots. One of them turned and gave her a nasty look. He had a scar on the left side of his lips that cut a jagged pattern down his chin and into a wiry, crow-colored beard.

Paige felt an odd prickly feeling at the base of her spine. She straightened her back up but the uneasy feeling didn't dissipate as she watched the strangers advance towards the edge of the marketplace. While it was common to see strangers from all over the Wild come to the market, these men did not look like the native people of the wilderness villages. They had fair skin and black hair while most people in the Wild had more ruddy complexions with shades of brown hair. She scowled and fell into step behind them, taking care to dip and slide behind carts and various booths as she did so.

Paige followed the strangers till she came to the edge of the marketplace. The cloaked men stopped by one of the last standing Elder trees surrounding Kapernaum, looking it over and placing their large gloved hands on the trunk.

Paige shrugged and turned to head back for the market. It wasn't uncommon for some of the traders and travelers to come from the south and pay homage to the Elder trees by praying to them. Many of the eastern tribes worshipped many gods rather than just the Creator and often came to pray in what was left of the ancient places. That explained why they had been so rude—the southern pagans had often been less than agreeable to her people when they came through town.

Yet this explanation for some reason did not sit well with her. In fact, the tingling didn't go away until she'd headed well beyond the sight of the strangers and back to the pump house. But after a few moments of idly looking into vendors' tents, she quickly pushed it from her mind and found herself bored as she awaited her Papa's return.

"Paige?"

Paige turned around to see a young man with stunning green eyes approach her from around the corner of one of the shops across the way. He was tall and well built with long, straight brown locks tied back into a ponytail, with bangs outlining his thin face. A thin, dark chinstrap of facial hair graced his strong jawline. Paige recognized him as one of the Fauxbre boys from Oak's Bough, a village to the north. He wore a shirt the color of a summer sunrise that bore ornate embroidery around the collar and cuffs. His tunic was tucked into a wide brown belt studded with brass tacks, on which hung a dirk. His boots came up to his knee, with a deep cuff that was embossed with oak leaf designs, the tight green pants accenting well-built legs accustomed to running through the hills of the Wild.

"Paige, daughter of Chief Alaire?" he asked again. She nodded, looking him up and down several times.

"You don't recognize me, do you?" He laughed.

Paige laughed uneasily.

"I'm sorry, I do, I just cannot for the life of me remember your name," she replied honestly. The young man snickered, brushing a lock of hair behind his ear.

"Derak, m'lady," he said with a bow, never taking his eyes off her. "We met last year at the Solstice feast."

"Ah, yes. I do remember now. You didn't have a beard then!"

"Correct!" He smiled, stroking his chin. "Glad you noticed!"

"What brings you to town?" she asked, reaching back and adjusting the leather cord holding up her hair.

"Father brought some carts of gourds for the Harvest Moon Dance tomorrow night, so we'll be at the market all day and then stay for the party tomorrow. I suppose you will be in attendance?"

"Naturally." Paige smiled as sweetly as she could muster.

"Then might I be so bold as to ask the daughter of a chief for a dance this far in advance?"

Paige felt her cheeks flush red. She laughed awkwardly for a moment.

"Um, I don't see why not!" she stammered, unconsciously fidgeting with the end of her braid. Derak smiled, nodding his head in a slight bow.

"I look forward to it then, Princess," the merchant's son said, slowly backing up and finally turning and jogging around the corner of the street where he disappeared.

"He seems nice."

Paige whirled around to see her father standing with a tall, dusky man who wore baggy pants and a simple leather vest over his bulging muscular frame. His piercing hazel eyes were unwavering, and his chiseled jawline looked as if it had never held a smile.

"Oh, stop," Paige scolded, adjusting her quiver and bow as she walked over to them. Her father's face spelled mischief, but he didn't press the matter further. He clapped the darker man on the shoulder goodnaturedly. The man didn't smile.

"Alright, well, my little princess, let's get old, grumpy Xandla Up Top. Can't keep the Burgesses waiting!"

"This is not my idea of a good time," the man spoke in his rich, deep accent. "A bunch of men arguing and chattering in a room. Like squirrels."

"Then maybe it needs to be our job to throw a couple nuts into the muck, eh?" Paige's father chuckled, ushering them both to the eastern edge of the village market.

Past the bakers' tents they came to the second great accomplishment of Alaire's rule as chief. Gone were the days of relying on huge rickety stairs to get Up Top. A series of lifts sat on the easternmost edge of the village in place of stairs and old rope ladders. Each lift took eight people to operate. With the exception of the single old staircase at the northwest corner of the village—not far from Paige's own home, and fondly called "Old Widow Wickets"—the Lifthouse was the main way to get to and from Up Top from the market.

Paige, Alaire, and Xandla all boarded the right-most lift. Paige leaned against the rail as her father, Xandla, and several other burly males insisted on raising the platform to let the women on board sit back. Normally Paige would have protested such a thing, but she was beginning to feel the long hike in her legs and was happy for the reprieve.

It only took them a few moments to winch their way Up Top, which towered five stories above the market. As soon as they lined up with the loading platform, several lift attendants locked the lift in place with large iron poles and forged latches. Paige hopped down onto the loading platform with the help of her father's outstretched hand. They quickly moved along as a group of down-travelers loaded the deck to descend.

"Ala, darling, why don't you head on back to the house? Xandla and I have to meet before the Burgesses to discuss some fixes to the water system," Alaire said, handing his empty pack to Paige. "Tell your mother I'll be along shortly."

"So, by that you mean you have no idea when you'll be back home?" Paige smirked.

Xandla snorted. It was about as close to a laugh as she'd ever heard from him.

"Pretty much," her father sighed. He chuckled, pulled Paige by the back of her head into a warm embrace, kissing her gently on the forehead. "Thanks for keeping me company this morning. I won't be long... I hope!"

"Alright, love you, Papa," she said, squeezing him back before letting go. "Goodbye, Xandla. Enjoy your meeting!"

She heard the man grunt and her papa laughed. As they began to walk away, Papa tapped two fingers to his temples and then saluted her with a grin. She returned the motion, a private parting gesture they had shared since she was young, before turning on her heel and heading home.

Each house in Kapernaum had a deck surrounding it wide enough for two people to walk abreast. Each deck was connected by an assortment of rope or timber bridges as well as stairs to get to lower levels. All of these pathways allowed people to take multiple routes to get to the same destination, making for a less crowded walk across town.

Paige made her way around several houses heading towards the northwest side of Kapernaum. The second-to-last of the larger platforms before her house was a square deck about twenty paces along each side. Several groups of men stood about beginning to prep oil lanterns to place on the walkways to the Great Hall for the next evening's festivities. Other groups of ladies gathered about, sewing everything from tablecloths to buntings while a few small children splashed in the public fountain in the center of the platform.

The gaggle sitting right beside the bridge caught her attention—a covey of ladies just a few years older than Paige herself, twittering like schoolgirls, even though Paige knew several of them were already married off. In fact, two were with child. Some of these young women spent time with her older sister, but Paige typically did her best to avoid this particular batch of girls.

The girl at the center of the roost was a slightly plump young lady three or four years older than Paige, who had rosy red cheeks and bright teal eyes accented by her dark lashes and locks. A spattering of freckles adorned her nose like the belt of stars that surrounded the night sky on the clearest evening, and her prim mouth held a twisted smile that looked as if it had permanently soured ever so slightly.

"Oh, Paige!" she exclaimed as she looked up from her sewing, making eye contact with the chieftain's daughter. "Dearie, how are you!"

"I'm quite well Matildra, thank you," Paige muttered, trying to brush straight past the group. The other girls looked up and and immediately began whispering to each other in hushed giggles. Matildra's smile made Paige's stomach turn. No matter the occasion, these girls always made it a point to make her feel self-conscious, whether that be a backhanded compliment about how manly her attire was or how the bloodstains and rabbit fur on her arms really kept her fair complexion from looking too pasty. Paige tried to ignore this bevy as often as possible when she was younger, caring more about being in the forest with her father than with Olivian and her friends perfecting needlework and cooking.

"Is your sister feeling better, Princess?" one of the other girls asked.

"She is. Luckily for her it was only allergies that kept her inside yesterday."

"Dreadful this time of year!" Matildra said, clicking her tongue in sympathy. "All the leaves falling really does play havoc on my eyes. They itch like wool!"

"I'm sure the princess loves this time of year. Makes the deer easier to see, or so my brother tells me!" another added.

"He's not wrong," Paige said, hefting the pack to a better position on her arm, taking a couple small sliding steps past them to try and exit the conversation.

"Well, I'm glad Olivian will be able to make it to the dance tomorrow night," Matildra said with a smile. "What about you, dear? What are you wearing this year? Have you saved enough of those hare skins to make a skirt?"

"She'd only need one of those pelts that hunter with the dreadful beard brings to the market!" one of the pregnant ladies chimed in.

"My mother has been making our dresses this year," Paige snapped. "I'm not sure what else I'll be wearing."

"I just got an absolutely dazzling sash yesterday from a Frantish trader who came from Couldena," another of the girls said.

"My husband bought me a woven shawl from a trader on the river!" the second of the pregnant girls bragged with a sly smile.

"Good, maybe it will hide how fat that baby is making you look!" another said with a laugh. The girls all acted appalled at the jab, followed by laughter that set Paige's tapered ears on fire with annoyance. She took a tentative step forward but apparently Matildra wasn't finished with her quite yet.

"Paige, what about you? Surely you must have something to bait your hook for a young man tomorrow!" She laughed.

"It's not too early to start thinking of marriage!" one of the married girls admonished. "I was only a year older than you when Hazek asked for my hand. And Gruetta only been married for six months!"

"I haven't given it much thought," Paige said absently, rolling her eyes.

"Better get a start on quick!" Matildra encouraged, waving her slightly chubby hand. "We'd hate to see you wind up being an old maid!"

Paige would have ignored the entire rest of the conversation, but she couldn't leave and ignore Matildra's last comment.

"Is it really all that bad, Matildra?"

There was a stunned silence as Matildra's cheeks went bright pink and she pursed her lips into a hard line. Paige smirked.

"I appreciate your concern that I might suffer your fate of being an old maid at twenty years old, but you needn't worry! I'll have you know Derak of Oak's Bough just this morning asked me to dance. What about you, Matildra? Have any eligible bachelors asked you to dance a day in advance?"

The girls gasped. Horror and indignation etched themselves onto Matildra's rosy face.

"That's what I figured," Paige snipped, with only a trace of regret. But she was too annoyed to offer an apology. Instead she adjusted her belt quiver, turned her back on the group, and marched across the bridge towards her own home, satisfied that she'd put all the whisperings and gossip to rest, at least for a while. She felt the three Cops jingle in her pocket and decided she'd have to make it back to the market tomorrow. She smirked, pleased with herself for the exit line, and stepped up onto the deck of her home.

The chiefs home stood at the northwest corner of the village, only a couple platforms away from the Burgesses' house where all the matters of state were addressed. Paige adored the house which was built around one of the few Elder Trees left within the confines of the village boundaries. It was a two-story circular home made from the finest red cedar hauled from the southern marshlands of the Wild, near Orellion Lake. The window shutters were painted a crisp green with carved runes of dragons, griffons, and winged horses dancing about the frames. Both stories had a large deck—the bottom one being available to foot traffic, which was shaded by the chief's personal deck above. Many chiefs before had used the upper deck as a place for excessive merrymaking, but Papa was a simpler, more resourceful man and had some dirt hauled up to turn a large section of the deck into a garden for Elenass. Various vines spilled out from their boxed confines, winding around the support pillars to provide passersby with a light snack in the early summer months.

Paige strode up to the double doors she'd been walking through nearly all her young life and dropped her pack in the vestibule. The doors were both a half of a beautiful arched frame with ornate knot carvings, filled with the mythical creatures that had once inhabited the Wild many years ago: satyrs, fauns, centaurs, unicorns, and sphinxes, among others. Hand-chiseled vines wove in and out of the design as if it had grown there, and stains transformed the door into a beautiful patina brown that reminded one of freshly upturned humus after the first plowing of the season.

She twisted the giant iron ring, and the door swung open noiselessly on well-oiled wrought iron hinges as Paige grabbed her pack and stepped inside. The smell of freshly-brewed herbal tea filled her nostrils as she breathed in the smell of home: the aroma of her mother's herbs mixed with the smell of a warm hearth, fresh bread, and newly laid parchment. She sighed contentedly as the late morning sun streamed in through the shimmering glass windows. She set her pack under the coat rack on the wall and gently swung the door shut.

Paige slipped off her moccasins and let her bare toes wiggle into the bearskin rug. In front of her was the giant, barky center of the home, the Elder Tree, its bark cascading up towards the second floor and above in a vast array of wild shapes and twists. To her right, a grand, log staircase ducked up into the second floor with the sleeping quarters. Below it, beyond the carved timber door, lay her father's study. To Paige's left heading around the tree to the back of the house was the sitting room, which was decked out in rustic log couches with cushions sewn from sheepskin, draped in hand woven tapestry. The parlor nestled itself around a small tea table crafted from solid, grey granite beneath which were stacked old leather-bound books and rolls of parchment. Beyond the sitting room, curling around to the back of the home, the kitchen and dining room basked in glorious sunlight as the wall surrounding that section of the house was more window than it was wood.

"Alwasu? Is that you?"

"Yes, Mother," Paige responded, looking up to see Elenass descending the stairs, the train of her slim-fitting, sky-blue dress slipping down two steps behind her. Her fair hand barely touched the banister as she glided into the parlor. Her waist-length hair, so blonde that it was nearly white, was pulled back into a single braid, similar to Paige's own hair. This style brought attention to her pronounced, tapered ears that were slightly longer in the point than Paige's own. Elenass's face was symmetrical in every way, with a complexion most women in the village would slay a dragon to have.

Paige grinned and walked over to her mother, embracing her and kissing her on the cheek.

"You're home much later than I'd expected. Did everything go alright?" Elenass asked, her steel blue eyes searching her daughter's, which was very nearly like looking in a mirror. Paige nodded. Her mother swiped away a pesky loose strand of dirty blonde hair from her daughter's face, tucking it behind a tapered ear.

"Papa just had to finish up some business and then get off to the Burgesses," Paige explained. "We saw Gerik in the village, and Papa invited him to supper tonight."

"The rabbit slayer?"

Paige nodded.

Elenass laughed softly under her breath. "Such a strange man. I will never understand how your father can make so much fun at another's expense and somehow still be best friends at the end of the day."

"I think it's a 'man thing,' Mother," Paige said, smiling. "I hear they can be punching each other over drinks one moment, then buying them for each other the next."

"How vile," Elenass muttered. "We'll need to be sure and set another place at the table. Olivian!"

Paige heard the door to her room open and close with the tell-tale squeak that had been there as long as she could remember. The sound of soft footsteps padded towards them as her older sister entered. She was a tall, beautiful young woman only two years Paige's senior. Olivian was built like her mother, tall and slender with dirty-blonde, straight hair that fell almost to her waist.

"Yes, Mother?" Olivian asked, reaching behind her head and tying her hair back into a loose ponytail. Her eyes were a dead ringer for their papa's: solid sapphire blue, compared to Paige's almost grey blue. She wore a dark blue gown with long, loose sleeves and silver trim, a black leather corset holding it snugly around her waist.

"Set another place at the table tonight."

"Can't Ala do it?" Olivian protested.

Paige glared at her older sister, although she was, by this time, used to her trying to shove off chores on her. Olivian had become the graceful, poised, refined young woman the village expected a chieftain's daughter to be, but since Papa refused to hire any household servants, she had tried to settle for bossing her little sister around whenever she could.

"Did I ask her to do it?"

"No."

"Then please do as I ask. Gerik is coming over for supper."

"Yes, Mother," Olivian muttered, rolling her eyes slightly. Paige giggled. Gerik wasn't Olivian's favorite person. Her nature gave her little patience for "those brutish, vile ruffians" Papa kept company with.

"And be a dear and watch the tea, will you?" Mother added. "I'll just be a moment more upstairs."

"I can watch it, Mother," Paige volunteered. Her mother looked at her skeptically.

"Darling, you should probably wash yourself first... Wait, are those bloodstains on your sleeves?"

Paige stopped halfway up the stairs.

"Papa's are worse, just for the record."

"What?"

Paige chuckled. With all her grace and poise, her mother was overly meticulous about her housekeeping. Papa said it was an elf thing, and that's why they got along so well—because her father described himself as a "rustically handsome, adventuring scalawag who has a slight tidiness problem."

Paige lunged up to the second floor steps, which led to several bedrooms and a washroom. She passed her parents' door and their washroom coming to the entrance to the room she and Olivian had shared since they were babies. It was carved with roses so lifelike one would almost be tempted to smell them.

The room was spacious, with a lunette window that stretched from the ceiling to the cedar baseboard. The interior of the room had been whitewashed over the cob stucco that danced in fancy patterns all the way to the ceiling. A chandelier made from contorted antlers hung above the girls' goose-feather beds, which sat along either side of the room. A hastily made quilt tossed over the rope-tensioned frame denoted Paige's bed from Olivian's perfectly flat, meticulously smoothed comforter.

Paige ran over to her side of the room to the mahogany vanity sitting at the foot of her bed against the wall. She slid open a collection of drawers under the dresser and removed a clean linen shirt and some baggy fisherman's pants. Mother wouldn't be overly fond of the choice, but Paige wasn't particularly worried about that. It had been a long morning, and right now she felt like snuggling up on a couch downstairs in comfortable clothes wrapped in her father's bearskin throw while sipping on some hot tea. She might even take a book out of Papa's library.

She eagerly changed and then went to the small washroom down the hall she and Olivian shared. No time to boil water for a hot bath—that would have to come later. So she splashed her face and scrubbed her hands in the wooden washbasin, dried her hands with a wool hand towel and rushed back downstairs, her baggy linen trousers whooshing as she descended the stairs a daring two steps at a time.

Olivian was in the kitchen setting the small stone table in the parlor for tea. A wooden tray held some small scones made from raspberries in mother's terrace garden, with some small maize-meal cakes sweetened with honey and topped with chopped walnuts. Olivian brought over the teapot and set it down on a small cushion to keep the porcelain from scratching.

"Would you like honey, Paige?" Olivian asked.

"Sure."

Olivian set a cup down and poured a small spoon of honey into the bottom of a clay mug. Then she poured tea over it. She handed Paige the cup, placing a tiny teaspoon with a unicorn's head on the end of the handle.

"Did Mother say you could use these?" Paige asked, glaring at Olivian as her sister put an identical spoon in her own teacup.

"No, but what's the point of having an enhanced set of teaspoons if you can't use them once in a while?"

"Liv, we're supposed to save them for company," Paige insisted. Olivian shrugged.

"Gerik is coming later, and he won't drink tea, so think of this as getting to use it because our company today won't." Olivian snapped her fingers and her spoon leapt to life, the unicorn head letting out a soft whinny and shaking its sparkling mane. It began to try and gallop around the teacup, stirring the honey into the tea as it trotted about in the steaming herbal brew. Paige rolled her eyes but snapped her finger too, allowing her own spoon to trot about and stir in the sweetener.

Her unicorn whinnied at her, and Paige nodded a "thank you" to the horse, offering it a crumb of a maize-cake in gratitude. The horse nibbled the crumb up happily and turned it's head away as if it were bashful at being recognized for its service.

"They're just so cute!" Olivian giggled, letting her own spoon lap up a drop of honey from her finger. Paige half-smiled. She was right: they were cute. Mother possessed a precious few enchanted items she'd bought from several traders as they made their way through Kapernaum from time to time. Paige didn't know a ton about magic, but she knew enough to know there hadn't been a magician in the Wild for over a century, and so with each passing year enchanted trinkets and commodities became harder and harder to find. Many in town suspected Paige and Olivian's mother of being able to use magic since she was an elf, but her mother claimed she could not; Paige had never pressed the matter.

After a moment of reflective sipping, Paige asked Olivian, "What are you wearing to the dance besides the gown?"

Olivian looked thoughtful for a moment. "I don't know. I have several green shawls that might go well with it. And maybe some beaded slippers. You?"

"I don't know," Paige said, tucking her legs underneath her and spreading one of the wool throw blankets on her lap. "I may go to the market again tomorrow and actually do some hunting around."

"You could get a red sash, that would look wonderfully striking with the white dresses!" Olivian suggested excitedly. Paige smirked, suppressing a giggle. Olivian became a schoolgirl again any time she got excited about the latest fashions. It could get annoying, but Paige was trying to take more of her sister's advice recently.

"That could work," Paige said, sipping her tea. It washed down her throat like a warm enveloping blanket, circling around inside her and spreading its warmth to the tips of her tingling fingers.

"You might go see if the Gyhughs traders are in tomorrow," Olivian suggested. "They often have some good scarlets from the eastern side of the Wild available, and they are almost always in Kapernaum for the bigger festivals."

"I might do just that," Paige said, finishing what was left in her teacup. A telltale 'squeak' in the second stair told her someone was descending the stairs. She glanced up to see her mother. One look at the tea table and her flawless, angled face screwed up in the contortion only a mother can achieve when she is about to scold her child.

"Honestly, Olivian, how many times must we go through this; practical magic only when there are guests over!" she scolded. Paige tried to hide an I-told-you-so smile by taking a fake sip out of her empty cup. The unicorn spoon nuzzled her nose and blew a tiny breath out through its nostrils.

"Sorry, Mother." Olivian sighed in annoyance at being caught. Paige had never understood Olivian's fascination with magic. It wasn't like she could use it outside of previously enchanted objects. Mother said there were very few humans left in the world who could, so few that even living among her own people she had never met one.

Elenass opened the silver chest that housed seven other identical spoons and held it expectantly at Olivian. The princess reluctantly pulled her unicorn from it's bath. The creature whinnied in protest the whole way to the box. Paige gently took her own spoon out and it brayed pitifully as she slid it into the velvet sleeve it was kept in. Mother shut the box and the noises instantly stopped as the spoons returned to their natural state. She silently tucked it away on the stone mantle of the fireplace.

"Well. I have a surprise for you both," the elf said, smoothing her skirt and taking a gracious seat on the edge of the couch near Paige and Olivian. "They're on your beds now."

Olivian's face lit up while Paige grinned smugly. Though she was nearly twenty winters old, Olivian was every bit the little princess she'd always been.

"I'll try it on right away," Olivian chirped, trying to contain her excitement behind some form of decorum.

"Wait, how did you know—"

"Thank you, Mother!" Olivian interrupted, leaping to her feet. She almost immediately remembered her manners and turned, setting her teacup down gingerly before she nearly skipped upstairs.

"You both knew the whole time, didn't you?" Elenass said, staring at Paige through azure eyes squinted in suspicion.

"Well, not the whole time," Paige said, taking another sip from her empty cup. Elenass huffed, her bottom lip pouting slightly.

"Don't lie to me, Alwasu."

"I'm sorry, Mother, you just aren't very good at keeping secrets." Paige giggled, downing the last of her hot beverage. Elenass looked slightly offended, then smiled smugly.

"I suppose I mustn't be. Well then, my little ray of sunshine, go try it on and make sure it fits, yes?"

"Thank you, Mother. You really didn't have to," Paige said graciously, setting her tea mug on the stone table. Elenass smiled taking a sip of her own tea.

"It was my pleasure, Alwasu," she said. "Even if it wasn't a surprise for very long."

Paige stood and tossed the sheepskin back onto the couch before crossing over to her mother and hugging her tightly. Elenass returned her warm embrace with her slender yet surprisingly strong arms.

"Love you," Paige whispered, squeezing her mother appreciatively.

"I love you too, darling." Her mother's smile took on a mischievous glint as Paige straightened up and turned to return to her room.

"But Paige?"

"Yes, Mother?"

"Don't think I've forgotten about the stained shirt, young lady."

Paige sighed, but smiled as she headed upstairs.

"I'll get it soaking, don't worry."

With that, she bounded up the stairs to try on her new dress, more eager than she'd ever admit for the dance the following night.

CHAPTER 2

CINNIKNOTS

AND HIDING SPOTS

*P*aige jogged across the village platforms, the wood bridges rattling with every bound and leap. Hardly anyone else was up and about at this hour, but the chieftain's daughter wanted to be sure she got on the first platform heading down to the market. She could hear the sounds of sleepy traders pitching tents and the clanging of pots below as the village slowly woke from slumbers in the pre-dawn that peeped through the canopy above.

She listened to the chirping of the birds beginning to try and rouse the forest from the clutches of Mother Sleep, the fanciful fairy that supposedly enchanted children's dreams, or so the old stories said. Soon she was in the line for the platforms and on the first lift down with a few drowsy hunters, a baker who was late getting to his marquee, and a couple of rowdy boys looking to go get into some sort of mischief, no doubt.

"Princess, so wonderful to see you!" one of the hunters said as he helped turn the crank.

"Good to see you, too!" Paige said cheerfully, not remembering the man's name but smiling warmly. The village was filled with people who knew Paige by name, but if she had to guess, she only knew about half the population well enough to remember what family they belonged to.

They continued down to the forest floor without any incident, aside from the baker yelling at the rowdy boys to sit down before they fell off the platform. As soon as the platform touched down, Paige quickly headed to the southern area of the market, where more of the visiting craftsmen tended to set up shop. There were a few from yesterday already hawking wares, but at least ten new vendors had pitched tents and were laying out tables filled with fine goods from the far east and southern border of the Wild.

She started with a group of Venomitain jewelers who were selling various hairpins and accessories of carved bone studded with brass and semi-precious stones. Nothing there really caught her eye, so she stopped by several more tailors and milliners, perusing their wares and hearing every typical sales pitch.

"I promise you, m'lady," urged a gangly man wearing glass spectacles that made his eyes look four sizes too large for his head, "there is no other vendor with such corsets. An hourglass figure the likes of which this village has never seen!"

"And for good reason," muttered Paige, suppressing a disgusted snort. He was proffering a waist brace made of canvas and bone. They appeared to make moving a chore itself, not to mention dancing the wild motions of their Harvest Moons traditions.

"What can I interest the noble woman in, then? A new mirror, perhaps? Or how 'bout a lovely pair of earrings for your lovely..." he trailed off as he noticed the slight taper on her ears, confusion melting into a dawning realization. Paige didn't mind—she was used to such stares from the newer traders that came into town.

"No, I'm really only looking for something that would complement a white dress, thank you."

She turned to go, but the merchant seemed to find his tongue.

"Ah, but give me a mere moment of your time, lass, and I will make it worth it to you, I promise!"

He turned to another small table behind where he was keeping his wares and opened a little chest with a key. He sorted through several objects that clinked and jingled and was soon back before her with a blue velvet cloth clutched tightly in one hand, peeling back the corners as if it were a pastry and all he cared about was the raspberry tart in the center.

"I got this chain from a fellow south of the Great River. Swears up and down it's Elvish, though I've no provenance to prove that."

He opened a knobby fist to reveal a beautiful silver chain that immediately had Paige's attention. It was thin, exquisite wire craftsmanship. Each link was an identical replica of a silver rose, its thorny stem looping around in a figure-eight pattern, connecting to identical links on either side. The craftsmanship was undoubtedly wonderful, and it certainly would look good with her mother's Elvish-style dress.

"How much are you asking?" Paige asked hesitantly. The man scratched a scruffy three-day-old beard on his square, cleft chin.

"I'd be able to part with it for fourteen Farthards."

Paige thought of the three copper coins in her vest pocket and sadly shook her head.

"We use Cops here," she explained, closing the merchant's hand around the velvet and necklace. "And of those I only have three to spend. Thanks anyways."

"Wait, miss, hold on—maybe we can still barter?"

"Barter for what, Paige?"

Paige turned to see Matildra and three of her friends advancing towards her from across the street. The princess felt a fire light in her gut, ushering the morning chill right out of her bones.

"Good morning, Matildra," Paige managed to force out through a smile hiding her disdain. The other girl walked right up to the table, her dark pink heavy wool cloak and white fox fur scarf wrapped tightly about her so passersby could barely see her curly hair and cherry red cheeks.

"What have we here?" Matildra asked, her false sweetness laced with a condescending edge. The merchant looked the bundle of wool up and down, then looked at Paige.

"I was just—" Paige started, before the merchant interrupted.

"I was just insisting how much I love this young lady's hunting dagger," he rushed in, gesturing to Paige's sheathed tool that rested on her right hip. Matildra looked genuinely interested in this development.

"I see!" she said excitedly. "Have you found something for your dress after all?"

"The finest chain in silver I can offer!" the merchant said, displaying the silver for Matildra and her friends to see. They huddled around it like a flock of sheep about to get the local brewer's mash leftovers.

"It's exquisite!"

"Most magnificent!"

"Does it come in gold?"

Paige looked at the merchant curiously. He raised his eyebrows with a knowing look, and nodded down to her dagger.

"Alas, ladies, this is my last one, and the mistress here just offered me a knife and three Cops, was it?"

Paige pulled her hunting knife out and set it on the table and fished in her pocket for the three copper coins, placing them by the antler-handled buckskinner.

"It's lovely, Princess," Matildra chirped, wrapping her cloak around herself even tighter. "I can't wait to see yours and Olivian's dresses at the feast!"

"And I yours," Paige fibbed, secretly pleased to hear something that didn't come off as condescending escape Matildra's mouth. The girls tittered on down the line of sleepy merchants, the odd squeak or two erupting and letting the world know they had found something else they thought adorable.

"Thank you for that," Paige said, reaching to scoop up her three coins. The merchant smiled at her and held out the necklace.

"I know what it is like to be bullied, and it's up to us to stand up for those who may not have the tools to stand up for themselves." He held out the necklace expectantly, and Paige looked at it wistfully.

"I can't afford a price for such an artifact," she said sadly. The man grabbed her hand and dropped the necklace in it, closing her cold fingers about the chilled silver.

"If you are willing to part with the hunting knife, I will make you that deal."

"It's not a very good knife, just the one I use when I'm out and about," Paige warned, looking at the old antler handled knife she'd received as a birthday present several years ago.

"I do not wish to take it if it is sentimental to you," the man assured. "But if you can bear to part with it, I will take the three Cops and give it to my son."

Paige searched the merchant's expression, but the only thing she could see beyond the glass spectacles was a look of sympathy and kindness.

"It's not... but only if you're sure?"

"I'm sure, my lady."

Paige handed him the Cops and slid the knife over to him, taking the sheath off her belt and tossing it beside the blade. He grinned and nodded his approval as she put the circlet of silver around her neck and slid the clasp shut. He reached under the table and pulled out a polished bronze mirror, holding it out for her to see. She failed to hide a grin. It was beautiful; all it needed was a pendant and it would be perfect for tonight.

"Incredible, my lady," the merchant said, returning the mirror to beneath the table. "I hope you outshine every one of those young ladies at the festival tonight."

"Will you be attending?"

"Probably not. I'm too old for dancing about like a young buck!"

"But not too old for feasting and drinking!"

The man laughed cheerfully at her response.

"Perhaps not. I shall have to consult with 'the Boss,' you know."

He glanced back at his wife who was wrestling with what Paige assumed was a tired and cranky toddler. The man turned back to her and winked from behind his spectacles.

"Well, I hope to see you all there if you get the chance!" Paige said, shoving her cold hands in the wooly pockets of her vest. "Have a good rest of your morning!"

"You too, lass!" the merchant said, waving as Paige began to jog down the street.

The smell of cinnamon wafted into her nose as she passed Dirgah's tent, her favorite baker. She made a hard right turn and skipped over to a large tan marquee with the sides dropped down, a tall cob chimney poking straight out the top. A wooden sign dangling from a twisted iron pole read "Dirgah's Loaves a' Plenty" with the 'e' in 'loaves' painted backwards. The princess chuckled as she did any time she sidled past the bakery, ducking into the marquee's opening as the warm, rich smells of spices, yeast, and burning hardwood embraced her.

The interior was packed with people, all chattering and laughing gaily as they waited for their various orders. A ring of wooden plank tables circled a large, dome oven made of cob that stood in the center of the marquee, its chimney stack poking out through a hole in the roof. Around these tables, six young bakers were working furiously, kneading dough, dusting proofed loaves with flour, and sliding baked goods in and out of the giant oven. No sooner would a round, whole-grain loaf appear out of the dome, a customer would rush forward and take the piping hot bread into their basket and they'd be on their way. Standing round back of the oven, the hefty, tall, bushy head baker, Mr. Dirgah, pronounced orders. His rosy cheeks flushed with the heat of his operation but his coal black eyes twinkled in the crackling light the oven cast dancing around the room.

"Harry, I need three more loaves for Mr. Albbus, please. Ronny, get me some more Cinniknot dough, if you would! Herman, how many times do I have to tell you the loaves don't have to be perfectly round, just get them in the oven!"

A young baker with wild, untamable hair that fell beyond his knobby shoulders rolled his eyes and continued to sculpt a loaf that was perfect enough to serve to a king. A lad with large blue eyes and a mop of close-cropped strawberry-blond hair hurried over to Dirgah's table and deposited a large wood bowl filled to the brim with a white, fluffy dough that had risen up to look like a perfect dumpling for a giant's stewpot. The baker plunged his ham-sized fists into a copper vat of flour and clapped them together to shake off the excess material, then ripped himself a hefty lump from the main doughball. The mountain of puffy proofing dough sank into its container as the master baker began slapping the dough back and forth between his hands. Paige pushed her way to the front of his table, flashing him her biggest smile.

"What did that dough ever do to you, Dirgah!?" Paige teased. The giant of a man looked down his voluminous black beard at her and winked.

"Ms. Paige! Right good to see you, it is. How's your father? Busy getting ready for tonight, I expect?"

"He is. I think he's seeing to the Great Hall's preparations now!"

"Right! Well, when you see him next, tell him the one hundred Cinniknots might actually be more like one hundred and fifty!" He chuckled, jabbing the strawberry-blond apprentice in the ribs. "Ronny here thought we'd want a little extra, so he accidentally dumped an extra half bowl of flour into the mixing vat!"

"I said I was sorry," the apprentice muttered, handing Dirgah a bowl filled with what smelled like cinnamon and allspice. The baker deftly sprinkled some on top of the dough ball and began kneading the ball with his large hands. Soon the ball became a rope that he nimbly tied off into a knot and let fall atop a large wooden peel with a plop. He grabbed a jug of what Paige took to be maple syrup and began drizzling it ever so lightly on top of the dough knot, finishing the piece off with another dusting of cinnamon.

"So that's what smells like heaven!" Paige marveled. The baker shoved the peel into the oven and laughed, yanking the paddle out so the knot stayed inside the heated dome. He then took out a similar knot that had just finished baking on the other side of the oven and dumped it onto a parchment napkin on the table. The maple sugar had caramelized and soaked into the knot's golden brown top, the steam from the bread's honey-amber crust rising up to caress Paige's frost-nipped cheeks. To finish the masterpiece, the baker sprinkled some finely ground flour over top the loaf and and folded the edges of the paper over top. He wrapped the package with a thin square of leftover linen and extended it to Paige.

"Cinnamon come in, then?" Paige asked.

"Aye, the spice traders made it just in the nick of time!"

"Lucky for you!" Paige smiled, snatching up the warm parcel.

"You aren't kidding!" The baker winked. "Do see this gets to the chief, Ms. Paige, won't you? Need to know if they are acceptable tasting, don't you know?"

"I'll see he gets most of it!" Paige said. "But I can't promise some will go missing on the lift..."

"What a mystery!" Dirgah chuckled. "Best not to spoil your appetite or get too full for all that dancing and carrying on later!"

"Oh, trust me. I'll be fine for dancing."

"Oh, ho, now? Ms. Paige finally got herself a suitor worthy of her favorable gaze?"

Paige felt her cheeks flush a bit more.

"Oh, Dirgah, you know you're the only man who really gets me!" she teased, shaking the ever tantalizing Cinniknots package at him.

"Princess, I may not be a poet, but I am versed in the true language of love. And there aren't many paths to a woman's heart as short and easy as a fresh honey cake or some Nutter Fluffers!"

"You aren't wrong." Paige laughed, tucking the parcel under her arm. "See you tonight, then?"

"I'll be saving you a dance! If my wife lets me, that is!" The baker laughed, waving goodbye with his flour-covered hands. "Herman! This isn't a sculpting contest, just get the loaves in the oven!"

Paige popped back out of the marquee into the early morning light filtering through the trees, the leaves sparkling like jewels. There were more people about now, preparing for the feast. Children were causing mischief in their frolicking, taxing their mothers' patience as the women tried to both corral children and get their shopping lists checked off for the big evening.

Paige stopped by several more shops on her way over to the lifts just to gaze at the array of fine trade goods some of the new merchants had displayed. One band of troubadours were setting up a tent splattered with greens and blues that matched the dancing peacock. Another tent had a rather brassy woman exclaiming it was the "last chance you or anyone would have" to snatch up one of her fine copperware kettles and pots. The sound of wood chopping told her the coopers and wheelwrights were chopping firewood for the evening's festivities. Paige could smell the sawdust as she passed their shops. Through the gaps in the tents, she could see all the apprentices dragging timber from the forest to the craftsmen, expressions of boredom slapped onto their tired, young faces.

Paige made it to the lifts just as the first load of firewood was being hoisted up to the upper levels. Each day, the families of Kapernaum were all responsible for hauling their own firewood or buying it off the woodcutters, but on feast days everyone chipped in and helped collect the mounds of cordwood needed to sustain a bonfire all night long. The last lift was designated all day for just such a purpose, so Paige hopped in line for the second lift and soon found herself slowly ascending, nibbling off a small piece of her Cinna-Knot.

Once Up Top, Paige quickly made her way to the southern end of Kapernaum by means of the bridges and platforms now humming with the din of hive-like activity. Women were sweeping the freshly fallen leaves off the platforms while men with wheelbarrows collected everything from firewood to stools and chairs in preparation for the feast. Some ladies wove garland together from bundles of spruce branches someone had cut and hauled up early that morning, twisting the the evergreen boughs around the platform railings like graceful serpents of emerald green. Paige ducked under a bench two older men were hauling to the Great Hall, who made comments about the "youth of this town ruining the village." She found her father standing in the center of the platform with his secretary, a tiny feeble old man named Pontus, who was scribing on a slab of slate nearly as wide as his oversized head.

"I think it would be better to have the whole floor cleared and not just half of it, wouldn't you agree?"

"Of course, my lord," Pontus said in a droning, high-pitched monotone. As Paige's papa turned and saw his daughter walking over to him, a wide, bright smile broke out over his face.

"Alwasu! What brings my little ray of sunshine out this early?"

Paige rolled her eyes but embraced her father's open arms with a tight hug. His surcoat smelled like the light, sweet pipe tobacco he smoked on occasion, mixed with the lingering scent of the hide. The soft, buffed leather felt cool against her cheek as she breathed in his warm, rich smell. All that was missing was the smell of the old pages of parchment in his library and she would have had the trifecta of what she considered the manliest of scents.

"Dirgah wanted me to bring this to you and let you know we'll have more than enough Cinniknots for the feast," she said, handing him what probably only amounted to two-thirds of the original knot. Her papa's eyes lit up as he inhaled the sweet aroma dramatically, feigning a fainting spell.

"Oh, good ol' Dirgah, always pulling through for me!" Papa laughed, scarfing down half the roll before handing the rest back to Paige. "Here, you eat it. I have to watch my figure or I'll never fit into those tight hosen your mother makes me wear to these things."

Paige didn't argue, nearly inhaling the rest of the roll. Papa looked downright impressed, while Pontus seemed indifferent to her existence as he muttered and scribbled on his slate with a piece of chalk. She looked about the Great Hall as men moved benches and prepared for the evening's festivities. Several of the village's warriors were hanging surplus shields of various paint schemes on the roof supports of the seating areas, with blues, whites, greens and yellows standing out in stark contrast to the weathered wood.

The platform itself was exposed to the elements, save for an awning that circled its rim over the benches and seats that helped make up the railing. There was enough space to comfortably seat almost two hundred people hip to hip along the benches running the length of the platform, with space for a hundred along its width. This didn't include all the space across the table on the countless wooden stools, benches, chairs, and stumps being brought in from all around the village. Tonight they would seat nearly the entire village on this one platform, with room enough to dance as well.

To Paige's left was a small dais built where the Burgesses and chieftain's family sat at raised tables. Before these tables, in the center of the platform, a stone fire trench was being stacked with wood for the bonfire, its ancient-looking boulders carved with all manner of effigies depicting griffons and dragons fighting amidst a tangled mess of vines knotting their way in and out of the design.

One of the young boys filling the stone trough looked up and caught Paige's eye as he dumped an armload of dried tree-branches into the trench. The ruddy, freckled lad made a face and stuck his tongue out at the princess. Paige returned the gesture.

"Bentley, are you making faces at my princess?" Papa exclaimed, interrupting his own instructions to Pontus. He pulled off his glove and shook his three-fingered hand at the boy menacingly. "Draw your weapon boy, for I will not suffer my lady's honor to go thusly offended!"

The boy, who wasn't any older than eight, grabbed a stout stick and brandished it like a bastard sword, trying to contain his laughter. The chieftain marched dramatically to the woodpile and armed himself with an equally formidable stick. He saluted smartly and then advanced on the boy, flailing his stick about whimsically. The boy charged him and began swinging wildly, laughing all the while. Paige chuckled as her Papa swung comically around and let the boy get a few taps on his arms and legs, crying out in mock pain.

"OH! Oh, good heavens! Bless me, I am failing you, my sweet!" he cried out to Paige as he pretended to stumble backwards. Some of the other boys had also grabbed some small stick swords and were encroaching the mock battle, eager to have in on the fun. Paige jogged over and snatched a branch up for herself, flailing it above her head.

"I'll rescue you, Papa!" she cheered, and began to fence with Bentley and the five other young lads, allowing him to get up.

"Ah, but the joke is on you. I AM IMMORTAL!" Papa shouted. He dropped his stick and snatched one of the lads up by the belt, then deposited him into a heap on the newly swept deck. The other boys all shouted protests as they leapt and scrambled on Alaire's back. Paige laughed and jumped on the pileup, pulling off a couple boys and tackling them to the floor. She pinned one under her arm and began grinding her fist into the boy's dirty blond hair, amidst his thrashing and howls of protest. Another of the boys grabbed her moccasin and tried pulling it off her foot, so she dispatched him with a swift kick, followed by catching his midsection in a scissor lock. The boy flailed and kicked, laughed and tried to crawl away but only managed to drag his captor along the deck with him a few feet. Paige was laughing so hard she failed to notice the deep-cuffed boots embossed with oak leaves planted just a foot behind her head.

"Why, Derak of Oak's Bough, fancy running into you here!" her father pronounced.

Paige felt her neck flush with embarrassment as she whirled around and saw Derak standing behind her, his emerald shirt and trousers only serving to highlight the bright green in his eyes. Paige leapt to her feet, dumping the boys onto the ground and trying to straighten out her wrinkled clothes. Derak looked at her with confused interest before bowing in front of the village chief.

"M'lord," he said courteously.

Papa waved off the bow. "Oh, enough of that. What can I do for the Fauxbre boys this fine day?"

"My father sent me to ask where you want all the gourds to be delivered. He brought the cartload you requested."

"Perfect!" Papa grinned, slapping the lad on the back. "You may deliver them to the Pump House. Xandla will inspect them and then see to it they are filled and distributed."

"Of course, m'lord," Derak said with a nod.

"My lord, we really must finish the seating arrangements for tonight," whined a wheezing Pontus as he tapped his slate impatiently. Papa chuckled and rolled his eyes.

"But of course, Pontus. Lead on, you miserable old sot!" the chief jabbed, tossing his long arm over the short little man's thin shoulders and walking back towards the end of the platform, leaving Paige alone with Derak.

"It's good to see you!" she blubbered, trying to fix her now unkempt hair. He nodded, regarding her curiously.

"Is it common practice in Kapernaum to scrap with the junior village ruffians?" he asked with a coy smile.

"It's, um, I usually..." Paige stuttered, trying to think of anything she could say to save her shriveling self-esteem. It was evident that, while not repulsed, Derak regarded her behaviour as odd. Words whirred around Paige's head, but she couldn't seem to string any of them together coherently.

"It's alright." Derak laughed, trying to reassure her. "Just surprised, is all. Not something you see girls participating in every day."

Paige knew he didn't mean it in a condescending way, but she couldn't help but feel a slight stinging sensation in her chest as the words hit their unintended mark. She was odd, and right now in her life, she wanted more than anything to feel like she wasn't an outcast. The incessant backhanded compliments and constant ostracization because of her interests had finally rubbed her calloused, carefree attitude to a raw spot. And now it wasn't just the village girls commenting on her odd behaviour, but an attractive and desirable bachelor.

"Well, I suppose I'd better be off. Have to get all those gourds to the Pump House for what's-his-face."

"Xandla."

"Yes, Xandla. That's the one."

"Alright, then will I still see you tonight?" Paige asked, realizing only after it had left her mouth how desperate it sounded. But Derak merely smiled and nodded.

"I promised you a dance, didn't I?"

Paige smiled sheepishly as he winked, turned, and jogged away towards the lifts. She stared after him until he was out of sight, then she sighed in exasperation, smacking her head repeatedly against the closest support.

"Stupid, stupid, stupid," she muttered to herself, keeping rhythm with her self-deprecation till she heard a soft chuckle.

"Careful, Little Dove. You'll dent the support beam, and wouldn't it be tragic to have that fall on someone during the party?"

"Why can't I live up to any of their expectations, Papa?" Paige muttered, feeling just the slightest hint of a sniffle coming. She turned and gave her father a big hug. He patted her head softly and rubbed her back. She inhaled his smell again, smiling as she felt the nub of his missing finger slide across her back.

"Who cares what they think, eh?"

"I mean, I don't want to care, but somehow I can't seem to stop from caring," she muttered into his shirt. The chief laughed.

"That's called 'adolescence,' Bobcat. I've been there. It's rough. But I promise tomorrow night will come and go, and in ten years you'll look back on that harvest dance as a mere blink of time that really didn't matter much in the end."

Paige smiled, wiping her nose on her sleeve, which brought a sparkle to her father's eye.

"All you need to know is that you have always exceeded my expectations, Alwasu. Never forget that, no matter what anyone else tries to tell you. Okay?"

Paige laughed and nodded as her father sighed and patted her shoulder.

"You'd best be off to get ready soon, yes? Isn't that the women's way? To need six hours to get ready?"

"Why are you asking me? How would I know?" Paige laughed, giving her papa one more hug.

"Best be off, then, just in case," Papa said with a wink. Paige nodded and chuckled before turning and heading back in the direction of home, eager to begin preparations for what was sure to be a night to remember.

Olivian ran the hairbrush through Paige's long hair as the two princesses prepared for the most eagerly anticipated social event of the season. Now that the storehouses were filled to the brim with the year's harvest safely dried and tucked away in the grain stores, they could begin to settle in and prepare for the long winter of the Wild.

To thank the Creator every year, the tribe held an annual Harvest Moon's Feast, complete with wild dancing, banquet tables overflowing with food, speeches from the Burgesses, theater entertainment, and rough sparring battles on the floor of the mead hall as the hours slipped by late into the night.

"Ouch!" Paige cried as Olivian hit a tangle in her flaxen hair. "Could you yank it any harder?"

"I might if you don't quit whining," Olivian warned. "Hold *still*, Ala!"

"This is so stupid. Hair should not be this troublesome!"

"It isn't, unless you move around like a squirrel in a burning tree!"

Paige rolled her steely eyes. Though she'd be more comfortable in pants and a practical shirt, her mother's dress was perfect. It was a dazzlingly white with a scooped neckline and lace trim, with sleeves that went just past her elbow and opened up elegantly. The back laced up with a dark blue ribbon and a matching sash she'd borrowed from Olivian.

Olivian wore the same style dress, but with a gold ribbon and a circlet of gold atop her head. She had already spent hours curling her own hair in twisted bits of paper. Once the older princess had finished her own dressing, she then attempted to prod, push, jab, and yank Paige's hair into submission for what seemed like an eternity. She curled the bottoms of Paige's locks that cascaded down to the middle of her back, then wove thin vines of baby ivy into several small braids to catch the majority of loose tresses. As a finishing touch, she was currently attempting a crown braid in Paige's hair.

"Now behave!" Olivian scolded the obstinate locks that fell to Paige's mid-back. "I have to get you in place so I can go finish getting ready!"

"Big plans?" Paige queried, wincing as yet another clump of hair was wrenched from its natural spot.

"Yes, actually," Olivian said, tearing out another tangle so hard it felt like she was trying to snap a fresh rope. "I have a dance to see to! Honestly, Ala, do you ever brush your hair?"

"Is it the dance you're really worried about, or will a special someone be attending?" Paige asked absently. Olivian always had a new crush that Paige kept a running tally of in her head.

"Derak of Oak's Bough is in town. Oh goodness, Ala, those green eyes of his? I can hardly handle speaking with him without stumbling over my words! I heard he was finished seeing that girl from Hayen's clan because she wasn't worth the two-hour walk through the mountains."

Paige felt her jaw tighten. Olivian set the brush down on the table and handed Paige some ribbons to tie into her hair. As her sister skipped across the room to her own vanity and began braiding her own hair, Paige turned to glare at her.

"It's odd you mention that, because I talked to him yesterday, and he said he'd be dancing with me," Paige replied tersely. It had taken many interactions with girls like Olivian and Matildra to do it, but she had perfected the appearance of civility laced with a dripping dose of sarcasm.

Olivian laughed.

"What?!"

"Oh, nothing. Just that I saw him only an hour or so ago by the Pump House with his brothers. He agreed to dance with me as well. Did it occur to you when he asked you that the first dance is always the Elder dance?"

Paige frowned. She'd forgotten about that. The firstborns of each household were the ones that traditionally started the dancing. Usually it didn't bother her, but this meant that her sister could corner Derak.

"So what? Maybe he'll say 'no', eh?" Paige snipped.

"Oh, please, Ala. Boys don't just say 'no' to me. You know that."

"Well maybe they should," Paige muttered. Olivian sniffed, putting another ribbon in her own hair.

"Don't be daft, Paige."

"He asked me. You can't just overrule that because you don't like it!"

"I have the right to dance with him first, and let's be honest, we both know I'm the better dancer."

Paige's face flushed. Olivian spoke the truth, and there was little Paige could do about it. She wasn't surprised, though; it was just like Olivian to manipulate the system to get her own way.

"So what?" Paige huffed through clenched teeth. "It's a stupid custom! Old laws for old people."

"I believe this is what is commonly referred to as 'your problem.' Word from the wise, Ala—don't try to steal him from me, or go running to Papa like you always do. Father won't risk upsetting the Burgesses just because you went crying to him like a daddy's girl." With a flip of her perfect hair, the older princess pulled on her shawl, patted Paige on the head condescendingly, and walked out of their room.

Paige glared at her fists in her lap, her knuckles turning white with the pent-up frustration. She had never been able to compete with her sister when it came to matters like this. Olivian had all the looks, all the refinement. Paige? Well, she'd managed to be the son her father never had. She took pride in knowing how to spar and hunt. She didn't mind that at all, but when it came to these womanly things, Paige always felt like she came in second place. If the other girls in town were around, she moved even further down the list. Though she told herself it was all right, deep down she doubted herself. Maybe she did need to start acting more like Olivian and Matildra?

"Stupid customs," she muttered, tossing the brush onto her nightstand. She stood, looking wistfully at her reflection in the polished steel. Usually, dressed in her boys' pants and everyday hunting attire, she always thought she looked like her father. But now, with her hair down and her new dress on, she looked every bit her mother's daughter. Paige didn't consider herself a vain person, but tonight she felt as beautiful as

Elenass looked. She would show them. She'd stood down hundreds of wild animals in the forest; what were a couple of twittering gossips with painted faces to worry about? She pressed her lips together and shook her head defiantly. Olivian would see. They'd all see. More than one star can shine in a night.

Paige tugged the bottom drawer open on her nightstand and retrieved the necklace from this morning. It went perfectly with the dress mother had sewn, and she smiled as she put it around her neck. The roses were beautiful against her fair skin, and the entire ensemble really seemed to accent the elven features she'd inherited from her mother.

"Of course," she muttered, touching the bare spot below the necklace where a locket would have hung. She needed a centerpiece to pull the whole thing together. She looked over at Olivian's bureau. Immediately she imagined how her sister would persecute her if she borrowed something from there without asking, and she certainly was not going to ask now. No. It would have to be something else.

She thought long and hard. If she couldn't use any of Olivian's silver, and her own nearly bare jewelry box would not suffice, perhaps her mother had something in her dresser that she could use.

She stepped out of her room carefully, making sure her bare feet hit only the spots on the floor she knew would not creak. She knew the sound of each floorboard by heart. Even though her mother might not mind if she borrowed one small item from her nightstand, at this point in the evening, she didn't want to risk asking. The princess looked about carefully; better to beg forgiveness than ask permission. After making sure no creeping peepers were about to witness her, she slid through the open door into the bedroom.

The humble room was adorned with two delicately-carved wardrobes, a vanity, and a four-poster bed. Each bedpost was carved as if it was a tree growing up from the ground, with wispy-thin sheets of green linen draping down around the frame like willow branches. Her father had commissioned it years ago to remind Paige's mother of the forests she had grown up in far to the southeast. The wardrobes stood against the wall opposite the foot of the bed. Paige inhaled the smell of the cedar panels deeply as she wiggled her bare toes on the soft, wispy sheepskin carpet that adorned the floor of the entryway. Between them was mother's own mahogany vanity, with a small bench upholstered with a soft sheepskin cushion, similar to the rug.

Paige tip-toed over to the dresser and began searching the small drawers and several clay and glass jars neatly placed along the back of the desk in front of the polished silver mirror. Nothing grabbed her attention as she shuffled through the various trinkets and jewelry. Everything from some brass rings to carved bone amulets were arranged in multiple compartments, but none of them seemed to match the wirework of the roses in her necklace.

"Paige!"

Paige's heart tripled its rhythm at the sound of her name. She jerked her hands away as if the desk had been made of molten brass, but the lace on her sleeve caught one of the glass jars on the table. Her blue eyes widened with horror as the jar teetered off the vanity. She instinctively thrust her foot out and caught the container from crashing on the hardwood floor. It smacked her bare foot and rolled harmlessly across the oak floorboards and under her papa's dresser.

Paige let out a huge breath that she hadn't realized she'd been holding. She looked quickly to the door. The voice had been her mother's, but she hadn't yet heard the telltale squeaking of her mother ascending the steps.

"Yes, Mother?" she called out.

"Your sister and I are going to head out. Shall we wait for you?"

"No, Mother," she replied, holding her breath.

"Alright, we'll see you over there. Your father is already at the Grand Hall with the Burgesses, so make sure you lock the door when you leave!"

"Of course, Mother!" Paige responded, listening hard. She heard the sound of her mother and sister talking quietly, then the noise of metal softly tapping more metal as they opened the forged iron latch and then closed the door behind them.

Paige gasped a huge sigh of relief.

"Well, that was close," she muttered to herself. She looked down at the floor where the jar had fallen. It had apparently rolled so far under her father's black wardrobe that she couldn't see it. Paige pouted. Of all the times she'd have to crawl around on the floor, it would be when she was wearing a brand new white dress.

She kneeled down, being careful not to get the skirt caught underneath her as she peered beneath the broad cabinet. The jar had rolled over to the very back of the wardrobe. She reached around blindly till her fingertips brushed the glass. She grabbed the jar tightly and smirked, pleased with herself as she drew her arm back. Her knuckles scraped against the wardrobe's polished bottom until she hit a rough, sharp bump. Startled, she jerked her hand back, pulling the jar free from the tight space. The tiny scratch on her hand irked her. She wished to discover what injured her, so she looked under the wardrobe once again.

When she couldn't see anything immediately apparent, she slid her arm back in and began brushing the panel with her fingertips. She found the rough spot and prodded it. It felt like a sharp metal object that was tied to the bottom of the dresser by old leather lacing. Curious, she grasped it and pulled hard. It took a couple tugs, but eventually the object was wrenched free with an echoing 'thud.'

She stood, grasping the jar with one hand and the mysterious object in the other. Quickly, she set the glass back down on the vanity and looked at the curious object in her right hand. It was a thin silver key wrapped and tied into a small leather piece that had been tacked to the bottom of the dresser. It gleamed in the flickering light, with not a blemish nor even the smallest fleck of tarnish pitting its smooth surface. She pulled the crusty leather away and set it on the nightstand, holding the key up to the lamp on the wall between her mother's dresser and the floor. It was beautifully crafted; the bit was shaped like any other key, whereas the stem twisted round like a gazelle's horn till it reached the bow. The bow was shaped like two spheres, side by side, one a full circle, the other about two-thirds empty, a waxing moon. It was obvious they were the two moons of Eirensgarth, Taivian and Suntra. The dark and light areas of the moons had been expertly replicated.

It was perfect. Paige didn't even hesitate. She pulled the necklace chain off and slipped the key onto it, returning it to her neck. The bare silver felt cool against her pale chest. The key matched the necklace exquisitely. When she looked in the mirror, she turned to the left and to the right while stifling a squeal of delight. The best part was that she didn't have to bother borrowing from her mother. Clearly, this was an extra key to the wardrobe, long forgotten under the dusty dresser. Her father would not likely even miss it.

She tossed her hair behind her tapered ears and placed her fists on her hips, triumphantly smirking at her reflection with renewed confidence.

"All right, now, Paige," she said to herself, chin held high, the necklace and key dazzling in the flicker of the candles. "Let's go get you that dance."

Every outdoor lantern in the town was lit, the trees and bridges alive with the flicker of firelight and laughter as people made their way to the Great Hall. Children laughed and pushed their way through the steady stream of adults like trout pushing their way through a mountain creek's current. The sound of joy gave even the chilly early autumn night a glow of warmth that Paige looked forward to every year.

"Hello, Lady Paige!" a small boy called, tossing his arms about in a frantic attempt to get the princess's attention.

"Hello, Phaelun!" Paige waved back.

The young boy was hardly six-years-old, but he was tall enough to poke his small head over the rail of a bridge parallel to the one Paige was crossing. He waved cheerfully, a set of gold curly locks bouncing about his rosy face. "I'm going to dance at the party!"

"Oh, you are, are you?" Paige gasped in playful surprise. Phaelun nodded furiously, his grin as wide as a watermelon slice. The boy's father, who had a similar mass of curly blond hair in a thick ponytail, laughed as he picked the boy up so he could see Paige better.

"Yes! Yes, indeed! Can I... can... can I dance with you, Lady Paige?"

"Oh, Phaelun, of course you may!" Paige winked. The boy squealed with delight. The boy's father mouthed the words "thank you" to Paige with a smile of his own, and the princess laughed merrily.

The laughter caught in her throat after only a moment. Her spine tingled again, like it had the day before. Paige's gaze fell on the bridge to her left where she noticed two figures walking in the opposite direction of the party.

It was the same two strangers she'd run into in the market, the one's she'd assumed must be tree worshipers. She recognized them because of the white turbans. They were moving along the bridge at a brisk pace, both scowling and not speaking to one another. She scratched her back and tried to shake off the unusual feeling as she watched the two men stalk away. She pursed her lips and wondered if she should mention the two men to Papa or her mother. But as soon as the men disappeared into the sea of party-goers, she shrugged off the thought and continued to make her way to the party.

She entered the Great Hall from the the westernmost of the four bridges that connected the town to the primary gathering place of Kaprnaum's residents. The side of the platform Paige entered on was already cleared for dancing, a separate fire being started in a large, iron brazier. Musicians were setting up drums and harps in the corner, a few of them tuning lyres and practicing some flute notes before the official beginning of the party. People were laughing and calling out to each other as they began to claim spots around the tables and gather in cliques.

The crowd swirled about like the smoke from the fire now roaring in the great hearth while the smell of burning wood mingled with the scent of all manner of delicious treats being served: roast peacock, suckling pig, Dirgah's Cinna-Knots, and a plethora of other assorted goods that made Paige's stomach grumble. Beyond the main hubbub, all of the elected officials and the wealthier businessmen of the town had seats and tables reserved for their families on the raised dais. Paige's father and mother were already by the two large thrones from where they could see the entire village around the Great Hall. They were both laughing and talking to Laird Buckwig, a fat man with ruddy cheeks who ran one of the only public eateries in the village. Her chair sat beside her mother, but Paige decided to hold off heading over until she found Derak.

He was over by the edge of the dance floor, dressed in a bright blue tunic trimmed with white ribbon. His black pants made his newly polished boots stand shine like the moons that were rising high in the sky as the night fell. His hair had been combed, pulled back into a short braid, and topped with a wreath of pine. His bright, cheery smile made Paige's cheeks flush, but when he shifted his weight to his other foot, her cheeks flushed for a different reason.

"Oh, Derak, that's simply the most endearing thing I've ever heard!" Olivian was gushing, batting her long eyelashes at the handsome apprentice boy. She was flanked by none other than Matildra and three other young single ladies, all of whom were grinning behind their scarves and shawls with knowing smiles.

"Well, it's not every day someone gets to save a basket of puppies from being drowned in a well," one of the girls said, giggling. Derak smiled sheepishly, though his expression betrayed his secret pleasure in the praise. Paige had a moment of self-doubt, thinking she might just go sit next to mother after all, but her anger quickly overruled that decision. She marched up to the group with determination thudding with every step her moccasins made.

"Evening, Derak," she said confidently. The young man turned and looked at her, a mixture of shock and wonder crossing his face.

"By the Creator's hand," he said, sucking in a deep breath, "Lady Paige, you look... you..."

"My goodness, Paige, how simply brilliant!" Matildra said with a gasp. "That dress...you actually look respectable!"

Paige simultaneously felt a sense of smug accomplishment and a drive to choke Matildra. The older princess was glaring. She stuck her tongue out at Paige behind his back, and Paige felt the corner of her mouth tug into a satisfied smirk.

"Thank you, you're too kind, sir," Paige said, giving a slight curtsy, but not overdoing it. She had her pride, after all.

"Derak was just relaying the sweetest of stories to us!" Matildra piped up. "You simply must hear it, Paige!"

"I'd love to, but I believe the dancing is about to start," Paige commented absently, looking to where the musicians were beginning to assemble.

"Indeed!" Olivian said, suddenly more chipper. Paige saw the gleam in her eye and was about to ask Derak if he cared to head towards the dance floor when the loud sound of a deep drum thundered across the deck. All eyes turned to the head table where the girls' papa was standing to greet all the guests. He was wearing the crown of the chieftains, a solid band of silver studded with garnet and inlaid with intricate knotwork of carved bone in the shape of stags and wolves. A pair of stag antlers were riveted to the crown on either side of the head, wrapped in freshly cut holly sprigs, their blood-red berries hanging from the various points of the rack. In addition to his green tunic, a bison robe was wrapped around his already broad shoulders, making him an even more imposing and impressive figure.

"Kapernaum!" he shouted, arms outstretched. "Are you well!?"

The crowd cheered and screamed, stomping feet and beating fists on tables. Papa smiled at them all, making a motion with his hand like he was cleaning something out of his ear. The people shouted and clapped harder with enough fervor to raise the roof, had there been one. Papa smiled, and Paige was sure that a twinkle of mischief was dancing like a wild doe in her father's eyes.

"Good people! My friends!" He shouted above the din. The crowd immediately repressed the volume of their cheers to hear. "Tonight we celebrate, as one people, another year of success in both the hunts, the gathering expeditions, and the harvest!"

The people cheered again, and the drum began beating a slow, deep rhythm as the chief stepped high onto the table in front of him. Paige sneaked a look past him to her mother. She looked mildly mortified, shaking her head in her hand. Paige stifled a giggle. Her father was always going above and beyond the call of duty when it came to being dramatic for the people, and every time he did, Mother assured them all that she died a little on the inside from the embarrassment.

"We are here to thank the Creator!" he shouted, tossing the crown onto the table with a flamboyant flick of his wrist.

The people banged the table in agreement and slowly the crowd began to stop their feet in tandem with the beating of the drum. BOOM, thud. BOOM, thud.

"We are here to feast and make merry with one another, to be thankful for all that our labor and providence have brought us from this, our forest!" He gestured to the trees above.

BOOM, thud.

"The fishermen have brought us trout!"

BOOM, thud.

"The huntsmen; bison and stag!"

BOOM, thud.

"The farmers have clawed our roots and vegetables from the earth!"

BOOM, thud.

"And so for all this, I have but one question for you! Dare I ask again, Alatarians?"

BOOM, thud.

"KAPERNAUM! ARE YOU WELL!?"

The crowd roared and raised goblets high as the stringed instruments and flutes began to play a lively jig that made the boards beneath Paige's feet shake like a mighty thunder. Her father leapt from the table to the floor and began to dance wildly, screaming and hooting at the top of his lungs like a rooster whose tail feathers had caught on fire. The warriors of the tribe leapt up from their various tables, round shields in their hands and converged on the wild chieftain, slamming their feet to the rhythm of the drums as well, their long, wild hair and beards adorned in various festive arrays. They formed a circle and began chanting to the beat of the drum, their laughter and husky voices cutting through the chill in the early evening sky.

"Hear the drum beat! Feel our thunder!
Put our enemies asunder!
Light the fires! Kiss the ladies!
Dance with children! Feed the babies!
One! Two! Three! GO!
Reap the harvest, beat the SNOW!"

The men whooped and hollered, grabbing large logs and heaving them onto the central hearth, sparks flying up and dancing into the black sky overhead before evaporating into the pantheon of stars above. The crowd screamed and whistled as Papa danced back to his table and jumped back atop of it, much to Mother's chagrin. The drums pounded several more times and the tune halted with one last deep, bellowing *THUD.* The crowd erupted with applause as Paige's father took a bow.

"Thank you, good people!" he shouted above the clapping. "You are too kind. As your chief, I am now proud to announce the official beginning to the Harvest Moons Festival!"

All the young ladies cheered. Derak put his fingers to his lips for a shrill whistle of approval. As the chief raised his goblet high, everyone reached for their own glasses and held them likewise.

"And per request of my beautiful daughter, I'd like to declare the dancing to begin with the Elder Tree dance! Ladies, you know what to do—all firstborn women to the floor and pick your man! Bring on the feast!"

Paige felt her cheeks flush as the crowd cheered. Olivian took one sly look over at her little sister before grabbing Derak's arm and pulling him towards the dance floor. The drums picked up a moderate beat. The harp began to play as the dancers assembled and imitated the niaid's age-old steps in the flickering light of the bonfire.

Paige was furious. She hadn't even entertained the thought that Olivian might go to Papa about it, but she wasn't surprised. She glared at the couple as the dance began, watching the two young dancers bow and curtsey respectively as the music picked up speed.

"Such a shame, Paige." Matildra snickered.

Paige clenched her fist, but did not snap at the girl. Instead, she worked her jaw in frustration. She mumbled, "Two can play at that game, Liv."

The chieftain's two daughters played a cat-and-mouse game well into the night. One would snag the merchant's son for a waltz, the next for a reel, and so on. Meanwhile, Derak seemed to be relishing in the attention, trying his hardest not to show favorites and be as courteous as possible. As the seventh dance died down, Paige was grinning at the handsome lad as he spun her around the dance floor, then stepped away and bowed as the musicians wrapped up the song. No sooner had the last notes drifted away like bonfire smoke in a breeze when Olivian was back at his side.

"Derak, come, sit with us! They've just brought out the mince pies and wildberry scones!"

She didn't leave time for his protest; she simply grabbed his arm and pulled him over to a table where she was sitting with Matildra and the bevy of other well-dressed young ladies.

Paige stalked to the chieftain's table in disgust. She was willing to do many things to battle her sister, but enduring the ceaseless chatter from that particular group was a bit much, even for her.

The chief's daughter plopped down next to her mother in a huff. The chieftan's wife looked over at her with kind green eyes reflecting the light like a peaceful pool of seawater. She was clad in her favorite white dress, with a fine green sash made from the wool of wild mountain sheep. Her waist-long white-blond hair was braided and held in place with an exquisite silver hairpin designed to look like a thorny rose, with several small, silver buds about to bloom. She looked at her younger daughter, her thin, angled face and slanted eyes masking a quizzical gaze.

"You don't look like you're enjoying yourself, Alwasu. You and Olivian have been stabbing each other with your eyes all night. Do you harbor animosity towards your sister?"

"No." Paige sulked, slumping in her chair. She glared at the figures twirling around the platform, shadows from the center fire dancing across her face. Even the smell of the roasting boar on the spit couldn't please her tonight. It felt like someone had stuffed her gut with sawdust; the nasty feeling and taste still haunted her mouth.

"That's not what it looks like to me," Elenass commented, watching the Olivian and Darak sit and laugh with their group at the table across the hall. The hall basked in bright firelight.

"It's not fair!" Paige nearly growled. "She ran to Papa just to get her way. Did you see that? Now just because I'm younger, I have to take a second seat and watch Olivian be a total fairy about it." Paige didn't often invoke such an insult, but she was so angry tonight that she didn't even care.

"A fairy?" Elenass replied thoughtfully. "You mean you want more attention, and your sister is making it a point to rob you by becoming the center of the world?"

"No! Yes! I mean..." Paige sputtered, not liking the childish shadow her mother's observation cast upon her.

"Well, this mustn't go on. We can't have you two biting each other's heads off. It's not good for your teeth."

She leaned over to her husband and whispered something in his ear that Paige couldn't hear. Alaire, with a solemn expression on his face but a twinkle in his eye, nodded and filled his cup with more wine from the clay pitcher at his right. He rose steadily and motioned for the musicians to cease playing. As soon as the jig died down, he gestured for the couples on the dance floor to be seated. The chief lifted his goblet high above his head and shouted in a loud and boisterous voice.

"Friends! It is time we tell the tale of this year's bountiful hunt!" A round of cheers and yips leapt forth from the crowd, and they scurried to get to their seats. Papa grinned his widest smile as the little children of the village flocked over to his table and sat before their beloved chief, cross-legged, with large eyes that shone with wonder. He once again stepped up onto his table, and Paige saw her mother roll her eyes once again this evening.

"Why, I recall it was only two months ago on a ghastly day in the great mountains to the west. We pursued a great herd of mountain bison. You now feast upon some of them in your trenchers. Four-thousand and up, there were, some bigger than this platform! We climbed for days...."

Paige settled back into a more comfortable position, ready for the long and witty story that would certainly follow. She gazed around, surveying the beautifully lit mead hall with the shields tacked onto the supports for the seating canopy. Large carvings of stags and does decorated nearly every beam of wood in the building. It was cool outside, the breeze fluttering through the open forum like an ice blue butterfly dancing its way across the decks. She looked out to her right at the dark forest floor below and thought for a moment that she had seen a flicker. Animals often skittered about below, not fearing the humans so high above them. And it was far too late for any of the merchants to be milling about down there still. As her father's tale continued, she thought no more of it.

Paige glanced at Olivian as her father droned on. She was barely even paying attention to Papa, choosing rather to snicker with Matildra and her coven while playing with a lock of Derak's long hair. By the look on his face, Paige could tell

Derak didn't mind in the slightest. She knew she should take her Papa's advice; she really shouldn't care what the others thought of her, and she shouldn't feel a need to gain their approval. But seeing Olivian, Derak and all the other girls huddled up and indifferent to her put a knot in her stomach.

One night. Olivian couldn't let her have one night where Paige could be the belle of the ball. One night where, for once, she could dance with the most dashing young man on the floor. A sickening disgust gripped Paige's gut, and she turned to her mother.

"*Logheon te' ah yeigh orhn?*" Paige spat in Ehrenya, her mother's native language. They always spoke Elvish when they desired to keep a conversation private, as none of the other people in town could speak it. Are you seeing this?

But her mother wasn't paying attention to her. She was looking up at the open sky with a curious expression, her head cocked to one side as if she were listening to something far off. Paige put a hand on her arm, and the elf broke her concentration and looked at Paige with concern etched into her pale brow.

"I'm sorry dear, wha—" she began but cut herself short as her gaze alighted on Paige's neckline. She leaned forward, reached out, and drew the silver necklace to her face. She looked from the necklace back to Paige, alarm in her eyes.

"Paige," she said in confusion. "How did you...?Where...?"

Before even waiting for her husband to finish his story, Elenass grabbed and clutched the bottom of his robe and tugged it emphatically. Her father had just delivered a punchline that had the audience laughing and cheering, so he squatted down to one knee atop his table, laughing and wiping tears of joy from his face as he focused his attention to his beloved. She held the necklace out for him to see, and his expression froze then melted away. He stared first in disbelief, then in confusion, finally settling for grave seriousness.

"Where did you get that?" Papa asked her in a tone she'd never heard from her father: unsettled.

She was about to answer when she felt a sudden sensation in the base of her spine. It was back again, that tingling she'd had earlier that day, but more intense this time. It felt like an army of fairies were jabbing hot needles into her backbone over and over, yet her body seemed to be growing colder and more tense. The sensation spread quickly up her back and to her limbs. Then she heard a low groan quietly slip in over the din of her father's tale and the laughter of the gathering. It was a moaning of death in the trees, a long, sorrowful sound. Paige heard the deafening crack of splintering wood. Her skin froze over like a pond in winter.

A shadow loomed overhead, blotting out the moonlight. Paige looked up. Her eyes widened. She opened her mouth to let out a scream but it felt like sawdust had again filled her throat. She barely even managed a croak. But it was too late to warn anyone as one of the gigantic Elder Trees fell slowly towards the unprotected villagers.

CHAPTER 3

BURNING SKIES

$\mathcal{T}$he tree smashed into the southern deck with a deafening *BOOM*. She heard someone's blood-curdling cry as they plummeted to the ground four stories below; the remains of the bonfire's ashes flung in all directions. Where laughter had trickled through the night sky only moments ago, shouting filled the air as panic ensued. Paige felt the deck shifting underneath her as she jumped up from her seat.

Alaire immediately spurred into action, leaping off the table and grabbing both Paige and her mother by their arms. He pushed them towards the bridges on the western side of the deck. People flooded past them to the bridges. Fire spread faster than they could run. Some people screamed, others jumped to try and put out the flames engulfing the thatch canopy. A huge chasm formed in the center of the platform, splitting the three of them from where Olivian had been seated. Amidst the panic and the screaming, Paige couldn't see where her sister had gone.

"Go!" Papa shouted, shoving them forward. Paige tripped over overturned chairs and terrified parents as they corralled their children and called out for loved ones. But she couldn't hear anything other than a dull ringing in her ears. Everything sounded like it was underwater, and she felt her eyes locking onto the rubble, unseeing.

"Hurry!" Papa shouted, hs cries yanking her back into the present as he pushed her onward.

"Alaire! Olivian!" Elenass shouted, pointing across the ever widening chasm.

"I'll get her. Don't worry. Get Paige out of here!"

"Papa! What—"

"Alwasu!" Papa said, grasping her shoulders and looking deep into her eyes. "Listen to me. Those trees do not just fall over. This is an attack, and there will be soldiers here any moment. I've seen it before. Listen very carefully. Are you listening to me? Go with your mother. Get your gear and get to the forest floor. Run. Run as far as you can and don't look back. I will find you, but you have to trust me!"

Paige's mind raced to the movement she'd seen only moments ago on the forest floor: a flash. Moonlight glancing off a spearhead or a breastplate.

Soldiers? From where?

There were no large-standing armies in the Wild, only in the countries far to the east. But what purpose would any of those people have being this far into a wilderness woodland? And how had word of an army not spread to them? They would have had to march for weeks through the hand-cut paths and roads in the Wild. None of it made any sense to her, and she was beginning to feel panic increase the pounding of her heart. Papa looked hard at her.

"This is going to be a massacre," he growled. "Now listen; go. Get your sword, and—"

The deck bucked like an unbroken horse, causing everyone to lose their balance. They fell to their knees as the lumber cracked and settled, the gash in the wood widening. Paige saw several thick, heavy ladders being propped up with iron hooks on hinges set into the wood. Several of the Alatarian warriors instantly jumped up to knock them over, but no sooner had they set hands to the beams then they fell with dozens of arrows protruding from their bodies like porcupines.

"Olivian!" Elenass cried in desperation. Papa started to stand, hesitating only briefly as he gently touched the key on Paige's necklace. He looked swiftly to his wife.

"I'll get Olivian. You know what to do, Elenass. Get it from the study. I'll meet you at the house as soon as I get Liv. But no matter what happens, get yourself and Paige out of here. Do you understand?"

"Alaire, I—"

"Promise me!" he shouted, pulling Elenass and Paige to their feet. Elenass nodded furiously. Papa kissed her quickly on her lips. He began to turn towards the fray when he glanced back at Paige and saw the look of terror etched in his young daughter's eyes. He quickly tapped two fingers to his lips and gave her their little salute before rushing back towards the hole in the deck. The chief drew his dirk from his side and dove headlong into the sea of panicked villagers, making his way to the chasm.

A stream of shouting men poured out of the far end of the chasm from the heavy ladders, all wearing mail armor and white surcoats adorned with golden trim and sashes. Some held spears, while others held bows at the ready, loosing arrows into the helpless crowd. Some of the swords at the soldiers' waists were decorated with serpents on the hilt, coiled and ready to strike. The soldiers wore turbans of the same shade as their tunics, embroidered with an identical snake emblem. Like vipers upon mice, they set into the crowd of men, women and children, showing no inclination towards giving quarter of any kind.

"Get to the house!" Elenass shouted, grabbing Paige's hand and dragging her towards the end of the platform. Paige tried to swallow but couldn't manage past the lump in her throat.

"But Papa—"

"Paige, this is no time to argue. Move!"

The tone her mother used sent a row of chills down Paige's spine. She immediately lost any will to argue further.

With one last futile glance back at the sea of people where father had disappeared, she took off with Elenass as they began to shove their way to through a sea of screaming villagers towards their house.

Alaire felt his temples throbbing to the beat of his hammering heart. He glanced back to see two of the most important things in his world disappear into a sea of panicking people. He whirled about and grasped the rosewood pommel of his dirk, yanking it free of its scabbard. He quickly scanned the frenzied crowd across the gorge, trying to make way through the flames to the exit on the southeast corner of the deck. His gaze quickly darted back to the ladders in the ever-widening and shifting chasm in the Grand Hall's platform. Soldiers were flooding the eastern end of the deck, their gilded armor bearing the crest he knew all too well. A mixture of rage and horror welled up in his throat. How had they found him? Thousands of times, he'd considered this moment, haunted by the possibility they would find him. But in those thousands of moments, he had not believed this would actually happen. His worst nightmare was becoming reality, and there was nothing he could do to stop it.

"Alaire!"

The chieftain snapped his head to the side in time to see Xandla and Gerik also shoving their way through the crowd alongside him. Gerik had ripped one of the decorative shields from its handing grounds and was hefting his small axe in the other hand. Xandla had his own dirk drawn as well as a small steel buckler grasped tightly in his fist.

"Get out of here!" Alaire bellowed, pushing his way towards the chasm. "Get these people to safety."

"What about you?"

"I've got to get my daughter!" Alaire came to a stop by the edge of the chasm. He could see hundreds of torches below amongst gleaming armor. At least four hundred soldiers moved steadily to the ladders and crawled up like termites ascending a mound. Some of the warriors were fending off the first wave of attackers at the eastern end of the deck, but more ladders and more men were steadily flooding the chasm.

"I'll help you," Gerik shouted, joining Alaire at the lip of the chasm.

"Xandla, we have to get these fires under control. Is the switch system still intact?"

Xandla nodded, his bald, glistening head flashing in the firelight. "The deck parts are not, but I can access them from the Pump House."

"Do that. Turn on all the pipes, get the village saturated as best you can. It may buy the people some time to escape. We'll meet you down below."

Xandla nodded once more and took off towards the pump house. Alaire snapped his attention back to crossing the chasm. There was only one bridge Olivian could have gone down, assuming she had not fallen into the gaping maw of the platform. Alaire refused to consider this as an option. He had to get to the bridge and find Olivian.

"Think we can jump it?" Gerik asked.

"You're the rabbit expert. You tell me."

"Worth a shot."

"On three, then. One... Two... THREE!"

The two men took a running head start and at the very last moment, Alaire propelled over the deep chasm with a powerful thrust of his legs. He felt suspended in motion for a brief moment, catching a look at the chaos going on at the forest floor. The market was engulfed in flames, and his people were scattering to no avail as the soldiers hunted them down like dogs. Then he felt himself falling, and his feet landed at the very edge of the wooden canyon.

Alaire rolled forward onto his back then used his momentum to propel up and forward. He turned just in time to see Gerik slip on the edge of the platform. The hunter slammed his axe into the deck as he began to fall backwards.

"Gerik!" Alaire shouted, rushing back to the chasm. He grabbed his friend's arm and heaved till he could reach the rabbit slayer's belt, which he hauled with all his might. Gerik scrambled up, some floor planks giving way under him as he fought to get to his feet.

"Thanks," the hunter gasped.

"Don't mention it," the chief huffed, taking off for the bridge, the hunter on his heels.

"Olivian!" Alaire shouted as they rushed down the bridge to the lower level. He could see no blonde heads amidst the sea of people running and screaming.

"Olivian!" he shouted again.

"I don't see her!" Gerik shouted, jumping on one of the railings for a better view. No sooner had he done so, an arrow whizzed down through the forest and struck his shoulder with a sickening 'thud.' The blow knocked him off balance, and he fell down and tumbled down the last few steps to the deck.

"Gerik!" Alair yelled, hauling his friend to his feet. Gerik growled in pain and rage looking up to the Great hall's deck where several imperial archers were now standing, losing arrows into the crowd at random. Several women and men were hit and tumbled to the deck floor, crying out in agony.

"Get to the forest!" Alaire shouted to the villagers. He whirled about to see several soldiers armed with pikes now marching across the bridge and down the stairs. Gerik grabbed his shoulder and shoved him towards the platforms.

"Go, Alaire, find that girl of yours. I can handle these."

Alaire took one last look at his scruffy friend. His honor told him to stay and help Gerik fight, but every fiber of his being was screaming for him to find his daughter. He handed Gerik his dirk.

"You might need this. I'll see you down below."

"Wouldn't miss it!" Gerik chuckled, taking the dirk in his shield hand while flourishing his axe in the other, he whipped round and began to charge up the steps towards the oncoming soldiers. Alaire quickly jumped onto the deck and began pushing his way through the crowd as they stampeded to the southernmost point of the village, unfurling the emergency rope ladders to escape. He cried out for his daughter again and again, feeling icy cold desperation gripping his heart every time he called out to hear no answer.

"Liv! Olivian!"

"My lord!"

Alaire turned to see a young woman about Liv's age staggering over to him. She had a nasty cut on her upper lip and a bruise developing on her left eye. Her makeup was running from tears that were welling up and spilling over her cheeks.

"Matildra!" Alaire cried out. "Matildra, are you alright? Have you seen Olivian?"

"She got up and went to get some punch right before the crash! I haven't seen her since!" Matildra blubbered. Alaire handed her his handkerchief.

"Can you get yourself to the forest?"

"I think so, my lord," she sobbed, dabbing her eyes.

"See that you do. Take care and keep running south if you can. Understand?"

Matildra nodded, and Alaire took off towards the railing. If Olivian had gotten up to go get punch, there were only two real alternatives for where she was. One was at the bottom of the forest, crumpled under the remains of an Elder tree. Alaire again refused to acknowledge this as a possibility. The other was that she'd been swept up in the crowd and pushed towards the north side of the village, where his beloved and younger daughter were heading at this very moment. If Oilvian had listened to even one of his lectures on being prepared for a disaster, she would head back to the house.

When he reached the railing, he quickly surveyed the best way to get back to the north side of the village towards their house. The stairs and bridge were not an option, so he would have to improvise. There was one route the soldiers wouldn't know about: the pipes. Wood pipes from the pump house ran under most of the platforms. If he could get under the deck and get ahold of one, he could swing and crawl his way to the other side of the Great Hall, getting to the north side of the village. He looked at his hands. He was not the young man he used to be; he wasn't sure his strength would be enough to get him where he needed to go.

"Father Creator, hear my prayer," he muttered under his breath as he leaned over the edge of the platform railing, looking down. "Let me get my family to safety, and then you may call me home, if it be your will."

With that prayer, Alaire swung his legs over the railing and slid down into the night's inky blackness. He barely caught the pipe mounted to the underside of the decking joist, but he managed to get his hands around it tightly enough not to fall to his death. He clutched as hard as he could in spite of his missing fingers. The chief sucked in a huge breath and began to climb hand over hand towards the north end of the village.

Where he hung gave him a perfect view of the forest floor swarming with soldiers. They seemed more occupied with climbing into the village than the villagers trying to make their escape. Yet patrols of ten or so waited on the forest floor, hunting down stragglers. The market was in flames, as were the lifts, but Alaire didn't take the time to watch any longer. He kicked out so he could swing forward, and began inching his way towards home.

"Hurry, Alwasu!"

Paige dove after her mother as they shoved their way along with frightened villagers. Burning wood filled her nostrils. The haze of smoke whirling around her on all sides made her stomach sick. She could see men leaving houses all around the village, armed with spears and swords and whatever armor they could manage in their haste. She looked out across Kapernaum to the lifts as she sprinted, heading to the north end of the village. All four of the elevators were wreathed in flame, trapping everyone in the confines of the bridged city. Men she knew extended rope ladders and nailed them to the platforms as people rushed to get out of the nightmare that they had once called home.

Paige felt her heart stop as they made their way through the fountain deck. She caught the flash of light off a steel breastplate on the bridge parallel to them. Soldiers surged through the village. Several of the armored men had leapt onto a smaller platform, engaging several warriors. Tears stung in her eyes as she watched the strongest men fiercely protecting the fleeing women and children.

"Paige, you have to go," Elenass said, pushing her towards the next bridge.

"Mother, no!" Paige protested. "Papa said—!"

"Listen carefully: No matter what happens, you have to go. Do you understand? Go to your father's study. Second drawer of his desk. Break the lock. Take the scroll and find your father down below. I'll meet you there." She took one more moment to kiss her daughter gently on the forehead before placing her hand over the necklace and Paige's pounding heart.

"Guard this with your life." She shoved Paige forward and turned to face the soldiers that were hacking their way past the warriors.

"Mother!"

"I'll be fine! I'll meet you at the north end of the market! Hurry!" Without another word, her mother took a running start at the platform. Before Paige could shout after her, Elenass leapt into the night sky with a single bound from her long, strong legs and landed evenly on the opposite platform. She approached the soldiers from behind, drawing out her silver hairpin, which let her platinum-blond locks fall around her pointed ears like a waterfall. She said something Paige could not hear, and then to her astonishment, the hairpin spit hot, blue sparks from its end like slag spraying from a blacksmith's hammer. The pin elongated and twisted like soft dough from Dirgah's bakery, eventually sparking into a long, curved sword with an elegant silver handle. Elenass advanced on the men who had been giving chase to several young women and raised her sword high.

"You! Raven-heads!"

The soldiers whirled about and saw the elf striding towards them defiantly. This gave the terrified women time to get to the next bridge and make a hasty escape. The chieftain's wife leveled the tip of her blade at each of the four soldiers individually.

"Give chase to something that might bite back for a change."

The four men approached cautiously, their heavy boots clomping onto the wooden platform. Two soldiers held drawn swords, while another held a spear, all dripping crimson with the blood of innocent friends. The fourth, wearing a large feather in the center of his turban, stepped forward to take charge with a large mace in his right hand.

"Look at her ears, boys!" he snapped. "That's the one your prince wants. Take her!"

They all raised their shields and began to advance on Elenass.

"Best of luck," Paige's mother spat, holding her sword ready.

Paige felt panic grip her. She knew Mother had intended for her to obey and go right back to the house. But seeing her alone, outnumbered, and standing between the soldiers and the stream of people fleeing to the bridge, Paige couldn't leave her.

She frantically looked for another bridge to that same platform, but all the bridges were the same, packed with villagers stampeding to their dwellings and to emergency ladders to the forest floor. It was too far for her to jump. She looked about her for a rope or a vine, anything she could use to swing over. Her eyes locked onto a hanging lantern dangling on a rope strung up between the two decks. It wasn't much, but it was her only option.

"Out of the way!" she shouted, pressing through the throngs of people flooding the platform. "Move!"

She looked over worriedly to see her mother engaging all four men at once. Paige had never seen her mother harm so much as a fly, and now she fought like an acrobat in a carnival. Her sword made a whistling sound as she swung it left and right, parrying one blow while sidestepping another and ducking a third attack. Never had her mother expressed a hint of martial inclination; for all the secrets she couldn't keep, this one was as awe-inspiring as it was terrifying.

Paige shoved and pushed her way across the deck to the hanging lantern and stopped. Nothing but sky and the ground below stood between her and her mother, nearly twenty paces ahead. Paige took a deep breath and backed up four paces, waiting for a break in the frantic crowd. She lunged at the rail at a run, heart pumping. Without so much as a blink to the ground below, she vaulted her way onto the rail and jumped.

As she jumped, a panicked villager tripped behind Paige. Paige lost her balance as she hurled herself at the lantern.

Her heart lurched as she twisted in the air, wildly groping at the suspended lantern. She felt her fingertips brush the rough wooden base. Paige snapped her hand shut like a vise, her knuckles cracking as the whole weight of her body dropped down towards the forest floor and snapped the lantern's rope taunt. She cried out, latching onto the lantern with all her might as it swung slowly back and forth with her momentum.

"Alwasu?" she heard her mother scream, and Paige saw her falter upon locking fearful eyes with her daughter for a brief second. One of the soldiers took the momentary distraction and swung his sword quickly and efficiently, catching the elf under the rib cage. Elenass cried out as blood began staining her beautiful dress, her slender fingers pressing her side in agony.

"Mother!" Paige screamed. Elenass gripped her sword and quickly got her balance back, managing to catch the swordsman on the neck with the tip of her blade. The man dropped to his knees, clutching the wound.

She stepped on her attacker's spear and drove the iron head to the wooden deck. When he stumbled past her, she dispatched him with a quick slash to the abdomen, catching him between his steel breastplate and thick leather belt. He went down like a sack of stones, but the mace-wielding officer and the second swordsman quickly took his place.

Paige kicked with all her might and began rocking the lantern back and forth, inching her way towards the other platform with each swing. She flexed her abs and kicked her legs as high as she could, preparing to let go on the final swing.

Her mother fought frantically for her life now, both men engaging her with ferocity. She began to stumble with each step backwards. Paige knew she couldn't wait any longer. She took a deep breath, swung forward, and let go, flailing her arms to grasp at the platform railing. Barely grasping the rail, she pulled with all her might, heaving her small frame up and holding herself there with her crossed arms. Trying to catch a foothold, she looked up in horror, locking eyes with an officer noticing her where she hung helpless.

He disengaged from Elenass, striding towards Paige with heavy steps, spurs rattling against the planks of the platform. She tried pulling herself up, but she kept slipping on the smooth boards. The man raised his mace, quickening his step. Paige clambered and heaved with all her might, managing to push herself up on her forearms and then hitching her leg over the railing. The man began to run, shouting as he pulled the mace back for a strike.

His expression suddenly changed from fierce rage to blank shock as he fell face first onto the deck, Elenass's silver sword sticking out of his back through his mail. Paige looked past him at her mother, whose arm was still outstretched from the throw. For a brief moment she held Paige's gaze, her bright blue eyes welling up with tears as she clutched her bleeding side. Then the swordsman behind her brought the point of his curved scimitar down into the elf's back, and Paige screamed. Her mother slumped over onto the deck.

Anguish surged through her body with renewed strength. Paige clawed her way up and over the railing, hitting the deck and immediately lunging at the soldier, pulling her mother's sword from the dead officer as she did so. The thunder clap above was no match for the storm broiling inside her. Paige charged the soldier head-on, sword at the ready just as her father had trained her all those times as a child.

The soldier stepped up, a grimace across his scarred, bearded face. His eyes flashed in the lighting as the first few drops of rain began to cascade through the leaves of the canopy overhead. He held his sword ready, standing his ground and letting the princess come to him.

Paige let out a battle cry as she engaged the soldier, hacking and slashing at him with everything she had. He deflected the fierce blows with practiced ease. It became clear to Paige that even in her rage, she was not going to defeat him by technique alone. She would have to outsmart him. She began to slow, taking the defensive more and more.

Seeing her back off, the attacker became more fierce and confident. She began giving ground, backing up towards the railing. The closer she got, the more furious the man's attacks became. Paige waited till the last moment possible, inching her way towards the wooden barrier.

The swordsman pulled back for a powerful thrust, and Paige knew this to be her only chance. She slid her feet apart just like Papa had taught her and made her practice a hundred times over. As the man's arm descended, she crouched and caught his glove in her hands and deflected the man's momentum, causing him to lose his balance. Paige swept her foot under his leg. With the drizzle now pouring from above, the wood was slippery enough that the soldier's legs slid out from underneath him, and he landed heavily on his back with a thud. Paige brought her hands together and jumped, throwing her full body weight into the man's steel breastplate.

He gasped and coughed as the wind was sucked out of him. She rolled off of him, grabbed the extra length of fabric in her sleeve, and wrapped it around the man's neck, pulling as hard as she could. He kicked and thrashed, trying to grasp his sword again, but the princess put her foot against his shoulder and pulled as hard as she could. He kicked for a few more moments, then slowly became limp as he passed into unconsciousness, his body slumping to the platform.

Paige felt the tears slide down her face as she shoved the man to the side, crawling over to where her mother lay motionless looking up at the sky. She gasped with barely-constrained sobs at the sight of her mother, who lay still in a pool of her own blood mixed with the rainwater falling from the sky like tears of the Creator. Mother barely sputtered, unable to take full breaths. Paige pulled her up to a sitting position in her lap, the princess wiping the blood and wet, mangled hair from her mother's face.

"Mother? Mother, please!"

Elenass looked up at her daughter, trying to reach up and stroke Paige's face.

"Alwasu?"

"Yes, Mother?"

"You have to go," she sputtered. "You must... get the scroll... father's desk..."

"No, Mother, please, don't go!"

"Time is... almost gone. Alwasu. You must... go... Take... take *Klaíomh*. She... she will protect you." Mother was reaching for her discarded sword, and Paige grabbed it, handing it to her mother. The elf smiled feebly, clutching the beautiful saber.

"Soighren," she whispered, the elvish word for "return" lilting off her lips like a cool brook over smooth river pebbles. Blue sparks danced around the blade, as the sword morphed back into a hairpin that Paige's mother pushed into her daughter's shaking hands.

"Call her name... she will protect you," she coughed, heaving for her final breaths. Paige felt hot tears pouring down her face, contrasting with the rain drenching her now.

"Alwasu. Promise me... promise me you will run."

Paige gulped. "I will."

"The Shahir must never... leather scroll... understand?"

"Yes, Mother," Paige sobbed, her heart breaking into pieces.

"Alwasu?"

Paige looked at the light in her mother's blue eyes, which faded a bit more with each breath. She looked up at her daughter one final time, a faint smile tugging at her lips.

"I... love you..."

Elenass's head slowly rolled back as she released her final breath. Paige cried out in agony, gulping the huge tears that were welling up in her eyes and dropping onto her mother's still, peaceful face. She could hear the sound of more troops' heavy boots on the wooden platforms and bridges. She looked up and saw more of them, organized now and being led in droves from the Great Hall, breaking into homes and dragging terrified villagers out into the cold night air.

Paige took one last look at her mother, then stood shakily.

"I love you too, Mother," she sobbed, then turned and took off into the night.

Alaire's hands were raw, his arms shaking, his body drenched in sweat by the time he made it back above the platforms of Kapernaum. He decided then and there that he preferred crawling through sewage passages to shambling along pipes a hundred or more paces above ground, but he hadn't the luxury of reminiscing about past escapes and encounters. Heaving with one final effort, he climbed up and over the railing of a bridge that spanned the far west side of the village. Most of the fighting seemed to be directed at the eastern side of town where the Burgess's House, Lift Systems, and the Pump House all resided. The west part of town was made up of the smaller, more spaced-out homes. Many of the villagers were now rushing into their homes, grabbing whatever weapons and food they could carry and retreating down emergency rope ladders to the floor below, hopeful they could outpace the soldiers.

The chieftain dashed across the bridges and decks, pushing his way past panicking citizens, admonishing them to get to the lower levels as quickly as possible. Mothers with babies wrapped their precious cargo to their backs with nong shawls, while men did what they could to help smaller children down the ladders. Alaire helped in passing where he could but knew his own family took precedence, so he surged onward.

"Chief!"

He was about four platforms from home when the voice of a woman cut through the sea of haunting screams. He turned to see a young mother dragging a crying toddler behind her while trying to manage a sack filled with bread and blankets. Behind her, a group of three soldiers were advancing, swords drawn. The chief looked about frantically, his eyes alighting on a rope ladder hanging across the next bridge.

"Get to the ladder. Hurry!"

"Chief, I can't carry Toulya! Please, help me!"

Alaire's eyes flickered back to the soldiers jogging towards them. They were so sure in their complete victory that they weren't even bothering to run anymore, which kindled an anger in the chief he had not felt in a long time. As the men moved towards them, the chief grabbed the young woman's hand and dragged her over to the bridge between them and the rope ladder.

"Savahnah, where is your husband?" he urged.

"Dead."

Alaire's grip tightened on her hand, his upper lip twitching in an effort to contain another wave of rage crashing in his chest.

"Get to the forest and hide, you hear? Do you have a blanket? A towel?"

The woman nodded, her eyes red with tears. She pulled a thin quilt from her bag and handed it to him, her hands shaking. The soldiers were only about forty paces away now, making their way to the platform Alaire had just left. The chief felt a slight sense of panic setting in. He snatched the toddler up from the floor and tossed the kid onto his mother's back. The child cried as he wrapped his tiny arms around Savahnah's neck. Alaire yanked the quilt around both of them and tied the toddler onto her.

"Listen here, little man, hold tight to your mother and don't let go, alright?" He urged. "Savahnah, good luck, my dear. I hope we meet again in happier times. Now go!"

The sobbing mother nodded and scrambled down the first several rungs of the swinging ladder. The chief looked back up just in time to see the soldiers spot him from across the platform and began running. Alaire knew the disadvantage. He had no weapon, and he was running out of time. The jingle of the soldier's mail resonated in his ears as they charged. He balled his fists up, ready to play his odds, but a sound like a gurgling faucet caught his ears. He glanced up.

"Oh, Xandla, you miracle worker, you."

Water flowed through the wooden pipe hanging above his head about three feet up. Without wasting a moment, he leapt up and grasped it, pulling as hard as he could. The soldiers were only a stone's throw from him now, and he could hear them shouting at each other as they advanced. The chief let one last prayer escape his lips as he yanked once again, and finally he pulled the pipe out of its beeswax mould. A torrent of water blasted out of the pipe and hurtled towards the soldiers like a rushing river. The men had nowhere to run now that they were on the bridge. The water slammed into the first two assailants, tripping them up and knocking them backwards, soaking the deck around them. The others slipped on the wood, one of them hitting the rail hard enough to tumble over, grasping at the bridge planks for dear life.

Alaire immediately turned on his heel and dashed across the next bridge. Only three more to go before home, and he was running out of time.

Paige dashed across the village, now swarming with Imperial soldiers and fleeing clansmen. Choking on her own sobs, the princess tried to lose the shouting soldiers trailing her like a pack of hounds on a fox. She used all the secret passages and shortcuts she knew, fear rushing through her veins and driving her legs forward. She admonished every person she passed to make for the forest floor and run for the south, the direction it would be hardest for the soldiers to pursue.

Within a few moments of hard running, she reached her house and quickly unlocked the door. She bolted the heavy wooden beam across the entrance, her hands shaking.

"Get the scroll. Father's desk," she muttered to herself through the tears. She was having a hard time thinking clearly, but her mother's final words had burned deeply enough into her mind that she didn't need to be.

She ran to her father's study and threw open the doors, taking a candle stub from it's wall mount. She lit it with a quick flick of a match her father had left on the giant oak desk at the center of the room. Wasting no time, she began shuffling through the mountain of papers on his desk. But there was no leather scroll. Papa typically hated using parchment. Because his handwriting was so bad, he felt it was a waste of good paper. But with not a single leather scroll to be found, Paige began to feel panicked.

Get the scroll. Father's desk.

It struck her that perhaps it was not on her father's desk but in her father's desk. She checked all four drawers on either side. The first three only held more papers and envelopes, but the fourth one on the right hand side, bottom drawer, was locked. Paige immediately grabbed a letter opener and jammed it into the lock. With a quick jerk downwards, the princess broke the lock and pulled the drawer out.

Empty.

But why would Papa have a locked, empty drawer?

Unperturbed, she felt all around the bottom of the drawer. There! A small indentation just big enough for a fingertip in the back of the drawer. She pulled up and felt the entire bottom of the drawer give way, sliding up to reveal a hidden compartment.

"Got you," she spat. There, covered in dust, lay a single scroll bound with a thick cowhide thong. All in all the piece was only about a hand's length and the thickness of two fingers rolled up. She didn't take time to speculate as to what it was or why, but she knew she had to get moving.

She bolted into the room she and Olivan had shared as long as she could remember. She ripped her wet, tattered dress over her head and threw on the first shirt she could pull out of her wardrobe, tossing on a pair of men's trousers over the moccasins she was already wearing and stuffing the green cloth into them. She hurriedly used the enchanted hairpin and a leather cord to pull her hair up out of her face, then pulled her leather jerkin over her shirt and cinched her belt. The belt buckle jingled as she tried to strap it as tightly as her shaking fingers would allow.

A telltale creaking sound made her freeze in her place. That part of the floor never made that sound unless someone was standing on it. Paige sucked in her breath and held it, biting her lip to keep from crying out. She grasped her mother's pin in her hand and whispered to it as she moved to the side of the door.

"*Klaíomh*," she whispered, and a blue shower of sparks shot forth as the hairpin morphed into the elegant sword once again. She held it close to her rapid beating heart. She could hear the soft patter of footsteps outside in the hallway, and she gripped the sword till her knuckles turned white.

The doorknob jiggled and slowly turned, swinging open without a sound. Paige held her breath, set her jaw, then lunged around the doorway, swinging Klaíomh with all her might. Paige felt a strong, rough grip catch her hand before she had time to bring the blow home.

"Easy, bobcat!"

Paige let out a cry of relief that immediately turned into wrenching sobs as she collapsed into her Papa's arms. His hands were raw and bloody and his clothes were drenched in sweat, but he was here and alive. Her father squeezed her tightly for the briefest of moments before pulling her away to look at her.

"Paige, why do you have your mother's sword? Where is she?"

"She... she..." Paige tried to get the phrase out, but she found herself choking on the words that lodged themselves painfully at her Adam's apple. A horrified expression suddenly dripped onto his face, and Paige felt his grip tighten.

"Paige, where is she?"

Paige couldn't say anything. She didn't have to. Alaire sank to the floor, his knees shaking and buckling under him. Her Papa's eyes filled with huge tears that welled up and began spilling over to drip down his scruffy cheek and get caught in his beard. He began to sob, big, ugly, guttural sobs from the deep pit of his soul. He slammed his fist into the floor repeatedly. It took him a moment to compose himself enough to stand back up and look his weeping daughter back in the eye.

"What about your sister, have you seen her?"

Paige shook her head.

"Was she not at the lower end?" Alaire wiped his eyes with his bloody hands and shook his own head. "Matildra said she had gotten up before the crash. She was nowhere between here and the platform that I saw."

"Is she... could she be...?" Paige stammered, but her Papa shook his head violently.

"Until we track her down, we won't know. For now, we need to get to the forest. Are you set?"

Paige nodded furiously.

"Alright, I have to get something out of my study, you stay here."

"This?" Paige asked, yanking the scroll from her belt and handing it to him. For the first time since the invasion, relief flooded Alaire's face.

"Oh, thank the Creator," he breathed quietly. "Yes, everything depends on us keeping this safe. Now we must—"

BANG. BANG. BANG.

They both leapt to attention. Paige stuffed the leather scroll into her belt, her breath coming out in short, hasty gasps as her heartbeat pounded in her ears.

"Ala'haran! Come out, coward!"

The words cut through the air, and Paige and her father dashed over to the window that rested between her bed and Olivian's. Outside stood a body of twenty or so soldiers all dressed in bright crimson with crimson turbans wound about pointed helms. They carried torches and curved swords, while a group of about five held a makeshift battering ram at the ready. They were all standing about one man who was pounding the door. Paige couldn't distinguish many features through the ripples of the glass, but she could tell he was tall with a lean, fit frame. He was dressed in crimson and white robes, a white plume tucked into the center of his black turban, which accented his closely-cropped beard, black as panther fur. The man's gloved hands grasped a bloodied and broken villager by the scruff of the neck. The Alatarian had obviously been beat until he had given up the location of the chief's residence, thought to his credit it looked like he was only inches from death himself. The resplendent officer pounded on the front door again, barking at the occupants.

"Ala'haran, open up in the name of the Great Shahir! Come out now and I shall grant you a merciful death."

"Get to the balcony," Papa snapped. Fire was in his eyes now, replacing the tears he had been shedding with wild, barely controlled rage.

"But what about you?"

"I'll be along shortly. Grab some rope off the terrace and tie us two lead lines from the garden, but don't toss them over till I come out there. We'll have to make a hasty retreat. Can you do that for me?"

Paige nodded. Alaire planted a quick kiss on her forehead as he hugged her with one arm.

"That's my girl. Hop to. I'll be along shortly."

The sound of a ram smashing against the door snapped Paige into action. Her papa shoved her out the door to her room, and she dashed down the hallway to the double doors leading out into the terrace. She could hear her father shouting at the intruders as he ran downstairs to the parlor and grabbed his broadsword from the mantelpiece. Paige flung open one of the doors and leapt out onto the terrace, the cold night air slapping her in the face.

Normally, the view from the terrace would have been something she would have relished on a night this brisk. But before her all she saw was panic, terror, and absolute destruction. Kapernaum was filled with the sounds of screaming and the crackle of tongues of fire licking their way up to the heavens across the faces of buildings. Ice coursing through her veins, Paige wrenched the lid off a box with shaking hands. Digging about in the crate ever so briefly, she soon found the two coils of rope she'd been looking for. They were a bit old. but she didn't have other options at this point. She ran over to the railing and began tying each line to the support beam underneath.

As she cinched the rope in place, she glanced over the edge to make sure the path was clear. There was enough of an overhang on the balcony that, if they slid straight down, they had a fairly clear shot to the forest floor. Several lower decks were scattered to the left or right of their descent path, but it wouldn't be a problem, assuming the escapees kept a straight drop and the decks stayed empty of soldiers for the next couple minutes.

Laying the rope coils out, the princess dashed back inside. Her heartbeat skipped when she heard the sound of steel clashing on steel on the floor below, and she bolted to the stairs, screeching to a halt at the top. Papa stood steadfast, halfway up the stairs, hacking and slashing his broadsword at two of the crimson cloaked soldiers. A pile of dead and wounded invaders lay on the floor just inside the doorway, which was hanging by a single hinge amidst splinters and shards the battering ram had left behind. One by one the men were pouring in and trying to shove their way up the stairs after Alaire, but the chief had the advantage of the narrow stairway. Sweat dripped from his brow as he drove yet another soldier backwards with a wounded left side.

"Enough!"

The officer with the white plume muscled his way through the hole where the front door used to be, a gilded sword drawn. His coal black eyes glinted like obsidian, a look of pure disgust mixed with absolute vehemence. The soldiers backed away from the stairs, standing at attention as the leader strode forward.

"I love what you've done with the place." The officer waved his hand and gestured outside to the burning village. "Not bad for a traitor."

Papa began pushing Paige back up the stairs, his sword extended towards the officer.

"Against you, Feridar? Absolutely."

"Where is it!?" screamed Feridar, throwing a part of the door out of his way with a tremendous amount of force.

"Somewhere you will never get it," Papa spat, backing up a few more paces.

"Give it to me!"

"You know I'll die before that happens."

"THAT CAN BE ARRANGED!"

The man lurched forward, lunging at Paige's father. Not having much time to react, Papa hurled the broadsword with all his might. Feridar grabbed one of the soldiers to his left and yanked him off balance, the broadsword striking him in the gap of his armor where his cuirass met the pauldrons at the neck. The rabid leader pitched his soldier aside to bleed out but the movement had given Paige's father the window he needed.

"Hurry!" Papa shouted, charging up the steps. He didn't have to tell Paige twice. The duo bounded down the hallway to the terrace doors and leapt back into the cold night air. Papa slammed the doors shut and took one of the wooden benches beside Elenass's squash boxes and leveraged it against the door. No sooner had the wedge been placed when the sound of armored men shouting and banging against the heavy oak doors pulsated through the wood.

"Paige, here!"

Paige looked up from the rope coils to see her father toss an old pair of gardening gloves. Paige snatched them up and shoved her hands into the stiff weathered deerskin. She in turn tossed her papa his own rope and then jumped up on the railing of the balcony.

"Ready?" he asked, pulling on his own set of gloves. She nodded. Alaire leapt up onto the rail beside her. He glanced down at the void below them, letting out a low whistle. "Never took the time to notice how far down that is. Try not to let go!"

The sound of shattering glass startled Paige. Men were smashing the windows on either side of the door. Paige's papa looked at her and nodded. Paige gripped her rope tightly as she pushed herself over the edge of the rail. She felt her hands cramping as she gripped the weathered rope for dear life. She let herself down, hand over hand, as sliding would surely be far too much to control. She glanced up at her father, who was in the process of lowering himself over the railing. She could hear the men shouting and the sound of the door splintering with every blow.

"Papa, hurry!" she shouted. Her father must not have heard her clearly, because he glanced down at her, confused.

In that split second he looked down, Paige heard a hard thud as an arrow was driven into his shoulder. Alaire shouted in pain as he lost his balance.

"Papa, NO!" Paige screamed as her father began to fall into the abyss below them. She tried to reach out and catch his glove. Her heart stopped as she missed his hand, their leather-clad fingertips barely brushing as he plummeted towards the ground below.

Somehow, in a split second, Alaire managed to grab the rope with his right hand. He jerked hard and she heard him cry out in anguish. The speed at which he'd fallen caused him to swing back and forth dangerously several stories above the forest floor, which was now littered with patrols bearing torches.

"Hang on, Papa!" Paige shouted. "I'm coming!"

"Ala, get down the floor. *Now!*"

A tingling in the base of Paige's spine erupted. Everything suddenly seemed to slow down to half speed. Paige heard the distinct sound of fibers ripping and popping. The old rope she'd grabbed was fraying between them, about three feet above Alaire's head. One of the three cords had just snapped, leaving two more twisting about as her father swung dangerously back and forth.

She looked back down at her father, who was looking up at the rope, then his eyes met hers. He opened his mouth to say something, when another cord snapped, dropping him down a few more inches as the rope weaved back and forth like a pendulum. Paige screamed, but the only sound she seemed to hear was the final pop as the last twine of the rope crackled, creaked, and then snapped.

"PAPA!" Paige cried out as her father plummeted towards the ground. The rope had swung him far to the right, and as he fell he smashed into several railings. He landed on his back on a small housing platform some thirty or so feet below. Papa's head dangled limply over the edge of the deck.

The chief didn't move. He made no sounds. The only thing Paige could hear through the pounding in her ears was the roar of thunder overhead that clapped as if the sky itself screamed out in anguish.

The princess began pushing herself back and forth, trying to swing over to the platform where her father lay motionless. The rope she clung to creaked and whined in protest as she began to arc in an oval pattern several stories above the burning forest.

"He's on the deck below, sire!" she heard one a man above her shout. The sounds of clunking boots began to drum in her head as she heard the men stomping out of the house. She watched them make their way from her home to the nearest staircase leading to the lower tier of decks. Paige looked frantically back at her father. She could see his chest heaving, gasping for the wind that had been ripped from him.

"Papa! Papa, you have to get up!" she screamed. Her father rolled onto his side slowly, and Paige could guess by the expression on his face he'd broken something. He looked over at her, his hair hanging in strings around his face. Raindrops began splashing about him on the deck. Paige threw all her weight into her swing as the group of cloaked soldiers sloshed their way down the staircase. She strained hard against the old rope, shoving her weight forward. Only ten more feet.

Her hands cramped and burned beneath the now-soaked leather gloves.

Eight feet. Three more and she could probably make the jump down.

Six feet.

Suddenly, the muscles in her hand spasmed, and she lost her grip on the slick, wet rope. She began to spiral down the length of the twisted cord, sliding uncontrollably. She summoned all the energy she had left and clutched her lifeline for all she was worth. She skidded to a stop and felt the slack snap as her weight caught up with her fall. She cried out in pain as the rope slowed.

The princess glanced up, shaking the water form her face. She had slid to an even plane as the deck her papa now lay on. He was lying on his side, his eyes filled with tears of agony as he stared at her, face white as a snowcap.

"Pa—" she tried to croak, but her father shook his head.

"Go," he mouthed, although no sound came from his lips. The soldiers were pouring onto the platform now, with the one called Feridar marching towards Alaire with long, furious strides. Paige shook her head and reached her arm out, trying to will the rope to swing closer to the edge of the deck. The look of grief on her proud father's face rent her heart a new tear as he shook his head once more.

"No, NO, PAPA PLEASE! *PLEASE*, PAPA!" she choked through the sobs as the officer marched towards her helpless father.

"Run! Ala, Run!" he urged through gritted teeth. The officer was upon him now, his gilded scimitar drawn. He reached the crumpled heap that was Alaire and placed a heavily embroidered boot with a pointed, curled toe on the chief's back. Alaire groaned in agony as the officer pushed him back down onto his belly and lay the sword's tip on his back, right behind his heart.

"Leave him alone!" Paige shouted.

The soldier looked up and squinted at her in the darkness, the lightning casting a shadow on every line of his sneering face. His posture changed as he recognized something about her, and he jabbed a gloved finger towards the dangling princess. "You!"

Paige glared at the man through a veil of wet, stringy blonde hair. His eyes were locked onto her waist, where the roll of leather from her father's study sat stuffed into her belt. Alarm filled her father's face as he wildly shook his head.

"Paige, get out of here!"

"Paige, is it?" The man sneered down at the chief. "Seren Wahadi! A pike, if you please!"

Another soldier with insignias adorning his scarlet turban snatched a pike from another soldier and marched forward. For a moment, Paige thought the man was going to throw it at her, but when he reached the edge of the deck he extended the shaft out towards her.

"If you want your father to live, you will bring that scroll to me," the officer demanded. Paige looked from the pike to the officer and then back to her father.

"No, Paige, run!" her papa wheezed. Paige gripped the rope, not knowing what to do. She knew there was no way she could trust the officer, and yet she couldn't just leave her father lying there to be dispatched, knowing there was the slightest chance he might spare her father. Paige hesitated for a moment, and then reached out one arm timidly.

"No!" Alaire shouted. He struggled to sit, but the soldier pressed the scimitar harder into his back.

"Be still, you wretched bastard," the man spat, "or I swear to the gods, I'll run you through."

"Papa, please!" Paige pleaded. "I can't leave you!"

Her father looked her in the eyes, and for a moment she thought she could see a smile on his lips.

"You can do it. I know you can." he said, his voice cracking with emotion.

"Shut up!" the man spat. "Listen here, you crossbred little urchin, time is running out. Give me the scroll! I'll skewer him, I swear it!"

"Paige?"

Paige looked back at her father. He had a defiant glint in his eye now, and she could feel his gaze boring into her. He pulled one of his hands up to his lips, tapped two fingers to them, then saluted her, mouthing the words "Yeigh me threighan."

I love you.

Before Paige could scream, cry, or make any kind of protest, Alaire, the chief of the Alatarian people, braced his palms flat against the slick wood of the battered deck and shoved his body upwards, driving the officer's saber directly into his own heart. With a gasp, the chieftain's body quivered, then sank back down onto the deck. The water splashing around him stained with the color of his blood as the wind howled lamentations for the fallen warrior.

For a moment the officer looked shocked, then he whipped his head up and glared at the sobbing orphan.

"Kill her! Get that scroll!" he bellowed, and the man who had been holding the pike out to her hurled the weapon at her with blind rage. Paige had no time to cry, scream, or process what had just happened. She loosened her grip on the rope and fell, clutching to the worn hemp just tight enough to slow her plunge. Steam rose from the wet leather as the rope burned through the old calfskin and began to rub against her bare palm, causing her to cry out.

The drop down only took half a minute or so, but the soldiers had already begun blowing horns and trying to communicate to the other troops on the ground. Once she was about ten feet from the ground, she released her grip and fell the rest of the way to the slick, leaf-covered mud. She slapped the saturated ground with a hard thump and rolled to her feet, her hands aching and burning as she ripped the tattered gloves off and cast them into the bushes. Soldiers ran towards the north end of Kapernaum, chasing villagers in every direction. She heard the soldiers above shouting and soldiers below changing course for her. Bolting into the forest, she rushed south as fast as her tired and battered legs could carry her.

The chase lasted for hours. On and on she ran, strengthened by fear and pure adrenaline. She moved to the rhythm of her pounding heart, knowing that if they caught up to her, there was no chance of her survival. She began to lose sense of direction, but her knowledge of the terrain gave her an advantage and allowed her to stay just ahead of the troops. These men were no amateurs at hunting and killing things, it seemed. Just when she thought she had lost them and could collapse in a heap, she would hear their shouts or see their ugly yellow torches casting light across the darkness of the forest. Paige soon learned that even fear runs out eventually, and adrenaline only moved her body so quickly.

Arrows flew through the rain, narrowly missing Paige as she frantically tripped over what must have been her hundredth large stone since she'd set off. Her reasoning and directional senses were quickly departing, leaving only one instinct coursing through her splitting headache. Run!

She was vaguely aware of a tall boulder standing upright at the edge of the gully and decided she had to make it over to it and risk collapsing beneath its shadow, hoping the men would pass by her. She staggered forth, grasping the rough lichen-covered surface and ducking behind the stone, straight into something soft that jumped in astonishment.

"Ah!" she screamed.

"AHH!" an equally surprised voice squealed, a pair of bright blue eyes gazing at her in shock before she felt someone's fist connecting with her left eye. Sparks of light filled her vision, and the pain registered when she was thrown backwards into the muddy ferns. She heard two voices talking angrily back and forth in hushed tones for a moment before she felt her world spin and envelop her in a darkness as deep and black as an unopened tomb.

CHAPTER 4

BUSTED POTTERY

*T*hick haze surrounded Paige like mountain fog in the early summer. Her head pounded as if she'd been smashed in the face by a piece of cordwood. She blinked hard, trying to wash away warm, stinging tears. Her eye felt painful enough to be the color of an overripe plum. She shivered, curling up into a small ball beneath some sort of soft, warm blanket.

She was in nothing more than a man's thin nightshift several sizes too big for her. Puzzlement took hold of her as she tried to sit up to gather her bearings. The princess squinted, looking hard until the shapes began to swirl into solid forms.

Paige lay on a hanging box cot strung between huge tree roots, opposite the hearth. The dome-shaped hut she was in appeared to be made of a deep brown cob, sculpted by hand and smoothed to a flawless surface. Despite being on edge, she felt warm and cozy in the interior, save for the occasional breeze whispering through the open door. The cottage sat on many large tree roots jutting out in ornate contortions up the wall.

"Well, you certainly slept long enough."

The rough tone was definitely male, and though laced with sarcasm, did not seem unfriendly or threatening. She had been so caught up trying to get her bearings that she'd completely glanced over the figure standing near the fireplace. He sounded young—much younger than she would have guessed upon seeing his patched robes. His broad back was turned to her as he quietly attended.

Paige looked about for something to defend herself with, seeing her effects stacked on one of the rough chairs at the table between them. Her mother's hairpin sat neatly atop her jerkin, in plain sight. She bit her lip in frustration.

"If you're thinking about snatching that, I would seriously reconsider that decision in your condition," he said with a chuckle. "Not that you need it. I wouldn't have patched you up just to turn around and off ye."

He moved slightly, revealing a massive spear, at least six feet long, leaning alongside the hearth. The tip of the spear shone as brilliant as polished diamond with dragons, unicorns, and other magical beasts forgotten by time elegantly etched into the head.

Paige started to sit up again in the swaying box cot, but shrank back into the blankets when she remembered all she was wearing was a night shift. She pulled the rabbit-fur cover up to her chin, cheeks burning.

"Your breeches are at the foot of the trunk next to the cot. Your shirt was ripped to ribbons, so there is a new one with the pants," the man said, never turning to face her. "I'll step out a moment to allow you some privacy." He stepped outside, shutting the wooden door behind him.

Paige slowly eased out of the cot, gasping as bolts of pain blasted up the back of her leg. She sank to her knees, holding back fresh tears. Her legs felt like they were being seared from the inside with hot irons.

She suddenly felt a kick of panic and she clutched her chest. The chain and key were still there, but she saw no sign of the leather scroll. Had she lost it running? She wasn't sure, but the ache in her heart only grew as doubt flooded her mind.

"Papa," she choked, sobs clawing their way out of her tight throat. She felt every shard of her broken heart threaten to puncture her lungs and keep her from breathing at all. She had failed to protect the one thing her father had sacrificed himself to keep safe.

"Oh, Papa, I'm so sorry!" she wailed, bending over and touching her forehead to the earthen floor, her body convulsing with sobs. What was she to do? She now had no home, no family, and she was currently under the roof of some stranger. She cried out as many tears as she could, the sickening feeling of dread numbing her with every gasp. Remembering the stranger, and knowing he would surely return, she rose and dried her nose on the back of her sleeve. Turning to the chest to get her garments, Paige took a deep breath and pulled the shirt over her head.

Once dressed, Paige quickly braided her hair and inserted her mother's hairpin into the top. She felt yet another pang in her chest as her fingers touched the cool silver, her mind flashing back to her poor mother lying lifeless on the deck of a burning village. The paleness of her cold, beautiful face. The unblinking, lifeless eyes that had once held so much love. The blood saturating the dress she had made for her daughter as Paige had clutched her in her arms.

Paige sucked in a deep breath and clenched her fists. The scroll was still missing. Did the stranger outside have it? Had she lost it in the night? She needed time to think. First and foremost, she needed to get some answers, and right now the man was her only lead. After checking over her gear and attire one last time, Paige hobbled out of the open doorway, blinking in the sunlight.

The dwelling was a mound at the edge of a valley, vividly green in the sunshine. On top of the hill, a large pine tree grew, its branches spread wide to hug the warm rays of light cascading from the sky above. Along the edge of the valley's ridge, surrounding pines stood lush and flourishing. Pines were not very common in the deciduous forests near Kapernaum, so she guessed she had to be a great deal farther south in the Wild. The trees covered the valley edge and crept up the foothills of the mountains. A clean, crystal creek trickled down the gully in a natural mosaic of reds, browns, greens and greys.

Walking to the creek, Paige pulled out Klaíomh and shook her hastily braided locks free. She looked down into the running water that rippled like a moving looking glass as she stared at her own reflection. It was no wonder her eye hurt; whoever or whatever had hit her popped a blood vessel. She shook her hair out with her fingers, rolled her sleeves up, and dunked her head in the stream. She scrubbed it until her whole head felt raw and numb from the cold. As she combed her fingers through her hair, she caught movement in the corner of her eye and clutched the hairpin tightly.

She relaxed slightly when she recognized the stranger who was just down the creek. Getting a better look at him now, he was of medium height and stocky, with close-cut dirty blond hair. His pale skin was blemished with several dry, scaly patches. As she approached him warily, still gripping her hairpin, she saw his deep-set pale blue eyes, the color of the sky after a rainstorm. A proud, defiant chin and strong, clean-shaven jawline strengthened his expression.

The man looked at her, smiled a jagged-toothed smile, and waved. He sat on a log dangling a thin fishing pole over the water, teasing several small brook trout.

"'Morning!" he said cheerfully. "Oh, wow, that eye is looking downright demonic, isn't it? But I trust you feel a little better after that hibernation?"

Paige nodded, watching him. He noticed her sizing him up and let out a haughty laugh.

"There's nothing to worry about, missy."

"It's not missy. It's Paige," she muttered, reinforcing her stance, "and I'm not worried."

"No, of course not," he said with a hint of sarcasm sprinkled onto his tone, and winked. Paige felt her cheeks flush. She sat on the bank about five feet away from the young man, tightly clutching Klaíomh. He chuckled.

"Who are you?" she demanded. "Where am I?"

"My name is Robert, or Eöl, if you prefer Elvish. You do speak Elvish, I assume?" He gestured to Paige's ears and she self-consciously touched one.

"A little."

"Sort of what I figured." He laughed. "As for what you're doing here, well, I snagged you out of the woods and brought you to Glimmerglass Creek in the southern edges of the Wild. You were, eh... well, pretty banged up."

"It was a long night," she muttered, feeling emotion well up in her throat.

"I'll bet," Robert said quietly. An awkward moment of silence ensued as he continued to fish. Paige couldn't quite decide what he was. Though he could pass for a human, his ears were slightly tapered, but not as angled as those of an elf. Instead, they curled downwards. His teeth were slightly jagged as well—in fact, almost pointed.

Finally, Paige worked up the courage to say something. "I suppose I owe you some thanks," she began, looking the hermit in the eye. He snorted in amusement, but his expression grew soft and he smiled.

"No worries. I didn't do much more than provide a bed."

"Well, it was very kind, all the same. I feel as if I've been run over by a buffalo."

"I can't say I'm surprised."

"Last thing I remember was running into someone and then this blinding pain before I went unconscious."

"Oh, yeah. Sorry about that. Broadside gets a little ham-fisted when he gets startled," Robert muttered.

"Broadside?"

"A friend of mine. Can't blame him, though, not like he's used to running into sprinting women at three o'clock in the morning."

"What on earth were you doing in the middle of the Wild at three-thirty in the morning?"

Robert shifted uneasily in his seat.

"Nothing of consequence."

"Is that so?" Paige demanded, crossing her arms.

"Indeed," Robert said, as if that were the end of it. He teased the hook and worm he held in the brook a bit before continuing.

"How do you like the clothes?"

"It was most generous of you," she replied. Paige shuddered thinking that two men got her out of her other clothing and into a nightshift. As if reading her thoughts, the stranger piped up quickly.

"Also, just so you know, I was able to get that nightshirt on you over your other clothes, so your modesty is intact,"

Robert said, somewhat sheepishly. "I figured it beat hypothermia."

"I appreciate that," Paige said, still not sure if she believed him, but his slightly embarrassed look seemed genuine enough. He had stepped out to give her privacy earlier, so she decided to give the young man, or whatever he was, the benefit of the doubt. Robert smiled, but a jerk on his line distracted him. He pulled the line out of the stream. A shimmering green river bass nearly twice the width of Paige's hand splashed onto the bank. Its scales glistened in the late morning sun like emeralds in the side of a mountain.

"Best get on to breakfast. You must be starving after all that time you spent unconscious," he said, rising. Paige realized that her stomach was indeed gnawing at itself like a dragon clawing its way out of a cave.

"How long was I asleep?" She thought about the attack and wondered how many nights could have passed while she had been out cold.

"About two days," he replied, leading her up the stone path over the side of the valley to the hermitage. She wasn't too surprised—she must have been nearly dead of exhaustion when the stranger had caught her. She kicked a stone in the pathway and watched it skitter up to the mound as she tried to recall any other information she could remember, but she came up empty. She quickly rebraided her hair and inserted Klaíomh into the top of the plait. Then she followed Robert back to the cottage and they entered the low doorway together.

Robert dropped the fish onto the table and began to gut it while Paige seated herself in the chair at the end of the table. He threw the fish into a pot of boiling water on the small fireplace hearth and stirred it. He stood a while, stirring in silence save for the sound of his wooden spoon scraping against the sides of the iron cauldron. Paige glanced about for a way to be helpful. She noticed a small pile of scrawny-looking vegetables on the hearth.

"If you have a knife I can borrow, I could peel and dice these for you," she offered.

Robert eyed her warily, a sly grin sliding onto his face. "Promise you won't stick me with it?"

"Of course," she said, irritated. She held her hand out expectantly. The young man fished out a small paring knife from the drawer beside the hearth and handed it to her. Paige seated herself in one of the gnarly kitchen chairs and began peeling the carrots one by one, dicing them in turn and making a tiny mountain in the center of the table.

They worked in silence for a few moments, Paige letting the monotonous task of dicing the carrots lull her into a trance of her own thoughts. She hated carrots, but Mother had grown them in her box garden. Her mind wandered from the garden to the events of three nights before, the memories as clear as if they had been moments ago. She could hear the creaking of the old rope as her father had clutched on for dear life, the fibers snapping one by one, dropping him to his doom. Paige bit her lip, trying to keep from sobbing again. Should she have taken that rope? Was there another rope nearby she could have used instead? All the scenarios poured through her mind, but they all kept coming back to one theme, one singular, nagging thought that cut deeply into her very soul:

This was all your fault.

"Two?"

Paige looked over at Robert. "Excuse me?"

"Two scoops?" the young man asked, holding up a ladle and a bowl. The warm smell of fresh food hit Paige's nostrils and sent her stomach to aching like a broken heart. She nodded emphatically, the spicy aroma making her feel faint and slightly nauseous. Robert ladled her a bowl and garnished it with the raw cubed carrots as he handed it to the starving princess. Seconds later she had the bowl all but licked clean.

"Easy there, tigress, there's more where that came from!" He laughed.

Paige dabbed her mouth with the corner of her handkerchief gingerly. "I apologize," she mumbled as Robert dumped another batch of the stew into her tankard.

"Think nothing of it. You had a long run and a long few days sleeping it off. You need as much strength as you can get, I imagine."

Paige ate the second bowl more slowly, savoring each bite this time. Robert let her eat in peace.

Paige rested her spoon neatly on the bowl's rim. "I can't thank you enough, but I'm afraid I haven't anything to repay you with. All my belongings are... well... they're gone now."

"This is a home, not an inn." Robert tsked, scooping up the dishes and taking them to a wooden barrel in the corner, scrubbing them out with a bundle of twigs tied together with jute twine. "You can stay here as long as you want or need to. I know everything's got to be quite overwhelming right now."

"You've no idea."

Robert chuckled mirthlessly. "I've seen the Shahir's troops lay waste before. There's not much to walk back to and not many places to go afterwards."

Paige's head snapped back to face her host.

"Whose troops?" she demanded.

"The Shahir's?" Robert said again, confused. Suddenly a look of dawning realization spread across his face as he looked into Paige's eyes.

"You...you don't know who the Shahir is, do you, lass?"

Paige shook her head.

"Who are the Shahir? Why did they destroy Kapernaum!?"

"It's 'who is the Shahir,' not 'who are,'" Robert corrected, disbelief etched onto his face. "You seriously don't know? Your father never told you?"

"What do you know of my father!?" she demanded. Robert drummed his fingers on the table as he took a seat opposite Paige.

"I'm getting the sense you're behind on world politics these days."

Paige made a face to indicate she clearly hadn't the slightest idea what he was talking about, and the lad sighed.

"Okay, then, where to begin?"

"How bout you start by telling me who this Shahir is and why he, whoever he is, attacked my village?"

Robert nodded his ascent as he stood up, pulled a loaf of bread and a block of cheese out of the cupboard, then seated himself once more. He offered a hunk of each to Paige but she declined, too anxious to eat anything else.

"The Shahir is a king in the east, in a far off country on the edge of the Great Sea," Robert began. "Till the last hundred years or so, they were just another collective of city states, like out here in the Wild. But the last three kings they've had this century seem to feel the title 'Emperor' is more to their liking, and this one? He's the worst yet. He's been pushing his borders like none before him ever dared."

"And they've made it into the Wild now?"

"Well, see, that's the odd thing. The Wild has had too many pitfalls for them over the last decade of trying. They have two settlements, last I heard. One is just a small mining city in the far northeast of the Wild. I think it's called Frang-something-or-other."

"And the other?"

"That would be Aschin. It's a fortress city they built on the edge of the Raychel Ridge that serves as their westernmost outpost. I think they finished constructing it about two years ago, but until now they hadn't sent any kind of real army into the Wild itself, let alone as deep into the forest as Kapernaum was."

"I think they were after my parents."

"It's the only explanation I can think of," Robert agreed, reaching into his robe. "And I suspect it had something to do with this?"

Paige gasped as he pulled a leather scroll from the inner folds of his robe.

"Give me that!" she commanded, snatching it out of Robert's hand. She felt both shocked and elated to see it hadn't been lost.

"That's kind of what I figured," her host said, stuffing another bit of bread and cheese into his mouth. "Any idea why the Raven-heads would want that little trinket?"

"Raven-head?"

"Sorry. Shauds. The people the Shahir rules over."

"Oh. No, I have no idea why they would want it. It's just a bunch of old Elvish that I can't even read."

"That's unfortunate. I was hoping you'd have some more insight, since that's all I could glean off it as well." Robert sighed.

"Well, I'm sorry I didn't get to take the time for all that extra insight as my family was being slaughtered," she quipped.

"I didn't mean it like that," Robert said. "Whatever it is, your father felt life-bound to protect it. The Shahir must really want whatever secret this ancient text contains."

"But how did my papa get it? And how did this Shahir person know he had it?"

Robert shrugged. "We may never know, but one thing is for sure: it has to stay out of his hands."

Paige nodded, unrolling the leather and glancing across the ancient words. She thought she could make out the Elvish words "open," "earth," and "guard," but it was impossible to tell for certain. She sucked in a deep breath and let it out in a weary, exacerbated huff.

"So, not that I'm trying to run you out, understand," Robert added, clearing the table and scrubbing it with a semi-clean rag, "but do you know what you're going to do now?"

Paige sighed and shook her head.

"No relatives? Family in neighboring villages?" Robert asked.

"No, everyone I would have gone to was at that feast," she whispered, the gravity of those words hitting her like a millstone being dropped on top of her. "Now they're probably all dead."

"I'm so sorry," Robert offered, his face now etched with compassion. "I wish there was something I could do."

"I just... I need a moment to think." Paige kneaded her forehead.

"I need to go weed the garden anyways. I'll leave you to it for now."

"Oh, no, I didn't mean that! I'll go on a walk. Please don't feel like you have to leave."

"Oh, I don't. It is my house, after all." Robert smirked. "I just better get to it before I forget, that's all."

He ducked outside and headed around back. Paige sank back in her chair and rubbed her eyes, the ache in her left eye increasingly festering.

Her mind and her gaze began to wander, her eyes once again resting on the chest at the foot of the hanging cot. It was a beautiful piece, the iron bands accenting the dark patina of the old wood. She followed the intricate carvings and scrollwork about the black bands, noticing a peculiar carving on the front of the box: a dragon twisted into a circular knot, a blade weaving in and out of the artwork at an angle. A banner beneath the design was written in a more modern Elvish than the scroll that lay on the table, and she could make out the words "Ayghrast Urrem Gaer ahl urm Ihmparhem." "One must uphold honor for all." She wondered if it was Robert's family crest.

Paige gazed at the chest for a long while before losing interest. She meandered over to the far side of the hut and plopped into the giant bearskin chair, pulling her legs up and resting her chin on her knees. The weary pull of exhaustion tugged on her eyelids like a tower-keeper tugging on a bell rope. As the minutes dragged by she dozed in and out of consciousness, her mind flashing back to the attack. Her brain felt dull as the images played through her dreams; she saw her mother lying in a pool of her own blood. Then her father lying crumpled and helpless on a deck just beyond her reach. The last image she saw was of the commander with the black turban and the white plume, standing over his dead body, a savage look of contempt and gleeful hatred etched into his bearded face.

It was on this image Paige's eyes snapped open. The room was nearly dark now; the sky outside had slipped into the deep blue of late twilight. Boiling anger began to build up inside her stomach and creep its way up to her heart.

The Shahir was the ruler of the nation and the army ultimately his to command, but she doubted she'd ever get close enough to him to dole out justice, even if she could make her way to the Great Sea. But this commander, the man whose blade had pierced her father's heart, he was still out in the Wild somewhere. He might be easier to reach. Paige wasn't sure if she could get close enough to him to use a dagger or a sword, but if she could somehow get ahold of a bow, she might be able to kill him.

Kill him.

Those last two words branded themselves into her mind as she sat staring at the hearth's glowing embers. She'd never killed a man before. The closest she'd come was the soldier she'd choked trying to protect her mother. Was she capable of killing someone? She'd often asked this in her heart while out hunting in the Wild. But after the attack, she was fairly certain she would have no hesitation killing in self defence. But in cold blood? Would she be able to release an arrow into an unsuspecting target, no matter his crimes? Where was the honor in that?

Then again, where was the justice for her family if she couldn't?

Paige fingered the key around her neck, wondering what her father would have done. She thought about his kind blue eyes looking down at her, his face crinkled up in an understanding, compassionate grin. No. No, she was certain he wouldn't condone such actions. Revenge was not his way, and as much as Paige wanted to make the soldier suffer for his crimes, she knew her papa would never abide such thoughts.

Crashing pottery sounding outside the hut jarred her back into the present. It was dark outside, and she'd completely lost track of time while lost in her own thoughts. She reached up and clutched Klaíomh, pulling it smoothly from her braid and gripping it as she sat perched upon the stuffed chair.

For a moment Paige heard nothing. The stillness outside was only broken by the distant chirping of crickets in the meadow. She strained her ears while clutching her sword in her hand, gazing out the open doorway into the indigo sky. A jolting pop in the embers of the dying fireplace caused her to twitch, and she felt her knuckles tighten around the hair pin.

"Robert?" she called out softly. Paige wondered if he had perhaps dropped a pot on his way back from the garden. It was awfully late by this point, however, and she began to wonder where on earth he could be.

No one answered her, but then again, she had barely whispered the name. Dare she call out louder? What if it wasn't him? What if the soldiers had found the hut?

Within a moment or two, she could hear what sounded like a low grumble, or at the very least a baritone muttering. This voice did not belong to her host.

Paige quickly slid off the side of the chair and crouched under its stuffed arm, peeking around the table to see if she could get a look at whoever it was. The voice grew louder and more distinct as the seconds ticked by.

"... who leaves a flower pot in the middle of a pathway, honestly..."

The stranger continued to mutter and grumble inaudible terms. Paige craned just enough to look over the top of Robert's table. To her surprise, the only thing she could see through the open door was the point of a small leather hood bobbing up and down like a cork on a fishing line. Heavy boots stomped on the earthen floor.

Paige readied to spring into action if she had to. The movement, although as quiet as a raindrop, seemed to draw the attention of whoever had walked through the doorway. The little hood stopped moving and jerked about back and forth as if searching for the source of a sound. Paige bit her lip and clutched the hairpin to her chest, mentally preparing herself to utter its name. The hat slowly began to drift towards the corner of the table where Paige was hiding. The princess held her breath.

With a quick prayer for reassurance, Paige dove around the corner of the table and raised Klaíomh. The sight that greeted her startled her so much that she let out a small cry.

A short, fat little figure wheeled around in terror and ran straight into the thick oak table leg. The force knocked the creature on its backside and caused it to almost somersault into Paige's lap. The little being scrambled up to its feet and whirled around to face Paige, a set of pudgy, ham-sized fists raised in defense.

"*Klaíomh!*" Paige shouted, leaping to her feet as the sword shot forth from the hairpin. The creature went white as a sheet but kept his fist raised defiantly as he stared cross-eyed down Paige's blade.

"Who are you!?" Paige demanded, pointing the tip of the saber at the stocky creature. "What are you doing poking around here?"

"Poking around!? Well, I never!" he huffed indignantly, jabbing a sausage-shaped finger up at the princess, who now stood upright and towered at least two feet over him.

This person looked similar to a man but he had a giant bulbous nose and ears that stuck out from his head and tapered at the points. Unlike Paige's ears, his pointed down to the floor, almost like Robert's. He wore baggy, grubby, homespun clothes and a pair of wide-cuffed boots that appeared to be at least three sizes too large for him. He wore a leather arming cap with the chin straps dangling comically, outlining a pair of round, red cheeks, which sat beneath equally round blue eyes. Thick black hair poked out in tufts all the way down to a short but curly beard bereft of a mustache.

"Answer me quick, or I will dispatch you quicker!" Paige hissed. She raised the tip of her sword.

"Broadside," the little man grunted.

"That's it?" Paige asked, eyeing him with no small amount of skepticism.

"I think I would know my own name, now, wouldn't I?" the little fellow hissed, keeping his clenched fists raised. "Some of us do just fine with one, thank you very much!"

"Well, then, what are you doing here smashing up pottery and creeping around this hut?" Paige demanded. "It's a bit late for a social call, wouldn't you agree?"

"It would be, if I was here for a social call, but as it stands, I came here to check on your scrawny posterior!" Broadside muttered. "I daresay, I thought hauling your drenched corpse across that very threshold would warrant a little less hostility."

Paige narrowed her eyes at the creature who moved his clenched fists from a defensive stance to firmly plant them on his wide, stubby hips like a fussy mother scolding a small child. With such a great height difference, it was actually genuinely comical to Paige, and she found herself laughing in spite of herself.

"Now, what is so funny?" Broadside snapped. "I don't know about you humans, but it's considered extremely rude to laugh and someone's face in Dwarvish society."

"I'm afraid with the last few days I've had, I don't give two Cops what you think, dwarf." Paige chuckled, dropping her sword point.

The dwarf's face melted into a somber expression, and he nodded. "I suppose you are right," the little creature almost whispered, genuine compassion lacing his low baritone. "I can't say I blame you. After what I've seen today, you are handling everything quite well overall, if I may say so."

"You bumbling oaf! You've smashed my best pot!" Robert came stomping through the vestibule, slamming the thick door shut behind him. The dwarf turned and looked at Paige's host, indignant once again.

"Well, maybe if you didn't leave your pot in the middle of a bloody pathway, it wouldn't get stepped on!" the dwarf sneered like a cheeky toddler.

"Or you should watch where you're going like you had half a brain!" Robert retorted. "Like you said, it was right there in the middle of the pathway. It's not like it was hiding from you!"

"It still wasn't my fault!"

"It wasn't NOT your fault!"

"Boys, it was just a pot," Paige tried to interject, but both of them rounded on her, glaring.

"You stay out of this, missy!" Broadside ordered.

"It's not about the pot. It's about the principal," Robert snapped.

"Principle!? What principle am I missing? 'Don't leave breakable things lying about' seems pretty cut and dried to me!"

"It's my property and I'll do whatever I bloody well please!"

"Oh, shut up!" Paige snapped. She was feeling the exhaustion creeping back into her bones. It was all she could do to maintain her composure as she whirled back on the little dwarf. "What did you mean when you said I'm 'handling myself well' earlier? What did you see?"

"She sure asks a lot of questions, doesn't she?" Broadside muttered to Robert. Robert nodded but gave an expectant look at the dwarf.

"I went seeking answers, of course," Broadside said, his somber expression of pity directed up at Paige. He doffed his cap respectfully, his messy, wavy black curls springing free. "And it's not good. Quite awful, actually."

"Did you see the village?" Robert asked, raising an eyebrow, but the dwarf shook his head.

"I saw the smoldering remains of what at one time could've been a village, and the graves of men, women and children thrown together in giant pits."

Paige felt a sob choke her throat. Her knees began to buckle. She staggered backwards into the chair she'd been sitting in moments ago, her stomach feeling like it had been hit with a club. She felt her core clench to purge the sunken feeling in her stomach. Robert snatched up a vase off his bookshelf and pitched the water and some crumbling carnations to the floor. He thrust it at the princess just in time—she yanked the flowerpot from Robert and heaved.

After she finished, she felt significantly better physically, but the heavy, wet wool blanket of despair still hung upon her soul. Mental images of her friends and loved ones piled dead in a ditch remained, each one bringing a tear to brim over her lashes. Papa had always promised Mother that they would rest together, side by side beneath the Elder trees. Now they were probably stacked far apart, tossed in a heap with their friends and neighbors.

Broadside seemed remiss to say anything else. His face screwed itself into genuine worry. He took a step back and looked at the floor, but Paige got ahold of herself and clenched her jaw to keep from crying.

"What else?" she murmured through gritted teeth. Broadside looked like he was going to object, but Robert coughed, glaring at the dwarf.

"I must be honest; it does not get better. The army had set up camp in what was left of the forest. There are at least three regiments there, but I can't be sure. As best as I was able to ascertain, they had mustered out of Aschin, and that's where they were heading back to."

"Did they raid any other villages?" Robert asked. Broadside shook his head.

"No, best as I can tell."

"Which means Kapernaum was the target all along," Robert spat.

"Were there any survivors?" Paige asked.

"There were quite a few," Broadside said, a slight note of hopeful resolution in his tone, "but I can't be sure exactly how many. I saw at least fifty or sixty of them being roped together for the march. Mostly women and children."

"We can assume they're going to take them back to Aschin," Robert said. "If they don't stay there, they'll be shipped up the valley to Franghal to work in the mines, I'd imagine."

Paige pulled her braid over her shoulder and clutched it hard. She took a shaky breath.

"And the survivors. Did…did any of them have hair like mine?

Broadside hesitated a moment and then nodded.

"Yes, Princess, there was one girl with hair the color of mountain wheat. And, unless I'm completely off and pointed ears are now a *human* thing, I bet my best pair of britches she was a halfling."

Paige felt her heart skip a beat. She sank to her knees and let gut-wrenching sobs of relief engulf her. Olivian could still be alive; a miracle beyond miracles. She had no idea what sort of state her sister might be in or where she could be headed, but at least there was hope she was still alive.

Broadside shifted uncomfortably, but Robert moved over to her side and placed a hand on her shoulder, patting it gently. Paige felt reassured by this gesture and managed to regain her composure.

"I don't know how I can thank you," she said. "Either of you. That is the first piece of good news that I have heard since I left home."

"Well… she's being dragged off to a dungeon across some of the most treacherous terrain in Eirensgarth. That's not exactly good news," Robert cautioned. "So I'm not sure we should throw a party just yet."

Paige wiped her nose with the back of her sleeve and stood.

"Obviously," she said, straightening her hair and returning her trusted hair pain to its proper place. "If she is out there, I have to go find her. She survived the destruction. That's all that matters."

Paige moved for the door but Robert stepped in her path and raised an eyebrow.

"You can't seriously mean now?"

"Robert, I can't thank you enough for the hospitality and the kindness you have shown me, but please get out of my way."

"Don't be an idiot."

"You think I'm going to just stand by knowing my sister will die? I have to save her! If I hurry, I can catch them before they reach Aschin!"

"Listen, you were running around in the Wild on foot. It took at least a day to get you here, and two for you to wake up. That means they are three days ahead of you, even more considering horses, roads, and guard outposts you'd have to skirt around. You'd never catch up on foot, and more likely, you'll be captured long before you could reach her."

"I was good enough to keep from getting caught last night, or two nights ago, or whenever that was!"

"That's called luck, cupcake, and it does run out. You do realize that Aschin is one of the most fortified palaces west of the Imperial capital, right?"

Paige glared at him but didn't head for the door.

"How fortified?"

"Well, let's see—it's a castle with multiple walls and levels built into the solid rock of a mountain. In fact, the dungeon is carved into the mountain itself. It maintains at least a regiment of garrisoned soldiers at any given time, with countless guard houses and so many gates it isn't even funny. How do you plan to save her from all that? Are you going to just waltz right in and take on the entire force, which, by the way, is about, oh, one hundred infantry with a yeomanry four times that number?"

The grave, sarcastic voice with which he berated her only made her angry, but the facts presented reasoning with which she could not argue.

"I can't just let her be defiled by that accursed barbarian! Who knows what he'll do to her? I'll break the gate down if I have to!"

"Gates! Plural!" Robert corrected, but Paige was no longer listening. She yanked her mother's hairpin back out of her braid, energy surging through her veins.

"Again! Don't be an idiot—" Robert began, but she was too quick for him.

"*Klaíomh*!" she shouted, and the blue sparks sprang from the hair piece and shot forward into the long curved blade. She placed the tip of it under his jaw, in the soft, fragile part of his neck. He eyed her in cocky amusement as she glared at him, her cold steel eyes boring holes into his.

"Oh, gracious me," Broadside blubbered on the other side of the table. "Should I give you two a minute?"

"This won't take a minute," Paige spat. Robert eyed her coolly, his gaze unconcerned and unwavering. Page steadied herself with a deep breath before continuing. "She's the only one I've got left. If I hadn't run back to the hut, I might have saved her. If Papa hadn't fallen, we might have gotten to her first, and it's all my fault!" Tears were in her eyes now. Robert's haughty gaze slowly melted into sympathy.

"Easy there, half-stock. You aren't to blame. You committed no crime."

She looked at him, holding his gaze, tears spilling out over her cheeks. "You've no idea—"

"I know you aren't."

"I am!" Paige nearly screamed. She fought to keep her composure, dropping her sword onto the table with a "clang" as she grasped the edge to support herself. She took a deep, shaky breath and went on.

"Mother told me to run. She told me to stay safe! I didn't listen! I tried to help her and she got herself killed because I...if I had just gone, maybe she would have been able to defeat those soldiers and I would have someone here to help me think! And Papa!? If I had given him my rope, he would still be here with me and I wouldn't be facing all of this alone. It's my fault they're both dead and I can't do anything about any of that!"

"That's so much blame to put on your own shoulders," Robert chided. "You did what you could, and there's no way you can know the outcome would have been any different."

"It doesn't matter. I distracted Mother and she died. If I had only been more careful and paid more attention, Papa would still be alive. And now Olivian is being hauled off to some dungeon somewhere and I'm the only person she's got left. I won't, no—I can't fail her. Not like I failed our parents." Paige could feel her tender, aching heart tear apart all over again. She began to cry, trying her hardest to hold in the tears. Robert softly patted her on the back again.

"You couldn't have gone to get Olivian without being captured yourself. It turned out for the best, because now she has a hope of rescue."

Paige nodded, wiping the tears off her face with the sleeve of her new shirt.

"But," he added, "you shouldn't go alone."

"Who would go with me? You?"

"Sure," Robert replied. "It's been a little boring here recently, and anyway, I could use a good stretch of the legs. Besides, I might have a few friends that can help."

"I'd go," Broadside offered, raising his hand.

"I said *friends*, but you will do, I guess." Robert smirked. Paige looked from Robert to Broadside and then back to Robert.

"Your little group?"

"Well, that's slightly emasculating. We have big personalities," the dwarf scoffed.

"It's a brotherhood of sorts," Robert explained. "That's our crest on that chest over there."

"Fine. The Brotherhood?" Paige said, her eyes rolling. "But how do you know they will want to help me? I don't even know why *you* want to help me."

"*One must uphold honor for all!*" the dwarf piped up, reciting the phrase Paige had read on the chest earlier.

"Indeed. Because, I hate the Empire as much as the next free man," Robert said. "And it's the right thing to do. I know that, and so do the others. Now, I don't know for sure if they'll come. In fact, I can think of one moron who would probably resist the entire endeavor, but if we're going to Aschin, we have to walk that way anyway to get to the best mountain pass. Worth a shot to ask. They're not one to leave a damsel in distress."

"Sure you should be speaking for the entire group?" Broadside asked, his face etched with slight concern.

"Look, just because he *acts* like he's the leader doesn't mean he is the boss of me." Robert chortled.

"Who?" Paige asked.

"The person you're going to have to convince," Broadside mumbled.

"Does he have a name?"

"Obviously!" Broadside snapped.

"Broadside likes to think he's protecting Dinendale by keeping his name mysterious." Robert laughed. Broadside's ears turned red as he scowled up at him.

"You know he has a price on his head," Broadside snapped.

"And until this week she didn't even know there was an Empire who would cash in that reward," Robert retorted.

"Whatever. You don't think he'll be too keen on helping us?" Paige retorted.

"I think he'll come around. The others will come without him, but he's only one who has been to Aschin before. Knowing someone who knows the terrain and the layout would go a long way in helping make an impossible task merely improbable."

Paige searched Robert's face. His expression was softer now than it had been, and she wanted to believe she could see kindness in his soft blue eyes. But she bit her bottom lip apprehensively.

"And if they decide not to come, will you try and stop me from going after my sister?"

"Absolutely not. You have my word."

"But can I trust your word?"

"Guess you'll find out."

"Then it's settled," Broadside said. He grabbed a bottle off one of the shelves by the fireplace and pulled the cork. "We'll head out tomorrow."

"Or you could go now, since there isn't any time to lose. Gather the boys, and we'll meet you at sundown tomorrow," Robert ordered. The dwarf looked put-off as he re-corked the bottle and set it back up on the shelf.

"Fine. Where do you want to meet?"

"Willow Hollow. We've got most of the gear stashed there by now, yes?"

"Most of it."

"Then tell them all to meet there by sundown. We'll see you then."

The dwarf nodded then turned to Paige and made a slight bow from his pudgy waist.

"Until tomorrow, m'lady," Broadside said, before he secured the arming cap atop his head, saluted sharply, then waddled out the door and into the darkness while humming an off-key tune.

"We'd better get packed if we want to get to the Grove on time. We'll pack everything up tonight so we can leave first thing in the morning."

Paige nodded. She whispered "Soighren" to change her blade back to the hairpin, which she neatly tucked into her braid. Robert nodded his approval with an impressed look.

"Not bad. It's not every day you're lucky enough to find some practical magic enchanting a sword."

"It was my mother's. I had no idea she had it till..." She trailed off, and Robert didn't press the conversation further. He moved to the fireplace and picked up the massive spear.

"This was given to me by my mentor just before he died. Count yourself lucky you know how to wield yours. I know this spear has magic in it because I can feel it in my fingers, but till I can discover what power lies within it, it's just a heavy toad-sticker. But that spear is all I have of my father. He died before I got the chance to meet him. So I understand what it is to have something that precious."

"I'm so sorry," Paige offered. "I can't even imagine growing up without a father."

"The hermit took care of me well enough," Robert shrugged. "He was the closest to a father I had, and he didn't have to be. When I was old enough, he gave me Raegnah."

"Your spear is named Raegnah?"

"Dwarvish. Means 'gatekeeper.' No idea why it's called that, that's just what the old hermit who raised me told me."

"It's very beautiful," Paige commented, tucking the leather scroll into her belt and cinching it tight. Robert nodded then eyed the scroll, finally looking back up at Paige.

"Don't show that to anyone till I tell you to. Understand?"

Paige nodded.

"Good. Then we best be getting the packs pulled out and cinched up. There is a long journey ahead of us, and I, for one, am keen on being well-supplied for a trip of this magnitude."

Paige spent the rest of the night packing with Robert. He was a skilled packer, managing to fit everything into each satchel perfectly as they set their gear next to the door. For several hours, Paige gathered arrows, bread, water-gourds, carved shafts for arrows, rain gear, and other long-term travel provisions they would doubtless need for the several-week trek they were about to embark on.

It was late into the night by the time Robert announced they had all they would need. Paige was exhausted and felt like she was going to pass out atop the two packs at any moment.

"Get some rest, princess," Robert urged. "We'll be able to sleep in a little in the morning, but we can't hibernate all day. I'll be outside under the rowan tree if you need me," Robert announced, grabbing a thick wool blanket off the pile they had accumulated.

"Are you sure you don't want to spend the night in your own bed? Might not see it for a while."

"You need your rest far more than I. Besides, someone has to stay on the lookout, just in case any other unannounced visitors crash some more of my booby traps."

"You left the pot out on purpose?"

"I should have figured that little oaf wouldn't be able to navigate his own two feet, let alone my yard."

Paige nodded, a slight smile tugging at the corner of her mouth. Robert chortled under his breath before picking up his pack and hefting it onto his back and grabbing his spear. As he turned to go, Paige called after him one last time.

"Do you think we have a chance?"

Robert paused for a moment, then nodded.

"Rest easy. We'll find your sister, but that's tomorrow's problem for tomorrow's Paige."

And with that, he left her alone in the hut to turn in for the night. Paige took a last minute check through her things, then slipped into the hanging cot under the rabbit fur quilt. The last thing she heard was the popping of the fire as she lulled herself into a deep, exhausted sleep.

CHAPTER 5

The WILLOW

TIME FORGOT

"*A*cob, princess?"

Paige nodded as Robert handed her a piece of charred corn. The husk wore dancing red lines where the singed corn had been sitting on the hot stone. She quickly shucked the singed ear, the purple kernels glistening and steaming in the chilly morning air. He offered her a tiny bowl of goat butter which she spread onto the glistening bluish cob with a finger, biting into the sweet vegetable that was as juicy as a peach.

"And some fry bread?" Robert shoved some crispy, yellow flat-cakes smothered in dark marmalade at her, almost dropping them onto her sleeveless jerkin.

"Is that brambleberry jam?"

"Enjoy it while you can. Won't be much but biscuits and wild game once we get on the trails, let alone jam." Paige took a crunchy bite out of the fry bread and the sweet flavors of wild brambleberries cascaded across her palette.

"Oh, goodness! I could grow to miss that from the comforts of my own cottage." She laughed. "You've quite the culinary skills, it would seem!"

"Heavens, no, I trade for all my sweets. I'm not bad with a spatula, but I'm not an artist when it comes to preserves, like old lady Winterwrapp off by Nobbs creek across the valley."

"Do you have many neighbors this far into the Wild?"

"Not really. She's the only one who lives within ten miles of this place." Robert scarfed the rest of his fry bread and wiped the crumbs off his bare chin. "It's about a day's journey on foot to the closest village. I only make it to market once a moon or so."

"Which village is that?"

"Davadish, almost straight south."

"There were traders in the Market at Kapernaum from Davadish, but I've no idea how far from home they were."

"From here, Kapernaum is...er, was about fifty miles northwest of us. We'll have another fifteen miles to go farther south today and then we'll keep pressing east from there."

"Just how far is it to Aschin from here?"

"I haven't a map, but we'll ask the others tonight."

"Best guess?"

"If we cut north just a wee bit and then get through the Dalestrom Meadows and cross the Kaela at a ford up that way, we may be able to make it in three weeks, assuming the snow doesn't set in early this year."

"Three weeks!?" Paige had never traveled that far and that long; she wasn't sure her legs would make it three weeks hiking up and down switchbacks.

"Aye, but it will be much better than trying to go south. The Raychel Ridge lies to the south and not many men have ever made it through the mountains in summer let alone right before winter. But like I said, the others will have a better idea once we get there."

They finished their breakfast in relative silence before rinsing off their dishes and putting them away in the cupboard. Paige felt a great debt of gratitude towards Robert as they finished tidying up the tiny cottage. It was a lovely home, and he was willing to give it all up to help a near perfect stranger. She thought that type of kindness and honor only appeared in the books she would sneak down and read in her papa's study as a little girl.

"Well, unless you can think of something I missed, I believe we are finally ready!" Robert exclaimed, hoisting his pack onto his back. He winced under the load. "It's been a while since the last time I trekked out there. Might have over-packed just a little bit."

"I'm sure we'll both be pitching some non-necessities as we go," Paige grunted, heaving her own pack onto her small back.

"Aye, I know we will," Robert muttered as he trudged out the front door with Paige close behind him. The morning sunlight struck the dew and frost on the ground, scattering light like a cut diamond. She let the brisk breeze prickle her lungs as she sucked in the fresh air, her heartbeat quickening. For the first time that week, Paige had hope.

Robert took a rusty iron key out of his mantle and locked the door of his home.

"Best enjoy the sunshine while you can," he said, pulling a small sack from his belt. "Further east you go, the gloomier the mountains get this time of year."

He opened the little pouch and proceeded to pour out a small pile of whitish powder onto his palm. It looked like the crushed eggshells Olivian used to use to powder her nose, but rather than apply it cosmetically, Robert tossed it at the threshold of his hut and stepped back in a hurry. No sooner had the substance hit the dirt when the sod began to bubble like a boiling stew. It slowly rose up into a wall, and before Paige had time to blink, the grassy slope of the hillside had swallowed the door. She stuttered at Robert, trying to ask for an explanation. His smile broadened.

"Fairy dust. Won it from a leprechaun in a card duel last week," he bragged.

"What is a—"

"So many questions!" Robert cut her off as he headed for the east slope of the valley.

"But—"

"Spread them out! We have a long way to go!"

They reached the top of the valley within a half hour and immediately headed northeast into the thick, dense vegetation of the Wild. Paige had never been this far east, and although there was frost on the ground, the ferns and brambles still stood tall, green, and heavy along the forest floor. The brightly colored canopy above let in the yellow rays of sunlight like a stained glass window. The beams of light reached past the blindingly red maple leaves and stretched to the forest floor like tendrils of life to the little green plants.

They waded through the dewy leaves for several hours. Paige felt her toes turn pruney as the wet plants soaked her moccasins. The small pot and canteen Robert had strapped to his pack clanged and clunked against the heavy spear lashed to his back. He slashed at the foliage with a short machete, muttering under his breath at the mosquitos tormenting his uncovered ears. Paige trudged behind him, trying to ignore the sticky, sucking sound in her moccasins. She tripped over the uneven ground and her ponytail often caught in the branches of thorns and evergreens. In spite of the the harsh terrain, he showed no sign of stopping.

"If you and your friends knew about Kapernaum, why have I never seen any of you there?" she called.

"I've lived here my whole life," Robert answered, hacking at a low hanging branch. "Most of the boys are from all across Eirensgarth. We knew about Kapernaum, but the Mystics thought it better not to put a target on their backs by meddling in the affairs of men."

"Mystics? Like magicians?"

"Hah, not quite. Mystics are just what the magical races call themselves to differentiate themselves from men; elves, dwarves, and the like."

"So am I a mystic then?"

"Well, technically, you're only half mystic. That would make you a 'Geartha.'"

"Sounds like ghearrta," Paige noted. "It means—"

"Cut," Robert finished for her. "That's because it is. Geartha is the western Elvish dialect for ghearrta."

"Why use that term?"

"It's in reference to the bloodlines," Robert said, hacking another branch out of the way as they jumped down into an old, dry creek bed. He reached up, offering Paige a hand to hold as she hopped down into the gully.

"The bloodlines of the races?" she asked.

"In a way." He ducked under a dead log. "How much do you know about magic?"

"Not a ton. Mother was pretty secretive about her healing poultices and remedies. She promised to teach us one day, but..." Her breath caught in her throat. Oh, Mother. So many things they could never do together now. "That never happened."

"Well, she was right to keep that under wraps. Most men can't use magic anymore, and so all too often they get it in their head that if they can capture one who can, they can use that to some sort of advantage. Understand?"

"I could see that."

"A few thousand years ago, many people across the races could perform natural magic. As the humans and Mystics settled this world, some began to study the natural magic to figure out why some could and others couldn't. They finally linked it to several specific bloodlines tracing back generations. Some races, like the elves, decided for the good of their people, they would selectively breed those bloodlines to maximize the number of people who could use magic. It only took three or four generations to disperse the genealogy that way, so now it is very rare to come across an elf who can't use natural magic in some form or fashion."

"So the human kingdoms just let it die out?"

"Humans tend to think on an individual basis, not about the collective as a whole," Robert countered. "So as I heard it, human magicians and wizards became more sporadic when they tried and failed on multiple levels to do the same thing."

"You said there were other Mystic races too?"

"Yes, there are western and eastern elves, and all the small elvish cousins like the pixies and the sprites. Then there are the dwarves and the Fae."

"Now you're just making up words."

"Hardly. Faes used to outnumber men, elves, and dwarves combined, but now they stay in their own territories. They were pretty much driven out of the Wild, so the people who live here now think they are mere myths and legends. Tell me, princess, have you ever seen a satyre?"

"No?"

"A gnome?"

"Nope."

"Centaur?"

"Surely you jest."

"Not at all. They're out there somewhere. I've met a faun. Lovely chap, sold me an oil lamp years ago when my mentor took me south of the Great River."

"I had no idea..."

"It's a big wide world out there," Robert said, gesturing to the sky and beyond. "There's so much more to this land than just the Wild."

"So what are you, then?"

He turned and looked at her with slight annoyance.

"Don't give me that look. You're clearly not a man."

"I'm myself," Robert snapped. "And that's all anyone needs to know."

Paige looked him over again and then it dawned on her.

"You don't know?"

Robert didn't answer her, rather just kept trudging ahead in a sulking silence. They continued on jumping in and out of dry seasonal creek beds, but Robert didn't talk for a long while. These little creek beds dotted the landscape like the thin webbing of a spider's roost. As night approached, Paige felt shaky. Her ribs were still sore, making the pack a cumbersome and painful thing to adjust back and forth with every step. Her feet were sore and cramped, adding to her ever-present headache pounding like a water-drum.

"Did you know my father?" She took a swig from a wooden canteen off the back of her guide's pack. Robert shrugged, continuing to hew the thick underbrush and tall grasses with his machete.

"Yep. I met him a handful of times when he came to visit my mentor. I wasn't much more than a child, but I remember him well."

"He must have been pretty young then."

"Ha! Not by much."

Paige frowned. "Just how old are you?"

"Not sure. All I know is, I'm older than you," he said with a mischievous wink. His expression softened as he took a more serious tone. "He was a good man, your father. He was always kind to us."

"Who is this mentor you keep talking about?"

"He was a great man and a fantastic teacher. Taught me how to fight, raised me to live off the land and adapt. Closest thing I ever had to a father."

"Where is he now?"

Robert's expression darkened momentarily before it was replaced by remnants of a grief long buried. "The one enemy we can never outrun is time, and sometimes... yours just runs out."

Paige felt a pang of sorrow. Her own loss still lay heavy on her. She began to feel little tendrils of fear creeping around her heart with icy fingers, and she tried to brush it off. What if Robert was wrong? What if the Brotherhood didn't want to help her? She knew she would have no choice but to forge on ahead and go it alone. Quitting was not an option for her. But the thought of also failing or being too late terrified her to her very core.

"So what makes you think this Dinendale character knows the layout of Aschin?" Paige queried.

"Because he should. He was there when it was built."

Paige's head jerked up in surprise.

"He helped build the fortress?"

"He didn't have much choice as a slave, now did he?"

"I didn't know that, you sarcastic twat," Paige spat, indignant.

"You're cute when you get snippy, anyone ever tell you that?

"No one more than once," Paige warned, grinding her teeth. Robert chuckled.

"Fair enough. Din is from the south lands beyond the Great River. He was captured when he ventured too far north, and from what I can gather, was pressed into service for the Sharadhen's construction efforts."

"An atrocity!" Paige hissed. "The very idea that someone thinks it's okay to own another human being is absolutely revolting."

"Welcome to the Empire," Robert grumbled. "I wish the Sharadhs thought the same way. Instead, they imprison the free peoples of the land and make them erect monuments over their own farms. I know the slaves they pushed to build Aschin numbered in the thousands."

Her stomach twisted. Her own countrymen would be added to that number soon. She silently promised herself that someday, if the Creator granted her the chance, she would do everything in her power to free as many of those poor souls as she could.

"So, since he was there to help build the structure, you think he will be able to help us rescue Olivian?"

Robert shrugged. "He'll at least have a better idea of the layout than any of the rest of us. So that's a starting point."

They continued on in silence for some time as Robert hacked their way through some the dense bushes that were quickly wilting in the autumn cold. Paige heard the honking sound of a flock of geese and stared high into the sky. Through the colorful quilt of fall leaves, she could see the familiar chevron formation passing over them as the birds headed south for the winter. Paige felt a pang of jealousy strike her as she imagined what it would be like to have no cares in the world, aside from flying south with a family. She longed for that sweet simplicity, that ability to roam free without kings and killings. Paige brushed a tear from her cheek as it fell warm amidst the cool evening air.

The sound of the birds began to give way to an orchestra of crickets. Robert stopped for a moment at a large fir tree and selected a young, springy limb towards the bottom and hacked it off with his machete.

"We're not far now," he said, tying the end of the switch into a course knot of sappy wood. "Best we keep quiet till I tell you it's alright to speak, you hear?"

Paige nodded as Robert finished his rough knot. He yanked a piece of flint out of his pocket and struck the back end of his hunting knife till a small shower of sparks cascaded onto the makeshift torch. The canvas caught, and the wood popped and spat as the fire spread around the knot, lighting up the dusky forest. Robert jerked his head, and Paige followed close behind as they walked deeper and deeper into the ever-darkening woods.

They walked for a while before Robert pointed to a large boulder. If he hadn't motioned to it, Paige wouldn't have seen it in the dense foliage. The heavy fog that was falling was not helping matters either. It twisted and curled about like a sea-green smoke, drifting to and fro. Paige wanted to grab Klaíohm but resisted the urge to pull the hairpin from her braid. Instead, she gripped the dagger tightly Robert had loaned her as they trudged forward.

CRACK!

Robert halted and stuck out his arm. She yanked Klaíohm out of her hair, her muscles tense. Her guide looked around them warily, peering into the foggy quagmire swirling around them.

"I can't see a bloody thing!" Paige spat. Robert hushed her urgently.

"That's one of the secrets to having a secret hideaway," Robert muttered. He then straightened up and pulled his spear from its strap, placing the torch into the ground.

"Jey, is that you?" he called out, pointing his spear into the mist. There was no answer in the heavy forest air. Paige combed the trees with her eyes, her ears lying flat against her head like a cat's. But there was no tingling at the base of her spine, which made her wonder if perhaps the sound they'd heard was a squirrel or a dead branch simply falling to the ground.

A slight sound just to her right. It was a faint slap, like someone had struck a rock with a leather glove. This was followed by a soft hum growing ever louder as the seconds ticked on. Suddenly, out of the darkness, a thin shape leaped through the fog, punching a vortex through the air. The long shaft of an arrow quivered in the ground inches away from Robert's foot. Paige was about to summon her sword when Robert caught her wrist and held it fast.

"Jesnake, it's Robert, you melodramatic prat!"

"I know it's you," a thin, low voice hissed through the fog. "Why do you think that arrow is in the ground instead of your gullet?"

"Could have lost your edge? It's been a couple months; for all I know you're missing a couple fingers now and that's the best you got!"

"Never." The voice chuckled. Paige imagined the voice would pair nicely with a talking fox. Thin, but not in a weasley way. A cunning tone that sounded like it was almost spoken through the nose. She heard a rustle in the branches of the trees above her and caught a flash of moving metal in the torchlight. A figure sat perched on one of the branches, his chainmail glittering in the light. His silhouette was tall and slender, with a pair of lean arms and what appeared to be a bow grasped in his left hand. His bearing reminded Paige of a panther lazily perched in a tree after a successful hunt and subsequent feast.

"The others here?" Robert asked. The slender man nodded, letting one foot hang lazily.

"Aye. Most. Is this the princess the short one spoke of?"

"Indeed," Robert said, nodding towards Paige. "Paige, this is Jesnake of Westfjord, House of Some Long Name I Can't Pronounce, Son of Someone-Important but not important to me. Jey, this is Paige of the Alatarians, Daughter of Alaire."

"I'm honored to meet you," Paige added quickly, bowing slightly.

"But what is your real name, child?"

"My real name?"

"Aye. The one your mother gave you. The one that matters."

"Alwasu," Paige said softly. The figure inclined his head in return and slid nimbly off his perch, landing on his feet with hardly a sound.

In the light of the torch, Paige could now make out more of his features. Although his pointed ears immediately gave his elven heritage away, he looked nothing like her mother. He was much taller than he'd appeared in the tree; the top of Paige's head would have barely come up to his chin, she guessed. His features were all more sharply pointed than her mother's had been; longer, pointier ears and thin, almond-shaped eyes the color of cool water. The only thing not angular about him was his nose; it was round and slightly bulbous.

"The honor is all mine, Alwasu," Jesnake said, bowing once again. "Though I wish you were here under better circumstances."

"As do I," Paige said softly. She felt that all too familiar ache in her heart threaten to spill over into her eyes. She bit her lip to compose herself. "But there's no changing that now. Only righting the wrongs done."

"Indeed," Jesnake said grimly. Robert yanked the arrow out of the dirt and handed it back to the elf.

"You'll come along, then?"

"It isn't me you'll have to worry about," Jesnake said, wiping the iron arrowhead off on his palm and returning it to its sheath. "You know me—I'm always in the mood to off a few Sharadhs."

"Din not wanting to come?"

"I doubt it. But I can't say for certain, as he's the only one not here yet."

Paige bit her lip. Robert snorted.

"He's always late. At any rate, you might as well meet the rest of the lads," Robert said to Paige. Then, turning to Jesnake, he said, "You waiting out here till he arrives?"

Jesnake nodded but didn't say anything further. Robert shifted his pack and jerked his head for Paige to follow him as they continued into the dense underbrush, Jesnake disappearing into the dark mist behind them. They forged ahead into the fog for another five minutes or so, the sound of the crickets muffled by the density of the cloud swirling around them. Paige began to wonder just how far out Jesnake had been standing guard when something damp and stringy suddenly slapped her softly in the face.

"Mind the willow," Robert chuckled as Paige pushed the branch to the side like a curtain. He held the torch further forward. Paige blinked as her eyes adjusted. The fog seemed to clear ever so slightly.

It was indeed a willow tree, but to call it 'huge' would have been an understatement. It was the size of an Elder tree, at least four stories tall, with a trunk so thick, ten men could have stood hand in hand around it and still not closed the circle. The branches around it draped down in a thick curtain over seven paces thick. The leaves had already turned to yellow but had not yet dropped from their dense veil, so Paige nearly had to swim through them with each step.

"This is magnificent!" Paige gasped. "I've never seen a willow this big!"

"Aye, not many Willow Elders left in the Wild, but we call it home when something important is on the wind."

Robert carefully guided Paige through the curtain and into the clearing by the tree trunk. In the light of the torch, Paige could see a series of wood timbers acting as steps from the base of the large root system and ascending upward around the trunk of the willow. They were solid and sturdy-looking, but Paige guessed by the way the tree had grown around and over the timbers, they had been in place longer than she or Robert had been alive.

"Up?" she asked.

Robert nodded. "Welcome to the Willow of the Wild," he said, taking the first step and offering a hand to Paige. She took it and hauled herself up onto the first step, appreciating the gesture, as her heavy pack threatened to topple her with one off-balance move if she wasn't careful.

"How on earth did you find this place?"

"Dinendale brought us here the first time we banded together. Apparently it used to be a pagan temple of some sort, but it's been long abandoned."

"There were pagans that worshiped the Elder trees back home, but I didn't know they used temples," Paige mentioned, feeling the coarse bark under her palm as they continued to ascend the stairs. Since the trunk of the tree was so large, the steps were spaced at a steep incline to keep the ascent as short as possible. Still, Paige could feel her thighs starting to protest, especially after an entire day of walking.

"They usually don't, but it's not like they left a journal for us to read. So we turned it into our meeting point."

"How far spread out are you all?"

"Not far. We each have dwellings about a day's walk in any given direction. Keeps us from being vulnerable at any given time."

"So how did you get the word out to meet so fast?"

"Pigeons. Broadside keeps a couple here just in case. He probably used them this morning when he arrived."

"Pigeons?"

"For all the innovations your father built at Kapernaum, you never used carrier pigeons?"

"We didn't exactly correspond outside the village," Paige reminded him. Robert nodded as if that explanation made sense to him as he helped haul her up another step. They stood two thirds of the way up the tree. Paige could see the end of the stairs ahead where they connected to a timber-framed deck that vanished over the top of the tree, giant branches looming around it and dipping low to allow the canopy curtain of willow leaves to cascade to the forest floor below. She felt a dull ache in her heart. This was so much like home in so many ways, and she would never see it again.

Flickering light emanated from beyond the dock. Paige could hear low voices drifting down from the dwelling. Robert reached the top of the landing first, his visage cascaded in dancing yellow light. The murmuring stopped and Robert waved briefly to whomever owned the voices above. He then turned back to Paige, reaching out to help her. Paige grabbed his hand, and he hauled her up and over the last step and onto the deck.

The sudden change from dark to yellow, dim, tavernesque light was enough to make her eyes strain to refocus. The ancient platform they stood on was polished to a dull ebony from use. A large doorway stood open to them with a spiked stockade wall extending around the top of the tree in either direction from the entry. As she followed Robert through the open doorway, she felt a jolt of surprise nail her feet to the ground. Ahead of them stood a flat, wide expanse the size of a ballroom. Walls ran twelve feet tall, with sharpened sticks at the top and a lofted platform set just tall enough to allow a man to peak over the wall if needed. A set of stairs to her left led up to the battlements, the same peg-style construction that had led up to the top of the willow.

As they stepped into the enclosure, Paige glanced down and saw that the deck had ended, giving way to the thickest carpet of moss she'd ever seen in her life. It covered the enclosed space like a blanket of snow as smooth and flat as a frozen pond. An assortment of chests, pots, barrels, and shelves of jars lined the walls, and several stacks of spears, swords, bows, and barrels filled with arrows lay scattered about. Several bronze braziers with glowing ember charcoal fires in them crackled and popped to Paige's right. Around each basin was a square arrangement of wooden and canvas cots, some empty, some with gear cluttering them. The only other piece of furniture in the room aside from these was a large oak table in the center of the circle enclosure, and around it stood three figures.

The first figure stood at the right end of the table. Or rather, he stood atop a stool at the right end of the table. Broadside now wore a baggy crimson shirt tucked into fur-lined vambraces lashed to his thick arms. Over the shirt he wore a leather vest that was a size too large for his frame. The vest draped comically over his pants, which looked like they were made of thick green wool homespun cloth. The trousers were neatly tucked into cuffed leather boots sporting steel-toed tips that glinted even in the dim yellow light. His arming cap had been topped with a shiny, unadorned steel helm.

Next to him, standing easily two feet taller than Robert, was a man with a set of broad shoulders and a thick waist like a boulder of granite. The gentleman wore a short-sleeved, double-linked chainmail halbert that Paige was sure weighed more than her and her pack combined. The armor was pulled over a white linen gambeson, and atop both of these he had strapped on a polished steel breastplate that bore a relief of a bear holding an olive tree in its jaws and front paws. On his belt he wore a plain, simple dirk that had a cutting edge almost as long as Paige's forearm. A small, wooden round shield with a large brass boss in the center covered his back, bearing the same heraldic symbol on his breastplate. His straight black hair was cropped close to his head except for a thin braided lock at the nape of his neck. His overall demeanor and bearing seemed

173

pleasant enough, and as oxymoronic as it sounded in her head, Paige could think of no better description for this character aside from jovial "little giant." He nodded at her, smiling a thin but wide grin.

The last person on the far left end of the table sat in a chair tipped on its two back legs. The heavy riding boots he wore lay propped on the ancient tabletop and were crossed lazily at the ankles. Despite his tall, lanky frame, he was well-muscled and lean. Unkempt, sandy hair fell to his collar and a scraggy shadow of a beard graced his wide smile. Prominent front teeth lent his grin a boyish look as he held Paige's gaze. Paige noticed a scar running across the bridge of his round nose and down his left cheek almost to his jawline, which looked out of place with his softer features. He wore a forest-green tunic under a leather vest; brown breeches and knee-high boots completed the outfit. Hanging on the back of his chair were two very plain, unadorned rapiers, held there by beaten, worn leather cross belts with huge silver buckles. He looked up and tossed his head back with a laugh when he saw the pair entering the glade.

"Well, well, unless my eyes deceive me, 'tis none other than Robert Eöl! And what be this? Has the hermit gone and gotten himself some female companionship for his wee little home?"

"Don't go there, Duelmaster," Robert muttered. "She might kick your—"

"I'm Paige," she interrupted, glowering at Robert. He simply shrugged. The one Robert had called 'Duelmaster' plopped his legs off the table and jumped to his feet, striding over to her.

"I've no doubt she would, Robby, m'boy!"

The fellow tucked his shoulder-length hair back behind his ears, which Paige noticed were long and pointed like an elf's but with three distinct points at the end that splayed like an oak leaf. Paige thought in that moment that this rugged individual was either oddly handsome or handsomely odd. Perhaps both.

Robert strode towards the table and beckoned for Paige to follow. "Now that we've all had a good laugh," he said dryly, "let's get on with introductions, shall we?" He gestured to the man who had just spoken. "You've just met Calebna of Stumpy's Hollow. Around here we call him Duelmaster. Obviously, he's cocky as a rooster, but don't let that reflect horribly on our group; the rest of these morons will more than likely do that individually anyways. Our resident lowland giant over there is Isaac Twostaves."

Robert then pushed Paige closer to the table and gestured to her with his free hand.

"Gentlemen, this is Paige Alwasu of Kapernaum."

"Just Paige," she muttered, staring as Calebna, or, what was it...Duelmaster, made a dramatic bow, pulling a tasseled cap out of his belt.

"And what could the fair maiden have come for?" he asked. "I doubt she's here to experience my handsome company and sunny disposition, though I would believe it if she said so!" He aimed a cheeky grin at Paige, who glanced

175

around, not knowing what to think. When Robert had said there was a "brotherhood," she'd envisioned at least fifteen warriors in some semblance of a militia organization. They clearly had the arms for one stockpiled, but this was barely a squad of mismatched young males, let alone a band of warriors.

"She's here for our help," Robert said, dropping his pack next to the table. "And I called everyone here to talk it out."

"A story? I relish in hearing!" Duelmaster said, with a dramatic flourish of his hand. "Does it include the harrowing tale that gave her royalness the Daemon's Eye?"

Paige touched the corner of her still slightly achy eye. "Oh, well, I apparently have Broadside to thank for that." Paige laughed. The dwarf looked confused and slightly stunned.

"What? But I never—"

He cut himself off and whirled on Robert.

"You told her I gave her that!?"

Robert looked embarrassed and slightly peeved.

"Let's not get mired down in the details," he muttered, shrugging the dwarf off, who in turn looked perturbed.

The other two snickered as Paige glared at Robert.

"Well, now that you are here, can we eat?" the giant Robert had called Twostaves asked, patting his breastplate impatiently. Duelmaster rolled his eyes but kept his toothy grin cracked.

"I suppose the latecomers will just have to run faster if they're going to get any food before you inhale it, Twostaves," the dryad said, approaching one of the barrels and cracking the lid open.

"Where are the others?" Paige whispered to Robert.

"Well, Jey is out keeping an eye on things," Broadside said, "and I'm not sure where Din is. I thought he'd be here an hour ago."

"So there are only five of you?"

"Well, six including Robert." The small giant pointed a finger the size of a spear shaft at Robert.

"So only six?"

"Did you expect an army, madam?" Duelmaster asked, pulling a salted pork haunch and tossing it to Twostaves. The giant snatched it and slammed it on the old table with a resounding 'thud' as he pulled his dirk out and began carving slabs of the meat.

"I honestly didn't know what to expect," Paige admitted.

Robert laughed. "Beggars can't be choosers, Paige."

"No, I didn't mean it that way!"

Robert continued chuckling as he pulled Duelmaster's seat out and beckoned her over. She hesitated, but as soon as she saw the dryad had happily perched himself on top of the salt pork barrel, she reluctantly took the seat. Her feet sighed with relief as the pressure of walking an entire day finally lifted. She realized this was to become a feeling she would know intimately in the coming days.

Twostaves slapped some of the pork slabs onto some trenchers while Broadside tossed some cracked wheat baguettes around. Paige took the food gratefully and began munching on the salty meat, alternating bites with the chewy bread.

"So, princess," Duelmaster asked between huge bites. "What does our holiday entail?"

"Your holiday?" Paige asked, confused.

"You aim to get us out of this state of boredom and stagnation, no?" the dryad laughed, shaking his hair out of his eyes. She thought she saw some tiny twigs caught in his tangled mane.

"I suppose that's one way to look at it?" she stammered.

"My dear, it's the only way to look at it!" Duelmaster laughed, almost manically. "An adventure! Finally!"

"Duelmaster, be sensible," the giant scolded through a mouth stuffed to capacity with bread. "This is a rescue mission after all."

Duelmaster nodded sheepishly, turning back to Paige. "I apologize, princess," the dryad mumbled. "Do fill us in, won't you? Broadside gave us the highlights, but if you're able, we'd like to hear your tale as you tell it."

Paige felt a slight lump in her throat forming, but she promised herself she wouldn't choke in front of an entire table of evidently battle-hardened warriors. She started from the beginning, telling them everything she could remember about the day leading up to the feast and the events of that night. She almost broke when she got to the part about her parents' deaths, but managed to take a shaky breath before continuing. The only thing she omitted from the story was the part about the leather scroll now bound tight to her stomach, as Robert had advised. She concluded with a plea for them to help her only family left—her sister. By the time she'd finished, all traces of a smile had vanished from Duelmaster's face, and the dwarf and the giant seemed to have lost their appetites, staring at her with gloomy, pitying faces.

"We're so sorry for your loss," the dryad said, reaching out and taking Paige's hand in both of his own. His palms were rough, filled with ridges that looked more like tree bark than fingerprints and palm lines. She smiled appreciatively.

"Well, there's nothing for it except to bust down the gates of Aschin and get the poor princess out of that barbarous prince's clutches!" Twostaves declared, jumping up and pounding his fist into the table so that all the wooden bowls clattered with the force.

"While I agree, I think bludgeoning down the gates is probably the worst plan we could have," Robert said. "If we want to live to fight another day, I think stealth is our only option."

"And for stealth, you need to know what you're getting into," a voice murmured from behind them. Paige turned to see the willowy figure of Jesnake flicker in the torchlight as he paced softly towards the table. His bow was unstrung and strapped into his quiver which now lay across his thin back. Broadside was quick to toss him a roll, which the elf caught deftly without so much as a sideways glance.

"Well, obviously," Twostaves muttered, his acerbic tone dripping with every word. "So we get a map."

"A map is only good for the landscape around a place, but to get to the princess, we'll need a full layout of the castle's inner sanctum, yes?"

Twostaves twisted his mouth up as he pondered this. Robert was nodding his agreement as Jesnake came around the table and leaned against the corner between Twostaves and Broadside.

"And it would appear the only person with that full layout has yet to arrive."

"He'll be here. You know he comes and goes as he pleases!" Broadside insisted.

"Unless he got lost," muttered Robert. Duelmaster and Twostaves snickered.

"That was one time, and you were supposed to be the one steering the boat!" Broadside snapped. Robert rolled his eyes dismissively, but the story behind the remark now had even Jesnake chuckling softly.

"Regardless, I think it would help to have all the gear packed for when he does arrive," Jesnake offered.

"You really so sure he'll help?" Paige asked, hopeful.

Robert snorted. "We'll get him to come. He'll complain and whine a bunch, but we can get him to come."

"Then we'd best make use of the time we've got!" Broadside ushered, hopping off his stool and hurrying over to a pile on the floor covered with canvas. "A pack for everyone! Chop-chop!"

"Never say 'chop-chop' to me again, dwarf," Jesnake said dryly.

Broadside pulled the tarp away to reveal a pile of assorted packs. They ranged in style from small baskets with tumplines to intricate leather packs framed with hickory staves. Jesnake, Twostaves, Broadside and Duelmaster all gathered around and began picking their own packs out of the pile and then heading to the gear that lay scattered about, selecting odds and ends and stuffing them into their satchels.

Paige stood to help, but Robert told her not to worry. They wouldn't need any help. "Perks of coming prepared," he chuckled, settling backwards into his chair.

The rest of the Brotherhood took about half an hour to pack up gear from the various piles. Robert explained that as they raided Sharadhen outposts over the last few years, they would always haul back as much contraband as they could, just in case.

"You never know when you might need to outfit a bunch of people," he explained. "A rebellion is useless without firepower. And it'd better be close to the firepower the enemy has, so why not take it from the enemy itself?"

"Do you think there will be a rebellion?" Paige asked, untying and retying the loose laces on her moccasin.

Robert shrugged. "I think they'd have to conquer the Wild first, which would be really hard to do, just because of how the societies out here are structured and spaced out. I think maybe someday someone will push back, and maybe even those in the heart of the empire will fight it one day, but for now it can't hurt to stockpile if that day should ever arise."

"They didn't seem to have a problem taking Kapernaum," she muttered, jerking the leather thongs on her calf tight.

"The only way I could see them pulling that off was with a well-supplied forced march," Duelmaster added. "There's no way they were able to cover the ground they did in the forest with a supply train behind them. They were probably running dangerously low on food by the time they got to Kapernaum."

"They can cut roads, and then what will stop them?" Paige asked.

"Maybe us? Maybe some child who is not yet a man? There's no way of telling," Robert said, scratching his chin.

"Hey, that's my bow!" Broadside shouted. He was clutching a small bow with both hands and pulling with all his might. Twostaves had it pinched between his thumb and forefinger on the other end.

"It was in the stack. Everyone knows gear in the stack is fair game!" the giant snapped.

"It's three sizes too small for you!" the dwarf shot back.

"Four, actually."

"Then why the bloody blazes do you want it!?"

"Because he's acting like a child to a dwarf that's acting like a baby," a new voice behind them muttered.

Paige turned around. A dark figure blocked the doorway of the tree fort, leaning against a post as if he'd been watching the crew for some time. He was tall with broad shoulders and a solid frame. She couldn't make out many of his features, yet his eyes reflected the light slightly, like Jesnake's had earlier.

"Hey, moron," Robert shouted. "Why not come out of the shadows? I promise you the only thing mysterious about you is why you insist on creeping about like that."

The newcomer didn't reply but swaggered into the dim light.

"Call it a force of habit," he muttered.

Robert rolled his eyes. "Well, Paige, meet 'Force of Habit,' known by the rest of the world as Dinendale Faoris. Din, this is Paige."

Dinendale approached the table with measured steps. He appeared to be a few years older than Paige, perhaps Robert's age, with bold features and shaggy brown hair so dark that it almost looked black. Thick, slanted brows marked his expression, giving him a stern, serious appearance, and his hair was swept behind the tapered ears of an elf. Judging by his angular features, strapping build, and dark hair and eyes, he was no kin to her mother's kind, but his features were not as pronounced as Jesnake's. He seemed a somber fellow, with a reserved, closed-off posture. After imagining all he must have been through according to Robert, she could understand that. As the elf drew nearer still, she could see his eyes flashing in the firelight; a deep, dark brown, the color of a bear's fur. Above them, adorning his head like the crown jewel of a diadem, was a web of thin, white scar tissue running from the center of his forehead down towards his left eye.

"So, then." Dinendale directed his words at Robert, halting with his hands clasped behind his back. "I take it we're all going on a trip?"

"You're rather observant," Robert said dryly. He stood and walked up to the elf, reached out and clasped Dinendale's arm firmly. They pulled into a short embrace before turning to join the others who had abandoned their packs to come to the table.

"Dinendale, it's been too long," Jesnake said, embracing the fellow elf in a similar fashion as Robert had. The others exchanged the gesture till they had all made the rounds, then Dinendale sat down across the table from Paige and stared her directly in the eye.

"I was summoned here by the briefest of explanations via a pigeon to arrive and see the band is already packed and ready to leave. So tell me. Where are we going?"

"I assume you've heard Kapernaum was sacked by the Sharadhs four nights ago?" Robert asked.

The elf shrugged. "I heard. You planning on moving in?"

"No. They took the chief's eldest daughter."

"My sister," Paige interjected meekly. The elf's hard, searching gaze turned to her. It was slightly unsettling, but she forged ahead. "And I need help. Your help."

"I tend to not bother myself with crusades of revenge," the elf said, his searching eyes scanning her warily.

"As much as I desire revenge, that isn't what this is about," Paige answered. "Olivian is still out there, and I have to get her back."

"So you would ask us to march on the greatest force in all the kingdoms of men?"

"Whether you come or not is immaterial to me," Paige insisted. Robert had a slightly worried expression on his brow, but he didn't interject. Paige continued, "I'm going with or without anyone; I am my sister's only hope."

"And just where would we be running off to save your poor damsel of a sister?" the elf demanded. Paige bit her lip, took a deep breath, then exhaled slowly.

"They're taking her to Aschin."

The elf's gaze hardened. She saw the corner of his mouth twitch.

"Indeed?"

"Yes. She's being taken there by a man called Feridar."

The elf's fist clenched.

"The crown prince has your sister?"

"Yes."

"So you intend to storm Aschin itself?" he asked. When she nodded, he shook his head. "That's a good one, that's really good. You should be a jester."

"And you should be a Burgess," she spat. The elf looked amused. Paige felt her heart start sinking. She quickly looked to Robert.

"Damsel in distress, a black-hearted prince, and a matter of honor—seems like our kind of adventure, Din?" Robert asked, staring the elf down. Dinendale barely blinked.

"It would seem so," the elf muttered.

"I know it's a lot to ask, but Robert says you know the layout. That you've been to Aschin before?"

Paige saw Dinendale's jaw clench as he turned his gaze to her own. His eyes were cold and unfeeling, a sort of steeled deadness only a life filled with anger could forge.

"Do you?" he asked through gritted teeth. "Do you understand how much it is you ask?"

"I can't pretend to know what happened to you there," Paige rushed, "or the things you had to endure, but—"

"But nothing, Alatarian," Dinendale hissed, knuckles popping in the fist he was clenching. "You are a fool if you think you can waltz right in to the dungeons of Aschin and then just slip away with your prize. That prison is a hell, and Hell does not give up its dead."

"It gave you up, didn't it?"

"I clawed my way out. That shouldn't have happened at all. It was a miracle."

"Which is why with your help, the more chance of success—"

The elf leapt up from the table. "If your sister even makes it to Aschin, she'll be dead within a month. The prince often tires of his playthings. He'll toss her in the trash pile the moment he's done with her."

"I can't just leave her to that fate!" Paige also stood. "I already told you, I'm going one way or the other, so I really don't give two Cops whether you come or stay here and let that Empire walk all over these lands and its people."

"You want some help? Some advice from someone who's been there? Cut your losses. Head out and find a new life for yourself."

"Like you?" Paige spat. She was angry now, beyond any notion of feeling desperate by this point. "I can't leave her to the hands of that barbarian! She'll be tortured, and it's my fault! He knows I have it!"

The elf glared at her, his brown eyes flashing.

"He knows you have what?" he growled.

Paige realized she'd said too much. She looked at Robert. He shrugged his shoulders and mouthed the words, "Go ahead." Paige took another deep breath to steady her nerves.

"They attacked my home because of this," she explained, reaching into her shirt to pull the leather scroll out, "and if she's still alive, who knows what he'll do to try and get it?"

The eyes of all of the warriors were glued to the ancient scroll. The elf reached out. Paige hesitated a moment before handing it to him. He gazed at it as his brow furrowed.

"Where did you get this?"

"My Papa..." Paige started, but she stopped, fearing she would start choking on any words to follow.

"Your father was the outlander chief?"

She nodded, and the elf looked over to Robert, concern and worry etched into his face.

"Alaire?" he asked. Robert bowed his head.

"So much blood for a single piece of leather," the hermit muttered.

"Whatever is written there, brother," Jesnake said softly, "it was worth dying for, and sending half an army to retrieve."

"Of that there is no doubt, Jesnake," Din replied, glaring at the scroll. "And Feridar knows you have it?"

"Yes," Paige choked. "He saw me with it right before... before...."

"And that's why we need you," Robert interjected before Paige lost control of her voice. The elf looked up at him.

"So for all we know, if she's still alive, Feridar could be using her as bait to draw this young woman out?"

"Aye," Robert said. "And you know what happens to people in Feridar's grasp. We have to break her out. You're the only one who knows the inner halls of the Keep. Without knowing that, we might as well knock on the front door for all the good it will do."

"They had only laid the foundation and structural walls," Dinendale said. "There's no guarantee I'll recognize anything even if we manage to get inside."

"Curse it, Din! That's still a better knowledge than any of us have!" Robert blurted. "And that girl? Olivian? This young lady's sister? She's going to be trapped there until she starves to death or he gets that scroll. Is that what you want?"

"Of course not," the elf snapped, pain seeping into his hard eyes.

"Don't let Feridar keep doing this. Think about what happened last time."

Dinendale rubbed his brow, a look of pain and exhaustion etched into it. "That was different—"

"No one left behind. That was what we said," Robert muttered. "She may not be our family, but can you in good conscience leave her in the clutches of that man knowing what you know?"

The elf turned and stared at Paige for what seemed like an eternity. The only sound around them was the occasional pop of the dim torches and the sound of the last few remaining crickets serenading the forest around them. Dinendale looked hard at Robert, as if he had said too much, then over to the dwarf.

"Broadside?"

The dwarf perked up, eyes alert.

"Is there a pack that will fit me in that pile?" Dinendale asked, his eyes glancing over to Paige.

"At last! Some action!" Duelmaster whooped.

The others chuckled and began to scurry around like ants on a forgotten breadcrumb. Paige felt gratitude and relief wash over her like a hot bath. For the first time since the massacre, she felt the tension ease a bit. Robert offered his hand to support Paige as she sagged to the table in relief.

"Pack up, then head to bed," Dinendale said mirthlessly. "It will be an early morning tomorrow. Call your cots, gentlemen."

With that, he moved to the far end of the room and began picking arrows out of a barrel and inspecting them. The others quickly addressed their own packs and began pulling blankets out and tossing them on the circles of cots, stoking the coals in the basins as they passed them.

"You alright?" Robert asked, beaming. She nodded, looking back towards where the elf was stuffing arrows into a leather quiver.

"More than I can say," she assured, giving Robert a quick hug of gratitude. "I'll be right back. I just need to go say a personal 'thank you.'" Paige turned back to follow the elf to the far end of the stockade. The moss beneath her feet seemed extra spongy, or maybe it was just that she felt so much lighter on her feet. She approached the elf who had just finished tying the retainer cord on his quiver and was now picking out a bow from a stack to his left. He looked up, his blank expression boring into her.

"Can I help you?" he asked in a calm, even voice.

"Actually, I wanted to ask you the same question," she replied, looking him straight in the eye. "Seems to be a lot to do, and I'm ready to do what it takes to get going."

"I can pack my own bag, thanks," he muttered, testing the arm of a small yew bow.

"Well, then, I guess I'll leave you to it," Paige said awkwardly after a few moments of silence. "But I wanted to tell you personally how grateful I am—"

The elf waved her off.

"You can tell me how grateful you are once we've broken into Aschin," he said. "I haven't done anything yet."

"You said you'd help, and that counts for something to me," Paige insisted, shrugging. The elf grunted but didn't offer any further conversation.

"I suppose I'll see you in the morning then," Paige asserted. The elf nodded and cinched the yew bow to the quiver with a set of leather thongs.

"Get some rest, Paige of the Alatarians," he said quietly. "We've got a long way to go, and if we're going to make it before winter snows start settling in, we'll have to make good time early while it counts."

Paige nodded and walked back over to Robert, who was adding the finishing touches to a giant nest of quilts piled up around his cot. He motioned to the cot next to his own, which had several of its own quilts stacked on top of it.

"Saved you a cot," he offered. "You'll want to bundle up; those coals will help but it's going to get frigid by dawn's first light."

After taking time to remove her moccasins, Paige unfolded the quilts gratefully and crawled in between them. She folded and placed her moccasins at her head so they would at least be warm in the morning. The other fellows were also stashing their gear near their cots and settling in for the night. Paige lay her head on her makeshift pillow and looked over at Robert, whose head was only an arm's reach away, burrowed into his quilts.

"Robert?"

"Mhm?"

"Thanks."

Robert looked up and smiled his jagged tooth smile from behind a molehill of patchwork blankets. "Happy to help."

"Wake me as soon as you're up," she demanded, lips pressed in a serious line that meant business.

He chuckled. "As soon as I can," he promised.

CHAPTER 6

INTO THE WILD

A sleepy sigh escaped her lips as Paige allowed her eyes to adjust to the morning sun. Warily, she wondered why it was so quiet and peaceful. For a moment, she feared the men had abandoned her altogether. A gruff sneeze dispelled her fear. Paige looked to her left where the men stood at the large table, packs at their feet, ready to be hefted. Loaded with provisions, they stood chatting in low voices.

Calebna, the Duelmaster, looked her way and grinned. "At long last, the sleeping princess awakens! And I didn't even have to kiss her!" The others chuckled as Paige's cheeks flushed with embarrassment.

"How long have you been ready?" she demanded. Twostaves looked at the sunlight streaming through the willow branches all around them.

"About an hour," he answered casually. Paige leapt up, flinging the toasty quilts away in haste.

"Why didn't you wake me?" she fumed, indignant and embarrassed.

"We decided you needed the rest," Robert said, shifting his pack.

"But you said you'd wake me when you were ready—" she started, breaking off as she noticed Robert's smug look.

"No. I said I'd wake you when I could," he replied, "and I couldn't bring myself to interrupt your much-needed slumber. Need I remind you that you're still recovering? The trail is gonna be rough and long. You'll thank me in an hour."

Paige stomped over to where they were standing. Jesnake held out her leather pack tightly bound with a cord of sinew. It now contained blankets, a quiver of arrows, an unstrung bow made of a hickory sapling, and a bundle of food that Paige hoped might last her a week. She begrudgingly took it from him, still fuming over being the cause of their delay. In haste, she slipped the pack over her shoulders and cinched the waistband snugly around her.

"Let's move out," Dinendale jerked his head in the direction of the forest. After treading carefully down the tree, they set out to a slow gait as they waded through the thick vegetation of the forest. Hiking through the dense growth did not lend itself to much conversation, at least on Paige's end. Uncertain around her new friends, she opted rather to study them and get a feel for how they meshed together as a unit. Twostaves and Broadside jabbered boasts or muttered complaints as fast as they could think of them, specifically to each other. When they weren't talking, Paige could only hear the soft tread of leather-soled boots and moccasins on the forest floor, and the sound of birds hiding high above in the shadows of the trees. At one point, a strong, fierce-looking hawk flapped high over head, silver feathers glinting in the sunlight as it soared on the warm winds just under the canopy.

After several hours of hiking, Paige fell into step with Duelmaster.

"So, exactly where are we going?" she asked.

The tall fellow looked at her and smiled. "Well, I figured we'd go for a bout around the pond and then have a spot of tea in the shade of a large oak." He grinned.

"No, seriously. I know the destination, but I've never been out of the Wild. Are you sure we're headed in the right direction?"

"I hope so!" Calebna winked. "But to answer your question, Aschin is in the southeast near the fork of two rivers. We must pass through a long, narrow valley that twists its way through the mountains to get to the fortress. It's a long journey and would be easier if we could go in a straight line."

"And I assume there is no road?"

"I've heard there is one now," Dulemaster said. "They just finished cutting a road from Franghal, an old mine the Shahir saw fit to 'liberate' about two years ago. But I'd wager it has far too many outposts and patrols along it to make it a viable route. We may wind up finding it eventually, but for now we will have to use the valleys and passes through the mountains."

They continued walking along as the sound of cookware clanged against a pack. She jumped over a particularly large tree root, taking the hand Duelmaster offered in assistance. She smiled at him, his toothy grin poking out from his tanned complexion.

"So, what's the story behind all this?" She gestured to the solemn group. "I've never seen men of such varied races intermingling, let alone cooperating in this way."

Duelmaster smiled. "The group has its flaws. Well, all right, the only big flaw is our insufficient supply of pleasurable company."

Paige chuckled. "I'd noticed. But I've never heard of elves and dwarves getting along at all, much less working together."

"We all have our own stories, our own reasons for joining the band," Calebna said, shifting his pack. "Me, I was born far to the northeast. My father and mother were of different heartwood."

"Come again?"

Duelmaster snickered.

"As I'm sure you heard earlier, I am a dryad—a tree nymph. My mother was as kind as the soft maple, and my father as strong as the weathered oak."

He dug around in his wild hair for a moment and pulled something out of the tangled mess, handing it to Paige.

"Is that... is that a twig?" Paige asked, slightly off-put. She held up a tiny twig with a single green leaf growing off the end. Duelmaster laughed.

"Told you! Tree nymph! Gotta keep those branches trimmed if I'm going to pass for a human in these parts."

"Do all of you grow like real trees!?"

"Sort of. We also have big families. I had two brothers, you know!" He paused. His expression grew more somber. "One was killed trying to stop a party of settlers from clearing the forest that was once my home. My other brother has not spoken to me for several years. Last I heard, he was in the south, past the Vidla-Dûn river, somewhere in the great plains. Why he went there is beyond me; that place is disgusting, flat for miles. You can see your enemy coming from a great distance. Where's the challenge in that?"

Paige shrugged.

Duelmaster continued, "After my home was destroyed, the rest of my family slowly disappeared. I migrated south, trying to find a new place to be miserable. One day while I was resting near a brook, pondering what would become of me, I spied a slightly chunky fellow picking mushrooms."

"So you met Robert?"

"What gave it away?"

"Lucky guess."

"Ha! Well, anyway, as we became acquainted, Eöl asked me if I'd be willing to help him and a few others do what little we could to keep the Shahir's forces out of the Wild. I agreed."

"So where'd the nickname come from?"

"Duelmaster? Well, let's just say it was a well-earned title, and the fourteen Sharadhen Cavalry officers I took on at one time would agree!"

"Fourteen?" Paige said dryly. "Really?"

"Okay, so five. Wasn't that many off!"

"Sure...."

The dryad feigned being shot in the heart with an arrow, then laughed, smacking the princess on the back good-naturedly.

"I like you, Princess," he chuckled. "I feel you and I will get along splendidly!"

"Likewise." Paige smiled.

Duelmaster wiggled his eyebrows, then dropped his tone. "Though, not so sure about these other pixies," he said mockingly. "Lot of weirdos in this crew, if you get my drift."

"Perhaps, but you've done a very good job at keeping to yourselves, it would seem"

"How do you mean?"

"Well, ever since I was a little girl, I've heard about dwarves and elves, of course, but I've never seen one, let alone met them all in the same place! The Wild hasn't had any magical creatures or races other than men in centuries, my Papa said."

"He's not wrong," Duelmaster admitted, taking a swig from his wineskin. "Not in this age, anyways. But the Wild is the gateway to the rest of Eirensgarth, so if we want to protect our own people, this is where the fight had to happen. And believe me, it's a lot harder to hide a giant in the Wild than you'd think."

"Wait, is Twostaves an actual giant?" Paige asked, astonished. She looked at the huge, lumbering individual ahead of her. One of his giant staves thumped on the ground as he walked; the other was strapped to his back with the round shield. She hadn't considered him as an actual giant, just a very tall man.

"Aye! And a curious one, indeed! A little strange in the head, if you ask me, which no one ever does, but a real chipper fellow when he wants to be."

"Are giants always that small?" Paige asked, keeping her voice hushed.

"Gracious, no, princess! Lowland Giants are much smaller. Word is, back an age or so ago, the really big giants in one clan started mating with the humans instead of eating them, and this is what you get after a thousand years of that kind of nonsense! Twostaves came from a wealthy lowland family in the east, on the edge of the Great River. Lowland giants had a few small clans about there back in the day, and Isaac was the son of the Bear clan-master."

"So what's royalty doing out here?"

"Not much different from you," Duelmaster said in a hushed tone. "Lowland Giants, if you didn't know, are the most hospitable and jovial creatures you'll ever meet. When Twostaves's family discovered a hunting party in the woods, of course they invited them to their castle for a feast. The hunting party was headed by none other than the Shahir himself. Isaac was weary of these strange men and their strange manners, but his father insisted on upholding tradition and showing them hospitality."

Paige's pointed ears perked at the mention of the Shahir.

Duelmaster kept talking, his voice hushed. "As the night waxed on, Isaac's unease grew, so he excused himself from the festivities to take a walk on the roof. He fell asleep under the stars at about the second hour, and that's what spared his life. When he awoke the next morn, all was unusually quiet. Upon entering the castle, he found every member of his house butchered, and the 'guests' gone with every article of gold and silver in the castle. Grieving, he buried his family, took up his father's two massive staves, and left his forest home. He met up with us early last spring."

"How dreadful!" Paige gasped.

"Tell me about it."

"That's got to be a heavy load to carry," Paige mumbled, looking at the little giant.

"Well, he's used to that," Duelmaster said with a slight chuckle.

Paige punched him in the arm. "Don't be so cruel!"

"I didn't even mention how horrible his cooking is. Only thing the poor twonk can make is muffins, which, somehow, are incredible. Might explain the gut."

The sun slowly sank low into the horizon, and Paige could hear the chorus of huffing and puffing escalate. One by one the men's backs began to round as their shoulders slumped under the weight of their gear, and even in the chilly breeze several began to show tell-tale rings of sweat around their collars and blotches on their sleeves where they'd wiped the perspiration from their eyes. Paige saw Dinendale at the front of the men keenly looking about them for a place to camp. Paige turned back to the dryad, sympathy in her blue eyes.

"Do you all have stories like that?"

"Most. Broadside was beaten until he gave up a dwarf mine to the army of the Shahir, barely escaped with his life. Robert can't remember anything from his childhood, but the hermit who raised him said the Shahir killed Eöl's family when he was a baby. Jesnake was a little different, in that he was exiled from his people because of a human."

"Wait, really? His own people exiled him?"

"He's a western elf. They've long been bred to hate all that is human."

"But why?"

"That is an entire history lesson for another day. But Jesnake has a better heart than the rest of his kind. They tossed him out when he openly objected to putting a young human captive to death. He met Broadside and Dinendale several years ago and was one of the founders of this band. Poor idiot."

"What about Dinendale?" she asked. The dryad grew grave, and she feared she'd overstepped the bounds. But he answered, a sad smile on his lips.

"Din? He's probably the most unfortunate of us all. He was a fun-loving fellow when we met him; he banded us together out of his thirst for adventure and untamable spirit. But he hasn't been that way for a long time."

"Why not?"

"When something you love is taken from you, you have two choices. Fight for it, or cave in to despair. You handled your loss one way. Din... he's handled it in his way. Can't blame him. But he's not been the same as he once was."

"What was taken from him?"

"A very dear friend," Duelmaster whispered. Paige was about to ask more, but suddenly Dinendale stopped at the head of the column. The rest of the group eagerly welcomed the halt after hours of constant walking. They had reached the edge of a small ravine. With a cliff on the left, a gully on the right, and thick shrubs all over, it was concealed from the rest of the path quite well.

"Anyone have an objection to camping here?" Dinendale asked.

"Let's call it a day, guys," Robert said. They dropped their packs in a heap near a large shrub off the path and began a chorus of yawns and groans. Paige spread out her elk-hide blanket-roll between two redberry bushes, her thighs and feet aching from the long hike with her heavy pack. It was chilly, and she was glad to have the warm fur sleeping bag that

Twostaves had supplied for her. The others had the same idea, each having picked a bush to sleep under.

"Someone start a fire, will you?" Broadside yelled from a rather small bush.

"You do it," groaned Robert from his pile of gear.

"I'm kind of in the middle of taking a—"

"For land sakes, Broadside, we have a woman with us now!" Twostaves scolded.

"... Sorry."

"Won't a fire be seen?" Jesnake asked, diverting the conversation. Paige noticed he seemed to be the most cautious of the group.

"Nay," Duelmaster said. "The gully shields us from the rest of the valley. The wind is blowing in the opposite direction of our enemy's travel, so they won't see the smoke either."

"Well, someone get one going quick! My toes are about to freeze off," Twostaves said.

"If you'd worn the moccasins like I told you..." Dinendale gave a slight smirk. Paige rolled off her bedding and began to gather dry wood for the fire. She had a full armload by the time she got back to where Robert and Jesnake were attempting to use flint and steel while having a heated argument. Duelmaster jogged over to where she stood and took the sticks she held.

"Allow me, princess," he said with a joking smile. She gave him a look, pulled the sticks closer to her chest and marched over to Robert and Jesnake's quarrel.

"You have to hold it at a sharper angle!" Jesnake insisted.

"Like I told you, I've got this!" Robert spat back.

"Oh, my apologies. I hadn't noticed the warmth spreading through my fingers. Oh, wait! There isn't any, because you haven't started the bloody fire!"

After several moments of no fire and all squabbling, Paige let out an exasperated sigh. She marched over and grabbed the flint from Robert and drew the dagger she'd found in her pack. In one fluid motion, she produced a spray of sparks that lit the dry kindling. She stood, noting Robert and Jesnake's genuine slack-jawed surprise. Someone started to clap, and she turned to see both Duelmaster and Dinendale applauding her. She shrugged.

"If men would just get things done instead of trying to prove who's right, we might actually get a fire going," she sassed.

Robert huffed but didn't argue further. They quickly set to making a meager supper of bread, dried fish, and some candied nuts. By the time the meal was over, Paige felt the waves of exhaustion hit her like a stormy gale.

"We should all get to bed," Robert yawned, apparently feeling the same storm washing over him. "It's going to be an even longer day tomorrow."

>>>O<<<

Paige opened her eyes and yawned. She pulled herself out of the elk hide bag, stifling the long groan only a person's stiffness can produce. Looking about, she noticed that Duelmaster was up and Jesnake was re-starting the fire from still-warm embers. No sounds disturbed the cold mist of the mountain morning, save for Broadside's loud, obnoxious snoring.

"It's a wonder we weren't attacked; I should have thought they'd have heard that sound from miles away," Paige muttered to herself.

"If I thought we would be in any danger, I'd have made him sleep on that cliff."

She whirled around and saw Dinendale sitting cross-legged on the ground a few yards away. He held a buckskin cloth in his right hand, polishing his large broadsword. She fleetingly thought that the cloth looked an awful lot like the leather scroll she kept tied around her waist, but since that was still intact, she felt a quick relief wash over her. Dinendale gave her the briefest hint of a smile as he worked.

"How long have you been up?" she asked.

He shrugged. "Sun-up." He tested the blade's edge with his thumb. Finding it sufficiently sharp, he breathed on the sword to reveal the smudges he'd missed. Satisfied, he sheathed the blade. "I'm off to get some fresh meat with Duelmaster, if you want to come with. "

"Shouldn't we be getting on the road?" Paige asked, lips pursed. Dinendale shrugged.

"We do, but we also need to conserve the cured foods as long as we can, so we should eat fresh meat whenever possible.

Besides," he nodded at the crew. "They wont be packed up and ready to move out for another hour at least."

"Well then being with you two beats sitting around here," she said, pulling herself to her feet and stretching. She walked over to where the packs were stashed and drew out the bow Jesnake gave her yesterday. After carefully stringing it, she picked up a quiver of arrows and joined Duelmaster, who was teasing Jesnake for the amount of time it took him to get the embers lit.

"Coming along, princess?" the dryad asked. Paige smiled back and nodded, strapping her quiver across her back. She paused for a moment, looking down at the bow. Only a few mornings before, she'd done the same thing with her papa. She tried to stop thinking about it before the throbbing pain settled into the pit of her stomach, but it persisted. She quickly bit her lip and finished getting her gear together. Dinendale joined them a few moments later.

"I saw some fowl heading a little east of here," he said, stringing his own bow.

"I could go for a fat hen before setting out!" Duelmaster exclaimed, almost giddy. He looked at Paige and winked.

"Duelmaster doesn't believe in eating plants," Dinendale explained.

"You wouldn't understand! It's like eating a cousin or your favorite pet!"

"But Duely, you had a pet cow last year."

"Okay, so bad example! No need to drag Mincemeat into this. She was a wonderful cow!"

It didn't take long before they heard the rustle of bird wings overhead. Duelmaster motioned them to stop. He stretched out his arms and lifted his head to the sky. Dinendale nudged her.

"This is one of his favorite tricks," he whispered, setting three arrows on his string. After less than a minute, a fat partridge landed on Duelmaster's outstretched arm. As the seconds passed, several more joined it. When five had settled on the dryad, Dinendale drew his hickory bow and aimed.

In a blink of an eye, four of the five hens dropped without a sound, two skewed on one arrow. The one lucky bird made it to the safety of the trees.

"Well, that's one way to do it," Paige sputtered in astonishment.

Duelmaster grinned. "Since dryads are truly wood sprites, the animals sense no danger. Comes in handy every now and then."

Dinendale scooped up the four fallen birds, removing the arrows from their carcasses with a single deft movement. He stuffed the fat hens into his game bag, and the three continued hunting. For another quarter of an hour, the only sound was the quiet padding of their moccasins on the forest floor. Duelmaster managed to nail a jackrabbit at thirty paces, which enticed approving glances from both Dinendale and Paige.

After a brief breakfast of roast hens seasoned with some wild garlic Broadside had found, Paige and the Brotherhood geared up and started back down the forest's natural path. Leaving the ravine in their wake, they continued in the same manner as the previous day. The mountains became steeper as they moved into late afternoon, which meant the sun was gone much sooner in the day now. The daylight stayed about the same, but no sun meant no heat. The chill of the air began to creep onto her skin as the day dragged into twilight.

A few hours after leaving their campsite behind, Paige fell into pace with Jesnake, his mail armor jingling softly as he plodded along. The tall western elf was breathing as if he were taking a waltz in a garden, despite the great elevation and steep path. His ebony bow was strung at his side. Paige had never seen a more magnificent bow in all her life. The deadly beauty was inlaid with a silver vine on both arms of the weapon, capping the ends of the arms in beautiful inlay. She admired the still beauty projected by the wooden limbs, the dark wood looking warm in the fading light of the mountains.

"You admire my 'bringer of anguish'?" he asked.

She jumped a little at his unexpected voice but nodded. "It's a beautiful weapon. It must have cost a fortune!"

"I made it. The tree grew next to my dwelling when I was a lad."

"Just where do you call home, Jesnake?"

His eyes gained a distant look, and it took a moment for him to reply. When he did, his voice was quiet.

"My people live in a great valley we call the Albamaugh. It is a beautiful place far west of anything you would know about. It never snows, but 'tis never too hot. The fields are gold with wheat, surrounded by mountains on all sides."

"It sounds wonderful," Paige said. She recalled the story Duelmaster had briefed her on earlier and felt a pang of sympathy tug at her heartstrings. "Why did they make you leave?"

Jesnake's eyes appeared to mist over for a moment as he looked up at the sky through the branches above.

"Unlike your kin, mine decided to put up a fight first. When the Sharadhs landed on the shores of this land, we were the ones living where their farms and cities lay now. Our cousins to the south retreated further into their forests, but my people stayed and fought. One by one, our armies were decimated, our cities plundered, until we were all but wiped from the history chronicles. But a band of twenty managed to escape."

"And they headed west? Are there so few of you now?"

Jesnake chuckled. "My dear, that was nearly a thousand years ago. We have grown since then. Our city of Liennen is a rival to any you would ever find in the east."

"And will you try and take back your homeland?"

"A homeland four generations have never known? Not my idea of a rational life goal. Even still, from the day I entered this world, I was taught to hate the human race for what it did to my ancestors so many years ago."

"The Shahir's evil hardly represents all men," Paige retorted.

The elf nodded. "I tend to agree. Six years ago, a young boy was captured by our riders. The elders decided to execute him for the crime of being human. He wasn't even Sharadhen.

His skin was fair like the men who live here in the Wild. I hate the Shahir and his people just as much as any of my brothers, but I knew it would be wrong to slay this boy. He was not to blame for crimes committed by a different human a millennium before he was even born."

"That's horrible..."

"I stood up for him, begged for his life, and even offered to buy his freedom. All my words earned me was banishment. The lad was burned at the stake even as they drove me out of the gate."

He gazed to the westward sun with longing grey eyes.

"So I wander with Dinendale," he concluded, lightly touching his bow with slender hands, feeling the dark hardwood with his fingertips. "The Brotherhood is my home now."

Paige smiled at him in pity. She touched the key at her neck, realizing that it was to her what the bow was to Jesnake.

"I know what it's like to be driven from your home, so I'm sorry that happened to you," Paige said, touching the elf's shoulder. The elf smiled and patted her arm reassuringly, then plodded on ahead in silence as they headed deeper into the craggy mountains of the Wild.

CHAPTER 7

BOGGARTROLLS

$\mathcal{T}$he tedious pace of their journey exhausted the group as one day turned to four, each day following the previous in a dull procession. Despite Robert's assessment that the cold would be upon them with a vengeance by now, the hot sun was hitting them with every ray it had, as if attempting to prove him wrong. As they began to climb the foothills, the cicadas sang their songs in the sweltering air. Paige listened, knowing that soon the winter would silence the bugs for a season.

All of the men had flushed faces and short tempers. Even Duelmaster and Twostaves were cranky for their typically jovial natures. Dinendale was more glare than talk that afternoon, and Paige herself was agitated. The more familiar she became with the men, the more she appreciated them. Yet, as in every relationship, she was discovering their little quirks that grated on her nerves. She was glad when Dinendale called it a day, despite their covering a mere ten miles.

Paige plopped down onto the large root at the foot of a thick oak tree. Her spine ached from the days of backpacking, her leather jerkin felt stiff with sweat, and her hair tangled in its ponytail. A clod of dirt by her right foot held her weary gaze until she felt a hand on her shoulder. She looked up and stared blankly into Broadside's green-blue eyes.

"There is a stream down in the brush to our left. If you want to go wash up a little, the rest of us will wait a while."

"How on earth could you possibly know that?" Paige moaned.

Broadside looked a little hurt. "I'm a dwarf. Got good hearing and we can feel water in our bones!"

"In your bones? Really?"

"We get all tingly inside when there's water close by. Helps keep from drowning when we mine deep."

Papa had often spoken of the dwarves of the northern Baorn Mountains, but she was discovering new and wondrous things about them every time she talked to Broadside. It made sense to her now that she thought about it. Just yesterday, Broadside had mentioned to Jesnake that his left boot sole must be missing some stitches, because the sound of the elf's stride was uneven. Jesnake had smugly told him to quit showing off, as it was impossible to hear that when walking three people in front of him. When they stopped for a break, however, Jesnake counted the stitches and apologized quietly to Broadside for disbelieving him. Broadside had beamed and rubbed it in all night. Until Jesnake cuffed him, at least.

The black dwarf plopped down on a nearby stump, tipped his conical helm over his eyes, and laced his chubby fingers behind his head. Paige sat up, wincing as the cramps in her calves clawed at the back of her leg like wild cats.

"My feet, they're killing me," whined Twostaves. "Are we nearly there yet?"

"Oh, go jump off a waterfall," spat Robert. "And if my headache gets any worse, I'll join you."

"Come on," Dinendale said, "you guys need to settle down. We're all pretty worn out."

"Since when did you become the magistrate?" asked Broadside in a huff, his voice echoing in the helmet covering his face.

"Since you and the others are showing signs of heat exhaustion," said Dinendale, sighing.

"Maybe we do need to cool off a little," Duelmaster suggested. He turned and smiled feebly at Paige, despite his exhaustion. "Did I hear word of a stream near here?"

"Aye," Broadside said, "I could hear the water running in the ground a ways back. Here, I can feel the vibration of the creek even through these boots." He lifted one boot to show to all.

"Well, hurry it up, princess," Robert said. "If you take too long to wash them lovely locks, I'll get a pole and fish you out from upstream."

"I'll hurry." She grabbed the small bag of necessities out of her pack and headed into the woods in the direction Broadside had indicated.

"Be safe!" Twostaves called out as she trudged off into the brush. Paige waved his way as she entered the thicket.

Her halfling ears caught the sound of trickling water flowing over a bed of pebbles, and soon a large, deep creek became clear through the canopy of tangled bramble bushes and oak trees. It was about a stone's throw wide with water as clear as a polished looking-glass. A flat beach's shiny pebbles of every shade of brown and red spread on either side of the babbling water, crunching as she made her way around the scattered boulders to the edge of the water. She could see a small recess in the stream where the water would be deep enough to come up to her waist. Dipping her hand into the clear water, she let out a small giggle of glee as the coolness of it erased the dirt and grime from her wrists with a simple touch.

She laid down her small satchel to take off her armor, unfastened the belt and the metal vambraces Twostaves had given her. The princess laid everything, including Klaíohm, on a large, moss-covered boulder a little ways from the shore. She almost set the leather scroll with the rest of the gear but decided to take the extra precaution by hiding it in a small opening under the rock. She scooped some of the tiny pebbles from the beach into the opening to cover up her hideaway.

Taking a deep breath of the fresh, clean air, she approached the pebbled creek bed and knelt into the crystal water, letting it lap up at her knees. She untied her week-old ponytail, shuddering at its grimy and gritty feel. Stepping into the cool running water, she attacked her hair with her bone comb, vigorously untangling it. Once it was a little less like a thrush's nest, she held her breath and plunged her head into the water.

Being underwater reminded her of the time she and her sister had been taught by their mother to see as clearly under water as they could on land. This worked because of their heightened senses. Paige stared at the stream bed, probing the sand for anything of interest. Seeing only a few minnows and a crayfish, she soon lost interest and came up for air. She began to hum an Alatarian lullaby, stroking her hair in time to the song's soft beat as she whispered the words.

"When sun goes down and moon rises high,
And the meadowlarks stir in the sky,
You will be my ain true one,
'Til the dawn comes with an endless sun."

Paige sang and scrubbed until her hair felt silky and clean again. Trudging out of the water, she sighed with satisfaction as she gathered her belongings. She'd always favored time with her father rather than stupid housekeeping lessons back home as well, to the dismay of her mother and Olivian. But just because she dressed like a man didn't mean she relished being as dirty as one.

She was so wrapped up in her thoughts and the age-old tune that she failed to hear the slight rustle of grass on the bank behind her. She hummed the last few bars as she pulled her jerkin over her head.

"'At was a mighty nice tune, eh, gents?"

Paige whirled around. Behind her stood a ragged group of the ugliest creatures she had ever beheld in her short life. Each one was about five feet tall, with long, thin legs and gangly arms. Their hands and feet could have been muck rakes, for their fingers and toes were enormously long, with pointed, chipped yellow nails. Slimy skin the color of a muddy, algae-riddled puddle was covered with dark splotches, much like patches of mold on cheese. A mop of oily black hair trailed down their backs, reminiscent of slimy, dead seaweed she'd read about in Papa's books. Their ears, though tall and pointed, were not elegant like that of an elf; these were bumpy and muddled with warts and coarse black hairs. The creatures had sickly yellow eyes and thin, pointed chins, accented by long, hooked noses. The rough band of ten or so wore ragged pants; only a few were graced with vests.

"Yessiree!" one said. "A pretty lully if'n I eve' did 'ear 'un."

"And sung by a regular beauty 'erself!" another said. Paige felt icy fear grip her chest. She took a step back, almost tripping into the water, her spine tingling in warning.

"Well, gents!" exclaimed one that seemed to be the gang's leader, "it looks like we've scared the bloomin' daylight out of 'er!" He smiled, the rotting grin making Paige feel queasy. Whatever these things were, they weren't the kind she wanted to mingle with. "You see, me an' me chums," the leader continued, motioning to his comrades as he walked, "have a little bet on!"

As he spoke, three of the foul beings slid into the water to Paige's left without a sound.

"I bet you have quite a bit of gold stashed in that pouch."

"If you think so, take it and move along, but I promise you it's only soap," Paige managed to say without her voice wavering.

"We shall see, because Jarep here thinks you have more 'soap' stashed on your person," the leader hissed. The three in the water were advancing quickly, and Paige tumbled into the stream as panic gripped her heart.

"I don't like to lose bets!" shouted another, staring her down.

One of the creatures lunged at her, his streamlined body skimming through the water like an eel. Paige punched him in the jaw before he could grab her arm. Another darted at her and she jerked her knife from its sheath on her leg, slashing up at his face in the same motion. The blade cut him under the eye, and the gash oozed a sludgy green fluid as he recoiled in agony.

She tried to do the same to the third as he latched onto her left arm, but he was too fast for her. He grabbed her fist with a slimy webbed hand and pushed her back under the water. She tried to kick her way out, but several other creatures dragged her down. She dropped the dagger as they held her under.

She shoved past the clawing arms and legs and sucked air into her lungs with a gasp. "HEL—"

A hand clamped around her skull and shoved her back into the stream. Even with keen underwater sight, it was hard to see anything past the bubbles escaping her lips. As her world began to fade into black with every heartbeat, she felt herself giving up and her body being hauled up to the pebbled shore, multiple pairs of slimy, webbed feet slapping up and down on the beach.

They dragged her, sputtering and coughing, before the leader, who sat atop the boulder on which she'd placed her belongings. Paige tried to kick loose, but her captors held on tightly, their vise-like fingers gripping her arms. The chief screamed with laughter.

"You're a feisty 'un! Right lit'le bobcat, ain't ya?" he sneered. She spat at his filthy feet and he recoiled, eyes flashing in anger.

"Looks like the bobcat 'as a lit'le temper!" One of them whistled. The leader stepped forward, reached out, and slapped her hard across the cheek. She took the blow without a sound, though her cheek burned as if it had been stung by a hive of bees. He smirked. Then he noticed her necklace and the key dangling from the silver elvish chain.

"Well, well!" he hissed. "Pre'ty voice, pre'ty face, and pre'ty jewelry! Yeh know, I've taken a fancy for that." He wrenched the key from her neck. A ball of fiery, raw anger seared through Paige's chest, and she managed to free an arm, striking at him. He flinched, but a smile touched his thin lips.

"Looks like she needs a lesson in manners! 'Ow'd you like t'play a lit'le game?"

He motioned, and the creatures surrounded her, shoving, grabbing at her, laughing like the thugs they were. Paige screamed in terror and rage as she wildly clawed at anything that tried to touch her. One kicked her down and another one stepped on her back. Crying out, she tried to shove its foot off, but it only pushed harder, trapping her wrists as well. She could feel the creature's hot, putrid breath on her neck as it cruelly cackled.

A noise all too familiar, like the hum of a bee, was followed by a sickening thud as her attacker was thrown backwards. Black-fletched shafts flew through the air. The creatures panicked, scrambling around in confusion. Soon, five more were on the ground, arrows protruding from their thin bodies. As the survivors fled towards the woods for safety, Robert and Duelmaster leapt out in front of them and pushed them back, Robert roaring like a lion as he swung his spear, and Duelmaster flourishing his rapiers. Robert's spear cut one in half like a knife through a casserole. Duelmaster impaled the other two as he charged headlong into the fray, leaving his two thin blades pinning them to the gravel as he smoothly pulled his bow from its place on his back.

What remained of the terrified creatures turned and ran the opposite way down the shoreline, but Jesnake and Broadside burst forth out of the bushes, bows drawn. Twostaves stopped the creatures who tried to double back, hitting the first with his staff so hard that the pathetic brute flew back into the remnant of the band. Having nowhere to run, the rest fell to the ground and begged for mercy.

Paige, sitting shocked on the ground, felt a warm, dry hide thrown over her shoulders. Turning, she found Dinendale standing behind her, eyes dark with rage.

"Are you alright?" he asked Paige. She nodded, pulling the hide closer to her soaked, shivering shoulders. "Good," he said, turning back to the prisoners. "It would appear you fell afoul of a band of Bogatrolls."

The men rounded up the prisoners with very little resistance after that, binding them all and forcing them back to campsite. Paige took a few moments to get fully dressed once more, this time deciding to lash the leather scroll securely to her inner thigh rather than her waist.

Remnants of the thuggish crew were marched back to camp where they were thrown to their knees in front of Dinendale. The elf was flanked by Robert and Duelmaster on either side.

"We didn't mean nothin' by it!" squealed one of the Bogatrolls.

"Sure you didn't," Dinendale retorted.

"Look, we apologized! Most o'our chums are dead, and you 'ave us tied 'and and foot, like animals!" whimpered one of the pathetic lot. "What more do yeh want?"

"Maybe a scalp or two," muttered Robert in a deep voice dripping with bitterness as he checked the edge of his skinning knife with his thumb. Dinendale nodded in amused agreement then turned back to the five prisoners.

"Who's in charge?" he asked. All the other nasty little creatures turned and looked at the Bogatroll who had stolen Paige's key. He glared at his companions.

"I, sir. Horrace of Whackwillow; of the house of Thumberbump the Noble."

"Noble, eh?"

"More noble 'an any of 'our bloodlines, I'd dare wager!"

"Please, can I sit on this one?" the giant begged, leaning down close to Horrace's head and looking him in the eye with a gleeful smile meant to scare the Bogatroll. Judging by its trembling lips, it was working.

"Actions, not bloodlines, are what make a man, or troll, noble," Dinendale sneered.

"Look, the lady was singin', we thought she looked beau'iful and she seemed like the kind as could take a bit o'fun, so we messed around a lit'le..." Horrace began, only to be cut short by Dinendale, who leapt to his feet and cuffed the Bogatroll's face.

"I will not stand for this lady to be insulted!" To make the point, the elf drew his dagger and slid the tip across the side of the creature's neck, just hard enough to draw a drop of sticky blood, which rolled down the knife's edge.

"Ey' didn't mean it!" another troll screeched in terror. Horrace paled.

"Dinendale, no!" Paige exclaimed. The thought of watching the elf cut the throat of a tied up creature was more revolting than Horrace's insults.

"They would have killed you, or worse," the elf snapped.

"I know," Paige's voice was shaking, fear still clutching her heart. "But not like this."

Dinendale stood for a moment, then released the troll's head and sheathed his dirk.

"You are fortunate the princess has a bleeding heart," the elf hissed. "Otherwise you'd be dripping wet again, and not with water."

"Enough, Din," Duelmaster said. "I think he gets the point."

"Oh, what a mess you got us into, Horrace," one of the band cried miserably.

"You're lucky we caught you when we did," the dryad continued. "Broadside thought he heard you call out for help, so we rushed down."

"We will let no man or beast do her any harm. She is our sister. And now we must decide what to do with you," Broadside finished. There was an uneasy silence as the dwarf picked up his hand axe and advanced. "Well, no time like the present!"

"We swear we'll never set our eyes on yeh again!" one of the trolls pleaded. Broadside glanced at Dinendale. The elf surveyed the other members with a silent question.

"Din, they've seen our faces," Robert growled. "They could sneak back here and murder us in our sleep. And what's to keep them from running back to an outpost? Then we'll have Sharadhens coming at us from every direction. You want to risk that?"

"We won't! Honest!" another Bogatroll sobbed. "We was gett'n away from t'east, we was! They was killin' our kind by our swamps! 'At's why we was a'runnin'!"

"And do you want to trust them after what they just tried to do?" Robert hissed, scowling at Dinendale. The elf looked at Paige, but she was unsure. Robert had a point, but could they simply execute these creatures like cattle?

After another long pause, Dinendale rose, walked behind the troll chieftain, Horrace, and drew his dirk. A few of the Bogatrolls actually began to cry. Dinendale kicked Horrace to the ground and set his boot against his thin, muddy green neck. The troll winced under the elf's cold stare, and he closed his eyes, whimpering. Paige bit her lip and covered her own eyes as she saw Dinendale plunge the dagger down. She could hear the sound of slicing sinew.

But when she opened her eyes, the troll was sitting up on his bony backside. Horrace felt his freed wrists and looked up at Dinendale, wary of the large dagger.

"Go," he spat, "or I'll have this dwarf finish what his axe was meant to do."

The trolls scrambled up as their bonds were loosed. Without another word, they bolted into the safety of the woods, the pitter-patter of their feet fading into the direction from which the Brotherhood come.

"I still don't trust letting them go, Din," Robert muttered. "Now we'll have to stay up and keep watch."

"We need to be doing more of that anyways. These are dangerous forests. I doubt a couple cowardly Bogatrolls are the only thing lurking in these mountains that will cause us grief."

"We should have just—" Robert started, but Dinendale interrupted him.

"If it means that much to you, I'll take a double shift tonight," he said calmly. Robert grunted but apparently had lost interest in arguing any further. Satisfied, Dinendale walked over to Paige and stood before her as she finished buckling on her armour, Klaíohm now securely back in her hair once again and her hunting knife now dried off and back in her moccasin. Thankfully, the ancient piece of leather was once more securely bound around her waist, and she was safe. He gazed down into her blue eyes.

"I think this belongs to you," he whispered, as he took her hand and closed it over her necklace. She smiled up at him, fighting to hold back the tears in her eyes, remembering this necklace as her last bit of home.

"Thank you," she replied.

"Some things can't be replaced," he said with a slight smile. "I'm glad you are alright."

"Well, if that's over, I think I'm going to go wash up," Jesnake said, laying his bow and quiver down but keeping his belt of throwing knives close to his chest. Twostaves elected to go with him to take turns looking out in case the Bogatrolls decided to circle back. The rest of them set up camp and got a fire going while Paige plopped down on her bedroll.

She smiled as she watched Broadside and Robert argue about a log and whether it was too punky to burn. Dinendale and Duelmaster went to work skinning a few rabbits they had shot earlier that morning, skewering them on spits to roast for supper. She felt a swelling of gratitude in her chest for each of these friends. They considered her one of their own, though she'd only known them a week's time. She felt confident that no matter what obstacle they would face, they would face it together. It wasn't enough to fill the hole she felt in her heart, but having the beginnings of a new family eased some of the empty feeling she had.

At a lull in Robert's and Broadside's argument, Dinendale said, "Broadside, why don't you go take advantage of that creek?"

"No, no; you go on. I'll, umm... stay here and work on sharpening! Yes, that's it! I'll do some work on the spare swords!"

Dinendale pasted a smile on his face and walked over to the dwarf, placing a hand on his mail-clad shoulder. "Now, Broadside, it would be unfair to not let the finder of the stream partake of its... refreshing qualities," Dinendale said, teeth clenched.

"No, you go on... take a second bath! Won't bother me in the slightest, I promise!" He forced a laugh as Jesnake and Robert quietly edged to either side of him.

"No, no, I insist! It's only right and fair," Dinendale continued, a slight edge in his voice.

"Oh, leave it, Dinendale," Broadside snapped. "What are you going to do? Wash me yourself?"

Dinendale smirked, leaning in so close that he almost touched the dwarf. "Broadside," he said softly, "I want you to remember something. I want you to remember that you said it... not I..." Suddenly the dark elf, Robert, and Jesnake all grabbed at the pudgy dwarf and hauled him high into the air.

"Put me down, you FIENDS!" Broadside screamed; anyone within a mile would have been reminded of a tornado with a bad sneeze. The trio dragged the floundering dwarf down the newly-worn path that lead to the stream. Shrieking and kicking the whole way, the dwarf bucked like a trapped fish while the others chortled all the way to the water's edge.

"All right, you lard-laden sack of fat," Robert snorted, "have a nice swim with the trout!" With that, they flung the hollering Broadside into the stream. The effect was similar to that of a stone catapulted into a still lake—the water flew high into the air with the sheer mass of the fellow displacing it from its proper place. Paige laughed until she felt tears in her eyes. Duelmaster was leaning against a tree, convulsing with gulping, gasping laughter as Broadside thrashed and sputtered as if an army of evil dwarf-eating merfolk were out to get him.

"Should we... go in... and get him?" Twostaves gasped through his loud, obnoxious heaves of ravenous chuckling. Robert crossed to stand by Paige, nearly choking as he hooted and hollered. He produced a bar of soap from his robe and tossed it into the water. Within moments, Broadside looked like he was drowning in the froth of a giant mug of ale.

"He might have a slight case of hydrophobia." Duelmaster laughed.

"Understatement of the year," Paige giggled. "When was the last time—"

"Not since the 'Log Over Nubly Pond' incident, I'm sure!" Duelmaster heaved, smacking his chest as he coughed out his now raspy giggles.

"Y'see," Robert said with a smirk, "the fool never goes near water unless he absolutely has to. I'd wager good money he hasn't actually washed in two years."

Camp was rather quiet after the bath. Broadside sat on his bedroll, a little damp and cross beyond reckoning, wrapped head-to-toe in Dinendale's thick woolen blanket. His chainmail hung from a tree limb, and his boots were steaming away by the fire. Outside of the occasional snort, he simply sat there, glaring at everyone from under his bushy black eyebrows in utter dwarven contempt.

Paige stretched out on her bedding as she gazed at the leafy canopy above her and took a bite of the chewy rabbit the boys had portioned out with some hardtack. Robert wasn't a bad cook. The meal, however, made Paige long for the culinary genius of her Papa. His skill in preparing wild game had been unsurpassed in Kapernaum. Anytime she'd shot a duck or quail, he'd roast it over a hickory fire with fragrant spices bought from the merchants housed in the spice tents that had frequented the Market. She smiled sadly at the memory of his mouth-watering fried catfish, the best to be had in the depths of the Wild.

"Well, I'm in dire need of some sword practice!" Duelmaster said as he stood, strapping his two rapiers to his back. The dryad moseyed to the center of the clearing and stood there as if expecting a challenger to pop out of the soil. After a second, Twostaves stood, his two signature staffs in hand. The dryad grinned and drew his swords.

"All right, let's see if we've still got it," the lowland giant leisurely replied. After bowing low to one another, the two began to circle, each looking for a strike.

The giant attacked first with a wide swing of one staff. Duelmaster retreated with nimble steps, parrying with a twirl of his rapier. Twostaves swung the second staff with enough force to crack a boulder in half. Paige winced in anticipation of the head-ringing blow she was sure Duelmaster would receive, but at the last second the dryad ducked, rising with a barrage of quick and fierce blows. Right and left, up and down the quick tree nymph struck. Although he bellowed with laughter, Twostaves barely kept up to block the rapid swings. The dryad twisted into a leap, landing with one boot on top of each of the staffs, balancing between them. Quick as a falcon diving for prey, he brought a rapier to the giant's thick neck.

"All right!" Twostaves panted. "I surrender!"

He dropped his staves, throwing his hands up in the air, which caused Duelmaster to topple backwards on his now unsecure stilts, landing on his posterior in the dirt with a heavy "OOF."

The boys erupted into laughter as Duelmaster stood, rubbing his smarting backside with the hilt of his rapier.

"Well, I'd say you still have something, that's for sure!" Duelmaster said with a signature grin.

"Got ya!" the giant bellowed, picking up his staves out of the dust. As he leaned over, the dryad whipped his sword back up and put it at the giant's throat once more.

"And that something is a complete lack of situational awareness!" the dryad teased, removing his blade with a flourish. As everyone clapped and laughed, Broadside remained huddled in his blanket, muttering something about the giant's clumsy size and how big people would always fall harder in the end. Dinendale stood, still applauding the two. The dryad grinned slyly at him.

"Care for a 'bout with the foils, Faoris?" Duelmaster enquired. Dinendale chuckled and shook his head.

"I fight with only one blade and ye with two? That hardly seems fair."

"Only because you know I can beat you!"

"Oh, I meant unfair for you." The dark elf laughed.

"Ah, bravely lying in the face of danger, I see! Then permit me to let one drop at my side, thus," Duelmaster replied, dramatically spearing one of his elegant swords into the dirt.

"For me?" Dinendale said, stepping closer with a lopsided smile. "You'd need a third arm for another toad-sticker, eh?"

Like lightning, the elf drew his bastard blade, whipping it downward with the momentum generated from his superb wristwork. Duelmaster immediately pulled his second rapier from the ground and crossed the two weapons above his head, catching the heavier blade. The two spun and parried, jumped and ducked. Despite the dryad's advantage in his twin blades, able to simultaneously block with one blade and stab with the other, the elf remained more confident in his footing. Paige was sure one of them would be killed at the pace they were swapping blows. Nevertheless, she cheered with the other boys who urged the two warriors onward.

In a brilliant maneuver, Duelmaster stepped into Dinendale's vigorous overhead swing, catching the hilt of the elf's sword at the last moment. Twisting his own pommel between Dinendale's hands, the dryad wrested the heavy blade out of the dark elf's grasp. Instead of surrendering to the dryad, though, the elf ducked the next blows. As Duelmaster advanced, Dinendale swept the dryad's feet from under him with a low kick. Duelmaster stumbled, desperately trying to regain his footing. The elf took his chance to grasp Duelmaster's wrist, twisting it so that he dropped one blade into the dust. Before Duelmaster had time to react, Dinendale swung around and held him in a headlock from behind. The dryad squirmed and kicked, so the elf simply threw himself onto his back and held tight, wrapping his boots around Duelmaster's abdomen.

"Give?" Dinendale gasped. Duelmaster smiled, despite his predicament.

"I suppose!" the dryad choked out. Dinendale released him, laughing. They both rose, shook hands and retrieved their weapons, dusting themselves off as they laughed and clapped each other on the back. The lot cheered at the duo, except for Robert, who handed coins to Jesnake. The Western Elf quietly smirked in satisfaction as he pocketed the winnings.

"So, does the great Dinendale fight like that against all that crosses his path?" Paige teased. "Tossing about in the dirt like a common school boy?"

The group's laughter faded as Dinendale turned to look at her, an intrigued mirth dancing in his brown eyes. This was something Paige had never seen in him, so she rose and advanced to the middle of the clearing. The others stood in silence, awaiting his reaction.

"Against men, yes," he replied with a slight smile. Paige took another step, arms folded.

"And not against women?" she asked.

"Well, no! They're women," the elf retorted, as if it was as simple as that. Paige felt her temper flare up and she clenched her fist. The nerve. She was not just some simple creature that would sit around like Matildra and her flock of followers. She wasn't sitting and hiding, waiting for someone to ride in and save the day. She had been prepared to march to Aschin regardless of whether or not this elf came along.

"So we're dainty? Fragile? Not up to your standards?"

The elf seemed to think this humorous, and stepped toward her.

"What would you do if I said yes?" he asked, smirking. Paige narrowed her eyes and the group gaped in disbelief, giddy with anticipation.

"Brother, when you step in it, you go all the way up to the belt," Robert said with a shake of his head. Dinendale looked at Paige's indignant face.

"Well, what would you do?" he repeated, cocking a dark eyebrow at her. Instead of giving a reply, Paige punched him in the chest as hard as she could. He winced, winded and surprised. There was a chorus of "Ooh!" from the spectators' gallery.

"You want to take all that back, or shall I prove I'm no damsel?" she asked through now gritted teeth.

Dinendale inclined his head. "After you, m'lady," he replied, drawing his sword again. Paige refused the boys' offers of weaponry, instead whirling around and marching to the edge of the woods. When she returned, she carried a large piece of well-seasoned oak, about twice as thick as her thumb, that had been lying beside a fallen tree. She snapped the twigs off the branch and broke it down to size over her knee. She smacked her stick threateningly against the clay earth as the two met at the center of the clearing.

"I want a solid entertaining fight!" Robert shouted. "None of that 'clean fight' rubbish, you hear?"

Dinendale began to bow to Paige in a mocking chivalric gesture, but the princess didn't feel like playing anymore. She swung her weapon, striking him a resounding blow against the side of his lowered head. He reeled and fell amid the shocked cries of the company. He sputtered, gasping in astonishment and pain. Paige brushed a stray hair out of her eye and pounded her staff on the hard-packed earth.

"Come on, sword-master," she taunted. "Duelmaster couldn't have worn you out that fast!"

She spoke too soon, as Dinendale leapt up to his feet and lunged at her. He slipped his right heel behind her ankle and leaned forward abruptly, causing Paige to trip over his leg and hit the dirt. She coughed as she hit the forest floor.

"Are you okay?" the elf was in the process of asking, a hint of genuine concern in his brown eyes.

"Build a bridge and get over it!" Paige snapped, rolling to the left and sweeping the elf's leg out from under him. He hit the ground as Paige rolled to her feet.

Dinendale stood, shaking his head, but Paige didn't give him the time to regain his footing before thrusting her thick stick into his gullet, knocking the wind out of him once more. When she followed up with a blow to his back, he was down again.

"Get up, Dinendale!" Robert mocked. "Don't you realize a damsel is beating you!"

The elf staggered to his feet, managing to block Paige's next blow. She spun out of the way of his attempted swing, whacking his hand as it passed before throwing all her strength into one well-aimed shot at his shin. He shouted in frustration, but as he reached down to rub the pain out of his leg, the princess reared back and let fly a forceful kick that caught him right in the fork of the legs. She turned smartly as

Dinendale hit the dirt with a thud, gasping for air as if it had been ripped out of his body.

Was it a cheap shot? Absolutely.

Did she care? Not at all.

"Lesson one in being a 'damsel,' just so you know, Dinendale," Paige said with a mirthless smile, squatting over the prostrate elf. "Regardless of his stature, there is always one shot that will equalize any man."

"Come on, Dinendale!" Jesnake called.

Dinendale rolled over, moaning woefully. "It's... so... peaceful down here, though..." the elf wheezed through clenched teeth, curled up in a pathetic looking heap in the dirt.

The others couldn't stop laughing, despite their best efforts; even Broadside was bellowing beneath his pile of blankets. Paige offered a hand to Dinendale, who took it with a grunt as she helped him hobble over to his blanket. He sat down and closed his eyes. Paige turned to go to her own bedroll, the others slapping her on the back.

"You feeling up for some rabbit there, Dinendale?" Duelmaster chuckled. The elf glared at the dryad from across the fire ring.

"Lost my appetite," he muttered.

"Sorry we don't have any crow to offer you," Robert snickered, "although you seem to have had your fill of that tonight."

The boys continued to tease Dinendale as the shadows grew longer and eventually melted into the darkness. Night awaited the two moons to rise up from their slumber beyond the horizon. Paige chose that time to take a seat next to the dark elf as he lay back and took it easy for a bit. She felt a bit guilty for injuring him, even if she still felt he'd deserved every inch of bruising and skinned knuckles for his chauvinistic attitude. The guilt won over her good nature eventually, though, and she sat next to him and held her hand out as if she was expecting him to place a coin in it. He looked at it in confusion.

"Can I help you?" he asked, bewildered.

"Your hand, give it here," she demanded. He placed his hand in hers, his chocolate eyes searching her face for a clue. His hand was rough and calloused but gentle in her own. She had skinned his knuckles enough to cause a few to bleed slightly, so she began taking a bandage out of her pack to wrap around the slight wound.

"Completely unnecessary," Dinendale interjected, but Paige ignored him. She knew it was barely a scratch but it was more about the gesture than anything else. They were quiet for a long time as she gently wrapped the cloth and tied it snug.

"Thank you, princess," he whispered. "I believe I owe you an apology."

She gave him a half-smile. "Safe to assume you learned your lesson?" she asked.

The elf chuckled. "I'd say so. But you didn't have to fight that dirty to prove your point."

"Sorry about that."

"Yes!" Robert cheered from across the campfire. Paige turned in time to see him slap Duelmaster on the back.

"What?" Dinendale asked.

"Come on! That's two for two on the apologies count!" Duelmaster spat in disgust. Paige's cheeks flushed and her brow furrowed in annoyance as the dryad tossed a laughing Robert a single gold coin. Robert gave her a teasing, smug look that irritated her, but she rolled her eyes and ignored him rather than picking yet another fight. Dinendale stretched back on his pallet.

"Don't let it get to you, Paige," he said, then continued to Robert: "Speaking from experience, if you know what's good for you, mate, you'll not jab this little bobcat."

"Oh, I'm not too worried about it." The hermit smirked as he threw his hood up, laying back on his own bedroll.

"He's the only person more arrogant than you, Dinendale," Jesnake chuckled.

"It's not arrogance if you know you're the better fighter," Robert snapped. "Which, I am, by the way."

Dinendale grabbed his sword.

"Well, we may just have to see about—"

He stopped speaking mid-sentence; his head snapped backwards, eyes staring wide and unseeing.

"Din?" Paige asked, concerned. The elf didn't blink. His stiff body, suddenly limp, collapsed onto his bedroll.

"Dinendale!" cried Jesnake, leaping nimbly to his feet. He ran over to the dark elf's side, but just as he reached the ashen-faced warrior, he fell face first into the dirt himself,

236

plowing a furrow in the dirt with his teeth. Paige heard Broadside cry out as he toppled off his perch on a stump.

"What in the name of—" Robert shouted, grabbing his spear and whirling about.

Paige jumped up and reached for her hairpin, but just as her fingers curled around the silver head, she felt something like a sharp bee sting stick her behind her left ear. Her head began to feel light and airy even as she swatted at the pain. She slumped forward, falling onto the leaf-covered earth as darkness enveloped her. The last things she heard were Robert's shouts and the sounding of a horn echoing in the distance.

CHAPTER 8

"GHAULGRA DIN"

*A*s Paige came to, she smelled the pungent smoke of a wood fire. Opening her groggy eyes, she saw nothing but foggy black shapes that faded in and out, swirling about her. She attempted to stand but found herself bound at the ankles, her arms tied around a large timber. She'd been stripped from her leather armor, and she could no longer feel her hairpin in her braid. Fortunately for her, whoever had taken those items hadn't found the scroll; it was still tightly wrapped around her inner thigh. For that, she was grateful. Her necklace, as best as she could tell, was also still around her neck, which surprised her, since she would have expected thieves to search for jewelry and gold first. Her pants were torn along her left leg, but apart from that, she was unscathed. Taking a moment to focus in the dim light, she attempted to study her surroundings as the shapes slowly settled.

A line of tall poles stretched fifteen feet to the peak of the slanted roof, which was thatched with deep, golden-coloured hay. The walls were made of the thickest bark she'd ever seen. Along each wall were shelves filled with furs and baskets. Near her feet, the embers of a fire glowed, emitting the only light to speak of inside. She appeared to be imprisoned in a longhouse. As far as Paige could tell, she was the only breathing thing there; she could not see any of the others with her and worried for their sakes.

During the next couple hours, Paige nodded off periodically, overcome with a residual headache from whatever stung her in the forest. At times she tried to muster the breath to shout, but she was too groggy, and her throat was so swollen that all she could manage was a squeak. As she was about to doze off again, the door opened. She squinted into the sunlight. A cloaked silhouette blocked the door frame for a moment before the door swung closed. Paige had to blink to clear her eyes, but when they focused, the figure was standing before her, his head concealed by a green cloak.

"Robert? Dinendale? Duelmaster?" she whispered. The figure shook his head.

"*Nofayne Alatawaigh. Nofay en elfhien nofay dryadah. Se midhien, augh cara,*" the man said in Elvish. Paige's foggy brain slowly translated it to say, No, Pretty One, I am neither elf-kind nor tree-man. I am man and a friend.

She narrowed her eyes, suspicious. *"Ef cara, wahyne me prisough en hempa?"* If you are a friend, why am I caged in rope?

The man lifted his cloak, revealing a head of grimy, shoulder-length blond hair with a single stripe of silver running down the center of his scalp. His eyes were shaped similarly to her own, but the color, if it could be called that, was the strangest she had ever seen. They were clear as the diamonds in her mother's earrings—unique, to say the least. The colors of nearby objects reflected in the man's eyes; when he looked at her, his eyes reflected the light gold of her hair. When he glanced slightly over his shoulder they turned the same dark green as his cloak. Paige shuddered.

He whispered, *"Me nofayne prisough en hempa son cara."* I am not he who has captured your friends.

She forced out in broken Elvish, *"Nofay en midheintodh?"* Don't you speak the tongue of men?

He nodded but said nothing, glancing over his shoulder as if afraid someone might see him. He briefly looked like he was about to answer, but a sound at the entrance of the lodge stopped him. Before the unseen people could enter, he dashed over to Paige's side.

"Take heart, princess," he whispered, foregoing the Elvish. "You have friends, even in this dark place."

Then, as suddenly as he had appeared, he was gone. Paige tried to see if he had merely stepped into the shadows so quickly that she'd missed him, but the activity at the other end of the room drew her attention away. A couple of figures entered and began lumbering toward her.

Two men had entered the dwelling, but they weren't at all like the one that had so swiftly vanished. They had large, muscular chests, and muscles rippled beneath their freckled, nutmeg-colored skin. Their braided auburn hair trailed down their backs; they wore white linen pants covered with furs for warmth in the brisk autumn morning. Their baggy shirts the colors of autumn leaves were topped by leather vests with thick deer hair. Soft-soled leather shoes wrapped and protected their feet as they plodded along on the cold, hard earthen floor.

One of the men stopped and began yanking at the knot to untie her. Before the rope was fully off, they each took one of her arms, restraining her so she couldn't run. Paige tried to fight back, but whatever poultice they had used to capture her had left her more exhausted than she'd initially thought. In fact, the two men nearly carried her to the door. The taller of the two murmured something to the other as he drew back the curtain door. With a sharp blast of warm sunlight, they were in the bright outdoors.

Paige shut her eyes in the harsh, blinding light. When she did open them at last, she was astonished to see a large, thriving village. Ten longhouses, like the one that had held Paige captive, stood before her in the large enclosure. A tall stockade fence made of countless sharpened stakes encircled the little community, providing a barrier between them and the surrounding mountains. The single gate seemed to be at

241

the east end of the little village, but it was high noon and hard for her to get her bearings from the sun in such a blinded state. There were paths made in the deep red clay, packed hard as stone. Sporadically placed tents surrounded the huts with open areas between the dwellings. Paige guessed these to be shops, not unlike the marketplace of her beloved yet lost Kapernaum.

The people, as a whole, were of a darker complexion than Paige had seen before, with warm brown skin and chestnut eyes accenting their wavy red-brown locks and dark freckles. The people wore sparse bits of armour, looking as if they had been collected from opposing tribes or clans they'd defeated. The women wore long, white leather dresses, many of which were adorned by vibrant beads and embroidery in elaborate designs of dragons, flowers, and rivers. Paige noticed they were all directing intense stares her way, an even mixture of profound awe and utter contempt. Just like her own home, she imagined this place must be very isolated out here in the Wild, and she must have looked as strange to them as they did to her.

As the princess stumbled on between the two men, heading for the center of the village, the talking on the roadside hushed to a low whisper. She could not hear them, but it was obvious they were all talking about her. With each step her feet ached. Her body felt limp like a dying fish pulled from water.

The three rounded what looked to be a smithy of some kind, and Paige saw a new building, unlike the longhouses all around it. It was a square building built out of huge stone blocks fitted seamlessly together by master masons long ago. They entered through the carved oak doorway and were once again in the same bleak light.

After her eyes adjusted once more to the dark light, Paige found about fifty men lined up against the wall, some sitting, some standing, each adorned in great fur robes made of mountain buffalo and brown bears. Hard expressions and fierce patterns of white paint adorned their faces, which amplified their accusatory gazes.

The room itself was empty of any objects, save for a single throne made of a large maple stump still rooted in the ground. Along the base of the trunk, Paige could see entwined dragons and demons of various shapes and expressions carved into the wood. A wrinkled old man occupied the chair, wisdom and years of hard ruling etched into the lines of his face. He was covered by a white bear skin robe, the only brightness amidst the abundance of brown and black in the room. He alone had no paint on his bearded face. Atop his hoary hair he wore a crown of gilded silver, which, on closer inspection, proved to be a chain of prancing silver horses. In his left hand, he held a bleached white staff with a single ruby set on the knobby top.

The leader extended the staff towards the men carrying Paige, summoning them. Before the throne, stripped of armor and weapons, with their hands bound behind their backs, were the Brotherhood.

The two guards made their way to the throne, throwing Paige down beside Dinendale and tying her hands behind her back. Amidst the murmuring of those surrounding them, she sat up, glaring at the men as they bowed to the man on the throne. Paige looked at the Brotherhood. Instead of their habitual garb, they all wore sleeveless shirts and baggy pants made of coarse, homespun fabric. At least they had let her keep her own clothes. Though the situation looked bleak, all the Brothers had a look of proud defiance on their faces.

"What took you so long?" whispered Dinendale.

"What do you think? I stopped to pick flowers," Paige shot back.

"Silence!" shouted a man standing next to the throne. He was tall and skinny, with his hair knotted into a scalp-lock that draped down his back. Aside from a scruffy beard, the lock of hair seemed to be the only hair on his thin frame. He wore a scarlet blanket over his bare chest, which was riddled with innumerable scars. Since his pants only came to his knees, his knobby legs were bare, painted with white and blue symbols. His hooked nose draped over his curled lip like a bird's beak and a gnarled pair of leathery ears held enormous studs of green wood. A cane reed in the crook of one arm looked like a suitable weapon for someone of his frame.

"Where are we?" Paige whispered to Dinendale.

"This is the earl's—"

The ugly man with the cane swung the reed at Dinendale's face with such force that the elf was flung off his knees and onto his back with a resounding crack. A streak of blood formed along his high cheekbone.

"Are your ears made of stone, creature? I said silence! You will obey Locamnen of the Heralde Clan!"

Dinendale struggled up, staring at the man in defiance. The self-proclaimed Locamnen turned to the white-robed man whom Paige assumed must be the earl.

"Great Earl Khaftamen, before whom all men...and elves...bow down," he said disdainfully, pointing at Dinendale. "I present to you the murderers of Yarvidt of Clan Heralde, Son of Larne the Red. We found them in the forest by the border stream, trying to make good their escape!"

"We told you!" growled Robert through his teeth, lips tight in rage. "We have no idea what you're talking about!"

The knobby spokesman hooked his reed cane under Robert's chin, jerking it up forcefully to look his prisoner in the eyes. Locamnen scowled, baring his yellowed teeth at the look of hatred burning in Robert's gaze.

"That's what any murderer would say," he sniffed. Robert glared even harder. The earl, called Khaftamen, straightened in his throne. His hair cascaded down his shoulders like silver waterfalls on a mountainside. He examined each of the prisoners with his piercing black eyes as if expecting their confessions. When his stare landed on Paige, she saw his gaze soften. She searched his face and wondered if he perhaps held reservations about Locamnen's accusation.

"Where is your proof?" Paige blurted out. The furious spokesman strode over to her, pausing for a moment, scrutinizing her with his narrowed eyes. His gaze made her uncomfortable, and she looked to the old chief, who returned her gaze with a somber expression.

"I concur. I demand you present the charges, false as they are!" Broadside bellowed. The crowd seemed to find the short creature amusing, because they all began to snicker until Khaftamen raised his hand high to demand silence.

"Three days ago," the earl said in a grave, soft voice, "a young boy called Yarvidt, son of Larne the Red, went out for a walk with his dog. He never came back, but the next day we found the dog dragging himself back to camp, nearly gutted."

Paige felt an ache in her heart beginning to form. The earl stood slowly, stepped down, and began pacing in front of his prisoners.

"Throughout the night, we searched for him. We didn't find him until the next morning, an insensible, bleeding mess from the innumerable gashes along his body. Despite the best efforts of our healer, he died yesterday. But before he passed from this world, he was able to tell us who had attacked him. He described men that were heavily armed and travelling off the mountain road."

Duelmaster spat, anger flashing in his grey eyes like lightning in a thunderstorm. "We only just arrived in these lands—"

"He said there was a blonde she-elf with them."

Paige felt a pang go through her heart and the tips of her pointed ears flush as panic pumped through her veins. Armed men with a blonde girl that looked like an elf; there was only one other band of people that could possibly be.

246

The chief sighed. Amidst the shock of knowing they were on the right path to Aschin, and Olivian was in fact still alive, she couldn't blame these people for the hostilities shown. They had lost a loved one and had little information with which to take vengeance for their loss. Even still, Paige was not willing to be blamed for the murder of a young, innocent boy.

Locamnen strode like a peacock to the side of the throne, twirling his cane.

"My lord, the evidence is quite clear; this rabble of half-breeds and despicable creatures are guilty! There's no one else it could have been."

Robert shouted, "Did it hurt when you pulled that pack of lies from so far up your—"

The man struck his cane across Robert's face, cutting him off. Barely fazed, Robert hurtled forward, barreling into his accuser with a shout of rage. The room erupted into chaos as everyone rushed Robert.

Paige saw an opportunity with the temporary chaos and began to work the ropes on her wrists, finding that the knots were not tight at all. With each jostle and tug she felt them loosen. Just a little more, and... there! She had one hand loose.

The guards who held her were now in the fray, so she slipped over to the wall on her right. Paige was about to break for the door when strong hands grasped her shoulder. Acting on impulse, she swung with as much force as she could muster. Her fist slammed into a rather pudgy face, and she felt the squish as her knuckles connected. The scribe teetered like a top and went down, cold as a snuffed candle, as Paige scrambled to get to the door. As she reached it, members of the nearby mob realized her intentions. The commotion shifted its attention. She was suddenly surrounded by men shoving and grabbing to get their hands on her shirt.

"Stop them!" she heard the high-pitched voice of Locamnen screaming. "They must be punished! They killed one of our own!"

The princess toppled the first guard to grab her wrist, proceeding to kick the shin of the next unfortunate man to cross her path and stomping down on his toes for good measure. Paige shoved them down, one by one, into the dirt, when a sharp rap smote her behind her left ear. She crumpled to the floor, crying out in pain. The savages continued beating her, their powerful fists raining down merciless blows. Her lip was cut now, and she didn't know how much more she could take. Gasping, she tried to rise to her knees. Every time she tried, another arm was driven down on her shoulders, and she was pushed back into the sea of fists and boots. She could hear the earl calling for order, but the yelling tribesmen were so loud that his voice was drowned. Her head pounded in pain to the rhythm of the bony fists that struck her.

The pummeling stopped abruptly as she felt someone throw themselves over her like a shield. Through swelling eyes, she looked up to see Dinendale protecting her from the scores of fists beating down upon them. His dark eyes filled with fiery rage as he winced, taking the blows upon his own back. The guards finally began to calm the angry men. Soon, order was restored, and the roar was reduced to a low growl. Paige faintly heard a deep, authoritative voice barking loudly as everything went hazy. She slumped in a beaten stupor against the cool, rammed-earth floor.

Dinendale was yanked to his feet. He had kept calm, hoping to increase their chances of release, but after Robert's raging attack, he realized that their captors weren't going to simply let them go. Once the men started beating Paige for trying to escape, Dinendale lost the vestige of his control.

He hadn't asked for this. There wasn't a single part of him that wanted to be on this journey back to the one place he'd hoped he would never see. He'd not planned to have to fend off a troop of Bogartrolls. And he definitely hadn't expected to be trapped a captive of some backwater tribe in the Wild. But the moment the first fist connected with Paige, he felt some protective instinct deep in the pit of his stomach rise to his chest and light his neck on fire.

His arms had felt like braided steel as he wrenched them free of the cords on his wrists. Pushing past the two guards behind him, he managed to push Paige to the floor and out of immediate danger, holding his body over her as a living shield. He saw her go limp as she passed out, but he continued to block the furious fists of the enraged tribesmen as best he could.

Almost as quickly as the uproar had begun, the room fell to a murmur and the brawl ceased; the fists stopped their pounding and the boots, their kicking. Hands hauled Dinendale to his feet, and the dark elf looked up. The men were quiet, staring with shock, contempt, and curiosity at the scene before them. A large figure stood in the middle of the floor; a burly man, with thick red hair and a curly beard. His pants of rough spun wool and baggy shirt were covered with soot stains and dirt marks from the years spent in this smoky backwoods village. His brawny hands rested on his hips, a posture which struck Dinendale as more suited to a scolding mother than to a man commanding authority.

"You button-headed, sniveling, donkey-hearted wretches!" he bellowed, reminding Dinendale of an angry bear. "You would accuse them of murder and injustice, then commit the crime yourself!" The men mumbled, thinking this through. The ruddy man crossed to the guards holding Dinendale. He studied the dark elf, then turned to the earl.

"I realize that I cannot vouch for these people's honesty, yet I would see them pardoned."

Shouting erupted throughout the room, with Locamnen's voice the loudest of them all.

"You would have murderers run free!" he raged.

"We have no proof that these are the true killers!" retorted the group's defender.

Another man stepped forward from the crowd, his braided beard covering his wide girth. "Hanburg, you fat ox, we need no proof! The boy's attackers were heavily armed, and accompanied by a blonde girl!"

"Have you even entertained the thought that this may not be the same party?" The hefty man tuned to the earl, huge hands outstretched. "Earl, there is no evidence! Let them go; forgive instead of condemn, especially on such shaky grounds."

"So, Hanburg, you genuinely believe in the odds of two identical parties in our woods are that concrete!?" Locamnen sneered.

"Oh shut up, Locamnen, we all know you are just after the reward Larne the Red offered for the slayers of his son!"

Locamnen seethed with anger, his fists balled up at his side.

"How dare you impune my honor, you—"

"Save it, you sniveling curr," another man spat at Locamnen. "We all know it was no honor nor love for Larne that drove you to the woods!"

"These have to be them!" Locamnen screamed, whirling to face the earl. "Surely, my lord, you see that the coincidence is too great to allow these people to live."

"We told you already!" Twostaves bellowed. "That group wasn't us! We are chasing after the same people here!"

"Shut up, Twostaves," Robert hissed through gritted teeth.

"It's true!" the giant pushed, the four men attempting to keep him restrained, struggling as he stood to his full height.

Several warriors lowered spears about him, wary and ready to finish the unarmored giant. "We seek the same group you do!"

"ENOUGH, you stupid, bumbling buffoon!" Robert snapped.

Locamnen eyed the group now, suspicious and calculating. The earl, meanwhile shook his head heavily, as if burdened with a great weight upon his back. He looked from the seven prisoners before him to Locamnen and then back.

"As much as I want to believe you," he finally said, "I cannot just ignore this. There is evidence, and, while not conclusive, it is at least convincing. I am sorry."

"Fetch the executioner!" Locamnen cheered, almost giddy.

"Wait!" cried Hanburg, protectively moving in front of the Brotherhood. "I cannot allow such barbarous actions to take place."

"Is this treason, Hanburg? Do you question the earl's judgment?" screeched Locamnen, fist raised.

"I would follow my earl to any end, unlike some, Locamnen. But these men cannot be condemned unjustly."

"They are as likely lying as speaking truth," spat Locamnen. "Half of these lot aren't even human. When was the last time you heard of an elf telling the truth about anything?"

"Last time our people heard about an elf in the Wild, our grandfathers hadn't even been born, so what makes you think your perception is even close to accurate?"

Locamnen marched forward, sticking his hooked nose a mere finger's breadth from Hanburg's own.

"I will not risk the safety of this clan on your hunch, Hanburg," the man sneered. Hanburg's lip curled in disgust.

"Pish-posh. You care about the gold. Your concern for this village runs about as deep as your concern for oral hygiene."

Locamnen reared his boney fist back for a punch. Hanburg smiled coyly. The man's fist connected with Hamburg's rosey, fleshy face with the sound of skin slapping skin. The big man winced briefly from the blow, then grabbed the back of Locamnen's scalp-lock and smashed his forehead into the scarecrow's face. Locamnen fell to the floor howling, a chorus of cheers and booing mixed in the stuffy air of the chamber.

"You will all bear witness, he assaulted me first," Hanburg bellowed, stepping over the crumpled, sputtering mess of a man now on the floor and turned to face Dinendale. Grasping the elf's shoulders, he stared directly into his fawn-brown eyes.

"Tell me, elf, looking into my eyes, that you are innocent," he said gravely. Dinendale never wavered.

"Neither my friends, nor I, slew the boy," he evenly replied. "I swear it upon the graves of my kin." The man looked at him for a moment, searching his face, then he turned.

"Can you explain what it is you were doing in our wood?"

Dinendale considered this. Every detail of their quest relied on secrecy and speed, and they were losing both, thanks to Twostaves' interjection.

"I can tell you we are heading east, tracking possibly the same party you seek revenge on."

"From where?"

"Do you know the village of Kapernaum?"

There was a murmur among the crowd. The earl looked genuinely surprised.

"Kapernaum is not unknown to us," he said, gesturing to the people around the room. "Many traders pass through here on their way to the market there."

"Well, there is no market there anymore," Dinendale said carefully. "That girl lying there. She is from there. The Shahir's army burned it to the ground two weeks ago."

The crowd began murmuring in disbelief, whispering to each other. Hanburg looked to the earl expectantly.

"What have you to say about that, your lordship?"

The earl looked thoughtful. Locamnen staggered to his feet, clutching his bleeding nose, his eyes spilling hatred at Hanburg.

"This is still not definitive proof, and Larne the Red's son can not go unavenged!"

"Oh, save it, you pathetic runt!" A tall, brawny man with red hair the color of cooking coals in a fireplace stepped forward, his long beard splaying out in all directions. "My boy is dead, and no one wants to see his killer's head on a pike more than I do. But I'm not shelling out gold on the chance that you of all people might be wrong!"

"What do you suggest then, Larne?" Hanburg asked, scrutinizing the man. The father of the slain boy kneaded his brow, weary lines etched into his face that hadn't seen a good night's sleep in days.

"I say we send a band to Kapernaum. Verify this elf's story. If they are telling the truth, we let them go. If not, I will have my vengeance. What think you, earl?"

"Ridiculous! That could take a month!" Locamnen protested.

"You'll not see a speck of gold until I know for sure you didn't just get lucky and once again try to cheat your way into a lucrative reward!" Larne the Red shouted at Locamnen. The crowd erupted in shouting once more till the earl raised his staff high over his head, demanding silence.

"ENOUGH! I will hear no more on this matter. Larne's suggestion is seeded with wisdom. Hanburg, do you agree?"

"I do, my lord," he declared, "but our gatehouse is no place to keep seven travellers, who may be completely innocent."

"We cannot just let them walk free, Hanburg," the earl said definitively.

"Aye, m'lord. Then as in the old days of our people, I declare the right of Ghaulgra Din."

The room hushed. Dinendale felt slight panic set in; whatever that phrase meant, it must not have been invoked very often. The earl looked askance at Locamnen, then stood, staff in hand.

"So be it. The prisoners will be sold in the square at sun-peak tomorrow." he slowly announced. Hanburg exhaled slowly, relief etched on his face. Locamnen fumed, glaring at Dinendale.

"Oh, great and mighty ruler, I thank you in sincerity of heart. May I ask but one boon more?" Hanburg added.

The earl looked at him warily. "Yes?"

Hanburg threw a leather purse to the ground. The clinking of metal as it landed betrayed its contents.

"I claim the elf as my property," he said simply. The earl waved his hand.

"Yes, yes; whichever one you desire. Just leave the matter at rest. I will hear no more; I grow weary of this debate." With that, he exited the stone building, trailed by several bodyguards. As he left, the room began to buzz as the remainder of the crew discussed this turn in events. Soldiers jerked the Brotherhood to their feet and ushered them out. One man unbound Dindndale and shoved him over to Hanburg, who took the elf by the shoulder.

"Come along, lad. We've some work to discuss, you and I." He leaned in and whispered, "Together, we can see to putting this right!"

"We are slaves now?"

"Yes, until the party can return from Kapernaum, I'm afraid," he said apologetically. "But don't you worry. We won't be waiting that long. Now we have more flexibility and can begin laying some semblance of a plan."

Dinendale felt his temper flare again. A slave once again. And all because of a mission he hadn't even wanted to go on in the first place. But his temper was quenched as he saw Paige lying on the floor of the hut. He sighed and looked the councilman in the eye.

"Sir, I can never thank you enough for standing up for us, but I would beg that you don't spend your gold on me. I'm strong enough to serve anywhere I am sentenced for a while, but the girl is still extremely weak, though she would never admit it. She would probably be worked to death with anyone else, unable to regain her strength. Your earl said to take whichever one you desire; if you have any heart, please; take her," Dinendale finished.

Hanburg considered him for a moment, then turned to the guard bending to lift Paige. He hesitated, then took one last look at Dinendale.

"Soldier!" he barked. The startled warrior almost dropped the unconscious princess, but he quickly recovered, straightening his shoulders.

"Yes, sir," he replied, his frosty tone betraying his disapproval. Hanburg glanced at Dinendale once more, then took his shoulder.

"I've changed my mind; I'll take the girl. I've a daughter her age, and the girl will make a good companion for her." The soldier shrugged, relinquishing Paige. He practically threw her into Hanburg's arm like a sack of potatoes. The hefty man nodded to the elf and gently carried the fallen princess out the door of the meetinghouse. Dinendale found himself sighing a breath of relief. Paige would be alright. He watched Hanburg leave with her, feeling the bruises pulsating on his back. The guard stepped forward with another set of ropes to tie up the elf's hands, but Dinendale stood fast, keeping his arms locked at his side.

"I won't run," he muttered. "Not without my friends."
Then the dark elf strode out the door, followed by a very
befuddled and speechless guard.

Paige moaned as she tried to raise up on her elbows. The
splitting ache down the center of her head pounded like a
woman beating the dust out of a rug, her temples beating their
own tune against her skull. Tears welled up in the corners of
her eyes but she refused to let them fall. The pain began to
abate as a cold, damp cloth was pressed to her brow. Paige's
eyelids fluttered open and began to focus in the warm light.

A young woman stood above her, holding a bowl of cold
water in one hand and a wet rag in the other. Her olive-colored
skin had just the slightest tone of reddish-brown the people of
this village all shared, and this warm color complimented by
her rich, charcoal-black hair and thick eyelashes. Her brows
were creased with concern for Paige as she applied the cold
compress. The slightest smattering of freckles spattered across
her rosy cheeks like the stars in the heavens on the clearest of
nights. The girl wore an ivory deerskin dress embroidered
around the shoulders with blue and green threads intertwining
into a wavelike pattern. A sash of golden homespun cloth
wrapped several times around her waist with various trinkets
dangling from it like a wind chime. She smiled down at Paige
with deep set, cocoa-brown eyes.

"Headache subsided at all?" she asked in a soft, silvery voice. Paige shook her head, grimacing with the movement.

"Here, then," the girl continued in a clear, kind voice. "Try this. What it lacks in culinary flavor it makes up for in pain management."

She lifted a wooden spoon brimming with a thick, red substance. The girl helped Paige raise her aching head to sip the syrup. As she swallowed the liquid, Paige sputtered at the bitter taste, yet the pounding of her head waned as she lowered herself back onto the bed.

"That is...so nasty," she coughed.

"I know, sometimes I'd rather endure the pain," the young woman smiled.

"Thank you," Paige whispered quietly. "You have no idea how much that helps." The girl examined her with gentle eyes.

"I can imagine."

Paige leaned up on her elbow to get a better view, surveying the small room that held her. Though made of stone and wood like the longhouse she'd been held in earlier, it was much smaller, probably meant for a single family as opposed to several. Through the foggy haze of her splitting headache, she could make out a large oak door hung on a strong frame on the wall to her left, and in the far left corner a tiny stone fireplace crackled, giving off a fair amount of heat in the small room. A single lamp sat on a small table near the bed, but aside from this the room appeared to be bare.

"Where am I? Who are you? Where are my friends?" she asked, worry lacing her words.

"Shhh, easy now. You're safe, and your friends are still about. You are in the house of Hanburg Feldjorn, Councilman of the Bear clan. I am his daughter, Abenya," she replied, placing a new cloth on Paige's forehead.

"What am I doing here?"

"My father bought your freedom from the tribe. Father said that dark-haired creature asked that you be brought here. So here you are, none the worse for wear!"

"I feel much 'the worse for wear,' I dare say," Paige groaned.

"Well, you'll have some bruised ribs, but I don't think they broke any bones. You were lucky the pale one shielded you when he did; otherwise you would've had several fractures."

Dinendale. He had shielded her. Abenya was right. Their strikes would have mutilated her if not for him. Paige smiled feebly. Although her head seemed to improve by the minute, her ribs felt as if they were alive with bolts of painful lightning. Even still, she knew it would have been much worse. She'd have to thank Dinendale for that one.

"Where is he now?" Paige asked. "Dinendale? And the others?"

Abenya's smile vanished. Hesitantly, she dipped the cloth back into the bowl again before placing it back on Paige's forehead. Paige's heartbeat quickened.

"Are they... dead?"

Abenya's head bobbed up. "Oh, no!" she exclaimed. "They're most definitely alive. It's just... they have more complicated situations at present."

"What is that supposed to mean?"

"Well, without getting into the political nuances and blatherings, they are essentially sold to other members of the clan."

"Slaves!?"

Abenya nodded. "It was the only way Father could think to buy you some time," she reassured. "The earl is sending an envoy to Kapernaum to check out your story. Till that is done, the earl will not pass judgment. Rather than house you all in a jail, the people put you all up for auction as servants to work for room and board till the envoy can come back."

"We... we don't have time for that!" Paige blurted, jumping up. Just as quickly she laid back down as pain shot through her abdomen and robbed her of any strength. She felt her heart sinking into the pit of her stomach. After only a few days of lost travel, Olivian would be well on her way while Paige remained trapped in a barbaric place with no escape. A desperate tear slid down her cheek. Abenya patted Paige's arm reassuringly.

"I know that. And my father does as well. This way, there's more of a chance for you to escape. I know he will find a way for you to leave. We just need a few days."

"A few days is too long! It will be too late!"

Paige let the tears that had been brimming in her eyes trickle down her face into her ears. She took a deep, shaky breath, looking into Abenya's confused eyes.

"It's my sister. The same men who killed your boy took my sister, and if we can't get to them before they reach Aschin, we may never get her out."

Abenya looked heartbroken for her. Paige sniffed as she heard the sound of a door opening outside their room in the main area of the hut. The latch on the entryway clicked, and the door to the room slowly swung inward.

"Father!" Abenya hopped up from her chair as a large man with a ruddy red beard swaggered into the room. She embraced him, and he gave her a huge bear hug in return, chuckling softly.

"Abi, my sweet," he said warmly. "Have you been taking good care of our honored guest?"

"Yes, Da," she said sweetly. "The poor thing has been fretting. I told her you have a plan to make it all better. You do have a plan, don't you?"

Abenya's father walked over to Paige's bedside and took the princess's small hand in his giant palms, patting it reassuringly. Paige swallowed the lump in her throat. Papa had done that exact thing when she'd fallen ill growing up.

"My dear, we will do everything we can to make sure you are on your way as soon as possible."

"Thank you, my lord," Paige gulped, trying to be polite. The man wagged a sausage shaped finger in her face with a tsk-tsk.

"There will be no more of that nonsense," he commanded. "It is 'Hanburg' to you, my dear, for we are equals. Soon enough I'll see you and your friends restored as such."

"Da, she said that band that killed Yarvidt was the same group that took her sister," Abenya offered. Hanburg's expression was one of worry and concern as he looked down at Paige.

"My dear, I am so sorry. I do not doubt for one moment you are all telling the truth, but my kinsmen seem to not want to take heed of my counsel."

"You must get them to let us go!" Paige pleaded. "Please!"

"They will never agree," the man sighed, stroking his beard and twisting a tuft of it around his finger. "Not now that they've invested money in you all. No, I think we have but one recourse."

"And that is?"

"Escape, naturally!"

Paige pressed her lips together in fear and skepticism.

"You think it's possible with everyone sold off as slaves?"

"It is possible," Hanburg said. "It will take a good deal of planning. At any rate, it's far more likely that they can escape as they are now than if you were all under lock and key in the jail."

Paige forced herself to sit up in the bed, Abenya rushing to her aid to help steady her. Paige grimaced as the ache in her ribs kicked up again, but she bit her tongue to keep from crying out. She would have to muscle her way through this if she was going to save both her friends and then Olivian; this was no time to take a rest when so much was at stake.

"Why is that vile man so intent upon seeing us executed," Paige demanded, taking a mug of water that Abenya offered her. Hanburg scowled.

"You mean Locamnen?"

"Is that the man with a vulture's face?"

Abenya giggled and Hanburg let out a snort of a chuckle, scratching his ruddy nose.

"Aye, that would be Locamnen. He used to be a healer among our people, but he got caught swindling a family of their silver for a 'potion' that was apparently nothing more than charcoal dust and honey. He's been in a low standing with most in the tribe since then."

"Then why do so many people seem to listen to him?"

"He pays off many influential men and families. Gold is a favorite motivator around here. It did not used to be that way. We used to be a proud people, but our earl is old and has no heir, so the men go where the coin points them. It's a miracle we've been able to retain any kind of law and order in the village for the last three years, let alone this afternoon."

"So we're stuck here because Locamnen wants to get paid?"

"If he had one, he would sell his own mother if it meant picking up a few bartering bars of silver," the heavy-set man laughed. He slapped his knee and stood.

"Now, you rest up, my dear. I'll get some supper going, and we shall begin making our plans. I think I know how we can get your lot out of here within the week."

"A week!?"

Hanburg smiled apologetically.

"I know it isn't exactly the timeframe you wanted, but we have to do this carefully or not at all if we're going to get you out of here."

Paige sighed. "If that's the best we can do, then we best get to work."

"Brilliant," Hanburg nodded. He opened the creaky old door and bowed to the girls. Then he stepped outside and left them alone once again.

The two girls sat in silence for a beat. Paige attempted to enjoy the quiet moments of peace for what they were. She tried not to dwell on the knot that had seated itself comfortably in the pit of her stomach. Paige guessed would probably stay there until they were free from this horrific delay they couldn't afford. But it was so difficult to clear her mind, especially when she couldn't be with the Brotherhood.

"Don't worry, dear," Abenya tried to comfort her, standing and walking over to the small stone fireplace in the corner. She tossed a few bits of wood onto the heap of coals and stoked the flames back to a healthy, cheery brightness. Paige watched as they licked the wood and cackled with the delight of a new meal.

"Where is all my stuff?" Paige asked, undoing her tangled braid. "I need my hairpin. It's very dear to me."

"All of that has been locked up in the grain storehouses, I think," she said, dusting the ash off her hands and standing up. "By the law, they cannot parcel it out until you are all convicted, although I'm sorry to say some of the warriors placed to guard them are not above a bribe if someone wanted to help themselves."

"How dreadful," Paige muttered, touching her locket. She could still feel the leather scroll bound against her thigh. Her mother's sword might be lost, but at least her father's secrets were still in tact. She whispered a quick prayer to the Creator, thanking him for her good fortune before returning her thoughts to the task at hand. She played back the morning's events in her head and was struck with a question for which she had no answer.

"Abenya?"

"Yes?"

"Have you ever seen a man with silver eyes?"

Abenya turned and looked at Paige, her eyes screwed up in confusion.

"Silver eyes?"

"Yes. Clear, and they shone like diamonds in the moonlight."

"Uh, no. I can't say I've ever come across anyone who had eyes like that. I'm sure I'd remember it."

Paige screwed her face in confusion and frustration. Who was the man who had come to her in the long house then? What had he meant when he said she had friends, even in this dark place? And aside from that, how on earth were they going to all get free without waiting for the envoy to get back? There were so many pieces of the puzzle pounding against her head that she kneaded her temples in concentration.

"Don't worry," Abenya reassured. "Da will have a plan."

"He'd better think up something fast," Paige said, voice quivering slightly. "We had no time to lose, and that was yesterday."

As if on cue, the door burst open with a resounding CRASH. Both girls jumped to see Hanburg once again in the doorway, red hair splayed out wildly, eyes gleaming with the reflection of the grin he sported.

"Girls, come to the table quickly! I think I may have a plan!"

CHAPTER 9

ALL THIS FOR A

LOAF OF BREAD?

*S*weat poured down Robert's back and dripped below his waist, seeping into his suede belt. The sun beat down on his head as if its sole purpose in rising that morning had been to make him miserable. Twostaves was tethered to his side, breathing heavy in the muggy forenoon sun. They had been bought at the auction block by a wheat farmer as laborers because of their size and obvious strength. One of his oxen had drowned the week before, so he simply strapped the two large fellows together and set them out to till the field for a second planting of autumn wheat.

Silent rage burned deep within Robert's chest. These people were repugnant in their treatment of those different than themselves, and it made his distaste for mankind grow ever more bitter in his heart. Still, he worked on because he could do nothing else. His legs and arms bore iron chains. A solid brass collar was locked around his neck, weighing his head low. His back ached with every movement, and despite the cool autumn breeze, sweat dripped from his face and stung his eyes. Twostaves fared no better.

"Hurry it up, yeh good-for-nothings!" yowled the driver of the small plow. The burly man with oily black hair and a pock-marked face lashed them with a horse-hair whip, cracking on their threadbare shirts. Robert winced but didn't cry out.

"If I weren't bound...," he muttered.

Twostaves looked over with a half-smile. "Look at the bright side!"

"There is no bright side, Twostaves. Anyone who thinks otherwise is a moron."

"Excuse me for trying to make the best of it. There's usually something you can take away from any scenario that is positive in some way."

"There is. I'm positive now that you are a moron."

"Well, think about this—you don't have to wear that humiliating robe anymore!"

"Don't even give me that! I was waiting to get to the traders for some new trousers. It was all I had lying around at home for the season."

"Living in that little hole sure made you lazy."

"At least I learned how to be lazy. You can't learn stupid."

"Okay, I have had just about ENOUGH of you, tiny mouth-breather!" Twostaves roared, pulling himself up to his full height, which was a whole head and a half taller than Robert. This pulled Robert up onto his tiptoes.

"Nice to know you watch me in my sleep." He smirked. A loud CRACK sounded behind them as the farmer snapped Twostaves in between the shoulders. The giant growled, glaring back at the man.

"We should just break his neck and be done with it," Robert hissed as they set back to pulling.

"We'll think of something, but we can't just bail on the others. They might kill the rest of them if some of us go missing."

"We'd better hope someone in there is coming up with a plan, then," Robert murmured, "because I don't know how much more of this I'm going to tolerate."

Dinendale rose, wiping his sweaty, coal-dusted forehead on his ragged cotton shirt. The iron shackles exacerbated the ache in his arms. At the auction block three days ago, he'd been the first of the Brotherhood to be sold. Bought by a filthy bear of a man with matted brown hair and tobacco-stained teeth, Dinendale had at first been relieved to find he would be working in a blacksmith's shop. He had always loved working with metal and was a decent smith. But the smith owning him now had him shoveling coal for the great furnace and manning the forge's massive bellows. Now his muscles shrieked in protest with each pump of air that whooshed into the coal-burning chamber.

Despite his altered circumstances, Dinendale was grateful to be at the smithy, considering the fates of his companions. Paige was safe at present, although Dinendale still worried about Locamnen and his apparent blind ambition and hatred for the man called Hanburg. He'd seen an evil look in the cur's eyes when Paige had been hauled into the room.

As for the others, Dinendale had heard that Twostaves and Robert were working in the fields while Jesnake had been bought by the miller to thresh grain. The last Dinendale had heard, Duelmaster was working for the village bakery; the dark elf was still trying to figure that one out. One of the council members had picked up Broadside as an entertaining dancing dwarf. If it hadn't attested to the humans' naïveté concerning dwarves, it would have been the funniest thing Dinendale had ever seen. Anyone with sense or even an inkling of knowledge of the other races would have chosen the dwarf to work in the forge, for a black dwarf's craftsmanship surpassed that of any man, and could have brought the smith great wealth. But humans craved novelties, and, much to Broadside's misfortune, he drew the short straw.

His thoughts were interrupted by the jingling of the small bell suspended above the door by an iron hook.

"Good mornin', Smitty!" Hanburg bellowed good-naturedly. His fiery beard was a tangled mess and his eyes glowed with enthusiasm. Giant, meaty hands rested on his hips. He filled the doorway with his substantial girth, blocking nearly all the light. Dinendale's master sauntered over to the age-stained counter, grimacing as if the very presence of customers in his store annoyed him. The fat councilman leaned on the counter, the wood groaning under the load. The two men were similar in size, but the blacksmith's corded muscles had been hardened by years of labor; the councilman's had not.

"What can I do for you, Councilman Hanburg?" asked the smith, wiping the soot from his meaty hands.

Hanburg smiled. "I seem to have a loose door-hinge at my home. Funny, it just popped off one day! Pop!" he said, snapping a finger for emphasis. He caught Dinendale's eyes and folded his hands on the countertop. "Anyway, I need a new one immediately."

"My hinges don't just pop out," the smith snapped. "They're solid craftsmanship."

"Oh, I heartily agree. I almost wonder if some mischief had befallen my household. As wonderful as all the hinges are in this village, it is strange how easily that pin slid out."

"I built every hinge in this village, Hanburg. It takes a fair amount of pressure to pop one of those pins."

"I know you did! And it was a fine job, too! In fact, I rather like my hinges loose. Makes for a backup plan should the door ever be locked!"

As the smith scrawled a note on a piece of paper, the councilman and Dinendale locked eyes for a brief second. The dark elf stared at Hanburg curiously, but the man only inclined his head slightly and winked. The smith didn't even notice as he finished his note and handed it to an apprentice.

"Your hinge will be ready at first hour tomorrow morning, Councilman," he grunted in obvious annoyance. Hanburg turned from the counter.

"Excellent; I'll have my slave girl pick it up. Have a good day, Smitty!" With one last glance at the elf, the councilman left.

Jesnake was sifting wheat when Paige entered the mill. Five days had passed since their trial, and the Western elf was glad to see her feeling well enough to be out and about again. She strode through the open doors of the dusty mill wearing a doeskin dress and carrying a market basket in one arm, produce poking out the top. Her hair had been scrubbed clean and pulled back into a single braid, and aside from a small bruise on her cheek, she looked better than she had since the beginning of their journey nearly a month ago. She was still wearing her old leather moccasins, and the slight bulge in one of them told Jesnake that the scroll was safely tucked away. Her other moccasin housed a small antler knife. Jesnake wished to be as fortunate as she, knowing he and the rest of the Brotherhood had been stripped of all armor, clothing, and weapons. Bereft of his mail and tunic, Jesnake now wore a simple tattered cotton shirt, baggy trousers, and crude sandals woven from thick hemp cord.

The elf studied his fair hands. These hands were an artist's hands and his bow had been his paintbrush. Now they were raw, red, and cracking. He wiggled his fingers as she examined them. Duties of the mill had not been kind to him. He'd been tasked with the dangerous chore of pouring grain into the three-ton grindstones. That work alone had cost his master three fingers on his right hand.

He pushed his gloomy thoughts aside as Paige approached the maple counter. The miller came out from the back room, wiping his flour-covered hands on his leather apron.

"Good morning, miss," he said politely. Jesnake smiled slightly, knowing full well that if any of the Brotherhood had called the princess "miss," they would have received a sharp kick for their attempted courtesy.

"Good morning," she replied. "My mistress sent me for a pound of your best flour."

The miller smiled kindly and left for the storeroom in the back. As soon as he'd left the room, Paige scurried over to where Jesnake was sifting the wheat grains. "How's it coming?" she whispered.

Jesnake leaned closer to Paige, dropping his naturally quiet voice even lower. "Here's the thing; it could be possible, but the probability of achievement is slim."

"Cut the big words, Jesnake," she snapped, looking into the storeroom to make sure the miller was not yet returning. "Can you do it, or can't you?"

The elf rubbed his neck uneasily. "I'd give it a two-to-one chance for unhindered success. Even if I did get out, I couldn't get back into the village to help the others."

"Forget about them. Hanburg has a plan for everyone. You just focus on getting yourself out. But he needs you to wait for his signal," Paige replied, reaching into her moccasin. "You may need this," she finished, slipping a small clasp knife into the elf's hand. He slid it up his baggy sleeve just as the miller returned.

"Here you are, missy," he said, handing her the small sack of flour. Jesnake smiled again. The misguided "missy" had turned Paige's face a shade darker as she paid the miller. She left, glancing once more at Jesnake. The elf allowed himself a slight chuckle as he threw the grain once more into the air. The wheat sounded like rain as it landed neatly back in the metal sieve, half of the chaff blowing away as the breeze wafted through the open door.

Paige exited the mill quickly, her basket weighing her down as she walked one of the dirt paths toward the edge of the village. She had seen half of the company while running these "errands for her mistress." She, Abenya, and Hanburg had schemed for the past four days during Paige's recovery, hashing out a plan that would get them all out within the week. Abenya had a unique talent for healing with herbs, and Paige hadn't felt this well since her adventure had started.

Their plan was simple yet risky; it would be at the mercy of circumstance, since there were so many moving parts. In three days, the village would celebrate the Hallowed Moons Feast to honor the rise of autumn. Abeyna knew that the dances would not be complete without an abundance of good wine and meade, which Paige knew made for slow swords and deep sleep. In the early hours of the morning following the festival, each member of the Brotherhood would attempt his own escape, meeting outside the palisade to disappear into the night. The only difficulty would be coordinating all the escapes to occur within the same hour.

So far, Paige had spoken to Broadside, Duelmaster, and Jesnake. Most of them had some doubts, but were willing to try. Paige trusted his ability to get out, even if the plan failed.

Paige now hurried to see to Robert and Twostaves at the barracks, where they were being held. It was more of a repurposed tool shed than anything, back behind the warrior's quarters. The farmer that bought the pair had spent the previous night getting as drunk as a fish swimming in a whiskey cask. Paige could hear him moaning in one of the longhouses, suffering from what she could only assume was the biggest headache in the history of the world.

Paige walked with her eyes downcast, looking at the path in front of her and wishing to give the impression of a defeated slave girl. Part of her wondered why she bothered, when everyone in town knew Hanburg's anti-slavery beliefs. Most even gave her a nasty look, knowing her to be as free as any of them so long as she lived under Hanburg's protection. But she didn't want to cause a riot over Hanburg's casual 'ownership' of her, so she kept her head low. She was so intent on her appearance that she failed to notice a thin shadow slithering behind her.

"You! Slave!"

Paige recognized Locamnen's voice before she saw him. She tried to continue onward, but the man slid in front of her, blocking her path. "Half-breed, I speak!" the tribesman spat. Although Paige tried to keep calm, the telltale angry flush was creeping up her cheeks. She gritted her teeth, clutching the handle of her basket harder. Her spine began to tingle with foreboding.

"Let me pass, sir. My master is waiting for me," she muttered.

"Do you think me such an idiot? I know that Hanburg has always objected to the ownership of slaves. He treats you just as he does any other member of his house, which means you are free to go as you please. No. No one is waiting for you, my dear."

As Paige's anger rose, Locamnen stepped forward, his foul breath making her turn her head.

"You will listen when I talk," he hissed. Paige noticed a few other men edging in closer to them, and judging by the expressions of contempt they wore, they were not coming to aid her.

"Little slave, you can't avoid me," the spokesman continued. "I am a powerful man and can make life... unfortunate... for your friends."

"Yes, that's why you were so successful in seeing us all executed last week," Paige quipped, taking a step back.

"A minor setback, my dear, I assure you."

"I'll tell you once; get out of my way or things will become unfortunate for you."

"What are you going to do, half-breed? Faint on me?"

Paige's only reply was a sly smile, baring her teeth like a wildcat about to spring. Before the scrawny man could twitch an eyelash, Paige swung her basket with enough force to put a dent in a sheet of iron. The blow caught the weasley man in the side of the head, and he was thrown backwards in a cloud of white powder.

Six other men began to close in on the princess. Last time she'd faced the ruffians in this town, she'd been half-drugged and exhausted; this time she was fully aware of her surroundings, and she had been itching to use her fists. All the anger and rage she'd been harboring since the night her parents died came to a boil. She felt her fists tingling and clenched them in preparation.

The men began to circle around for the kill while Locamnen laid in the dirt. There was a reason her mother named her Alwasu, the Elven word for 'bobcat.' Clearly, these men had never hunted anything like her before.

The first to jump at her was a mere youth that might have had three hairs on his face. As he awkwardly tried to grasp her wrist, he received a snappy punch to the forehead. The second man took no lesson from the first and found himself subdued by a roundabout kick to the stomach. Paige whipped the momentum into a jump kick that sent another to the ground, her heel smashing and breaking the cartilage in the third man's nose.

The remaining three attackers advanced simultaneously. She ducked the first man's blow, clearing a path straight to his comrade's jaw. He spat several of his teeth out and howled in anger. She threw a fist to the windpipe of the first, knocking him back into the last man with a thunderous crash. Both thugs gasped for breath. As the remaining man leapt from behind, Paige snapped her elbow back into his sternum, then thrust her fist up to his wide-eyed face. She heard the crack of the cartilage as she broke her second nose of the day. Long after the strike, she felt the adrenaline surge through her.

"You were saying?"

Locamnen struggled to his feet and returned the stare as he snarled at her like a wounded animal. His voice layered hate with madness.

"You insolent, pathetic—"

He took a step closer but Paige reached behind her and pulled her small knife from her moccasin and held it threateningly. The weasel hesitated a moment, suddenly less sure of himself.

"One day you will be alone, unarmed, and unaware," he growled, a bony finger jutted in the direction of her nose. "And then you will learn a lesson in knowing your place, elfling scum." He spat at her feet then turned and slunk away into a nearby alley.

The princess felt that icy shiver tingle down her spine as a prick of fear stabbed the corner of her heart. Paige shook herself, picking up her crumpled basket off the dirty, flour-covered road. She snuck a peek inside under the lid and pouted. The pies she'd meant to give as bribes to the guards were smashed into a gooey pile of cherry slop. But the loaves of bread she'd made for the lads were still intact. She fixed her hair, muttering chastisement to herself, and decided she would have to make do with what she had. She picked herself up, stretched out the last crick in her neck from the fight, and began jogging quickly to the warrior's barracks.

The dwelling was constructed out of an imposing square of stacked logs, the walls almost two feet thick. Excepting several arrow slits, the small fortress was covered with plaster wood chips and small stones. She approached it carefully, making sure to not stray from the marked path as she rounded the eastern corner towards the back of the barrack's grounds to the giant tool shed her boys were locked up in.

Two large guards equipped with heavy spears and round shields stood at the door. Brave as she was, there were few her size capable of toppling a six-foot-three mass of muscle, much less one armed with a weaponed designed to skewer a full-grown man. Rather than confront them, Paige decided to use a different weapon.

"Good evening, gentlemen," she drawled in the sweetest voice she could muster, dropping into a small curtsey. "I hear you've been out here guarding these slaves all night."

Other than a curt nod, neither responded.

"You must be so tired, standing guard all day!" she said with exaggerated pity. One of the guards grunted, and Paige continued, "I thought you might be in need of refreshment."

She opened the basket and carefully pulled out the bowl containing the remnants of what had once been a beautiful cherry pie with golden crust.

"I was so clumsy, I'm afraid it's a bit... smushed. It's a wild-cherry pie that Lady Abenya made. She wanted me to give it to you."

"Right nice of Lady Abenya," one of the guards remarked. "I'm sure it all tastes the same. Vlet, you have a spoon in your kit?"

"I'm sure I could have the wife bring me a couple. Just set the bowl over on that table," the other guard huffed. Paige did so carefully before reaching into the basket again.

"She also sent me with some fresh bread for the prisoners."

She showed them the rather large loaf of plain brown bread that was smeared with little bits of cherry pie filling. The guards looked uneasy, shifting uncomfortably. Paige smiled sweetly and batted her eyelashes just like Olivian used to back home.

"I don't know…" said one guard. "Maybe we should check with the Cap'n."

Paige tried to put on a pout.

"Please? It's just a loaf of bread. All I want is to see them for a moment."

One of them simply rolled his eyes. She felt like an idiot; these weren't young boys that would fall for girlish charm. If one could even call what she was doing "charming."

"Look," she said, dropping all pretense of sweetness, setting the basket down and placing her fists on her hips. "I've had a long day. I brought this pie all the way across town and had to beat that stupid, sniveling Locamnen and his little posse to a bloody pulp. All I want to do is give my mates something to lift their spirits, and I'm happy to stand here and wait as long as it takes because I've already whipped seven other people today."

The guards looked skeptical, but the first scratched his ruddy beard in interest.

"You punched a Councilman in the face?"

"He was extremely rude," Paige snapped. "Needed to be taught a lesson. Hence the smashed pie."

"Yeah, that sounds about right," the first guard muttered.

"I hate that prick," the other guard said with a chuckle.

Paige tapped her foot dramatically as the guards exchanged a look.

"Alright," the second one said finally, reaching for his keys to let her inside. "But make it quick."

The first thing that she noticed was the darkness. The little light of the arrow slits allowed her elf-like sensitivity to discern shapes through the pitch black. Then the smell hit her, a foul mixture of mold, wet plaster, mildew, thick sweat, and rotting wood. She gagged, trying hard to keep her breakfast down.

"Thank you ever so much, gentlemen. You're too kind. Really, Paige?" She couldn't see him, but Paige knew Robert well enough to picture his smirk. She strained her eyes in the darkness, and was rewarded with the shape of two bulky forms chained by the south wall. As she made her way over to them, she stumbled over the uneven floor scattered with farming equipment and assorted junk.

"Are you both alive?" she asked, tripping over a mule plow.

"No," mocked Twostaves. Paige rolled her eyes. She had thought the driver might have whipped some of the cockiness out of them. Fat chance, it turned out.

"Shame, guess you'll have to share the bread," she said dryly, a trace of annoyance in her voice.

"How sweet! Do we get tea to go with it? And maybe some of those kiwi slices from the Eastern jungles, while you're at it!?" Robert snapped. She threw the bread at the shape she decided must be Robert's head.

"Ouch! Hey! What gives?" yelped Twostaves.

"Sorry, that would be the two spades we baked into the bread." She smirked.

"Spades? Really?" Robert said, skeptical.

"That's our plan. You have a better one?"

"What plan!? Giving us two shovels the size of a squirrel's pelvic bone to tunnel out of here is not much of a plan!"

"Would you rather I snag one of the large ones off that wall over there and hope they don't notice you using it to dig a hole?"

"She has a point, Robert," Twostaves noted. "We can keep these concealed on our person much easier, and if someone bursts in we can pitch them a lot faster than we could those clumsy wood shovels."

Paige glanced at the door nervously. "I've only got a few minutes, so you two dunderheads listen up, you hear me?"

Neither of the dark shapes made any further commentary.

"Right. Hanburg said there is no real foundation to this building. The logs are set straight into the earth, so you could burrow right under it like a weasel in a hen house."

"And then what? How are we to get past the gates or up over the wall. Have you thought of that?"

"Do you need me to draw up an itinerary for you?" Paige spat. "There are ladders you could steal from the outbuildings, a pile of crates, pole vault with a wagon tongue, I don't care! That is going to be up to you two."

"Alright, fine. We'll improvise. What about once we're over the wall?"

"Head back towards the south. If you come to a dry creek bed, turn and go along it till you get to the crest of a gully. There is a clearing at the base of it with a large tree in the middle. That's our rendezvous point."

"And how long will we all wait before heading out?"

"When everyone gets there, naturally."

"I mean, what if complications arise? What if one of us gets caught? How will the others know we're in trouble?"

"Hanburg won't let that happen. We'll all get out. We just have to focus on the timing is all."

"He has a point," Twostaves interjected. "Say one group gets trapped. What will the other group do?"

"Well, like you said," Paige said, tucking a loose strand of hair behind her ear. "We'll improvise."

"Alwasu," Robert said, his voice tight with frustration. "We have to consider the very real possibility that one or more of our group might not get away. Are you prepared to move ahead if that happens?"

Paige glared at him. It was a problem she was all too familiar with, but she refused to believe they would fail like that. They couldn't afford to.

"Let's hope and pray it doesn't come to that," she said finally. After pausing a moment, Robert shook his head.

"It's daft."

"Yeah, well, this whole adventure is daft. That's kind of why you brought me to this lot."

A pounding on the door warned the princess that her time was drawing to a to a close.

"I must go. I have one more loaf to get to Din," she said, jumping up to exit the barracks. She groped her way to the door, ready to return to the beautiful sunlight beyond the stuffy, thick walls of the shed.

"Paige?" Twostaves called meekly.

She hesitated. "Yes?"

"Can we still eat the bread?"

CHAPTER 10

WHISPERS IN THE

DARK

*D*inendale peered through a crack in the door while he waited for the streets to quiet. He resided in one of the coal storage sheds behind the blacksmith's shop with nothing more than a hole-riddled wool blanket. The buildings of the village barely housed the villagers themselves, much less separate slave quarters. Because of this, the slaves were often times locked up in the shops in which they served. Dinendale was lucky. His master had chained one of his legs to the wall, but it was better than the complete shackling he'd been told some of the other masters practiced. Despite the predicament, Dinendale knew his fortune. This was being treated well compared to a slave of the empire; tea and crumpets compared to what he had once endured. He touched his forehead and felt the jagged scar tissue, his constant reminder of Shauden cruelty.

It had been three days since Paige had stopped by the shop for Hanburg's hinge. She'd sweet-talked a young apprentice into allowing him a "humble loaf" which, unknown to the young smith, hid a small chisel. Dinendale had found this out the hard way, much to his incisor's dismay. Though his tooth hurt, Dinendale felt grateful for the tool since each night the blacksmith polished and then locked away every chisel, swage, punch, and drift he owned.

Through the cracks in the wood planking of the coal shed, he could see the people gathered in the square. The sun set over the village. The people gathered tonight for the Hallowed Moons Feast in the center of town. The drums and pipes began to play gaily, and Dinendale had only to wait for the people to finish congregating at the center of town to enact his escape plan.

The elf had to hand it to Hanburg – the man was a genius. He had planned the massive escape heist for all of them in a matter of a few days, and had thought out every detail. If they succeeded, Dinendale would risk a later trip to this village to personally thank the councilman. If they didn't succeed... well that wasn't an option he could accept. After all, he'd busted out of worse dungeons than this tiny coal shed. And they had run out of time.

The stream of people began to die down as the panpipe and fiddle music penetrated the still night air. Dinendale pulled the tiny chisel from the crack in the stone wall where it had been hidden for the past few days. He slid as close to the back door as his leg shackle would allow him, looking carefully at the door hinge and preparing to enact his plan. The dark elf took a deep breath, then began to work the chisel into the pin on the hinge.

Paige and Abenya sat for a moment's rest after having helped the townspeople prepare for the feast all day. Watching the people gather in this manner brought swirling memories of the night her parents died. So many customs here reminded her of the home she no longer had. She and Abenya gazed at the rows of plank tables outside the council house, set to accommodate the entire village. This evening they all would feast on the rich food that cooked on every hearth in the town. White deer hides covered the tables, each hide decorated with small chestnut branches still sprinkled with their reddish-brown nuts. The fire roared in the center of town a little before sunset.

As the throngs of villagers gathered, Paige looked in awe at the array of dress; bright colors and woven tapestries of fine cloth adorned each person. Old women hobbling with canes and young toddlers barely able to walk without holding to their mothers' skirts showed off their festive attire. Red poinsettias decorated nearly every flat surface in the village center, while evergreen boughs wrapped around every post. Paige licked her lips as she saw tables laden with all assortments of meats, both skewered and grilled, on large circular iron grates.

Abenya had loaned Paige a dress of the purest white buckskin adorned with innumerable blue and sea-green beads. The beadwork formed shapes and swirls reminiscent of the riverbeds that dotted the Wild's highlands. The garment's sleeves fit to Paige's arm, from the shoulder to just past her elbow where they widened and draped to expose her forearms. She looked down at the painted tattoos drawn by one of Hanburg's neighbors. Paige's key shone brightly against the white dress as the flickering firelight licked her pale skin. Her hair was braided and wrapped around her head like a turban of coiled blonde rope.

"I can't tell you enough times how amazing that dress looks on you," gushed Abenya. Her own dress looked equally radiant, made from dyed scarlet cloth with gold trim and a mink fur collar. She gave a quick spin, enjoying the motion of the tasseled sleeves and the swirl of the heavily layered skirts. Paige blushed and shrugged.

"I've never really been one for dresses," she muttered.

Abenya smiled sweetly. "Not to worry. You'll be back in your old clothes very soon," she whispered, taking Paige's hand and patting it reassuringly.

Paige felt a tap on her right shoulder and turned to see a young villager with curly red hair and a face full of freckles. His dancing green eyes creased with his large, toothy smile. The lad couldn't have been any older than fourteen, but he grinned at the foreigner girl with zealous confidence.

"Yes?"

"I'm Cloudlah Yarven," he introduced himself taking a slight bow. He wore tan buckskin trousers held up by brown leather bracers over a crisp white shirt, with a golden sash tied around his waist.

Paige forced an awkward smile. "Paige," she replied, polite but utterly jargoggled. His grin broadened.

"Would you give me the honor of this dance?" he asked.

Paige's half smile froze on her face as she glanced to Abenya for help.

"Just one dance won't hurt," Abenya said with a knowing look. "We have a little time to kill. It'd be best if witnesses saw you in the open."

Paige couldn't believe she was even suggesting this, but the girl motioned her forward.

"Can't be at a dance and not dance, right?" Abenya nudged, and Paige tried to hide her nervousness behind an incredulous gasp.

"But, Abenya," she started to protest, but the girl shoved her forward with a grin. The boy pulled Paige towards the

291

dancing circle. The flute and lyre players whipped up a lively tune, while a worried, foreboding sense settled into Paige's stomach.

She felt out-of-place in the ring of dancers twirling around the fire. The drums thundered as she and Cloudlah spun in unison. Memories of her recent tragedy began flooding back, and it seemed that every time she spun about, Derak's face flashed before her. The image was not there of course, disappearing and leaving her with the grinning, red-haired youth before her. The music was new and the steps were slightly different from how she had learned them, but the activity wrent her heart in twain as the emotions hit her with a vengeance. Paige swallowed as she thought on how she would never see home again. In contrast, the curly-haired youth was enjoying himself immensely. The exotic girl in the village was dancing with him. All his friends gawked while their own partners looked as if they'd each taken a swig of soured milk.

At last the drumming stopped. Paige nodded politely to Cloudlah, eager to leave. She hurried back to Abenya, who smiled broadly.

"What?" Paige demanded sullenly.

Abenya hid a giggle. "Nothing," she smiled. "But you caught every young man's eye out there."

Paige's jaw dropped in disbelief. She turned and noticed several young fellows starting towards them.

"Abenya!" Paige hissed, "Do you have any idea of how badly this could compromise things?" The girl's smile waned as three young men approached them. Paige looked to Abenya for a rescue.

"May I have this dance, miss?" asked the first fellow. Paige could only nod, numb. As the young man led her into the circle, she glanced once more at Abenya. Realization blanched the girl's face. How would Paige slip away now?

"Come on!" Dinendale grunted, to no one in particular. The elf had the chisel wedged in the pin that secured the door hinge. The smith hadn't been joking; they were extremely well made. Just a little more and...there! He had it. Once he'd pushed it past the tight spot, the pin slipped through like a hot knife through a block of fresh cheese. Dinendale smiled, satisfied. He had only one more to go before scaling the wall to freedom.

He paused a moment as he looked at his dirty, rough hands holding the small chisel. It wasn't too long ago he had been escaping the very prison he was now escaping to return to. Was he absolutely out of his mind?

If he was honest with himself, there was a tiny part of him that wanted to get out and run in the opposite direction as far as he could. The hell he had been through at the hands of Shauden masters had left scar tissue all over his body and across his spirit. He'd spent months feeling hollow and empty after clawing his way to freedom from that stone chasm, as if the gaping maw of that castle's gates had taken a bite out of his soul as he left it beyond the horizon.

But there was more at stake here than his own personal fears and trauma. There was an innocent girl being held captive in a place where he'd already lost one friend. He knew what would happen to Olivian if he left now. There was also the matter of this ancient page that Feridar was so desperate to get his hands on. Dinendale couldn't leave Paige to bear that burden alone.

"Get over yourself," the elf muttered to himself, rising to his feet, ready to split the last hinge.

Jesnake felt squeamish. The trough was the only means of escape available. One chance, that was it. If he messed up, he was dead. If he didn't try, he was as good as dead. He slid his hand across the aged wood of the water trough. Pine, strong and durable.

As the miller closed the shop, Jesnake had stashed a rolling pin in the barrel of wheat still waiting to be ground. When the miller left, Jesnake retrieved it, waiting until he was quite sure all the people had left his area of the village. Once the soft sound of drums fluttered through the air, he deftly jammed the wooden rolling pin into the steel waterwheel, stopping it temporarily. The water began spilling out over the sides of the trough, washing the dust from the floor away as it headed to the door.

Jesnake took a quick breath as he drew the knife Paige had given him. This could go horribly wrong. If someone noticed the water pouring into the streets, it could blow the entire plan. He hesitated for one moment, then swung himself as high into the trough as he could reach.

The freezing water rushed down, biting at his fingers as the elf sank his blade deep into the pine. He hadn't realized how forceful the current truly was. It soaked his sackcloth shirt and trousers, making them heavy. He gritted his teeth and began to inch forward, grasping the side of the trough with his left hand as he withdrew the knife. Reaching forward as far as he could with his right hand, Jesnake once again stabbed the knife deep into the wood. Pulling himself up as far as he could, he repeated the process over and over, concentrating on the rhythm.

Reach, stab, pull.

In only a few moments, he'd climbed fifteen feet, almost to the top.

Reach. Stab. Pull.

He took his time and held his breath until he had pulled himself to the knife and wedged himself to a point he could take a breath. He dug his slender toes into the swelling hemp of his sandals, making sure to put pressure into them to keep them from slipping off; they were the only thing giving him traction in the slick trough.

Reach. Stab. Pull.

Only one more stab to go before the elf could reach the small opening. He smiled in spite of himself.

Reach. Stab. Pull.

"At last," he whispered, triumph edging his voice. He pulled his left foot up to get a grip until suddenly, his world shifted from dreamland to nightmare. In his excitement to be finished with his climb, he moved too quickly and one of his hemp sandals slipped off his foot. It had soaked up the water like an oil lamp's wick and now slid heavily towards the strained wheel. The sandal thudded against the carefully-wedged rolling pin, and Jesnake heard it snap, offset by the sandal and shattering under the force of the current against the blocked water wheel. Slowly, the gears began to spin, and the groaning of the giant millstones echoed forebodingly in the small mill.

Their motion caused the trough to vibrate, and the knife blade slipped out of the water-softened wood. Jesnake slid downwards. His heartbeat went ballistic. He clawed desperately at the slick wood as he fell towards the razor-sharp wheels.

Robert heard the beating of drums afar-off as he pressed his ear to the dirty barracks wall. With sweaty palm, he grasped the wooden handle of the small trowel. The sleepless work of the past few days was about to pay off. He nudged the dosing Twostaves. The lowland giant moaned in protest.

"Come on, Eöl, let a chap have some rest!"

"Get up!" hissed Robert. "We haven't spent the past nights digging under the wall for nothing!"

"The hole isn't ready!" Twostaves yawned nonchalantly. "It's not deep enough to roll under, and too small to squeeze through."

"We can make it, but we need to move NOW!"

"Why?"

"Because, you lumpy lard-jar, the guards just went for their rum. We'll have a few minutes tops."

Twostaves snorted. He didn't appreciate being compared to a lump of lard, but he was used to Robert's constant run of insulting comparisons.

"What about the leg shackles?" Twostaves said, shaking his chained ankles.

Robert sighed, agitated.

"Last time they locked us up, I slipped a pebble in the mechanism on mine. It kept the lock from closing all the way."

"Great!" said the giant. "What about me?" Robert thought a moment. He should have known the other wouldn't think this out for himself.

"Here," he said, pulling the other shovel and tossing it to the fellow. "Once we're safe and out in the woods, our dear little dwarf can knock them off or something."

The giant muttered something about being big enough to do things himself, but Robert ignored him. He quickly crawled to the small hole under the barracks wall, which led through the shallow dirt and plaster. Robert threw back the rat-gnawed tarp that hid their trench and smiled with smug satisfaction. This was going to make a great story someday.

He and Twostaves wormed their way into the shallow trough of moist, gritty earth. The giant had been right; it was a tight fit. Robert puffed as he shoved himself as far into their 'masterpiece' as he could. As near as they could figure, they had about half-a-foot of dirt left. Robert hoped to break through the last little bit of earth so that the pair could sneak along the wall until they got to a drain grate. Paige had assured them it would be an easy matter to break the wooden grate and join the others in the woods.

The most delicate part of the plan was the timing. If they waited too long, they would lose the distraction the feast had given them. But if they left too soon, the lingering twilight could pose the problem of being easily spotted.

"Ready?," breathed Robert. The giant nodded. Robert took a deep breath and thrust his spade against the soil.

In a matter of seconds, his fist smashed through the dirt. He inhaled the sweet night air, but he wasted no more than a moment on sentiment; if he didn't hurry, it wouldn't be a long breath. As he wormed his way out of the tiny hole, his shirt caught against the log wall of the barracks like sandpaper on splintery maple. Pushing his arms out of the tunnel, Robert grunted as he pulled himself out, then stopped abruptly.

"Go! Go! What are you waiting for?" urged the anxious Twostaves behind him in a hushed whisper. But Robert didn't move a hair in response. He didn't feel like exchanging sarcastic comments with a huge tribal guard aiming a sharp bone arrowhead at his forehead.

Jesnake slid down the chute so fast, he thought for sure that the blades would shred his body into ribbons. He had briefly prepared to meet his maker, when miracle of miracles, he heard the clink as the knife fell into the fast moving wheels. It had fallen faster than the elf, being scooped up by the spinning blades and thrown into the works of the mill as the blades came to a grinding halt. The water, having nowhere to flow now, began spilling over the side.

Jesnake slid to a halt only inches from the end of the trough. He sat stunned for a moment, then breathed a sigh of relief. That was close. Far too close. Jenake had endured his fair share of close encounters and narrow escapes in battle, but he couldn't recall a moment in time he had come that close to death. The elf took a long, haggard breath and waited a moment for his pulse to relax. Then, he turned back to the trough and slowly grasped the sides. With one more look back at the large, still water-wheel and grinding stones, he clutched the sides of the the slick trough and pulled himself up once again.

His progress slowed exponentially due partly to the fact that he was getting colder, and now he didn't have the knife or the traction of his sandal. He slowly pulled himself up the chute once again, reaching around the outside of the trough and grasping at the driest part of the boards he could find. It was slow-going and excruciating on his arms, and he clamped down as hard as he could while reaching around as far as he could manage. Eventually he grasped the opening at the top of the roof. It was slick with green algae, but his shakey grip held. With his last ounce of energy, he hauled his slim body out into to night air and rolled over onto his back.

He rested for several moments, facing the sky as he breathed heavily, the two crescent moons of Eirensgarth smiling down at him. Or were they frowning at him, he wondered. It all depended on his perspective. A meteor flashed across the midnight-blue pallor of the heavens, and Jesnake felt peaceful for the first time in many months. He let the cold water run over his shoulders. It felt more refreshing now, less icy and foreboding.

He would have stayed like that for a while longer, had not the sound of feet shuffling across gravel caught his attention. For a brief moment, he thought it had merely been his mind playing tricks upon him in the wake of his death-defying escape. Then a second scraping sound confirmed the reality of something else.

There was definitely someone below him. He caught his breath and held perfectly still. Soon, slithering whispers reached his ears from beyond the gurgling of the water in the trough. Jesnake strained to catch the hushed tones by lifting his head ever so gently out of the water.

"Is everything ready?" hissed one voice, unrecognizable to the elf. It sounded like someone had slashed the man's voice box with a dagger.

"Yes, Seren," hissed another. Jesnake had no trouble recognizing the voice belonging to Locamnen. "As soon as the party dies down, you will have your prisoners."

Jesnake felt his heart stop. His chest went heavy when he recognized the tell-tale 'clink' of chainmail moving. No one in the village wore chainmail that Jesnake had seen. The guards here wore fur and some leather plate-armor. The only rational explanation sent a knot through Jesnake's abdomen, a knot he was used to feeling. Fear.

A Shaud would have chainmail. And if he was a Seren, or captain, there would be at least fifty men under him, if not a hundred.

"We only need the girl," said the seren in guttural tones. "The others are expendable."

"You will have her, my friend," muttered Locamnen, his voice slithering through the air like a viper in tall grass. "But you will recall that our agreement, expendable or not, was a lump sum for a lump bunch of prisoners."

"I know very well the terms of our arrangement, you piece of backwater slime," the captain hissed. "Just be sure they are delivered by dawn's first light tomorrow, in the glade just south of the village. If you prove false, I am certain I will laugh over your grave as I burn your home and all your possessions to the ground."

"No need to worry on that account," Locamnen assured. "My services for coin. That was our deal."

"As if I would seriously trust a deal at your word."

"That is of no consequence to me, Raven head," Locamnen slithered. "I'm the only one who can get you what you want."

You blaggard-hearted, soulless piece of trash, Jesnake snarled in his head. No honor. There was no honor to be found in a single fiber of this man's being. Jesnake would have loved nothing more than to drop down and strangle this human with his bare hands. Evidently the captain held him in an almost equal amount of disdain.

"You simpering weasel, the only reason you're still alive is it is significantly cheaper for me to just pay you to usher the girl out than it is to raise this place to the ground. But do not think for one moment the thought of this place in a state of alarm worries me in the slightest. I would burn you and every soul in it alive on an altar to the gods before you even had time to string a bow. Do not test me."

"Just bring the coin, and you won't have to trouble yourself with such thoughts. One hour. Behind the storehouse. Don't be late."

Jesnake heard the crunch of the earth under steel-plated boots and leather sandals as the two walked away. He waited for a moment to make sure they had gone, then slid over onto his belly again. The water of the trough tickled his chin as he began to force himself through towards the wall where he could escape the confines of the stockade. All pain was forgotten; he had to get out and warn the others before it was too late.

The guard sneered at Robert with a dose of smugness as he leveled the arrow shaft at his prisoner's forehead. Robert gulped. The man seemed as solid as an oak tree, and his yew bow pulled at least seventy pounds at full draw. The man held it steadily at a full pull without so much as a twitch.

"Nice try," hissed the archer.

"Uh... Hello!" croaked Robert. Well, that was dumb, he thought to himself. In his panic he had no idea what else he could say. His breath came out in hard gasps as sweat protruded from his brow in massive drops. He'd felt this kind of fear only a few times in his life, but somehow he mustered a smile.

"Wild party, eh?" said Robert in a shaky voice.

The guard grinned slyly. "I'll say," the guard said, not even blinking.

"Sure you don't want to join in the festivities?"

"Sure do," the man snapped. "But some of us have a job to do."

" How inconvenient for us...."

"Agreed," hissed the guard as he aimed the deadly arrow just off to the left of Robert's sternum area. "But if you were to be shot while escaping, I wouldn't have to be here standing guard now would I?"

Robert wondered how much he would be able to feel before his body registered the shock to his brain and his entire system shut down. He closed his eyes for the impact and sickening 'thud' sure to follow. He silently prayed that Paige would make it out safe.

THWACK!

Robert's eyes flew open, and he beheld the arrow still quivering only a hair's breadth above his left shoulder. He looked up to see the guard out cold on the dirt pathway, crumpled like a broken spider. Behind him was a medium sized man, completely covered in a deep, pine-green cloak. His hood was pulled over his eyes, and he held a staff. But within the time it took for him to blink, the figure vanished completely, leaving only an unconscious guard to show he had been there at all.

Present or not, Robert realized that the stranger had just given him an opportunity to escape. He wiggled out as fast as he was able, then plastered himself against the wall of the barracks.

"What happened!?" Twostaves demanded, wriggling his head out of the tiny hole and seeing the crumpled guard, now immobilized.

"We have a 'friendly' watching over us apparently," Robert said, brushing the loose dirt off his clothes.

"Wow, that was close," Twostaves whispered as he hauled himself out of the hole. The sound of a group of men laughing sent them into a faster pace as they skipped over to the outer wall. They chose a pile of weathered and forgotten boxes near the barracks toolshed to hide them as they rested a moment. Twostaves and Robert attempted silence as best as their heaving would allow as they peeked from their hiding spot.

"Who do you think that was?" Twostave's big eyes darting about for more potential danger.

"Don't know, don't care. All I know is that whoever he is the only reason we both aren't living pincushions."

Twostaves started to let out his obnoxious laugh, but Robert managed to smash a hand over the giant's mouth. Twostaves stopped, and they held their breath as the sound of the partying guards came closer.

"What in heaven's name are you trying to do?" Twostaves demanded as Robert tried to plaster himself to the wall.

"Trying to blend in," hushed Robert, sucking in his gut.

"Eöl, have you ever seen a red tree-monkey try to hide on a tree trunk covered in green moss?"

"Are you implying what I think you are? Because if you are implying what I think you are implying, then you'd better imply something else, because I'm about to imply something like my fist into your face."

"I'm just saying, it's no use trying to flatten your-"

Robert cut him off.

"We forgot to stash the guard!" he hissed. He smacked his head with his hand over and over. Twostaves grew a shade paler, and they popped their heads up from above the pile of crates. But the body of the unconscious man was gone. For a moment, Robert feared that he'd gotten up and was stumbling back to his comrades. But then he saw a pair of leather-clad feet poking out of the hole they had just come from.

"A friendly, indeed," Twostaves muttered. "Come on Eöl, we aren't out of the frying pan yet!"

Dinendale stole around one of the huts as quietly as he could manage. He warily glanced behind him, his dark brown eyes surveying the area for any potential dangers. The air was filled with the soft lilt of far-off laughter, and Dinendale made it a point to run away from it as he stole from wall to wall. He stood fifty yards from the stockade, the only barrier between him and his freedom. Haunting memories followed him as the all too familiar stress of performing an escape from slavery gripped his chest. Dinendale swallowed the feeling. He couldn't afford to be weighed down now.

After checking once more for potential witnesses, he slipped out of the shadows and scampered to the log walls of the stockade. He stood still only for a moment, gazing up at the nine foot barricade that barred his path. Dinendale leapt against the wall, driving his chisel deep into the soft pine. With cool smoothness, he slid up and over the edge of the wall. He dropped to the grass below, landing on the balls of his feet like a panther. Then, with one last hurried look at his old prison, Dinendale padded off into the wood.

Paige's unease only mounted as the festivities wore on. No matter how hard she tried, the same three boys kept coming to dance with her: the foreign novelty. She'd never been much for vanity, but tonight she was wishing she was a bit uglier. She had to get out. She felt as trapped than her friends currently in chains. If she didn't get free soon, she could leave the boys stranded and defenseless in the middle of the wood.

Her latest suitor was grinning ear to ear with a set of teeth too big for his head. She had tried to slip out three different times during the dance, but every time he found her before she could get out of the circle. After what seemed like ages, the drums began to slow and she saw her window of opportunity. She nodded and curtsied to the boy and hastened out of the circle.

"We have to go," she hissed to Abenya. "This was a stupid idea. We should have stuck to the plan."

"We'll be fine." Abenya said, but Paige glared at her.

"We're wasting time. If I don't break away now, we'll run the risk of losing the window I need to-"

A tap on her shoulder interrupted her.

"Excuse me miss," started a young man with blond bangs and freckles as he stepped forward, but the princess was done trying to exit gracefully.

"No!" she snapped, trying to walk around the fellow.

"I insist!" he tried to press. With a quick movement, Paige sidestepped out of his waiting hand as another dancing couple blocked the boy's view. She dipped and wove in between couples and into the crowd on the other side of the firelay. In that moment, she dove behind a stack of crates to the side of a banquet table.

She peeked out to see if she could see Abenya. The girl was on the right side of the fire lay, about ten yards off, searching for Paige in the sea of dancers. Paige waited until Abenya was standing only a few yards away before she moved out of the shadows slightly. The light of the fire cast a golden glow across her eyes. Abenya saw her and quickly stepped between her and the boy still searching for her.

"Where are you off to, Henrick!?" Abenya piped up in a cheerful bantering tone.

"Abenya!"

While the girl was blocking the young man from Paige's view, an older man, one of the village elders, strode over to her. Paige felt a pang of panic. Abenya was supposed to be her backup in getting over the stockade wall.

"Yes, Lord Butterly?" the girl asked. The older man gestured for her to come to him. Behind her back, Abenya made a motion for Paige to go on ahead. The princess hesitated, but realizing that Abenya wasn't going to be able to break away easily, she seized the opportunity and silently slipped between the houses.

Paige stole across the deserted streets as dark. The cold night drowned the warmth and cheer of the bonfire in a frosty mist. The village was a ghost town with all the people out at the feasting fires and banquet tables, so much like that terrible night back home. She began to weave her way in and out of alleys towards the place she knew she would have to enact her own escape plan, unaware of the slippery shadow skulking deftly in and out of the darkness behind her.

Robert and Twostaves huffed and puffed as they pounded their feet through the forest vegetation. They now made for the rendezvous point, slowed by Twostaves' shackled legs.

"Where were we supposed to meet?" heaved the giant, struggling to keep moving.

"Paige said there was a small clearing to the east. There's an oak tree in the middle," Robert heaved as they barreled through the dense underbrush of the Wild's highlands.

They continued on for several minutes. However, the woods didn't seem to thin out into a clearing the further in they went. On the contrary, they seemed to thicken. Robert began to question the accuracy of Paige's information.

"Now, if I were a clearing in the middle of the thickest, darkest forest this side of the Whisperwood" he pondered, "Where would I be?"

Suddenly, the ground beneath Robert's feed shifted and crumbled, and he felt himself begin to topple forward. They tried to regain a semblance of balance, but to no avail as they plummeted down a steep hill, their rolling, bashing bodies making a thunderous commotion as they cascaded in a living avalanche. For the second time that evening, Robert was sure they were going to die. But just as suddenly as they had fallen, they rolled to a stop at the bottom of a ravine.

"*Ooohhhoooooooooowwwww,*" the giant heaved.

"I'd be at the bottom of a gorge," spat Robert, finishing his earlier thought.

He picked himself up, brushing the dead leaves and dirt off his rough sack clothes. They had crashed into a large clearing at the base of the surrounding hills. Lo and behold, in the center of the clearing stood a large oak tree.

"Talk about a grand entrance, sir," said a voice near the tree. The two turned to see Hanburg, chuckling at the base of a boulder, one of many strewn about the clearing. Robert limped over to him, Twostaves stumbling behind mumbling about not being a "ball and chain." Robert didn't care.

"Where is everyone else?" he demanded. Hanburg looked about in answer, his eyes concerned but his brow not yet worried.

"They should be here shortly. Come, I have your gear."

They followed him to the tree where he had several large rough-cloth sacks hidden in a low branch.

"Hey! That bag looks familiar. Oh yeah," Robert scoffed, "I'm wearing one just like it!"

"I am truly sorry," Hanburg said in disgust. "For years I have opposed the slavery customs of my people. But people don't change when they are set in their ways."

"That's not unique to your people," Twostaves said. "Humans in general seem to have an issue with change."

"Agreed," Hanburg nodded, opening the sack and scrounging around. "Ah, here are your things, noble giant."

He produced the white tunic, iron breastplate, targe, and double-link mail coat. The giants staves were cleaned and sealed with fresh beeswax by the look of them. In a heartbeat, Twostaves used one of the metal tips of his weapons to bludgeon open the last remnant of his bonds. He then excused himself to go change in the thicket.

"And here's your gear," Hanburg said, untying another sack. He tossed Robert his gold belt and soft brown robe. As much as Robert had wished it had not been recovered, it was a welcome change to the coarse sackcloth he had now. He pulled it on over his head and turned to see Hanburg holding out his spear.

"This," the man admired, "is one of the finest pieces I have ever had the privilege to hold." He handed Robert the weapon, which had been diligently been polished and oiled.

"Thank you," Robert said, taking the weapon. "It was the only thing my father ever left for me."

Hanburg smiled. "I'm sure he knew you would use it to accomplish great things."

Robert shrugged. He didn't like talking about his father; it bore the weight of too many questions Robert had no answers for.

"Eöl!" a voice cried out in panic. Robert whirled around just in time to see a drenched and heaving elf burst through the clearing. Robert had never seen Jesnake wet, nor panicked, but to see both at the same time alarmed him.

"What on earth?" Robert shouted.

The elf stumbled to them at full speed then collapsed five feet away from him.

"Get up, we can't dally!" Robert said, jogging over to him and helping to pull the heaving creature to his feet.

"Eöl-" the elf coughed. Robert hauled him up and began dragging him.

"I know brother, just a little bit further and you can-"

"*Eöl!*" The elf pulled away and waved his hands frantically.

"What!?"

"The princess," Jesnake gasped. "It's a trap!"

CHAPTER 11

THE PAST

IN THE SHADOWS

𝒫aige slid behind a wagon for a rest. From her vantage point, she could see the stockade wall. She smiled with relief. All she had to do was make it to the stack of crates Hanburg had assured her would be next to the wall, use them to climb over the stockade, then rendezvous with the rest of the Brotherhood at the clearing he'd described.

She peeked around the wagon wheel to make sure she was still alone, trying to calm her ragged, nervous breathing. The deserted street sat silently in front of her. The princess slowly rose to a crouched position, taking care not to rustle the straw that was scattered on the ground. She tiptoed towards the wall, her last barricade before her long awaited freedom.

A twig snapped behind her. Paige froze halfway through her step. She turned her head slightly, looking over her shoulder. Nothing. The night sounded quiet save for the sounds of merrymaking on the other side of the village. It might have been an animal. Then again, it might not. She thought for a brief moment, then decided that even if it was an animal, she wasn't going to take the chance that it was a villager. She took off, her moccasins skimming the hard-packed dirt and straw as she bolted for the stack of crates. She was only a score of yards away now. All she had to do was make it to the bottom box, then she could use her speed to propel her forward and up. If she could only manage to grab the tops of the stockade logs, she could leap up and over the top of the fence. She pumped her legs, closing the distance between herself and salvation.

CRASH!

She lost her footing as a figure stepped out of the shadows, tripping her with what felt like a long pole. She tumbled head first and scrambled to get up onto her feet. An iron grip latched onto her ankle and dragged her backwards. She clawed at the dirt and straw, only grasping hands full of matted heather as they pulled her back into the shadows of an alley. She felt her arm being wrenched behind her back and a bony knee pressing her to the ground.

"Hello missy," a voice slithered, one she knew all too well.

Locamnen. No! She struggled to get away from his vicious hold.

He squeezed harder and flattened her chest into the dirt. "You are mine now. You have no one else to save you, and you won't get a chance to try anything like last time," he smirked.

She kept struggling until she felt the icy blade of a knife catch her throat. He chuckled as he yanked her onto her side, her free arm now pinned between her body and the earth. She glared sideways as the vile creature held his gleaming knife just under her jawbone

"What now, you mix-blood halfling wench?"

In response, Paige wrenched her body in the opposite direction. As she moved, she felt the blade glance along the back of her neck. She felt panic and instinct seize her. Her limbs tingled with a newfound energy. She wrenched her arm free and walloped Locamnen in the side. The man gave a startled cry as he tumbled off her, giving Paige the opening she needed. She slammed her heel into his lower abdomen. He gasped, releasing her as he doubled over.

She turned to run, but felt his talon-like fingers grip her around her throat. Her cut burned as his bony fingers manhandled her until he could get her in a stranglehold. Paige thrashed about trying to get loose, but his fingers constricted like a coiled boa, cutting off her oxygen supply. She gasped for breath as he pushed her up against a longhouse wall, slamming her face into the rough wood.

"Gold or no gold, I'm sick of dealing with you!" he hissed, a mad fire in his eyes. "And they never made me swear you would be alive when I delivered you."

Paige felt lightheaded now. She needed air. She tried once more to get free, wriggling and kicking backwards like a mule but he held firm. She found herself panicking knowing that Klaíomh wasn't pinned into her hair even if she could reach it.

"Pity," Locamnen mocked, nuzzling her pointed ears with his hot, sweaty beak of a nose. "Such a pretty face had to be tainted by pointed ears."

Paige thought she heard someone calling out, but her vision was fading in and out. She could only describe what she beheld as black wisps of smoke before her eyes. There was a sound of a shout followed by a sickly slice. She felt Locamnen's grip slacken enough for her to gasp a breath. As she gulped air into her lungs, Paige turned to see the wide eyes of her attacker. A sickly pale look spread out across his face. He coughed, blood sprinking from his mouth onto her face. She recoiled in shock. His grip released her neck.

Paige slumped to the ground. She looked up. A blade protruded from Locamnen's chest, physically lifting the devil off the ground. A sickening sound resonated as the razor edge pulled back through his bony chest. Locamnen fell backwards. Paige felt her vision fog up as she hit the dirt. Her head reeled as she fought for consciousness then succumbed to the darkness.

Robert crashed through the forest. Only a half hour earlier, he'd been trying to get away from the village. Now his sole purpose was to get back so he could save Paige. He charged ahead, not flinching at the countless branches stinging his face and tearing at his hastily fastened robe.

He kept plowing on, slashing away with his spear as quickly as he could. In the corner of his eye, he saw a dark shape slipping from tree to tree. He only knew two people that slunked about like large cats, and Jesnake was at the oak tree with Hanburg.

"DIN!" he shouted, not breaking his pace.

"Eöl, what's wrong?" Dinendale shouted, immediately abandoning the shadow to catch up to his friend.

"Paige is in danger!" Robert shouted over his shoulder, not breaking stride. Dinendale was soon matching pace with him wearing a look that would have caused a nine-foot tall bridge troll to wither. Robert knew he was wearing the same expression. It was the look of a warrior with one mission: to rescue a comrade from harm.

They thundered to the edge of the woods at a full sprint. The lull of the feasting had lowered considerably in the time they had escaped, making it evident that many of the villagers were turning in for the evening. The two warriors searched the outside of the village for anyone that might be wandering around. No one. The walls were clear of any life.

"Ok, go!" Dinendale hissed, picking up a sturdy stick. Robert scurried to the wall, laying flat against the stockade. He slid along the logs, locating the same grate he and Twostaves had used to escape. It wasn't hard to find. He motioned to Dinendale and the dark elf padded over to his side.

"Where do we start?" Dinendale demanded.

"Paige was to come through that wall," Robert said, pointing to the left. "You go that way. I'll search the other. There's no telling where she could be."

"Aye," Dinendale affirmed.

Robert caught his arm as the elf turned. "What if one of us gets caught?"

Dinendale paused, then looked Robert straight in the eye with a sly smile Robert hadn't seen from him in a long time. "We don't get caught."

"Ah, right," Robert said, gesturing smugly to the village around him. "Except for that one time, remember?"

Dinendale rolled his eyes and made a shoving motion with his hand to ward this friend off. Robert nodded, and then they both entered into the village. Once in, Robert turned to give one more look at his friend. For a moment, blue eyes locked onto brown ones, filled with determination sprinkled with worry. Suddenly, Dinendale was gone, evaporating into the shadows. Robert also slipped into the darkness, his keen eyes and ears alert for his friend.

Dinendale stole quietly along the inside of the wall, careful to creep through the hidden crevices where less of the bright moonlight would give him away. His fingers gripped the stick till his already pale knuckles were even whiter. It would have to do, there was no time to find a blade. He'd lost a close friend once by not being there in time, and he'd sworn never to let that happen again.

The elf slowed as he heard the crunch of metal plated boots on the gritty earth. He stopped and crouched like a panther behind a well at the back of a longhouse. A moose skull sat atop the well's roof; its antlers cast an eerie shadow on the ground from the light of Taivian and Suntra high overhead.

The footsteps grew closer. Dinendale heard the distinct clink of chain mail on plate-armor. The elf felt the thrill of triumph, knowing no one from the village would have mail to wear, as he'd worked in the smithy's shop for a week and never saw a single riveted link fashioned. The footsteps stopped near the well.

"Locamnen, you sniveling wretch, where are you," the voice hissed. There was no mistaking the accent; this man was a Shaud. The elf gripped the stick in his hand loosely as he tried to find the balance point.

"Locamnen!"

"I'm here," Dinendale hissed, mimicking the medicine man's whining voice as best he could. "Let's get this over shall we?"

"You have her?" demanded the stranger. Dinendale felt heated anger surge down his arms and into his fingertips.

"Who?" the elf hissed with calculated malice.

"The Alitarian princess, you goat! Quit playing stupid!"

"My memory is a bit fuzzy."

"Inbred curr," the other spat, and Dinendale heard the tell-tale clink of gold in a sack as it hit the dirt. "Enough games."

"Tell me, soldier. Why should I give her to you instead of keeping her myself?"

"We've already been through this! Quit with the questions and hand her over!" the voice demanded in a menacing rumble.

"Is she really worth all the trouble? What about her sister?"

There was a slight pause.

"Oh yes, she spilled it all to me. Every word as I held a knife to her throat," Dinendale cackled in a low tone.

"You idiot. Her sister is in my lord's castle. She is in the dungeon even as we speak. Now hand over the other girl before I lose my patience..."

Dinendale heard the *'shing'* as the Shauden drew his scimitar.

"Come get her, Raven-head," Dinendale said in his own deep baritone. He sent shivers down his own spine as he stepped into the moonlight, stick held loosely at his side.

The Shaud in front of him was a middle-aged man wearing a seren's scarlet turban and Shauden armor. An embroidered golden serpent twirled across his white tunic that stretched over his mail coat and steel breastplate. In his hand rested a wicked, curved sword that reflected the moonlight on it's polished steel blade. His boots made a crunching sound as he braced his feet into his fighting stance on the straw riddled clay and pebble road.

If Dinendale hadn't known better, he would have thought twice about tangling with a captain in the army. There were two different types of serens: those that fought their way up to the rank by skill, and those that flattered a noble enough to gain the position. A normal person would have run away in ignorance; Dinendale chose to fight. The fact that the sword the seren held was in like-new condition told the elf it wasn't used much; Dinendale hoped that was an obvious sign that this one was of the flattering types.

The seren was taken aback at the sight of a towering elf holding a stick. But he quickly recovered and charged his opponent, sword gleaming.

When he was just in reach, Dinendale jumped to the side and brought the stick down on top of the Raven Head. The blow sent the man reeling into the dirt, landing on his face. But he leapt back up, hacking at the elf with fury. Dinendale blocked the blows, one of which nearly rendered the elf's hand short a few fingers. Despite several seconds of fierce blows the seren's blade eventually snapped Dinendale's tree limb in two. The fighters parted. The only sound besides the distant thundering of drums was the heavy breathing of the two combatants into the chilly autumn air.

"What a pity," the seren sneered. "By the way, not bad acting. You could almost pass for the lowest of human slime, even if you are an elf."

"High praise coming from an expert in that area," Dinendale stalled, his eyes darting around for anything he could use as a weapon.

"Is that so?" spat the seren. His even white teeth gleamed with a satisfactory smirk in the moonlight. Dinendale let his jaw-drop mockingly as he began to back up towards the well, judging his distance by the shadow of the moose antlers on the dirt to his left. The gleaming smile widened as the elf saw him raise his sword for a second charge. Dinendale felt the wall of the well behind him and smiled.

This time, Dinendale waited till the last moment to jump aside, knocking the sword out of his hand. In one fluid motion, he hooked his hand into the man's sword belt and jerked him forward and up over his shoulder. The captain hurled headfirst down into the well.

Dinendale heard the smack as the soldier as he hit the water far below. He could hear the shouting and sputtering as the seren surfaced. The elf sneered.

"Have a good swim, you intrepid little monster," he hollered as he slunk back into the darkness.

Robert ducked behind a nearby stack of crates. He'd searched up and down two rows of buildings with no success. The villagers were beginning to trickle back into the longhouses and cottages in small groups of three to five people sporadically. Sneaking around was becoming more and more treacherous the deeper he headed into the village, but by the stockade wall, it was still relatively deserted. He crept about as quietly as possible, wishing he had some eucalyptus balm to help him steady his breathing

"Come on, Paige," he hissed to himself in frustration.

Suddenly he heard the soft crunch of leather soles on the rocky path. He gripped his spear with sweaty palms, licking his dry lips. He didn't know what to do if the stranger was a foe; he would have to be fast, and dispose of the threat as quickly as he could. He took a deep breath and slowly peeked around the corner of the boxes.

His veins immediately turned into a hot, untamable wildfire. A tall man covered in a forest green cloak was stealing his way to the wall. Slung on his back was a limp body. Robert tried to make out features, and felt his heartbeat skip.

The limp body was Paige. The sight of her wearing a dress distracted him. The white dress was dirty and tattered in several places; her blonde hair, which appeared to have been done up at one point in the evening now cascaded down her back like an uneven laxen waterfall. The boiling sensation in his veins continued tenfold.

The cloaked figure looked around warily, summarizing the situation. Seemingly satisfied, he backed up a few paces from the wall. Robert knew if he were to move, he had to move now. He took one more deep breath, then leapt up behind the man with the ferocity of a wild animal, spear leveled at him.

"Put her down," Robert bellowed. The cloaked figure whirled around surprised. The dark green hood concealed a face save for a pair of eyes that reflected the moonlight back at Robert like a cat.

"What's in your head, boy?" the figure retorted in a low voice.

"The notion to waste you," Robert growled through gritted teeth.

The figure pulled back his cloak a bit to let one arm free. It was covered by a tooled leather glove that reached all the way up the forearm, covering everything but the tips of the fingers. Robert raised his spear to the defensive stance. It's large, polished head illuminated by the moonbeams that reached down from the sky like white fingers from the heavens clutching at the earth.

"Don't be a fool. If I wanted you dead, I'd have left that guard to put an arrow through your skull."

"Even so," Robert said, sidestepping to try and circle the stranger. "I don't know you from Eya, so I'll be thanking you to put the lady down now."

The glowing, silver eyes narrowed.

"I think not," the stranger said in a low whisper.

Robert could stand it no longer. He rushed the stranger, spear down and ready for action. In the span of time it takes a hummingbird to flap a wing, the man threw up an arm to deflect the blow. He stepped out of the way, as a long, thin blade slid out the back of the glove about a foot long. He had only to swing his arm to deflect the spear as Robert charged past him.

Robert caught the deflection well. He dared not strike too high for fear of hitting Paige. Balancing on the ball of his right foot, he swung around again, aiming for the cloaked figure's legs. This time, the man managed to jumped high enough to make it over the spear, landing nimbly and spinning his other leg out to catch Robert square in the jaw with the sharp heel of his riding boot.

Robert reeled back as lightning bolts of pain shot up his face and stung his cheeks. How he was able to do that without dropping the princess, Robert couldn't explain. Robert shook it off and readied himself for another lunge, but the figure made no effort to advance. Rather, he held up his forearm and retracted the blades into the glove, making a dash towards the stockade wall. Robert pursued him, stumbling forward as he willed his head not to ring with pain.

The figure kept running at the wall, no escape in sight. But to Robert's astonishment and horror, he heard the figure shout out something in what sounded like elvish as he leapt straight into the air and soared effortlessly over the stockade wall, dropping soundlessly down on the other side. Robert's heart stopped. The man had just hopped over a wall at least four times his own height, and he'd done it with the ease one might take if climbing a short, insignificant staircase. Robert broke into a dead run. He didn't care if the now sleeping villagers awoke and chased him. All he knew was Paige was in the arms of some unknown runner, and this runner apparently knew enough magic to help him soar effortlessly over vertical wall at least fourteen feet high.

Robert knew he himself would never be able to scale the wall like that; he only knew rudimentary magic, and he was no good at climbing. He bounded back down the wall opening he had crawled through twice now. He ran as quickly as his legs could carry him.

As he neared the hole, he saw Dinendale running towards it as well from the other direction.

"Did you find-" the elf started, but Robert cut him off.

"No time! Magician... princess... over wall..." he gasped, lunging through the door. He came out and saw a green cloak vanishing into the forest a bowshot away to their right down the fence wall. Robert took off at a dead run, with Dinendale right on his tail. Once more they found themselves crashing through the woods, traversing wherever the cloaked magician went. Up and under logs they ran; around boulders, through spider's webs and bursting past vines they flew on wings of fury fueled by their male instinct to protect.

On and on into the highlands of the Wild they ran. Dinendale began to feel his exhaustion catch up with him as they bolted on into the forest. The mysterious magician led them with a sense of direction and purpose, and something dawned on the dark elf.

"Where is he taking her!" Dinendale shouted to Robert.

"His gravesite if I have any say!"

"Eöl!" Dinendale called. "Don't you find it strange that he is running in the same direction we-"

His words were cut off as a tree root sprung up out of the ground on its own accord and hooked them both under their feet. Dinendale felt a branch the size of a caber smash into his forehead as he rolled down the steep incline. Robert was in the same condition, cursing the entire way down as if he'd been through something like this before.

After what felt like an eternity of bumping and crashing through the slope of a deep ravine, the two rolled to a halt at the base of the basin, moaning as they pulled themselves from the grass. Dinendale looked up as a pair of boots halted at his nose.

"You could have just marched in like the rest of us. You could have been normal. But *nooooooo*! You had to make, yet, another grand entrance! And you, Robert!? Twice in one night? Really, you have got to get your head looked at, Mate."

Dinendale looked at Duelmaster as his brain's groggy gears attempted to catch up from the fall. His head felt like it might explode. Robert tried to stand but sank down again instead, cursing out in pain.

"Paige?..." Dinendale called out, bleary in the eyes and slurring his words like an old sot in a tavern. His days as a slave had sapped him of nearly all energy, and the running, combined with the blow to his head by that tree branch finished off any reserve energy he might have held. After a moment of swirling surroundings and fading vision, he slumped back into a state of sluggish unconsciousness.

"If I had a silver half-tinny for every time someone in this company passes out, I'd have more money than the Shahir himself by now!"

Paige felt her eyelids flutter open so see Duelmaster tapping his foot in annoyance, staring down at her.

"Duely!" she cried out, struggling to stand up. Suddenly a hand was at her elbow, easing her to her feet. It was Hanburg, dressed in a maroon red coat with a thick wolverine fur collar and brass buttons. His round nose was cherry red in the frosty air of the morning, and he was quick to place the wool blanket Paige had been laying on around her shoulders as she staggered to her feet. Judging by the light about them, it was nearly dawn.

"Where did I.... how..." she stammered, tears welling up in her eyes. She reached the back of her neck and felt a gauze dressing sealing off Locamnen's cut.

"There there, lass, you're ok now. We're all here!" Hanburg soothed, wrapping her in a huge, warm bearhug. She sobbed a few times, grateful tears washing her smudged face as her heart swelled with relief. They were all here. Din and

Robert lay sleeping under the large oak tree to her left, Twostaves, Jesnake, Duelmaster, and Broadside sat about packing up gear back into packs from large sacks Hanburg had brought to the glade the day before.

"Hanburg, thank you. Thank you so much!" she sobbed, squeezing him back tightly.

After a brief hold on the embrace, she released him and ran over to where Robert and Dinendale lay asleep, dropping to her knees beside the elf. He stirred at the noise, cracking his brown eyes open slightly and blinking even in the dim twilight of morning. It took him a moment of grunting and blinking to finally focus in on Paige's face.

"Princess?..." he mumbled feebly. Then the realization of what his eyes beheld apparently jolted through his brain and he sat bolt upright, grasping her shoulders, eyes wide. "PRINCESS! By the Creator, you're alive! And here! But, how!?"

"I don't know," Paige said, smiling. Dinendale took her face in his hands, her soft cheeks flushing slightly against the rough texture of his palms as he looked into her eyes, a look of absolute relief and gratitude washing over his face. He wiped away a stray tear from her cheek with his thumb before embracing her in another solid hug.

"Great, glad to see you're safe and sound after all," muttered Robert as he stretched, waking from his own slumber. Paige hopped up and embraced him as well. He stiffened uncomfortably for the briefest moment, then wrapped her in his arms and returned the hug, squeezing her tight.

"I'm so glad you are both unharmed, " she said. Robert grunted, gingerly reaching up and touching a lump on his forehead which had turned purple.

"Well, almost unharmed," the princess chuckled. She gave both of them one more hug for good measure before collapsing back into a sitting position and turning so she could see Hanburg and the others.

"We thought we'd lost you when that devil took you and ran," Dinendale choked out composing himself quickly. Paige nodded.

"I thought I was a goner as well," she admitted, lightly touching the bandage on the back of her neck. Her last memories came flooding back, and her face screwed up in confusion.

"But... when last I saw Locamnen, he had a sword sticking out of his chest!"

She quickly reached up and felt several spatterings of dried blood still on her jawbone.

"See!?" She pointed to her cheek. "This is from him. He should have been dead. How could he have made off with me after I'd succumbed?"

"It wasn't Locamnen that we were chasing!" Dinendale urged.

"Then who?" Paige asked, bewildered. A soft cough sounded off behind her, and both of them looked over at

Hanburg. He cleared his throat again and nodded in front of him, to the left of Paige and Dinendale.

Upon a log, not ten paces away, sat a stranger that looked somehow familiar to Paige. He was almost as tall as Dinendale, with an average build like Duelmaster. He had pale skin, with hardly a blemish on it. His hair was a shaggy, dirty blonde, except for a silver streak going through the middle, gleaming in the sunlight. He had a young face, yet wisdom that comes with great age etched into his eyes. The man wore a pair of leather knee-high boots dyed a deep maroon color with a knife and sheath sewn into the side of each one, housing antler-handled daggers. He had two more identical knives and sheaths sewn onto his belt, which was buckled over a pair of moss green trousers. His shirt was woodland brown, covered by a leather doublet and buried under a forest green cloak and hood that draped over his shoulders like moss on a tree. Additionally he wore full length leather gloves the color of walnut wood. Intricately tooled, they covered his whole arm from the elbow to the second knuckle on his fingers, the thumb being fully enclosed and well padded.

The man carried an almost indifferent, sullen air about him. He sat on the log, whittling on a stick with one of his belt knives, making no noise and offering no commentary. Paige looked from him to Hanburg and back again.

"Who the blazes are you?" Robert demanded after a moment of silence. The man ignored him for a moment, cutting a smooth, clean sliver of wood off the stick he whittled on. The curly wooden discard floated gently to the soft, dewy grass below, bouncing briefly on the carpet of clover before settling into the tangled mess of greenery.

"They call me 'the Woodcarver' here in the Wild."

"I've never heard of you," Robert countered.

"The Wild is a big place, boy."

"Who are you calling boy!?" Robert demanded.

The man looked up and stared at Robert with unblinking, crystal clear eyes which immediately caught Paige's attention; they were clear as a pair of polished diamonds. Right now they were illuminating the pine-needle green of his cloak. When he glanced over at Hanburg, they shifted to a dark reddish brown. Paige suddenly connected the dots and gasped aloud.

"You!"

He looked at her, his crystal eyes reflecting back white as they alighted upon her dress, dirty as it may be.

"You were the man who spoke to me in the longhouse, the first day we were captives here!"

The man nodded, the corner of his mouth twitching slightly in almost a half-smile.

"Aye, that was me."

"Wait, you've met this guy before?" Robert asked incredulously.

"Briefly. We had so much going on in all the excitement honestly I'd forgotten all about it!"

"It is good to know I made an impression, m'lady," Woodcarver chuckled.

"Ha! 'Good to know' my bodacious backside!" Broadside snorted, waddling up closer to the group and inserting himself into the middle of the cluster of conversing individuals. "Still doesn't explain who you are or what you're doing here, now does it?"

"No master dwarf. I suppose it does not," the stranger smiled, sheathing his knife. He looked at Paige with those eyes that appeared to be made of glass. "I told you m'lady; you have friends even in this dark place."

"Enough of the cryptic talk. Why are you here? And why did you help us?" Dinendale scrutinized. "I've seen those eyes before, but not on a human. Warlock? Sorcerer? Out with it, man!"

Paige was surprised by the hint of venom in Dinendale's tone. She looked at the man curiously as he smirked, tossing his whittling stick off into the woods and dusting the shavings off his lap. He placed his fingertips together thoughtfully as he regarded the dark elf with interest.

"Just a humble magician, that is all," he said, smiling for the first time. Dinendale seemed unsatisfied with that answer.

"Natural born human magicians have been extinct for three centuries," the elf said, eyes narrowed in suspicion.

"With all do respect, Dinendale Faoris, son of Aedard, till a month and a half ago, I thought the Dark Elves of the Cullodren bloodline were also extinct."

Paige had no idea what any of that meant, but by the shock on Dinendales face, she gathered it was something that Dinendale had not expected this stranger to know. He was in a shocked stunned silence, struggling to get to his feet as he stared at the man in disbelief.

"How do you know those names," the elf said evenly. The man actually chuckled, standing up and gesturing to the entire group.

"I know all of you. I know who you are and where you come from. I know what it is you seek to do!" he laughed. The Brotherhood all looked uneasy and suspicious as he walked circles around Dinendale and Paige. He scanned the princess up and down with a coy smile.

"I also know what you carry, princess."

Paige looked hard into his mesmerizing eyes. He glanced down at her feet, then back up at her face.

"Left moccasin, I believe?"

"What?"

"Your left boot, my lady," he said, bowing his head slightly in respect. "I believe you are currently housing something of great value there."

Jesnake, who was by now back in his mail armor, stepped closer, nonchalantly playing with one of his throwing knives, eyes fixed on Woodcarver. The others all shifted uneasily as the magician stared expectantly at Paige. She hesitated, unsure of what do do. Should she acknowledge his assumption, or try and play it off? Something told her he was completely sincere in his statement, and that he would somehow know if she tried to fib her way out of admitting her precious scroll was stuffed in her moccasin.

"How do you know I have something in my moc?" she asked, trying to read the stranger's expression. He smiled again, taking a step forward.

"Because, I know everything there is to know about you Alwasu, second born of Alaire, chief of the Alatarians and Eleness the elven maiden of the Whisperwood. You've no idea how good it is to meet you after all these years."

"Sir, I don't know how you know all that but I request that you explain yourself immediately," Paige stammered, her breathing in short, anxious breaths.

"I've been searching for you for a long time. In fact, I've followed your lot since you set out on this journey a month ago," he said, gesturing again to the group. "I know the price you have paid, Paige of Kapernaum. I know about Olivian. I know about Aschin. I know it all."

He paused for a moment then looked Paige directly in her eyes. "And I know about the leather scrap you carry in your boot because I was there when your father tore it from the Book of Death."

CHAPTER 12

TEARS IN THE RAIN

*P*aige stared at the stranger in absolute shock. Her expression matched that of every member of the company, including Hanburg. Her father had stolen this scrap of leather scrawled with ancient gibberish from the Shahir? But why?

"How... how...?" she tried to force out more, but she couldn't seem to formulate a sentence from the million and ten questions exploding through her mind. How had she never heard of this from her father?

"My dear, it is a very long story that we don't have time to get into at present. Morning is breaking, and we need to put some considerable distance between us and this wretched village." He looked toward Hanburg. "No offence meant, Councilman."

"You can't just make a statement like that and not explain!" shouted Paige in frustration. She yanked the leather out of her moc and shook it angrily at his face. "My father and mother, my entire village suffered because of this, and I don't even know what it is! Now you tell me this instant or I will gut you myself!"

"*Claigvaghn heylagh*," the man said in a soothing elvish tone.

"Don't dare to tell me to 'calm down' sir," Paige hissed through gritted teeth, her eyes flashing. The magician regarded her almost with amusement but also admiration before he sighed.

"Alwasu, you've known such pain these many weeks. But take some slight amount of comfort, if you can, in knowing your father single-handedly stopped the Shahir from wreaking havoc across this entire world by taking that piece of parchment. I cannot tell you what it says. You think it's hard finding a human-born natural magician, try and find a one that can read spells written in Archaic Elvish from a book over two thousand years old. But I can tell you this: whatever is on it was worth the Shahir marching three divisions of soldiers into the Wild to find it, and you single handedly have foiled an empire this last month. I am here to ensure that his sacrifice and your suffering are not done for naught."

"So that's it then? We're supposed to just trust you and let you walk away?" Twostaves said, taking a menacing step forward. He stared down at the man in clear indignation.

"What you believe is of no consequence to me," Woodcarver said, walking over to the oak tree and picking up a particularly gnarled and knotted staff. "But I am not planning on walking away at all, Mr. Giant. In fact, just the opposite; I'm coming with you."

Robert snorted.

The man glared at him with those piercing clear eyes. "The fact is you've lost the element of surprise with your enemy. They are actively hunting you. You can see that by the presence of a seren in the walls of the village you just escaped from. The main path to Aschin is too dangerous now. You'll be caught the moment you step too close to a main road or well-known pass."

"If what Jesnake heard is true," Hanburg commented, "this man is not wrong. If the Shauds have come this far and sought out my village this deep into the Wild, they will have all the main routes of travel blocked or ambushed for you by now."

"So what are we to do?" Paige asked, worry etching the edge of her voice almost to a quiver. "Going back is not an option for me."

"I can take you," Woodcarver said, leaning against his staff. "I know a way around the main roads and passes."

"How?" Duelmaster asked quietly, staring at his boot in heavy contemplation.

"I know these lands better than any," he said. "I've seen the Wild from vantages most men can only dream of, and I tell you plainly, there is a way. If we hike through the highlands and go over the ridges south of us rather than follow the passes due east, then circle back, we can get to Aschin undetected and possibly make up for some lost time."

"Go through the Raychel Range?" Dinendale scoffed. "Those mountains are as barren and desolate as a dragon's cave. You're suggesting we try and cut across them?"

"I did not say it would be easy," Woodcarver countered. "But the best way to avoid the soldiers is to take the path they will not travel."

"And we're going to just have to take your word as truth and let you lead us blindly into the Wild?" Broadside laughed. "Dinendale, you can't seriously be considering this as an option!"

"He did go out of his way to save the princess," Duelmaster said, still in his pondering pose. "He didn't have to warn us. And we frankly owe him Paige's life."

"I would have gotten to her in time if he hadn't nabbed her first," Robert grunted.

"No, actually," Paige said curtly. "Duelmaster is right. I would be dead right now if it wasn't for this... Woodcarver."

"May we have a moment to counsel your proposal?" Dinendale asked.

The magician rolled his eyes but nodded with some annoyed reluctance. He took his staff and walked beyond the oak tree's shade and into the first rays of sunlight the morning had to offer. Hanburg excused himself and opted to go stand beside the man and engage him in conversation. The group congealed together and began discussing their options in hoarse, hushed whispers.

"Can we trust him?" Jesnake asked bluntly.

"I don't think we should risk it. What if he leads us into the middle of nowhere? What if it's a trap? I say we risk our route and just take extra care." Robert argued. Twostaves nodded a gruff agreement. Dinendale looked at Paige, uncertainty etched into the frown lines on his forehead.

"Princess, he saved your life. But he appears to know much more about your business than even you do. This either makes him a Creator-sent miracle, or a very dangerous enemy. Regardless of what we think about him, you are the one that has the most to lose in this adventure. If you do not want him to come, then we will end this here and now and leave him tied to a tree or something. It is your call."

"He's also a human magician," Jesnake hissed. "They have always been volatile. You know that, Din. What's to say he won't cast a spell upon us in the night and take the scroll for the Shahir?"

"Again. I'm leaving this to the princess. It is her burden and her safety that are paramount. On that can we at least all agree?"

There was a chorus of grunts and ayes from the men. Paige thought long and hard. On the one hand, she had no particular reason to trust the stranger. That alone was a good enough reason to wash their hands of the magician. However, he'd had several opportunities at this point to do her harm if he'd wanted to.

"If he was after the scroll, and knew where it was this whole time," she reasoned, "he would have had every opportunity to let Locamnen kill me and then take it. Or drag me off into the woods and take it. But he brought me to the very spot I needed to be. And he's right. The way we would have taken would now be crawling with guards on the lookout. Because of that, I think we almost have no choice but to trust him."

"I still am not a fan of that plan." Robert muttered.

"We will have to be very aware. If there is even the slightest indication he proves false, we sack him. Agreed?" Dinenedale asked.

The others nodded assent. They broke their little huddle, walking over to the edge of the tree. Hanburg and Woodcarver stood chatting about the coming winter.

"Master Magician, we would be happy to have you accompany us," Dinendale said, extending a hand for the man to shake.

"Under one condition," Paige interjected.

The magician eyed her up and down. "And that is, my lady?"

"You will tell me everything. About my father, about this scroll, all of it," she demanded.

The man cracked a half smile. "On my word my dear, I will give you the full narrative. But on my own terms, and not before."

"Why can't?"

The man's smile vanished. His brow creased and furrowed. "There are things in motion right now I can't tell you about. The more people that know the whole story, the more danger people would be in. I swear I will explain it all, but for the safety of everyone in this company, you have to trust me to tell you on my own terms." He lowered his voice and looked directly at Paige. "Do you want them all in danger?"

"We're kind used to that at this point," Robert snapped.

Paige shook her head.

"No. I've put everyone here in enough danger. But you will explain this to me. Swear it."

"I swear it. Do we have an accord?"

Paige nodded, and the man took Dinendale's still extended hand and shook it firmly.

Hanburg clapped his hands together. "Well!" he said, energetic as ever. "Now that this has all been sorted out, I must concur with the magician. Time is growing short my friends. We must get you further on your way before the village sends the whole garrison out to find you!"

"Agreed," Dinendale affirmed. "Lead on."

The band of riff raff, now counting eight in their company, finished getting their commandeered equipment from Hanburg. They were quick about getting packed up and dressed, taking only a momentary pause for a hunk of bread and cheese for breakfast at Hanburg's insistence.

Paige was quick to discard the dress in favor of the shirt and trousers once again. Her leather jerkin had been oiled and scrubbed clean, and her britches were white once more, complementing the new dark blue, long-sleeved shirt she wore under the leather padding, the sleeves tucked into a new pair of leather bracers. Her knee-high moccasins were new, a parting gift from Abenya. She pulled her flaxen hair back into her classic single braid allowing it to cascade down her back like a waterfall. A new belt wrapped around her hips, and she had an antler-handled knife tucked into it before she checked herself over.

"My dear, I believe you are missing one thing," Hanburg said, a twinkle in his eye. With a flourish he removed a small object from his robes, flashing in the sunshine of the morning as he proffered it to Paige.

"Mother's hairpin!" she squealed with delight.

"Abenya knew where it had gotten off to and was quite insistent it was very special to you," Hanburg smiled. Paige felt tears brimming up into her eyes. She threw her arms around the man's beefy neck and kissed him on the cheek. The man chuckled and returned the embrace.

"I don't know how I can ever thank you, Hanburg, " she cried into his coat.

"My dear, just stay sharp, be careful, and come visit me once before I am an old man, won't you?" he chuckled, scratching her back comfortingly with his beefy fingers. Paige could hear his heartbeat through the coat and was quite sure she'd never met another person, barring her own father, with a heart so kind as dear Hanburg's. She felt all the pain and emotion she'd been struggling with for a month burn within his warm, fatherly embrace. She could feel the tepid patches in his coat where her hot tears were wicking into the fabric before they had a chance to slide down her cheeks.

"It's a deal," she said, wiping the tears from her face and sniffing quickly to regain her composure in front of the boys.

Dinendale smiled over at Paige as she stuck her magic hairpin into her braid and secured it safely.

"You know I never got to hear how the rest of you all got out. Were there any other difficulties?" he asked the others as he finished getting his pack ready to strap on. Broadside grunted something unintelligible, but Hanburg clapped his hands excitedly as he laughed.

"I don't mind telling you, Dinendale, there was more than one harrowing close call last night. Enough to make my hair turn grey!" Hanburg laughed. "Jesnake told me about the plans he'd overheard in the trough after he crawled all the way out to Puddledew Stream on a hill outside the village. He stumbled through the woods to meet us in soaked clothes to relay the plot he'd uncovered."

"I would have stayed to fight but I hadn't the strength to be of any use should she be in danger," Jesnake added bitterly.

"Jesnake, if you hadn't done what you did, I wouldn't be here at all. Do not spend another moment kicking yourself, do you hear?" Paige demanded sternly. She looked at the Jesnake with great gratitude, and he smiled slightly, though he still wore an expression that told her he was annoyed with himself.

With that Dinendale turned to Hanburg and held out his hand. The man grinned as he took the elf's extended arm with his own in an embrace of camaraderie.

"We can never repay you for the kindness you've shown us, Hanburg," Dinendale said seriously. "We are forever in your debt."

"There is no debt, my friend. I like to think there is still good in this world," Hanburg said. "Good that needs no alternative motive. Just one person helping another person because, simply, it's the right thing to do."

"I hate to rush this cheery reunion," Woodcarver muttered. "But we don't have time to waste. The best way to get through the Raychels without going all the way around them is to pass atop a small plateau not known to many in these areas. That will be the quickest way to get to Aschin without taking the main passes and pathways there. It's a long, hard road and we have who knows how many soldiers nearby."

"Quite right, of course," Hanburg agreed.

"And this plateau. You're sure it exists?" Broadside queried.

"Like I've said," the magician smirked. "I've seen this land from many vantage points most men could only dream of. It is there, and it is the best chance we have."

Paige lashed a bedroll to her wood framed pack she'd quickly constructed. Hanburg was getting nervous; they were not terribly far from the village at this point, and he feared that by now they had probably discovered the slaves were gone and were mustering the warriors.

"There are no more than a hundred able-bodied men to be honest," Hanburg said, glancing back in the direction of his home. "So it could take them a few hours to even venture this way."

"It's not the village I'm worried about," Woodcarver said, scanning the treeline around the gully. "It's the soldiers. A seren doesn't come back, that tends to get noticed at an encampment. And where there is a dispatch of one hundred, you can be sure the three regiments that raised Kapernaum are not far ahead of them."

"Either way we can't tarry here," Paige said, tying the cord tightly around the scratchy wool blanket. Her brow was so furrowed in concentration, she didn't see Broadside come and sit beside her until he belched loudly. She jumped, and he grinned, wiping his hand onto the back of his trousers.

"Are you done yet?" he asked.

Paige gave him an annoyed look and he raised his hands in mock defense.

"Don't stab me with those Paige. I'm just trying to make conversation!"

She rolled her eyes. "Fine. Do you need something?"

"No," the dwarf said. "Just bored. I finished packing earlier."

"I see," she said. She glanced up, spotting Dinendale. He was stuffing some blankets into the leather satchel he used as a pack. He looked stronger now that he was back in actual clothes with a sword strapped to his hip. She also noticed he hadn't looked so haunted in recent weeks; his eyes seemed less empty than they had been when she'd first met him nearly a month ago.

"Hello?" Broadside said, waving a hand in front of her face.

She blinked. "What?"

"By my beard, princess, were you staring!?" Broadside gasped in fake astonishment, wiggling his dark, bushy eyebrows mischievously. Paige felt her face grow hot.

"I was not," she said defiantly.

"You were, princess!"

"Shut up," she snapped. "Surprised you can see anything being so close to the ground."

"At least I'm not as low as a blow like that!" Broadside said, sticking his tongue out. "That's the lowest hanging fruit, Paige!"

"Have some experience with low hanging fruit have you?" She laughed.

The dwarf chuckled. "Just thought you'd be above that."

"I'm not above anything except your stature, Broadside," she smirked. "So either way, I have to stoop to your level."

The dwarf cracked a smile, winked, and skipped away, whistling. She blew a stray lock of hair out of her eyes in exasperation. Robert walked over a few minutes later, his new gear all packed and shouldered. He sat down next to her as she began adjusting all her straps and pack preferences.

"Still not finished?" he teased. "Goodness, you're such a woman."

She swung a punch at his shoulder, remembering too late that he was now wearing chainmail under his robe. She cried out as her knuckles hit the riveted metal links. Robert smiled with obvious glee.

"Blazes and rubbish!" Paige cursed, rubbing her knuckles trying to work the pain out of them

"Oops!" Robert laughed, his eyes sparkling.

"I guess I deserve that." She looked up at Robert, pursing her lips for a moment as she surveyed his jagged-toothed smile. Despite his rough, sarcastic exterior, there was a real quality to this man, or whatever he was. She took a deep breath then let it out through her nose. "Look. Thank you. For coming back for me," she said. "Even though you didn't wind up needing to."

Robert glanced about quickly to make sure no one was eavesdropping on the two of them. Satisfied that the others were too busy finishing up packing their sacks to overhear them, he leaned in closer to Paige, looking her straight in the eye.

"Paige, you are one of the best friends I've ever had," he said evenly. "And there is literally nothing, save death, that could have prevented me from coming to find you. I'll always be here for you. You know that, right?"

Paige smiled warmly, feeling grateful. For a reason she did not understand, she felt a tad bit flustered and uncomfortable. She nodded, then waved her still smarting knuckles as if trying to shake off the ache.

"Ugh, bloody ashes!" she spat. "I think you may have bruised me."

"Well, I apologize for my rock-solid muscle tone. I guess you shouldn't try to dent biceps of iron."

"You don't need to apologize for something you don't have, Robert," Duelmaster jabbed as he jumped up from where he was sharpening one of his two rapiers. Robert scowled, picked up a rock, and tossed it at the dryad. The tree sprite caught it just before it hit him. Then, quick as a flash, he chucked it back.

The next few moments became a bit of a blur. The rock hit Robert in the forehead with a smack, and the husky fellow leapt up. He wheeled back his right fist and slammed it straight into Duelmaster's rounded jaw. The two were soon in a frenzied cloud of fists and elbows. Immediately, Broadside dropped what he was doing and threw himself into the brawl with something that sounded like a dwarvish battle cry, followed close by Twostaves.

"BOYS!" Dinendale shouted, "This is hardly the time to be..."

"Shut up, Din," shouted Duelmaster, grabbing the elf and throwing him into the frenzy. Soon there was nothing but a cloud of dust as the boys brawled, with the occasional cries and shouts escaping from the tangle of flailing limbs and clouds of dust.

"Do they do this a lot?" Woodcarver asked, puzzled and clearly impatient. Between that inquiry and the sight of the four males punching and kicking, it was all too much for

Paige. She burst out laughing once again. Huge gasps of melodious laughter erupted from her chest, and she clutched her side.

After a good five minute brawl, the boys parted, each one laughing as if for a moment all their worries and stress had melted away. Jesnake and Hanburg watched, smiles on their faces, and Woodcarver just looked on indifferently. It took a few minutes for everyone to calm down. When Paige finally got a hold of herself, the rest were still rolling in the dirt, or holding on to a tree branch for support. She looked up, still laughing, and saw Jesnake smiling at her.

"What?" she asked.

Jesnake walked over a few steps and nodded at Dinendale. "Look at him," Jesnake said.

"What about him?"

"Princess, he hasn't laughed like that in years. I haven't ever seen him happy in a long time."

Paige felt a warmness cover her, a feeling of happiness she hadn't felt for a long time. It was the same feeling she'd had when she had helped her mother heal a sick friend, or when she'd assisted her father in visiting the old warriors that were too restricted by wounds of decade's past battles. It felt good for her to help people, and Jesnake's comments made her beam.

Hanburg was chuckling a deep, husky laugh. He moved away from where he sat against a big boulder. His broad smile was cheery and rosy as he got up.

"Well gentlemen, and m'lady," he said, a slightly sad smile on his face. "This is where we must part. I need to get back to the village."

"Won't you be thrown in jail?" Paige asked, concerned.

"A hefty fine at worst." He looked at each of the men, and the princess. "A small price to pay to see justice done. I feel privileged to have been able to help you all. I only wish I could have done more."

"Again, we cannot thank you enough," Dinendale said.

"Pish-posh. It was nothing. All I ask in return is that you reunite this wonderful young woman with her sister. Do that, and all my work will be worth it." He went to each of them, shaking hands and wishing them the best of luck.

When he came to Paige, his eyes sparkled.

"The best to you, Paige," he said. "Remember your promise!"

"I will," Paige said, trying to keep her voice from shaking. "Do tell Abenya I'll miss her, won't you?"

"I will," the heavy man said. There was a momentary pause, then Paige threw her arms about him and hugged him hard one last time. The giant man returned the squeeze.

"Take care child," he said kindly. With a few more parting words he turned and headed back towards the village through the dense brush of the wood.

Rain fell from a cloudless sky as Dinendale flipped the hood to his cloak over his head. They had been walking at a brisk pace all things considered, letting Woodcarver take the lead as he began to turn them south and east of the glade. Now, tromping about, Dinendale sent up a silent prayer to the Creator that Hanburg's kindness would not go unblessed in this life.

The drops of rain pattered upon the brown and yellow leaves of the forest. The group climbed the rocky crags of the highlands. The Wild around them felt eerily still. Except for the occasional splash of boots and moccasins upon soggy ground, accompanied by the cold, runny sniffles of those wearing them, the forest had neither insect nor bird calling out into the dense undergrowth. The company's breaths came out in foggy plumes now, and wool cloaks wrapped ever tighter for warmth against the crippling chill.

Yet with the discomfort of the cold, a bigger problem lay in the ascent of this slippery slope of rocks. In slick boots and moccasins, the muddy leaves became a hindrance. Each of them had their turn slipping and sliding on this gradual slope. Obvious gashes and slide marks in the mud appeared following each poorly-placed foot. Twostaves, the giant that he was, left a particularly deep gash when his monstrous knee dug into a patch of muddy moss following his biggest decent. He'd tried to cover it back up with leaves, but Woodcarver demanded he leave it.

"We can't stop and fix every mark on the terrain," he insisted. "Stealth should always be our method of choice, but in conditions like this, hiding the tracks will only waste time."

The hours slipped away like raindrops sliding off waxy leaves. They slugged through the slick, leaf-covered slopes for the entire afternoon. Paige pushed herself forward, getting her aching muscles into a rhythm of push, then relax. She let out a sigh, re-tying the bandage on the back of her neck as they continued to push on. Woodcarver showed no sign of stopping any time soon.

Suddenly Jesnake halted. He clustered the line behind him so abruptly that those in front stopped to turn back and look. Jesnake held two fingers, motioning to his ears for them to listen. Paige focused her hearing, hoping to pick up whatever sound had caused Jesnake to pause. All she heard was the pattering of raindrops on the leaves. Jesnake's piercing eyes darted around the forest, searching for the origin of the sound he'd heard.

"What is it?" Broadside asked.

Dinendale motioned for the dwarf to be silent.

The group was as still and quiet as the forest itself. For a moment, there was nothing, just the sound of the rain splattering against their hoods. Paige strained her ears to hear. Silence. But then, ever so softly, she picked up a sound, echoing like it was in a far-off cavern of cave. Though it was faint, she knew the sound. It was muffled yelling mixed with the crashing of bodies through the forest. A tingling began to build at the base of her spine, and she tensed.

"Soldiers!" Dinendale spat. Jesnake immediately drew an arrow and trained it at the direction of the approaching noise.

"We can't outrun them, Din," Robert said sideways to the elf, quickly pulling his own bow from his pack and stringing it.

"We'll have to fight," Woodcarver said, tossing his green cloak over his shoulder. He flexed his elbow and two blades sprang out of his gloves at the center knuckle on each hand. Paige pulled the hairpin out of her braid as the others began dropping unneeded gear.

"*Klaíomh*," Paige whispered. Blue sparks began to dance down the length of the hairpin as it enlarged and curved outwards, fitting itself perfectly to her grip.

"Oooh, *shiney!*" Duelmaster exclaimed, jaw agape.

"It's... *Klaíomh*," Woodcarver muttered in astonishment.

"I expect you to explain how you know that," Paige tossed her own cloak over her shoulder, rain flinging off it as she freed up her arms to fight unencumbered. "You know, when we aren't fighting for our lives."

The group dove for cover, dashing into the shadows to prepare for a fight Paige knew they were in no shape to endure. The princess slipped behind a large tree root, sliding on the muddy moss covered ground. She pressed her body to the large, damp tree, listening hard. She tried to ignore the moisture wrapping its cold tendrils onto her clothing, reaching to touch her already shaking body.

The crashing continued to grow louder till Paige guessed they were within two bow shots of them. She scanned the forest with sharp eyes, picking up anything out-of-place. She noticed a large boulder near her had acquired an extra growth that looked suspiciously like a dwarf's chainmail-clad backside.

Just as she was about to lurch from her concealment, the wall of foliage to her left shattered as a horse galloped into the steep hillside, whinnying in the rain. She gripped the sword with both hands, ready to strike, but felt her eyes widen in shock upon seeing the rider.

"Hanburg!" she shouted in surprise.

"Where is Dinendale!?" the man heaved. He looked awful; his clothes were now a shredded and mangled mass of muddy cloth and patchy fur. A sickly mixture of blood and mud was streaked across his round face and a large gash in his left arm soaked his coat fabric in blood. He gripped a bloodied, short saber in his right hand, the sticky, wet leather reins in his left. Paige felt sick at the sight.

"Hanburg," Dinendale cried. He jumped out from behind the concealment offered by a tall oak, alarm etched into his sharp features, "What is it?"

"Dinendale, get out of here now. The soldiers are hot on your trail!" the man heaved. "Got back home....torched. All of it. Gone! I've been racing the soldiers to get to you first. You have to make for the high crags!"

He'd barely gotten the words out when a whizzing sound like a horsefly on a hot summer day shoved its way through the darkness. An arrow slammed into Hanburg's ribs, driving the steel head through to the other side of his body. He gasped in shock, blood spurting from his mouth. He toppled off the screaming horse, which took off running. Jesnake leapt past the fallen man and drew his bow back to his chin. When the hidden Shaud scout popped up from the shrubs within bowshot distance, the elf released an arrow that drove through the Shaud's steel breastplate like it was made of paper.

Paige screamed, running to the side of the fallen tribesman. Robert skidded along the wet hillside to join her.

"We can't help him!" Robert shouted, grabbing Paige's arm, but Paige ignored him, wrenching free to kneel beside Hanburg. The councilman struggled to breathe, blood pouring from his wounds and sputtering out of his mouth with every agonizing breath.

"What can I do!?" she cried, trying to apply pressure to the wound. "Hold still. I can help!"

"Go..." the man sputtered, grabbing her hand and pushing it away from the wound and onto her sheathed sword. "You... you must..."

"No! I can fix this, let me fix this!" she screamed, pulling a bandage from the side of her pack.

"Free...your sister. Leave... me!"

She sobbed in agony, trying to stop the bleeding. Suddenly Robert jerked her up to her feet as dozens of soldiers began to pour from the forest, brandishing their various scimitars, pikes, and bows. With a sinking realization, she saw that there were far too many to ever hope to fight. As they charged towards her, she gripped Klaíomh in numb indecision. But before she could brace for a fight Robert grabbed her around the waist and slung her up onto his shoulder. He took off running south, charging uphill with the others.

"No!" she screamed, as they left Hanburg's still body in the bog of mud. Arrows from The Brotherhood's bows covered Robert's retreat. Paige felt hot tears mix with the cool rain as they escaped into the darkness of the forested highlands.

Robert heaved as the group retreated uphill in the rain, and Paige kicked free to run herself, tears still streaming down her face. They would take turns firing into the ranks of the Shauds' if ever they got too close, keeping the distance between them to a bowshot.

"We can't keep going like this!" Jesnake yelled. "I'm running out of arrows!"

"I'm thinking!" Dinendale shouted, scrambling up the rocks. The hills of the mountainside steeply jutted in all directions as they continued up the crags.

"Their armor will slow them the further up we go," Duelmaster shouted, picking up a large rock and tossing it down the embankment, tripping a Shaud who was gaining distance towards the group.

Paige suppressed a gag as they crawled through the narrow pathway cut into rock, her insides churning with sorrow, guilt, and adrenaline. The Shauds were closing in the space between them.

"Follow me!" Woodcarver shouted as he made for a steep, jutting embankment that dropped off as the path narrowed.

The gully became a cliff as it rounded the side of the mountain and led into the heartland of the Raychel Range.

"Everyone get ahead of me!" Woodcarver ushered. "I have a plan!"

"What plan?" Broadside shouted back.

"It's a *semblance* of a plan!" Woodcarver snapped, shoving the dwarf up the path. "An idea more or less if you really feel the need to get specific, Master dwarf!"

After Jesnake cleared past him, taking up the rear, Woodcarver clenched his fists and muttered something Paige couldn't make out. As the Shauds closed in, he got louder and louder, raising his fist to the sky. Paige noticed the wind pick up and a blast of thunder echoed through the crags and cliffs now surrounding them.

The Shauds ran along the ledge racing up the hill. Woodcarver waited till they were less than a bowshot away, then slammed his palms against the face of the rocky path.

The earth groaned and mixed with the howling of a sudden raging wind. Paige's eyes widened in horror and amazement as the ground began to rumble then break apart as if a giant stomped on it. The Shauds yelled as the earth in front of them crumbled forcing them to slide down the steep pitch of the mountain. Woodcarver bellowed in rage as the ground heaved and pitched harder with every moment, rocking like waves on a stormy night. He flung his arms up and down, again and again. Each blow cracked the stone with a sickening moan as he reshaped the entire mountain.

"MOVE!" Jesnake shouted, shoving Robert and Paige up the hill. Though Paige felt in too much of a daze to register his words, her body obeyed the command. The group bolted forward, the sounds of the Shauden soldier's shouts and curses drowned out by the noise. Paige cast one last look back, seeing the cliffside slide away from the mountain with a deafening roar. Woodcarver leapt away as the billows of dust rose high into the sky around them. The company escaped around the next bend, leaving their enemies to curse at the wind.

Numb.

It was the only word that adequately described the spectrum of emotions Paige was experiencing. The buntings and swallows chirped in the twilight of the evening, their mournful tones echoing the aches she felt in her heart. The chill nipped at her red runny nose as she wiped it with the back of her sleeve. The days were getting colder; winter was fast approaching this season, another dent in their already dire situation. She took a deep breath and felt the chill of the dawn sear her lungs as she stretched, attempting to bring her aching muscles into painful submission.

They were still in the forests, but a definite and drastic change was occurring as they continued to ascend away from the main valley passes and into the rocky crags of the Raychel Range. Each step took them further away from the Shauds, but also deeper into the wilderness. The pine trees became taller and more dominant, and the ground was rockier than in the forests back home. Boulders of immense proportions became more of a hindrance now, blocking the deer trails and small paths they used as often as they could find them.

The princess shielded herself from the elements by a small outcropping of rock above her as she leaned against the rough boulders around the campsite Woodcarver had chosen. She laid on a sweet smelling bed of pine needles Broadside had made for her and pulled her heavy wool cloak tighter around her. Robert laid his spare cloak atop her, hoping to aid her violent shivers.

Soon enough, she stood, wiping the tear stains off her cheek. But fresh, hot tears trickled down her face to the ground below.

Hanburg.

The man had only met her days ago, but in the short time she had been with him, he had shown kindness she'd thought left this world with the death of Papa. Now Abenya would never see her father again either, if she was even still alive. Woodcarver guessed the village had been raised to the ground like Kapernaum, otherwise Hanburg would not have just left to give them a final warning. The thought of Abenya dead made the ache of losing Hanburg all the worse, and she clutched her cloaks about her neck tighter than ever.

The others sat soberly around a tiny, pathetic fire that hissed and popped with the wet wood being added to it. The pine wood was so damp in the moist, foggy, mountainous air that the little flames wheezed and sputtered like a dying man's last breath. Like Hanburg's last breath, constricted and gurgling with his own blood. She tried to be engaged in the conversation; they were discussing their next move, but they were all so tired and grief stricken that it was becoming more difficult for anyone to concentrate.

"If the soldiers were able to track down where the princess was, it means the prince must know she has the scroll," Dinendale said glumly. "Which means he's expecting us to come after Olivian."

"So it is the scroll they are after," Twostaves muttered. "At least we know for sure now."

"But why?" Jesnake queried. "If it's elvish. It's so old we can't even read it. What use is that to a human?"

"I assure you, Master Jesnake," Woodcarver said darkly, the firelight's reflection dancing as it turned his clear eyes into orbs of flickering yellows and reds, "he is very capable of knowing what kind of secrets are contained on that page, and he will stop at nothing to unlock them."

"You said my father tore this from some sort of book," Paige reminded him, staring at the embers in the fire. "The way I see it, you still have an awful lot of stories to clear up."

"Here, here," Robert muttered, glaring at Woodcarver.

The magician stared into the fire for a long moment. "If anyone has a right to know, it's you lot," he said. "I will not go into the story of how Ala'haran and Eleness got the page, but I can tell you what I know of it's contents."

"Alaire."

Woodcarver looked up at Paige who stared at him.

"What?"

"My father's name is *Alaire*, not Ala-whatever," she said, more questions flooding her brain. Woodcarver suddenly looked uncomfortable; he clasped and unclasped his hands, uneasy.

"Well, when I knew him, he was going by Ala'haran. I apologize," he said deliberately. "Anyways, I was there when he and your mother escaped from the Shahir's palace together with that page."

Paige opened her mouth to let a flood of questions pour out. "Escape? My mother? Why were they in the Shahir's palace?"

Woodcarver held a hand up to fend her off.

"We will have that conversation. I promise, princess. But you must trust me when I say that conversation is one you do not need on your mind at present."

"It can't be much worse than what I've already got going on at this very moment," Paige snapped.

"My dear, there are so many things at stake here; so many threads to the tapestry of the world as it stands today. You must understand I do not do any of this lightly," Woodcarver said, unswayed.

Paige glared. She pursed her lips, but kept them closed.

Woodcarver continued, "What I can tell you is that the scroll you carry is not a singular text, but rather only one of many pages to the Book of Death, a text nearly as old as life on this world. It is part of a spell that the Shahir has been trying to replicate for over twenty years. Your father and mother managed to cut out one page of that book and have kept it hidden away in the Wild longer than you've been alive, my dear."

"And you were there when they took it?" Jesnake asked softly.

Woodcarver nodded. "I was. I helped Ala'ha- I mean- *Alaire* and Eleness escape that night but I was separated from them. I've been trying to find them ever since, but it wasn't until the Raven Heads had already attacked Kapernaum that I found out he'd made it into the Wild. So I stayed quiet, following the course of events, and eventually found your band just days before your capture. At that point, I knew the only way to protect that page was to help aid in your escape."

"This presents a potential problem for you then, I assume," Dinendale said quietly.

Woodcarver glanced at him with a somber expression. "Indeed."

"How so?" Broadside asked, a puzzled look on his face.

Robert, who sat between the dwarf and Paige, rolled his eyes.

"Because, moron; our current course of action is taking that scroll, page, or whatever it is and potentially placing it right in the lap of the very man who has already proved he'll stop at nothing to get it."

The group was silent for a moment, but Paige glanced at the magician quickly. "You could have made off with that scroll at any time in the last three weeks if you truly only wanted to protect it. Yet you came back to see me safe, and then helped us escape capture."

Woodcarver glanced up at her, his eyes somber as he looked her up and down briefly.

"I think it's more than this scroll. I think you wouldn't leave Olivian to die just as you didn't leave me."

There was another pregnant pause as Woodcarver smiled and snorted.

"You may be the spitting image of your mother," he chuckled. "But, you have your father's wit about you."

"I got that a lot," she muttered.

"Your parents were my friends. I owe them my freedom, my life, my very existence," he continued softly. "So I will not be abandoning you, my dear. I could never look at myself in the mirror again if I saved the whole world only to have left a debt like that forever unpaid."

She felt a brief, momentary wash of relief roll over her. But it was not enough to ease the pain of loss that burdened every portion of her being. She stuck her left foot by the fire, feeling the leather soles of her moccasins suck in the warmth and ease the cold nipping at her toes. Duelmaster tossed another stick onto the fire, a shower of sparks splaying into the air.

"Well, now that we've gotten that out of the way," he said, sitting back on his heels. "About this new route? I've no idea where we're going at this point, I've never ventured to this portion of the Wild."

"Well, there is no going back at this point," Dinendale said, raising an eyebrow at Woodcarver.

"Yeah. The new guy kinda already made sure of that when he brought down the mountain, Din," Robert said.

"Every outpost along the normal roads and paths will be watching for us. The prince may already know of our whereabouts, and he will expect us to come. He's counting on it," Duelmaster said. "But Woodcarver is right; he may not expect us to come through the mountains. And yet, once the survivors from that regiment get out of the rubble you caused, he'll know we had to go deeper into the mountains."

"This is true. But fortunately, even with having to cross the mountains, we may yet be able to beat the news they carry. It will be at least three days before they can get to the nearest outpost, and after that a week to get riders to Aschin even using the rough roads. I think if we push ourselves, we can beat them," Woodcarver said.

"I'm sure he feels confident his patrols will intercept us in the lowlands," Dinendale added, tossing a piece of semi-dry, punky wood on the fire. It rolled off the main flames, sputtered and popped atop the soggy pile of struggling ash, then hissed as the heat steamed the moisture out of it.

"Aye. But even still, he will expect us to break in, even if we come from a different direction," Woodcarver stated. "He wants the page, and fully expects us to try to get the princess without surrendering it to him. He will expect us to try and break her out and he knows there's no way we'd mount an attack on the castle itself."

"So we need to do what he doesn't expect," Twostaves stated. Paige saw Robert open his mouth to make a snide remark about stating the obvious, but he closed it, biting his tongue.

"But how?" Duelmaster asked. "How do you do something unexpected that is more unexpected than the unexpected the person is expecting?"

There was a long, confused pause.

"Well, we have to rescue her. There is no question about that," Broadside said, shifting his pack. "We'll just have to risk a break in."

"And now we have to think about this page from the Book of Death, or whatever it is," Robert muttered. "One more thing to account for in the list of things that could go horribly awry."

"Not if there is no page," Paige whispered. She reached into her moccasin, and drew out the dirty animal skin. "Why not destroy it?"

"Well for one, it is our only bargaining chip if everything falls apart to our worst case scenario," Dinendale said. "If the prince knows the page is lost, there is no reason for him to keep Olivian alive."

"He won't know we've destroyed it," she pointed out.

"That's hardly the only reason to keep it intact," Woodcarver snapped. "You have no idea the power contained within that page."

"I thought you said you couldn't read it?" Twostaves said, his eyes scanning the magician, sceptical.

"I can't. But I know enough to know the power contained within those pages is not something to just be cut up or scorched," Woodcarver said. "Between the two books, there are secrets we can't even imagine waiting to be unlocked some day."

"Wait, there are two books!?" Broadside exclaimed, clearly bewildered.

"It stands to reason if there is a Book of Death there would be a Book of Life, would it not?" Jesnake mumbled. Woodcarver nodded.

"The books are said to have been written by Ayan and Iyan at the Dawn of the Word," Woodcarver said, staring at the scrap of leather in Paige's hand. "They were entrusted with the power to create and destroy. Such Deep Magic created this world. That kind of raw power makes enchanted swords and healing spells look like parlour tricks."

"Then all the more reason to end it here and now," Paige said, shaking the leather in his face. Before he could argue with her, she threw the scrap into the fire as hard as she could. The flames roared to life as if strong ale had been poured directly onto it, and sparks shot out in all directions. The men all jumped up in surprise, smacking the sparks out before they could light their wool cloaks and linen shirts on fire. The page curled up in the heat, but then began to slowly unfurl again like a rose coming into bloom. The words on the page began to glow a hot, white color.

"What in the name of all subtropical fruit tree species?" Duelmaster gasped.

Woodcarver grabbed a fire poking stick and pulled the leather from the heat. No scorch marks, charred bits, or even ash dust could be seen on the leather as the Magician picked it up in his gloved hand and waved it about for all to see.

"I told you," he said, a smirk on his young looking face. "Deep magic."

"It was ripped from the book; could it not also be cut up into tiny bits?" Jesnake asked. Woodcarver shook his head.

"You'll see there are no torn or cut edges," he said, holding it up to be examined. "The book is not bound together or rolled like a scroll. It is merely a collection of pages, numbered on each side, that are stacked and locked in a box. There is no way to destroy this, which means keeping it safe is our only recourse."

Paige sighed. She didn't fully understand everything he was saying, but she was growing too tired to even demand more answers; she was sure based on her track record for asking thus far that she would merely be met with half an answer and a promise of more information at a later time. She stuffed the leather scroll back in her moccasin and sighed, staring into the sputtering campfire.

"So," Dinendale said, standing, "we'll go over the mountains instead of along them. Maybe, just maybe, we'll have the edge of surprise on our side."

"Best get some much-needed, much-warranted rest then," Twostaves muttered. "My calves feel like they are about to fall off the back of my legs."

"I don't even want to hear it, Twostaves," Paige hissed angrily.

"Hey! You must remember where I'm from!" the giant spat back. "I'm a Lowland Giant, remember?"

"Oh, shut up!" Robert shouted. The bark was louder than any of them expected, causing several of them to jump in surprise. Twostaves looked incredulous, staring at Robert who had leapt to his feet.

"It's not like we just escaped certain death at the cost of an entire village and the life of a man who literally lost everything to help us."

"Robert," Dinendale tried to interject, but Robert wasn't having any of it.

"No, I'm sick of this! Twostaves couldn't pour water out of his boot if the instructions were written on the freaking heel! He doesn't think before he opens his mouth! People are dead, and all he can go on about are how much his feet hurt!"

"Now see here," Twostaves leapt up with a face flushed with rage, but Robert cut him off.

"Shut your face, giant, or I'll shut it for you!"

Then, before anyone could stop him, Twostaves punched Robert's face so hard it physically threw Robert back four paces. Robert landed on his back, sputtering. The giant made for the fallen comrade, eyes ablaze and huge fists clenched like mighty hams.

"Twostaves, no!" Dinendale shouted, but the giant didn't stop. He was just about to pick Robert up by the collar of his chainmail for another face bloodying punch, when a shout echoed above the Brotherhood.

"Fhaighr me vghindur!"

369

The giant's body hurled several feet into the air and flew backwards as if pushed by an invisible hand. He landed on his back, knocking the wind out of him as his large body rolled and hit a boulder with a heavy thudding sound. He gasped for air as he rolled back onto his elbow slowly, looking about wildly in confusion.

They turned to see Woodcarver standing behind them all, his staff extended towards Twostaves, his free hand outstretched behind him. His eyes were glowing an opaque white but slowly faded back into his normal colorless hue.

"Enough of this nonsense. You are all worse than little children!" He paced over to Robert and muttered some words. Paige worried for Robert laying there with his body mangled from Twostaves' strike. Pulling his gloved hand back, Woodcarver smacked Robert with an open palm across the face. Paige gasped, but Robert's bloodied face suddenly seemed less contorted and broken, eventually working itself back into place. His broken nose straightened itself and his missing teeth filled back into their normal jagged places. He was not smiling however; he had a glare plastered on his mended bloody face that could have melted a brick of iron.

"Things are going to get a lot less pleasant in the next few weeks, so get a grip on yourselves. Quit complaining and act like men!"

"Not something I'm exactly striving to achieve," hissed a heaving Twostaves, who struggled to his feet.

Woodcarver glared at him. "Don't start with me, giant," the magician growled. "Your prejudices are not going to get the older princess free, are they?"

"No," Twostaves simmered, shaking himself. Dust floated from his cloak and gambeson to the ground.

"Now," Woodcarver snapped. "If you are all quite finished, I recommend getting some sleep. We've a long walk ahead of us tomorrow."

The Brotherhood grumbled among themselves, but one by one they began preparing makeshift sleeping areas to turn in for the night, though several of them spread out a little further than normal. Paige wrapped herself in her damp wool cloak. Her nearly dry wool blanket spread atop her as the others tossed their gear unceremoniously into bedrolls. Robert took first watch as the others wrapped up for what small amount of slumber they could afford.

Sleep did not come to Paige regardless of her fatigue. She could hear the sounds of crows and owls calling out in the night. The heavy weight of grief still festered within her. The more she lay still, the more it began to gnaw away at her heart. Soft tears welled up in her eyes. There she imagined the two villages that now lay in ashes beyond the cold grey chasm she and the Brotherhood has passed through on their journey, a little corner of the world wiped off the map because of one man's greed.

She had no idea how long she'd been laying there when she drifted into a fitful sleep, but slowly the black corners of her mind filled with flashes of light, like lightning in a thunderstorm. She saw flashes of her parents' faces covered in soot and blood, fire surrounding them on all sides. She saw dark, faceless spectres swoop in and hide them from view, screams of fear and torment echoing in her head and reverberating off the walls of her thumping heart. She then saw the same sort of flashes with Abenya and Hanburg. Finally, she saw Olivian reaching out to her, covered in blood and crying, swallowed up by the morbid, cruel chuckle of Prince Feridar.

"NO!" Paige screamed, flying up to an upright position screaming, tears flowing freely from her eyes as she sobbed in the dark. She sat straight up into a pair of strong, firm arms.

"Paige, calm down. It was only a dream." Robert was saying, squeezing her tight. She held in her sobs for a moment, then released the floodgates, her whole body shaking into his damp robe in the steady drizzle that surrounded them. She cried until her throat was raw, her lungs hiccuping to pull in enough breath. Her heart felt as if it had finally splintered into a billion pieces, and she was left with nothing to keep the feelings inside any longer. All the while Robert kept holding her tightly.

"It's alright. I've got you. Let it out. Let it all out. I'm not going anywhere."

"I can't....I can't let him keep doing this!"

"Who?"

"The prince. He's taken everything from me!" she sobbed. "And he's not going to stop!"

"No he won't," Robert agreed, stroking her damp hair reassuringly. "But we're going to get Olivian out. I promise."

Paige sobbed softly for a moment then pulled her face away, sniffing and wiping her nose with the back of her sleeve.

"It's not just her though," Paige said as she looked up into Robert's concerned expression. "He's going to keep destroying lives if we don't do something. He's wiped out so much of the Wild trying to get his hands on that stupid scroll!"

"You're absolutely right."

Paige paused for a moment, holding her breath. She let her hot, angry tears drip down her nose and stain the fabric of her already muddy shirt.

"And nothing I've done has once helped keep that from happening," Paige whimpered. "I'm too weak."

"Don't say that," Robert said softly. "Paige, you are the strongest woman I've ever met."

"That's just it," Paige said, sitting up a bit straighter and looking at Robert in the eyes. "I keep trying to be. But I failed my mother. She died because of what I did. And I couldn't save my Papa, even though I tried. I couldn't even get out of that stupid village on my own. Someone had to drag me. And now Hanburg is dead, and it's all because they are hunting me. It's not Olivian who's the damsel in distress. It's me. It's always been me." Paige hiccupped and felt her cheeks flush with embarrassment which made her even angrier. "See, I can't even pull myself together. This is stupid!"

She choked out the last few sobs she had in her. The patterning of the rain on his robe was the only sound aside from Paige's occasional sniff.

"Paige, do you know why I agreed to help you?"

Paige shook her head. "I figured it was pity, or honor, you being a good person or some such rubbish," she muttered.

Robert chuckled. "Well, yes. But the thing that sealed it all together for me?"

Paige shrugged.

"It was this," he said, thumping his chest. "That heart that beats in your chest is the bravest, most selfless heart I've ever seen. You don't have to be emotionless or tough to be strong. I wanted to help you because I saw the most honest person I've ever seen decide she was going to march to hell and back for someone she loves. For family. That kind of loyalty? That kind of bravery? That is the kind of thing that people are willing to follow."

"But all the pain? All the loss?" Paige said.

Robert inclined his head. "Life happens. There was nothing you could do about any of those losses, but you keep letting that unnecessary guilt hold you down. That's a burden you don't need to carry, Alwasu."

Paige shrugged again, but his words brought a soothing measure of comfort to her pounding, aching heart. She felt the tears continue to burn paths down her cheeks.

"Never think that being who you are is a weakness," Robert whispered. "It's that honesty about you that we all love, Paige. You should never be ashamed to be you. You're allowed to cry, you are allowed to grieve. Because it's your tenacity to keep going that shows your strength. Never forget that, okay?"

Paige nodded and closed her eyes. Eventually she cried herself to sleep in Robert's reassuring arms and did not wake up till the next morning when Woodcarver had tapped her foot to rouse her.

"I'm sorry my dear," he said, sympathy edging his urgent tone. "But we simply must get moving. No time to waste."

Paige nodded and numbly put her soggy gear back into her soaked pack and cinched up for the journey. She glanced at Robert before they set out, who gave her a half smile before putting his own pack on and following Woodcarver. They slogged through the muddy ground and back onto the trailless, steep cliffs that were now their only pathway to saving Olivian.

They trudged on for hours, the rain sputtering on and off into a slight drizzle. The trees were so thick they could see only a various sickly gray patch of sky filled with droopy clouds. The boulders and ravines were becoming steeper, and there were now more cliffs. Rather than march straight through the mountains up and over to the other side, they were having to skirt around them and zig zag up and down natural switchbacks and game trails.

On and on they plodded, one step at a time. Paige felt like dropping constantly, but she knew if she stopped, she wouldn't be able to get back up. She resolved to keep moving despite her feet turning as raw as a young tree scraped by a buck's antlers in the spring. The tired and worn out crew called it a day just as the twilight faded through the grim sky, although the day had been gloomy enough it was hard to tell how fast the sun was actually setting. They set up a fireless camp, too weary to find wood that wasn't damp.

Paige sat with her back to a mossy tree. She had wrapped herself in her wool blanket and cloak to fend off the cold that nipped at her body. A few surviving mosquitoes lazily buzzed into her ear, the noise. She shooed them away and bent over to pull off her muddy moccasins, as a sickly smell hit her. She gagged at the sight of her bloody foot coming out of the wet leather. She could make out the dark red areas that had formed deep crimson blisters the size of her thumbnail. They were now bloody, raw wounds, as if her shoes had been made of cheese graters. She bit her lip as she removed the other moccasin to the exact result.

"By the Moons!" Broadside exclaimed as he walked past and caught sight of her feet. "What happened, Paige?!"

The men swooped to her aid, concern flooding their faces. She felt embarrassed at the attention but touched by the sentiment.

Questions flooded out of their mouths all at once:

"Do you need some water? I saw a stream a ways that way."

"Oh! That looks painful! What should we do?"

"Can I help?"

"Oh, that's nothing. You want to see mine?"

"You want me to cauterize them for you?"

"Stand down, you tottling hens!" Woodcarver scolded in a tone that immediately hushed everyone to a silence like a sealed burial chamber. "Give her some air."

"Well then why don't you do something about it, mister sorcerer?" Broadside asked, placing two fists the size of hams on his robust hips.

Woodcarver glared at him. "I wouldn't expect a dwarf to remember such trivial details, but I am a magician, not a sorcerer." He knelt beside Paige.

"Big difference, that!" mocked Broadside.

Robert smacked him upside the head. "Sorcerers use human sacrifice for their spells, you dolt," he snapped.

Broadside's eyes grew wide with surprise and his cheeks flushed red. "I'm horribly embarrassed. Forgive me, sir," he muttered. Woodcarver ignored him.

"This won't be pleasant, but it's far better than searing your shredded feet with hot iron," Woodcarver said, looking over Paige's torn feet. "You're lucky it's cold, princess," he said, gingerly holding one of her small, bloodied heels. "The chilling numb is the only thing keeping you from excruciating pain."

"It still hurts," she winced.

He smiled with compassion. "I fear it will sting a little more yet, but I promise it will be worth it. May I?"

Paige thought for a moment, then sighed and nodded. Woodcarver took off his green cloak and rolled up his baggy, natural wool colored shirtsleeves, and took her two oozing feet in his hands. He took a deep breath, and closed his eyes.

"Ithniegh," he whispered. Paige watched in wonder and fascination as a light began to generate from his hands. It was a grayish-blue, foggy kind of light. Paige suddenly felt all the feeling go out of her lower leg. It was replaced by a cold tingling as the light faded. Woodcarver let her still bloody feet lay on the rocky earth.

"What's wrong?" she asked.

"Nothing. The Mist has entered your blood. It..." he hesitated.

"What?"

"I said it was better than cauterization, but, the irritation is about the..."

SNAP! Paige felt blasts of pain hit her feet. She cried out as a wall of stinging, searing sensations rushed up her legs. She felt like fire was burning up her feet, and no thrashing could ease it. Her bare legs radiated a bright light as the magic sped up the healing process, replacing torn and tattered skin and tissue with new.

And as suddenly as it had begun, it stopped. It had taken no more than a few seconds, but she had never in her life experienced such physical pain. She lay on the ground, nearly sobbing as she coughed, trying to force air into her lungs. Hot tears rolled down her cheeks.

Broadside bent down to her, concerned. "How do they feel?"

"Hang on," she said with gritted teeth, and then, before anyone could stop her, delivered a kick so violent it might have made the dwarf lose his supper if he'd had any. Broadside fell down with an "oof" and rolled twice, then coughed and moaned in pain.

Even with her own lingering discomfort, Paige smirked. "They feel just fine now."

CHAPTER 13

CRAYMOGHR CLIFF

It took another three days for the rain to clear up, but even after the downpour had ceased, the mountains remained misty and cold like the deep dungeon where Paige pictured Olivian. That thought drove her on as they climbed and trudged through the grey atmosphere of the wild highlands. Birds became scarce now, just like the wild game they had been relying on for food. With no lack of effort, they still managed to catch rabbits and other small creatures to keep them fed and energized each day.

On the morning of the fourth day, Paige wrapped up in her wool blanket and staggered to her feet. Her breath came out in clouds now, and it felt like her lungs were coated with the frost of the late fall. She looked to the sky, eager to see the sun crest the ridge and warm her bones. She flicked some of the rebellious strands of blonde hair out of her eyes, looking towards the men lying around their own campfire.

Judging by the sound of the snoring, she assumed they were all still asleep. Paige smiled at the rhythmic cacophony that resounded from across the sloped campsite, courtesy of the camp's resident dwarf and giant. Her mother had always teased her father for sounding like a bear, but they put her Papa to shame.

Paige swallowed another round of grief as those memories slithered across her heart. She found herself touching the key at her throat, the ache amplified with each heartbeat. She missed her parents so much, and the raw emotional ache that Hanburg's untimely death had brought to her made her miss her family all the more. She closed her eyes and imagined her mother, sitting on her bed when she'd been but a child. She remembered her mother's merry laugh and fanciful stories about the great forests of the Whisperwood. Every night she would tell the girls tales of her own childhood and the fantastic beasts that roamed the country.

A tear began to form in the corner of Paige's eye, but she refused to let it fall. Right now, she needed to focus. Paige tossed the blanket aside in a forsaken wad, biting her lip in defiance to the cold. She took a length of hemp rope and a few tight rolls later, she had the crumpled mass lashed to her wood frame pack.

"Ready?" a soft, but deep voice asked from behind her. She didn't have to turn to know it was Dinendale. For someone so big and tall, he had an uncanny knack for sneaking up on people.

"Are you?" she asked, not bothering to look up at him as she slid her hunting knife into her finally dry moccasin. She heard him slide off his perch on the gigantic boulder and land nimbly on his feet.

"I am always ready," he said, walking up to her.

"I guess you would be, living like this all the time."

The elf chuckled, walking up alongside her. "I didn't always live like this, I'll have you know," he said, his eyes glinting like obsidian.

Paige felt her cheeks flush. "Is that so?" she said with mock haughtiness. "Well, you certainly could have fooled me."

The elf smiled a one-sided grin, noting her sarcasm. "You are quite strange for a princess, you know?"

"Oh, so you've been acquainted with many princesses, sir elf?" she scoffed, turning to face him.

"I've met my fair share," he said, rubbing his chin, a mischievous glint in his dark brown eyes. Trying to stifle a chuckle of her own, air escaped through her nose in a snort. Her embarrassed cheeks flushed crimson as Dinendale lead a round of contagious laughter, grinning ear to ear. The silence took hold for only a few heartbeats before the elf cleared his throat.

"Well, I guess I'd better get these vagrants up." He stretched with a good natured sigh leaving his lips.

"Good luck," Paige rolled her eyes. "They could sleep in the middle of a battlefield, given the chance."

"Some of them have," Dinendale said grimly, immediately changing the tone of their jovial moment.

Paige held his eyes with sympathy, until that impish grin came back.

"Want to see something funny?" he asked.

"Is that even a question?" she laughed back.

"Follow me."

As they approached the camp, Paige saw that Jesnake and Woodcarver were already up. Dinendale walked over to Duelmaster and bent over the him. The dryad slowly opened his eyes and sat up, his autumn hair in so many tangles that it looked like a bird's nest cluttered with leaves from the ground where he slept.

The elf whispered something in Duelmaster's ear. The dryad looked surprised then delighted as he nodded emphatically in agreement. Dinendale proceeded to waking Robert while Duelmaster straddled Twostaves' heaving, snoring, chest. Then he delivered a loud slap across Twostaves' face. The giant jumped up, cursing and swinging. Robert, who'd been jostled by Dinendale, resorted to descriptive name-calling.

"Cut it out you tree-hugging, pond-drinking, jerk-faced son of a pixie!" he shouted. Dinendale shushed him and jerked his head at Broadside, the last remaining sleeper of the band.

Robert immediately shut his mouth, and a glint flashed in his eyes as he smirked and pulled himself out of bed.

Dinendale crouched and crept up to where Broadside lay snoring like a behemoth. His tawny hair and fast growing, matted, tangled beard shook with each raspy breath. A large puddle of thick drool hung out of his mouth and pooled in the folds of his makeshift pillow of helmet lining. His large backside pointed to the treetops, and his feet poked from underneath his cloak like hairy, wriggly butternut squash. Paige let out a soft giggle of amusement.

The dark elf took his water-skin and pulled the cork out with is teeth, leaning its mouth just over the dwarf's bulbous nose. He shook it once, allowing just three or four drops to splatter on the dwarf's nostril.

"FLOOD!" Broadside leapt up from his precarious position and began to thrash wildly in the tangle of cloaks and armor. "DROWNING! HELP! HEEEEEEEEELP!"

The dwarf leapt up, his body held hostage by his own cloak. Blinded by his woolen prison, Broadside ran about like a drunken madman who'd just had his bottom lit on fire. He screeched in a tone so high-pitched that Paige wondered if an elk somewhere in the craggy mountains might mistake him for a female looking for a sweetheart. The dwarf face-planted into a large fir tree, dropping immediately on his backside, then flat on his back, lying still and whining like a wounded duck. Paige gasped, laughter clawing its way out of her using her ribcage as a ladder.

"Oh my moons," Robert stammered, wiping tears from his eyes. "That is the most beautiful thing I've seen in my life!"

"That was somewhat mean-spirited, Dinendale," remarked Jesnake.

Dinendale's hand fingered the brooch Hanburg had given him. He looked down at it, and Paige felt an ache in her own chest as she followed his gaze.

"We needed to laugh," he said.

Jesnake looked at him, puzzled, then nodded, slinging his bow on his back and tending to his things.

"I didn't!" came a gruff, muffled voice from under the cloak and dwarf pile lying in the dirt. "Could have found a way to get that laugh without scaring me half to bloody death."

"We absolutely could have," Robert snorted. A new chorus of laughter let out on all accounts as they began to break the camp.

In a short while, everyone stood readFy to embark. All the travel of the last few weeks made the events of stowing, strapping, and cinching their assorted gear to the wood packs an easy routine.

"Ugh! What the devil!?" Broadside shouted, tossing his helmet off his head and ruffling his hair. "My liner is sopped!"

Paige felt a giggle explode from her lips like a suprise sneeze. The others roared with another round of laughter as Duelmaster picked up the liner with two fingers, holding it at arms length.

"I meant to mention it, but it must have slipped my mind!" the dryad laughed, plopping the dwarf's drool saturated cervelliere atop Broadside's head before patting the little creatures rosey cheeks like a child.

They hiked the craggy pine forests with an eager haste. Every moment they delayed was one more moment Olivian didn't have to spare. If the soldiers returned to the Aschin stronghold and reported Paige's confirmed existence, there was no way to know what might happen to the older princess.

The hills became steeper; the soreness burning in Paige's upper thighs and calves was a testament. More and more Paige found herself dodging large, lichen-covered boulders that dotted the sloping hillside. The trees grew taller and thinner, the trunks reaching high up into the sky. Their branches grasped for the misty clouds looming overhead which occasionally drifting low enough to envelope the tops in a dense fog. The ground was covered in a century's worth of pine needles that padded the sharp, rocky ground like a king's fine carpet. Eventually the mist of early morning finally gave way to a bright filtering sunlight that streamed through the branches, reached through the mist, and gripped the earth as if for dear life.

"A two-piece for your thoughts, princess?"

Paige turned to see Woodcarver plodding beside her, his staff slung across his shoulders like an oxen's yolk. He smiled a lopsided grin that didn't show his teeth; his eyes crinkling in the corners and betraying his young face with the sparkle of a man who had seen a good many years on the earth.

"The mountain forests are so beautiful," Paige said as she observed a great ponderosa basking in the pale yellow light. "Not at all like the forests I called home."

"It's the fairies," Woodcarver said, his eyes twinkling. "They help keep the mountains beautiful."

"Fairies?" Paige laughed, her skepticism quite evident. "I'm sure they do!"

"You laugh?" he commented more than questioned, amusement tugging at the corners of his mouth.

"Oh," she said, her laughter halting in the air. "You mean fairies exist?"

"Of course they exist." Woodcarver sighed as if he'd explained this fact a million times. "They are the guardians of the seasons, endowed by the Creator to watch over the earth and keep it beautiful."

"I've only ever heard children's stories about them," Paige defended.

"You are a halfling. Your mother was a full-blooded elf. I know of Shauds that believe Elves and Dwarves are also just stories. Are you a story?"

"No," Paige said. "But why don't we ever see them? The fairies I mean?"

"Because that's all you are doing. Seeing," Woodcarver said softly. "Maybe you've never been looking."

"Or maybe I've just never experienced what you have," she countered.

The magician chuckled. "Truth is truth my dear, regardless of what you've experienced."

The group trudged on and on, hour after hour. The day grew long and surprisingly hot as they wound their way around, up, and across the endless mountainside. They passed several small streams and waterfalls that allowed them to fill up their canteens and wineskins. At one point, a hare bolted out of a bush near Paige. She had her bow in hand and attempted to lose an arrow from her belt quiver at the creature. A sharp twang filled the clear mountain air, and one of Jesnake's swan fletched arrows struck the rabbit in its small head before her arrow had cleared her belt.

"You almost had that one, princess," Jesnake encouraged. She glared at him. "I was almost too late on that shot."

They continued the begrudging trek for several more hours. No one really felt like talking much, except for Duelmaster and Broadside, who never seemed to lack something to talk about. Paige half listened to them, but the bulk of her concentration was put on keeping a cadence in her head to keep up with the group.

"Got-ta get-there, got-ta get-there," she whispered to herself, forcing her cramping legs to keep in step with her young companions.

By late afternoon, Paige could see the crest of the slope plateauing off in front of them as the woods began to thin out, breaking into a clearing. The sunlight dimmed as it began to set in the east, sending tendrils of bright golden light into Paige's eyes as she trudged to where Woodcarver had halted.

The magician beckoned urgently as he stood along the edge of the treeline waiting for the others to catch up.

"Please tell me were done," Broadside heaved. "Please, can we be done?"

"Not quite," Woodcarver muttered. "We have a bit more to go, Master Dwarf."

Paige felt her heart sink at the thought of more walking as she and the others cleared the treeline. Then her spirit sank even lower as an audible groan lifted up from the Brotherhood.

"Oh don't get your knickers in a twist. It's just Craymoghr Cliff," the wizard scolded, gesturing before them to the steepest wall of rock Paige had ever seen. It was at least four hundred feet high, and had sharp crags and edges jutting out like the back of an agitated porcupine. It was so tall, one had no possible hope to see what lie behind it. The sheer size of the rock astounded the princess, stretching as far as her eyes could see in either direction, standing directly in her path.

"Well, this is an unexpected twist," Robert spat tartly.

"Actually, there is no twist. It goes straight up," Duelmaster joked.

Paige couldn't laugh. The sick lump in her throat wouldn't let her even think to chuckle.

"How in the name of all that is good and green in this world are we supposed to get up there?" queried Twostaves.

There was a long pause.

"We'll, I suppose we'll have to climb it," Dinendale stated in a matter-of-fact tone.

"Mm-hmm," Jesnake muttered, his tone drifting into the waters of sarcasm. "How?"

"There is one spot that has a small ledge that can be climbed to reach the top," Woodcarver explained. "It zigzags up the cliff but it beats trying to go straight up that rock face with no ropes or gear designed for such a task."

"As someone who is not okay with climbing any more often than I have to," mumbled Twostaves, "I'm thinking a road filled with Raven-heads would be better than this!"

"This is the shortest route to the east. The road to Aschin circles much farther north," an exasperated Woodcarver sighed, pinching the bridge of his nose like he had a headache at the giant's words. "No Raven Heads will follow us past that even if they've managed to get past the roadblock I threw up. They'd take one look at that wall and soil themselves."

"I think I might have soiled myself," Broadside gulped.

"This is hardly my idea of a shortcut," Robert said dryly.

"Can we even make it with the daylight we have left?" Jesnake asked. "I for one don't want to be on a cliff face when twilight hits."

"We have five hours of daylight left, give or take," Woodcarver said. "If we really want to get out of danger of being followed, I recommend doing it now."

"It would put the hardest behind us," Jesnake admitted.

Woodcarver chuckled mirthlessly. "Well, believe it or not, there is good news that comes with this situation."

"What's that?" Broadside bemoaned.

"I can count on one hand how many mortals have actually climbed this cliff and lived."

"And that's good?" Paige gasped.

Woodcarver's sly smile spread across his face. "Aye. Because any Shauds trying to follow us will be in the exact same predicament."

"And you're sure we can climb this, magician?"

"I am. I'm one of the ones who climbed it and lived, and the Shaud's have no such guide."

Paige grasped the sharp rocks with every ounce of her strength till her fingertips felt like they were on fire. True to his word, Woodcarver led them to the ledge he'd spoken of. Paige had decided that the group needed to have a meeting about vocabulary terms because the wizard's idea of a "ledge" was only about six inches wide in some spots and no wider than two men's feet. She gulped and looked up towards the cliff's tip high above. The ledge angled a little to the right and rose gradually to the top. From there it immediately switched directions about a third of the way up and repeated the pattern till the top. As long as the group didn't lean back at all, they might make it. This required a balance that made carrying packs a rather difficult challenge, especially for Robert, Twostaves, and Broadside; their body frames didn't exactly produce good balance to begin with.

Paige was behind Jesnake, who was behind Woodcarver. Dinendale followed her, and Robert came behind him. Broadside and Duelmaster came next, and Twostaves took the tail end. Despite his abundant apprehension, the giant had volunteered to take the rear in case his extra weight caused the ledge to break or crumble. They each had a partner connected to them by safety ropes; in the event one slipped, the partner could assist that person, but the whole group would not be in peril of falling. The thought of that possibility made Paige's stomach churn. As ready as they would ever be, they began to climb, or rather scratch, along the thin ledge heading up. They took little steps, calling out to each other with tips on the best hand grips for the person behind them.

About an hour into their climb, one of Broadside's canteens popped a strap when he rubbed too aggressively against the sharp stone wall in front of him. The little wooden barrel popped off and tumbled until it hit the rock face halfway down and splintered into a thousand pieces which rained down into the dirt.

The cliff seemed to have no end, the realization of which made Paige dizzy. Her toes hurt from digging into the rock's face, and her fingertips were rubbed raw and bleeding in several spots. She glanced at Dinendale, careful not to look down.

"Hand hold four inches to your right," she said, nodding her sweating brow to the hand hold she'd just used.

"Thanks," the elf said, perspiration dripping off his face. Paige turned and took another step to her right, continuing up the rock face.

"Almost there!" Woodcarver heaved for them all to hear. "That wasn't so bad, was it?"

"Shut up and keep climbing, Mr. Mystical," Robert screamed.

"Relax, Eöl!" huffed Jesnake, taking another step.

Just then, the Western Elf's foot slipped. The rock beneath his feet gave way, and he began to tumble backwards.

"Jesnake!" Broadside screamed. The elf fell into the abyss of air behind him.

Paige didn't even think about what she was doing. As soon as his foot slipped, she leapt to his side. The elf reeled backwards waving his arms and crying out for help. She barely caught hold of his left arm bracer, hooking her fingers into the cuff. But he was too heavy for her grasp. Jesnake's weight pulled her of balance, and she slid like a horse cart with no hand brake.

"Paige!" Robert bellowed. She cried out as she grabbed for a hand hold and clutched a small jut in the face of the rock wall. Jesnake stopped short, Paige still holding to his bracer. The weight yanked hard against Paige's joints. She screamed as she felt her shoulder dislocating. Jesnake hung there, at least three bowshots' distance, if not four, from the ground far below.

"Hold on, Jesnake!" she strained through gritted teeth. She could feel her hands slipping and wasn't sure how long she could hold on. She looked down into the elf's eyes, wide with fear. Then she saw the ground far below, and nearly fainted.

"Paige! Don't move!" Dinendale cried. He whipped out his dirk and drove it into the rock face with all his might. It stuck fast in the craggy stone as he grabbed Paige' arm with his free hand. She gripped his strong wrist, and he began to pull her and Jesnake up inch by inch.

"Jesnake! Grab hold!" Robert yelled as he held the end of his spear out to the elf. Jesnake quickly grabbed the shaft with his free hand, clutching to Paige's wrist with the other.

"Okay! Robert, pull up on your side!" Dinendale called out, "Jesnake, release Paige and climb up the spear to grab hold of the ledge. Do you think you can do that?"

"Does it look like I'm planning on not doing that?" Jesnake yelled.

"Alright, on three! One!"

Paige felt Jesnake's hand tighten on her wrist.

"Two!"

Paige took a quick breath and breathed a quick prayer.

"Three!"

Robert pulled on the spear with all his might. Paige let go of Jesnake and felt Dinendale grab her arm and haul her up to the ledge. Jesnake swung to the left from the swinging spear. Hand over hand, he pulled himself back up to the ledge.

"Is everyone alright?" Woodcarver called out.

"I think my lunch is plastered all over this rock face," quivered Twostaves.

"That was too close," Dinendale said. "*Way* too close."

"Um, Dinendale?" Paige said.

"Yes?"

"You can let go now."

Dinendale turned a shade of pink and released the princess. She smiled at his embarrassment.

"Beg pardon," Dinendale looked away, turning even redder.

"Nice try," Paige heard Robert scoff. Dinendale didn't offer a reply to that jeer but Paige could see him bristle slightly. She rolled her eyes, trying to ignore the buffeting in her heart as they once again began inching their way to the left. Her steps were small and shaky, and it was all she could do to keep her hands from quivering under the rush of energy and fear that still thundered through her veins with every heartbeat.

The sky darkened to a deep magenta by the time they rounded the last switchback and began the final leg of the journey on the cliff face. The sun had long disappeared in the east by the time they had reached the top, it's farewell painting to the world for the day cast in glorious pinks and oranges across the sky.

"Grab hold, Paige," Woodcarver said as he extended his gloved hand to her. She reached for it and held tightly. He pulled her up with relative ease, and she collapsed at the edge of the cliff, thankful to be done. She lay with her head in her arms, breathing hard and trying to endure the cramping muscles and fear she still felt from their deadly fall. Then she felt a hand on her shoulder.

"Look up, princess," Woodcarver encouraged. She did, and what she saw made her catch her breath.

They had reached the top of a large plateau where the surrounding landscape was covered in pine forested highlands not unlike the ones they had just come from. The mountain ranges surrounded them from horizon to horizon, their snow capped peaks filling her vision and stealing her breath away. They looked like old, bearded men, staring down with wrinkled scowls as they seemed to dare anyone to traverse their white beards and creviced eyes. The sight was beautiful and terrible at the same time.

Paige sank to her knees and lay on her back looking up at the sky as the last rays of pink light faded away and the stars began to assemble one by one, as if waking from a deep sleep. Slowly the two moons rose from the west and began climbing high into the sky, weaving in and out in their slow dance across the heavens. She didn't fall asleep but lay there in a tired daze for what seemed like hours.

Eventually her stomach let forth an inhuman utterance as she smelled the aroma of roasting meat waft over to her. She rolled stiffly to her side then pushed herself up onto her palms as she looked to where the men gathered around a small fire pit. Robert roasted the rabbit Jesnake had shot earlier, along with two other little bunnies someone must have snagged while she was lying in her exhaustion.

"She lives!" Duelmaster cried with joy. Paige stood and limped towards the group. Her joints and muscles creaked with aching pain; her fingers felt numb from grabbing the rock crevices. She plopped down next to Duelmaster and watched the coals with a dazed, stupid expression.

"Dinner?" Robert asked, concern filling his blue eyes. She nodded, and he cut a strip of the juicy meat off the spit and handed it to her on a shaved wood skewer. She bit into the tender meat and closed her eyes with the wonderful taste that ensued. Robert cut the rest of the fat hare up and divided it amongst the rest of the men.

"This is delicious," she said, ignoring the fact that her mouth was full.

"Isn't it?" Robert said. "I rubbed it with a spice concoction we created. Dinendale found the wild onions, Broadside found some berries, and Woodcarver cut us some sappy pine wood to cook it over. Best meal we've had in some time."

"He did alright," Twostaves grumbled, following his begrudging praise with an enormous belch.

"Oh, yeah?" Broadside said, standing up and drawing up his full height. "You call that a burp!?!" He sucked in his breath, and pushed out his stocky chest as his face screwed up and contorted turning a slight shade of red. The men all cried out, "NO!" at the same moment, and ducked for cover.

All Paige remembered from what happened next was that Duelmaster shoved her to one side and covered her ears. The ground seemed to vibrate with earthquake-like tremors. There was the feeling of a mighty rushing wind, and a sonic boom hit the little group. When it was all quiet, they slowly sat up.

"Wow," Broadside said, a dazed expression on his pudgy, and now red face. "That one surprised even me."

They heard a slow rumble and glanced back towards the cliff they had spent all afternoon climbing and saw great plumes of dust from what had apparently been a minor rockslide.

"I....I apologize!" stammered the dwarf. "I saw it going differently in my head."

"Way to go, moron," Robert spat, decking the little man in the back of the head. "You put my fire out!"

After the men had restarted the fire and settled down, Paige walked the short distance to the edge of the cliff wall. She sat down, tucking her knees under her chin and gazing out at the hilly highlands they had traversed. Somewhere in that sprawling blanket of vibrant yellow and orange leaves dotted with green patches of conifers, two villages lay burnt to the ground. Yet, from up here, the Wild sprawled out behind them as savage and untamed as ever. The view was breathtaking. The night stars and two half-moons cast a bluish glow on everything. The white caps of distant peaks sparkled and glowed in the moonbeams. She knew they still had a long way to go but took heart in the many miles she and the Brotherhood had already put behind them.

"Hey," Robert plopped down beside her as he pulled out his knife and an apple from his robe.

"Hey, yourself," she greeted back.

"I found an apple tree when we got wood," he explained. "Want some?"

"No thanks," she said, flipping her braid over her shoulder.

"Come on," he probed. "You've had a steady diet of crusty bread and wild game for the last couple weeks. It will do you good."

"Fine," she said, more to get him to stop talking than for the apple.

He cut the fruit into two pieces and handed her one. He wiped the blade of his hunting knife on his robe, putting it back in the inner folds of the brown material. She bit into the slice and felt the sweet nectar enrapture her taste buds. It had been so long since she'd tasted something so sweet, so wild. Since it was the end of the season, whatever apples had been left on that tree must have gathered every bit of sweetness left in the tree as the season changed, and she could taste every note.

"You and Twostaves make up yet?" she asked, taking another bite.

"Yeah, I guess you could say that," Robert responded, tossing the apple core over the cliff.

Paige watched it fall to the dark ground hundreds of feet below. She shuddered to think that that could have been her or Jesnake only a few hours ago.

"Apparently," Robert chewed the last few bites of apple, "we should only have another week or so to get to Aschin."

"Only?" Paige muttered. It seemed like ages ago when they had set out from the willow tree, and now they had at least seven days before they would reach the city. And then there was the time needed to break Olivian out, and who knew how long that would take?

"Yeah, it's not exactly a shortcut, not at the rate we've been going." He wiped his hands off on his robe. "But... the enemy won't be at our back now. We'll get to Aschin unseen, so we've regained at least some element of surprise."

They sat in silence for a moment. It was a quiet night, and the cool breeze soothed Paige's aching muscles. Robert looked at the stars, and then, to Paige's surprise, began to sing.

"Through the mist,
The Naiads weep,
Along the brook,
They bend and creep,
The fairies sob,
In war-torn land,
All because a tyrant,
Burned forests to sand."

"That was nice," she said, smiling.

He turned to her. "Was that a compliment, Princess?" he asked with sarcastic surprise.

"Yes, I suppose it was," she said.

"Well, I should very much like to compliment you back."

She looked at him for a second, and then caught his meaning.

"No. I'm not going to sing," she said turning her head away.

"Oh, come on. That's no fair! Here I give you a nice serenade to entertain you, and I wasted all my breath for nothing!"

" No!"

"Come on then, sing!" he insisted.

She blew a puff of air, blowing some stray hairs out of her face. "If I hum a few bars, will you leave it?" she asked. She folded her arms across her middle.

"Of course," he said with a wave of his hand.

Paige took a deep breath. "You can't laugh," she said. She thought for a moment about what song to sing, and then began to let the elvish words lilt off her tongue. She sang an old lullaby her mother had taught them when she and Olivian were young. The words told were about a hero who went off to battle, promising his true love he'd come home; how he thought about her every moment while at war. Her voice was soft, but not quiet; rather it carried out to the Wild and it's craggy highlands. In the darkness, somewhere afar off, a lone wolf howled to the blinking stars above. She let the final chorus fade as she came to a close, and then there was a moment of silence. She looked over at Robert. He was staring in absolute shock.

"That was....incredible," he said, staring into her eyes with wonder and admiration.

"Don't put your foot in your mouth, Eöl; after this week, it wouldn't taste so great," a voice said from behind them. Paige turned to see Dinendale standing behind them. She hadn't heard him come up.

"How long have you been standing there?" she demanded.

"Doesn't matter. He's snooping all the same," Robert growled tartly under his breath.

Paige glared at Dinendale feeling a mix of annoyance and violation at his intrusion. No other ears were meant to be privy to her performance.

"I think the halfling has you beat, sir," Dinendale said with a smile. Robert stood, and Paige did likewise.

"I'm tired," Robert grumbled. "I'll see you in the morning."

He trudged back to the campsite, and Paige started to follow.

"That was a beautiful song," Dinendale said to her as she walked past.

"Thank you," she mumbled, embarrassed, as she continued to walk past the dark elf.

"I mean it," he reached out and lightly touched her elbow. She halted her retreat and looked up at him. He stood there gazing at her, a small smile on his face. "You are full of surprises."

"Everyone has surprises," she looked up into his eyes as he chuckled.

"I guess we do," he gave her another smile. The lone wolf howled again, and Paige shuddered. It was an eerie, cold sound. Dinendale smirked as he looked off into the distance.

"Sometimes I wish I were a wolf. Free to roam these lands without any bounds. It must be nice to have no one chasing you; no one wanting you dead-"

"All alone," Paige added.

He stopped and looked at her. "Being alone is not a terrible fate. Sometimes, it's the only way to survive." He let out a long breath. "I had to do it for years."

"But not everyone can be you," she said, looking down. "I won't leave my sister alone. I'm all she's got."

"Paige, I didn't mean-"

"I know you didn't. But still, there are people that love you here," she gestured towards the camp. "To wish you could be free of all of them is selfish."

With that, she walked back to her pine tree, leaving the elf at the edge of the cliff, with the wolf howling alone in the distance.

CHAPTER 14

RIPPLES

They awoke late the next morning, worn out from the previous day's climb. Broadside whined and asked why they couldn't have one day's rest as they all massaged the kinks and knots out of their swollen muscles.

"After all," he reasoned, struggling to cinch his belt and wincing, "we covered quite a bit of ground yesterday, and we could use the rest."

"No," Woodcarver snapped, hefting his own small pack. "We covered vertical ground, much less liniar ground. We cannot delay. If you rest, your muscles will toughen and become stiff. Then you will want to delay another day, and that is just as good as giving up. We must keep moving."

The dwarf huffed his disappointment but didn't press the matter. As much as she didn't want to admit it, Paige agreed with Woodcarver. Her muscles ache down to the bones, but they had to press on. She was growing more and more worried for Olivian's safety with each passing hour. What if they arrived a week, a day, or even an hour too late? What would she do? How would she forgive herself for not pushing herself harder?

Jesnake had gotten up earlier than the others, and brought back some mountain berries for a meager breakfast. They were sweet to Paige's mouth, considering she'd grown used to the wild game dinners. Quickly pacing themselves through the morning earned them a remarkable distance. By high noon, they were setting out onto the plateau.

The steppe was a nice change from the steep mountain slopes they had endured. Their feet were grateful for the temporary downward slope. The thick growth of the alpine allowed a soft blanket of pine needles to walk on, as well as shrubs and ferns. Today's sky was overcast, keeping the air chilly and slightly damp. They walked on for several hours, chatting about the difference in the weather and the abundance of pine. Around mid-afternoon, they stopped to have a bite to eat.

"What food do we have left?" Dinendale asked Robert, who was carrying the supplies.

"We have about four day's worth of bread," he said, pulling the wrapped loaf out of his pack. "After that, it's whatever we can shoot."

"The game will get scarce after we pass into the highlands," commented Jesnake. "I vote we go out and get some heavy meat today."

"Uh oh," Robert said.

"What is it?" Twostaves asked.

Robert held up the loaf for him to see. "Make that two days worth of bread," Robert tossed the bread behind him, pulling out another loaf.

"What's wrong with it?" Paige jogged over to where he had thrown the bread. Robert made a face. She jogged back after seeing maggots in the inside of the broken, moldy, loaf. The sight of the wiggling, white grubs made her stomach crawl, and the thought of biting into the writhing, pus-colored maggots made her near ready to lose the few berries she'd eaten for breakfast. "That's so gross." She stifled a gag.

Robert drew his hunting dagger and began cutting a different loaf. He sliced the bread into nine pieces, one for each person, and passed it out. After everyone made sure their bread had no trace of the devilish worms, they ate in silence. Paige chewed the staling bread as she observed the pines surrounding them on all sides, the creak of the bread crust against her teeth matching the groaning of the tree trunks un the wind.

"We should keep our eyes open for fresh meat then," Twostaves said. "We can smoke it overnight. I can build a big smoking rack at camp tonight."

"You're not afraid someone might see the smoke?" Broadside questioned, skepticism etched into his face.

"Anyone behind us won't be able to follow," Woodcarver assured. "And no one is ahead of us till we cross the Raychels and begin descending into the valley where Aschin lies."

They all agreed, finishing their bread by washing it down with large gulps of lukewarm water that in no way made the experience any more desirable. Once they were all finished, Dinendale, Jesnake, Robert, Broadside, and Paige herself strung their bows and drew themselves each an arrow. The rest of the crew drew hunting knives and dirks to assist in the hunt. They continued walking down the plateau, spreading out along the way to cover more ground. They stood about a bowshot apart, keeping their distance, but not out of sight from each other.

Paige tiptoed in her moccasins. They felt good now that they weren't soaked and rough with water. They still were not as soft as her old buckskin ones, but with the ground becoming more rocky she was glad they were made of stouter leather for these mountains.

She gripped her bow tightly, an arrow now resting against her bow hand. She looked about the woods with an expert eye, paying attention to wind direction and all the other little details Papa had instilled on their many hunts together.

Her mind drifted back to their last hunt together. She could still smell the leathery, woody smell that clung to him as tight as her mother did. She could still see his grin flashing in the sunlight as he pitched pine cones at her and wound up flat on his back. She shook the thoughts from her head like clingy cobwebs on a broom; she needed to focus. They had to keep moving forward, Olivian was all that mattered now. That was the only thing she had even remotely in her control, and even the task before her threatened to overwhelm her if she thought too long and hard about it.

They kept moving forward as they looked for any game to come down. They continued on this path for an hour or two. Then Paige became aware that Robert had stopped a ways on her left. She paused and stared into the forest, scanning the treeline for any irregular movement. It only took a moment to see the slight shifting in shades of brown to pick out the creatures Robert had spotted.

The creatures were about the size and shape of an average whitetail with a rusty grey coat that sported bellies of white hair. The bellies matched the hair that made up the short mane on their necks like that of a mule. They had long, slender faces and looked similar to the deer Paige grew up hunting, but she had never beheld creatures like this before. Three of the animals stood with horns shaped like half a recurve bow pointing backwards away from their heads. In addition to these magnificent crowns, small beards of thick hair draped under their chins like a goat, but with a longer tail that hung almost to the ground that had a tuft of the same thick beard hair at the end.

Robert drew his arrow and pulled it back so that his thumb barely touched his jaw. Paige watched him sight the shaft to the foremost creature, narrowing his eyes as his calculated the distance. His mouth twitched, ever so briefly, then he fired.

The instant the arrow thudded into the deer's ribcage, the other two fled in opposite directions. One bolted towards Paige. She stood from her crouch, drawing her own bow back to it's full draw. The deer's wide eyes saw her, and it attempted to change direction mid-bound. She released the arrow as she exhaled smoothly, just like Papa had taught her. The arrow hit the deer in-between the second and fourth ribs as it collapsed, and its chin drove into the ground. The animal slid to a stop a few feet in front of her, heaving and struggling to get up. She drew her knife to end the deer's suffering, but at the same moment she stepped forward, a swan-feather-fletched arrow struck the deer's forehead with a ear splitting crack. The skull shattered.

"Nice shot!" she called to Jesnake. He ran to where the deer had fallen, crouched by the animal, and drew his arrow out of the deer's head with one hard jerk.

"I believe you beat me on that one, princess," he said, smiling.

"Can't win them all," she said. She pulled her own arrow out of the deer and checked the steel arrowhead to be sure it hadn't nicked or shattered on impact. She looked down at the deer. "What is it?"

"It's an Impasca, or *Bayneharn* as the elves call it," Jesnake said, examining the animal.

"Bayneharn? I don't know that one," Paige commented.

Jesnake stood. "Different dialect. In the west we speak a whole other language from your mother's kin. In the eastern dialect, it would be *Boghehern*," he said.

"Ah," she said, looking at the beautiful creature now dead at her feet. Again her mind flashed back to the last buck she and Papa had taken down together. She shook her head again and looked up at the sound of running footsteps. Duelmaster and Woodcarver, who had taken the rightmost flank of the hunting line, trotted over to the pair.

"Aw, acorns," the dryad spat. "I wanted a shot at that sucker."

"Sorry," Paige said without an ounce of sympathy. What was left of the group joined them soon enough. Robert carried his own quarry over his broad shoulders. Dinendale followed along behind him. Twostaves and Broadside carried the smaller buck between them. If she'd have been a gambling princess, Paige would have bet Twostaves had done the killing. His chubby, jovial face held a grin the size of one of Eirensgarth's moons at half season, and the skull on the animal had been bashed in by a large, blunt object. The mess reminded Paige of the squashed pies she'd given Twostaves' guards back in Hanburg's village.

They all pitched in the butchering process. Dinendale, Robert, and Broadside cut up the carcasses into large chunks of meat. Duelmaster, Woodcarver, and Twostaves cut those into smaller strips and gave them to Paige and Jesnake, who wrapped them in some fern leaves they cut from nearby brush. They worked hard, and an hour later, they put the meat in everyone's packs. The hides were kept folded and placed in Dinendale's pack while Twostaves carried two of the Impasca's heads on one of his staves like a yoke. Once the dirty business was complete, they shoved the carcasses under a tree and marched out again.

It took a couple more hours of walking before they came to the end of the plateau. The ground sloped into a gigantic valley between two ridges that made up this section of the Raychels with pines and bushes growing thick in all directions.

"I see a river!" Twostaves cried out as they descended the valley slope to the bottom. The heads of the Impasca were bobbing on his makeshift yoke in a comical, yet gruesome cadence as he stomped along.

"I thought I felt a wee trembling in my toes," Broadside said, adjusting his pack as they trudged for the riverbank.

"It's a feeder to the Great River to the south," Woodcarver explained. "We can store up on water and camp here for the night."

The crew finished jogging down the slope and reached the river just before sundown. It was about as wide as a bowshot with a steady flow of deep, sapphire blue water that looked cool and refreshing. They dropped their gear in exhaustion when they reached the sandy bank, taking long, deep drinks from the cool river. The icy water felt amazing as Paige splashed her sweaty, tired face with the clean, clear liquid.

"I can't remember the last time I was this exhausted," Dinendale moaned, laying on his back.

"I hear ya," Duelmaster said. "I could use a steamy, hot bath right about now."

"No time for that. We have meat to smoke!" Twostaves said, dropping an armload of wood he'd gathered from nearby.

"You said you'd smoke it, so I'm leaving you to it," Robert yawned, a smug grin on his face.

"Oh, come on you guys, more hands means faster finished," Dinendale grunted as he stood up again and stretched, beginning to also search for more wood. Paige huffed and stood up. She began helping them pick up dried pine branches to make a good smoking fire. She caught up a large stick and began to gather the kindling.

"Duelmaster, got your flint?" Dinendale asked once the threesome had built a firelay.

"No," Duelmaster sobbed in mock distress. "I do believe I lost mine back in our latest scuffle."

"*Famengher*," Woodcarver muttered, waking his fingers at the fire in a lazy gesture. The wood made a popping sound, smoked, and then little flames licked at the seasoned wood like baby birds popping their heads from the nest to get a bite at the worm their mother had brought.

"Impressive," Robert muttered, but his tone conveyed a hint of annoyance. Paige figured he probably thought the magician was just showing off now.

"You seem to be mighty useful to have around," Dinendale chuckled as he tossed more wood on the fire.

Woodcarver eyed him. "Am I wrong to assume you can also wield the Mist, Dinendale?" the wizard asked.

Dinendale's smile melted off his face as quickly as it had appeared. "I've had some... complications with magic in the past," Dinendale muttered.

Woodcarver nodded but didn't press the matter. He turned to Jesnake, an eyebrow raised.

"I unfortunately was not one of the lucky bloodlines," Jesnake said, almost bitterly. "So no, I cannot wield it either."

"What's the Mist?" Paige asked, no longer able to control her curiosity. They all turned to stare at her, astonishment written on every face.

"What?" she asked.

"Your parents never told you about the Mist?" Woodcarver asked, disbelief laced in his words.

Paige shook her head and looked them each in the eyes, getting frustrated at their shocked and stunned silence. "Well!?" she snapped after a few moments. "Don't everyone fill me in at once!"

"Princess, do you know how the world even came to be?" Jesnake asked quietly, searching her up and down with his eyes.

"Obviously the Creator made it," Paige said, indignant. "But what does that have to do with-"

"My dear, the Mist is what the Creator used to create this world!" Woodcarver exclaimed. "The Mist is all around us, the magic breathed into this land on the day the Creator spoke it into existence. When you wield the Mist you wield the very power of creation, the fabric of existence!"

"So, the Mist is magic?" she clarified.

Woodcarver rolled his eyes but the rest all nodded assent. "I suppose if you are going to use broad, lose definitions, yes," he admitted.

"Well you could have just said that," she muttered, blowing a stray strand of hair out of her eyes. "So why can't some people use it?"

"It's all about the bloodlines," Jesnake muttered.

"It goes back to the very beginning," Twostaves said. "To Aya and Eya."

Paiges' ears perked up. She recognized the names but couldn't place where she'd heard them.

"Who?"

"My dear, when the world was created and new, the Creator put two of his angels in charge, Aya and Eya, the Stewards of Time," Woodcarver explained. Duelmaster stacked a few more logs around the fire to begin making a bed of coals for smoking. "Their task was to see to it the new races and creatures filled the earth and to create environments for them to thrive. So the Creator gave them the Mist to wield and use to shape the land and create what would become Eirensgarth."

"But Eya was emboldened by his new power," Duelmaster added, spreading the logs of the fire out to let the new logs begin smoking. "He began using it to create things the way he wanted them."

"Quite right. His greed led him to pervert the new, clean world the Creator had made. In doing this, Eya created the Darkness, a part of the Mist where all manner of vile, evil things lurk and practice perverted, dark magic," Woodcarver continued.

"What happened to him?" Paige asked, soaking in these new tales like a sponge, wonder and confusion both mixing about in her head as questions began piling up.

"Aya confronted him, and they battled on the Plains of Gharath," Broadside interjected quickly. "They still have the scars in the earth where the angels fought!"

"Not only that, they brought with them armies that fought as well," Woodcarver explained. "Men, beasts, elves, and dwarves all fought the perverted servants of the Darkness that Eya had twisted and moulded in his own, greedy, power-hungry, vengeful image. The battle was hard fought and went on for days."

"A battle that went on for days," Paige gasped, her jaw agape in disbelief.

The men all nodded solemnly.

"From our youth they told us of the great heroes that fought and fell there," Broadside said, staring into the coals Duelmaster and Twostaves were raking into a pile.

"It was the same for us," Jesnake said, pulling one of his throwing knives out of his strap and began polishing the edge with a whetstone.

"So what happened to Eya?" Paige pushed.

"Eventually he was defeated by Aya, at a heavy heavy price," Woodcarver said, a somber expression in his face. His eyes reflected the dim, red glow from the fire Duelmaster was now rigging a wooden smoke rack for. "Eya was imprisoned in a tomb, buried alive and deep in the Barbial Desert far to the west of us, where the sun rises from everyday, baking the sand into an inferno no man could ever withstand long enough to release Eya and his evil."

"So angels, or Stewards, or whatever, could use the Mist. But what has that got to do with bloodlines?" Paige asked.

"After the battle and Eya's defeat, his servants scattered, waiting in the dark to terrorize the world with the evil they had been bred to spread. Eya was gone, but not before he had left his servants with a tool of absolute evil, the Book of the Dead," Dinendale said, opening several packs and laying strips of meat across the drying racks. "The people here needed a way to fight against the Darkness when Aya had gone."

"So before he returned to the Creator, Aya built the people of this world the World Doors," Woodcarver said pulling off his bladed gloves and stashing them in his small satchel. "He blessed ten males of each race with the ability to wield the Mist so they could use the World Doors to battle the creatures and servants of the Darkness until they were no more."

"So anyone who is descended of those original magicians has the ability to use magic?" Paige asked.

"More or less," Jesnake said. "It did not take long for some of the races to begin maximizing this potential. The elves began arranging marriages and trying to selectively breed all our people so they would all have the power to wield the Mist. I am one of a handful that still remain that cannot wield it."

"There's hardly any dwarves that can use it," Broadside pitched in. "Our mages tended to die unmarried and so we had to resort to our craftsmanship and wits."

"And even 'wits' got lost in the those bloodlines somewhere," teased Duelmaster. The group laughed as Broadside scowled at the dryad.

"And what of these....these World Doors?" Paige asked. "Are they still around?"

"No," Woodcarver sighed, clearly growing more and more tired as he lay there gazing up at the stars. "They were magical contraptions that helped the races cover great distances quickly, but no one alive today knows how they worked. All we know is they were destroyed over twenty-five hundred years ago."

"Boy wouldn't that come in handy right about now," Dinendale chuckled. "How bout it Duelmaster, those coals ready for the rest of this venison?"

They continued putting the meat on the drying rack as Paige and Robert kept adding green wood to the fire to let the smoke begin building and billowing up to the sky.

"So, how do we plan to cross this river?" asked Robert, who had been abnormally quiet during the discussion about magic Paige now realized.

"I tested the depth a few minutes ago when I went to fill my canteen," Duelmaster said. "It's at least eight feet deep in most places, but there is a small strip of shallow area downstream about a quarter of a mile away. We can ford it, easy."

"Wait. You don't mean actually getting in the water, do you? I mean, we're building a raft or something, right?" asked Broadside, in a shaky voice.

"Oh, suck it up, bloomer-boy," Robert cried out.

"You know I had no control over the pants I was forced to wear in my captivity. And that's rich coming from a guy who basically wears a brown dress!"

"I'll carry you, little man," the giant offered.

The dwarf turned beet red with embarrassment. "I may be slightly concerned about water," he started.

"You mean 'terrified at the slightest sign of dampness,'" interjected Robert.

"But I will not have anyone carry me across a stream," he finished with conviction. His eyes narrowed at Robert, who merely smirked. Paige caught his eye and glared at him, but Robert kept on smiling. She laid back on her pack and gazed out at the twilight sky, taking a breath of clean mountain air.

A shooting star dashed across the sky as if chasing the moons, and Paige thought of the summer nights she and Olivian had spent wishing on stars from their garden deck back home.

She felt for the scrap of leather in her moccasin and touched it gently. No wonder the Shahir wanted this page; so much pain, suffering and death accompanied such an evil power. Her stomach ached with the flood of realizations hitting her all at once. Her father and mother had died trying to keep it out of the world, and she silently vowed she too would do all she could to be sure such and to keep such an evil at bay, starting with freeing her sister from it's clutches.

"I'll find you, Olivian," she whispered. " I promise."

Dinendale knelt down next to the riverbank, untied the top of his shirt, and began splashing cool water on his dirty neck and collar. It felt good to get the grime off; he wasn't one to enjoy being dirty. He dunked his head into the icy river, shaking his long hair free of grime.

He stopped after a while and looked up at the night sky to stars that had shone down on his forebearers. As trivial as it might seem to some, it gave Dinendale a great deal of peace and comfort to know despite all the twists and turns his life might take, there were a few things that would never change. Losing himself gazing at the celestial wonders above him, he failed to notice soft footsteps coming up from behind him.

"Dinendale," a soft voice said. He stared as the willowy figure of Jesnake materialized through the brush to his left.

"Aye?" he answered, composing himself and taking a short but deep breath to whisk the momentary fright away. The western elf slunk over to him and crouched on his heels beside the dark elf.

"Something wrong at camp?" Dinendale asked. The elf shook his head, looked over his shoulder looked Dinendale straight in the eye.

"No. But... I have a very bad feeling about this river," he whispered. "A gathering shadow has been gowning in my heart ever since we reached it's shore."

"What do you think it is? I've not noticed anything out of the ordinary," Dinendale asked, sceptical of his friend.

"I can't quite articulate it, but... I feel as if someone... or something... is watching us."

"Just a gut feeling?"

"Aye. It may be nothing, but I don't think it wise to cross here. I think we need to find another way."

"There is no time, Jey," Dinendale said. "We cannot delay in getting to Aschin. You know as well as I do what will happen to Olivian if we don't get there soon. What might already be happening to her. And where else are we to go? Back down the cliff and to the main trails and roads?"

Both of the elves crouched as a sudden and resounding splash echoed across the river, the sound resembling a stick snapping when it cracks with too much tension. They froze for a few moments, waiting for another sound. None came.

"Probably just a fish?" Dinendale offered. "Could have been a beaver."

"Or it could have been something a lot bigger than a beaver. I'm telling you Dinendale, if we cross tomorrow without knowing what's in this river we may live, or rather not live, to regret it."

"We'll be fine, Jesnake. We'll try to be quick and not linger in the river longer than absolutely necessary. It's shallow and it isn't terribly wide. We'll be fine."

"For all our sakes, I hope you are right, my friend," Jesnake said soberly, slinking back into the rushes.

Paige awoke the following morning to the smell of hickory burning. She had fallen asleep where she had lain gazing at the sky, but she had had the good sense to wrap up in her wool blanket and cloak. She yawned and sat up, her joints creaking with stiffness as she sucked in a deep breath of air heavy with the smell of the sweet wood smoke. She rubbed her sore limbs to life, trying to get them warm in the early morning chill.

The men were busy bustling around, breaking camp. Robert and Duelmaster were lashing long poles together and, in turn, lashing the men's packs to the pole stretcher. Twostaves and Dinendale were seeing to the fire, and Jesnake was checking everyone's weapons. Woodcarver sat on a large rock, just watching.

"Good morning, my liege!" Duelmaster said with a mock bow. Paige stood up to stretch her short legs.

"Duelmaster," she said, " if you insist on talking to me as if I were the queen of the world, I may just have to start acting like it!"

The fellows all laughed as Paige walked over to the fire to warm her partially numb fingers. Dinendale threw another log onto the fire, and he, too, began to warm his hands.

"Where's Broadside?" she asked him.

He inclined his head upstream. "He went out to go fetch some of the fresh meat out of the creek."

"You stash it there to keep it cool?"

He nodded.

Paige gazed about at her busy companions as they stowed all their gear. Since she'd fallen asleep as she was the night before, Paige's own pack was more or less intact and ready to go.

"Is there anything I can do to help?" she asked.

"No. Those two can handle the packs. The rest of us are just killing time," Twostaves said with a yawn.

"We do not have time to kill," Jesnake said in a low tone, not looking up from examining the edge on one of Duelmaster's rapiers.

"What are you doing?" Paige asked.

"He's... uncomfortable about the river, so he wanted to check all the weapons himself," Dinendale told her. He then proceeded to tell Paige about Jesnake's gut feeling about the river last night. Paige listened with interest.

"You know, Jesnake may be right," Paige murmured.

Dinendale shrugged. "Maybe so, but it's not like we have any other viable options," he said, strapping his sword belt to his thigh.

"I'm serious. Sometimes I get this tingling feeling in my spine and it only happens before something bad is about to happen. Maybe Jesnake gets that, too?"

"But does it happen every time something bad happens?" Dinendale asked. "Like last night, did you feel anything like that happen?"

"Well, no," Paige stammered.

"Then it's hardly a perfect science, and you of all people know we don't have time to waste. Woodcarver isn't worried. I spoke to him about it this morning. "

Paige felt uneasy, but nodded, glancing once again at Jesnake who had moved on to Broadside's short sword, checking the edge one more time just to be sure. As if on cue, Broadside thundered into the clearing, carrying a sack of cloth that looked like it might have once been a shirt.

"Here's breakfast!" he said.

Dinendale looked down at the little fellow. "Where's the other one?" the dark elf asked.

The little man looked surprised. "There was only one," he insisted.

"Uh, no.... I tied the other one to the same tree branch," Twostaves insisted.

The dwarf shrugged. "Well, it must have slipped into the river or something," he said, tossing Dinendale the bag.

"Stubby giant's fingers never were very good at tying knots," muttered Robert.

Twostaves shot him a nasty look, but didn't chose to argue this time. Paige felt grateful.

"Unless something else took it." Jesnake's face turned pale.

Within moments, the meat that hadn't washed away was sizzling on a greenwood spit. While it roasted, they took turns lashing packs to a stretcher Twostaves had cinched together with a staff on each side. Once the gear was secured, they all sat down and ate the Impasca meat with relish. They polished off the meat and were also pleasantly surprised to find wild raspberries for dessert, thanks to Woodcarver, who had procured them on a walk he'd taken early that morning.

Once they put the fire out, the troop headed downstream to the spot that Duelmaster had scouted out the night before. Upon a brief inspection of the bank, it was agreed upon that the water here at about five feet deep was as shallow as it was going to get.

"Best take off the footwear if we want to keep both shoes for the rest of the journey!" Duelmaster said, scooping up a handful of wet slimy mud from under the surface of the river.

"Wet clay. Delicious," Robert groaned. "Nobody get stuck, okay?"

So off came the boots and moccasins and into the water they plunged.

Duelmaster led the procession with a tall sapling prodding the path in front of them to find the best route. Jesnake followed next, his ebony longbow held high in one hand, a throwing knife gripped in the other with knuckles as white as an Impasca's belly. Paige followed behind him, Broadside after her, his lip quivering as he braved the water with as much dignity as he could muster. Robert and Twostaves followed behind the whimpering dwarf, holding the gear stretcher between them on their shoulders; this was also to give Broadside something to grab hold of once they got to areas too deep for the dwarf to keep his head above water. Woodcarver came up behind them, and Dinendale took up the vanguard.

Paige winced at the chill of the water when she first stepped in. She was surprised to feel a strong current despite the rather peaceful looking surface. She felt her toes start to go numb. Though the water only reached her chest, it was fast chilling the rest of her body.

"This is a rather strange river," commented Robert, looking down at the water, their footsteps making bubbles appear from the mud below.

"How so?" asked Twostaves.

"This water is blue! I mean, look at it! I know it looked blue on shore, but in normal water, we'd be able to see our feet and the bottom. I can't!"

"He's right," commented Jesnake. "I've never seen anything like this before."

"Ouch!" Paige's bare foot slipped on the bottom of the slimy, mirky riverbed. It felt like something had pulled her heel loose, and she assumed it to be the current. She slid and started to fall. In the second it would have taken a bumblebee to flap a wing, Jesnake snapped his upper body around and caught her wrist, keeping her from getting all wet, while still holding his bow.

"Are you ok?" he asked, his tone direct and urgent.

"Yes. Just a loose stone," she said as he practically drug her towards the opposite shore. They were making a slow go of it with the bottom being so sticky with the wet, clay-ridden mud.

"Aw, acorns!" Duelmaster spat, coming to a halt.

"What happened!?" Jesnake demanded, worry lacing his tone.

"I've gotten my foot stuck."

"Well, pull it out! We've gotta get out of this water!"

"If I could get it out, Jesnake, wouldn't that, by its very definition, be quite the opposite of stuck?"

"Don't get snippy with me. Hold on," the elf snapped, pushing his way up to Duelmaster. He pulled hard, trying to help the dryad's feet out of the soggy, soppy riverbed. The rest of the group stood in the current, water up to their chests, in uneasy silence. All except Broadside, who clung to the gear stretcher like a man in a shipwreck clinging to a bobbing headboard.

"I don't like this. I don't like it one bit!" Broadside was muttering to himself over and over again.

"We get it!" Robert sighed, exasperated.

"AHHHH! SOMETHING TOUCHED ME!"

Paige whirled around to see the dwarf thrashing and clambering atop the pile of packs and attempting to crawl up Twostaves to sit on his shoulders. The giant protested loudly, as he could not swat off the hairy parasite without dropping all the gear into the river.

"Stop your yappering, you moron!" Robert shouted.

"Easy for you to say. You can reach the bottom! I'll sink! Sink like a rock! And I'm telling you something slid past my leg!"

"Enough dwarf. You'll drown us both!" Twostaves bellowed. Broadside stopped squirming, coming to rest atop the giant's shoulder like a fat, hairy parrot.

"Look," Robert said, jerking his chin downstream. A small branch was bobbing along the surface of the river, disappearing from view temporarily as it was sucked under by the current, then reappearing. Broadside grumbled something about sticks not wriggling but was largely ignored.

"Got it! Alright lads, tally ho!" Duelmaster called out as he and Jesnake began pushing forward towards the opposite bank again. Soon Paige could feel the clay growing stiffer underfoot and eventually became mirky sand and pebbles until she reached dry ground. She turned and watched as the others made their way to the bank. She rubbed her ankle where the current had pulled her foot loose, feeling it sting as the chilly air dried it out with a slight breeze.

"What on earth?" she exclaimed aloud. There were tiny scratches along her ankle, deep and bleeding like a dozen parchment cuts. Jesnake appeared by her side in an instant.

"What is it? What's wrong?" he demanded. He followed her gaze and didn't even wait for her to respond, bending down to examine the small wounds.

"It's not so bad. Just looks like it's bleeding a lot because my foot is still wet," she tried to reassure him, but the elf didn't listen. He leapt to his feet and dashed towards the river where Woodcarver and Dinendale were still slogging towards the shore.

"Din, get out!"

Dinendale looked up and made a questioning face as Jesnake waved frantically.

"Get out! There's blood in the water!"

"What?"

"THERE'S BLOOD IN THE WATER!"

Paige felt her spine tingle. Her heart stopped. She screamed as absolute primal terror gripped her by the heartstrings and squeezed her chest till her knees felt weak.

Behind Dinendale, gliding through the water like an arrow on a windless day, was the most terrifying creature she had ever seen. It was serpent-like with a long, slender body that must have been at least twenty paces long and as thick as a cypress tree. It's skin gleamed a slippery white as it's tight interlocking scales skimmed the water with speed and agility. It had the head shaped like a cougar bereft of ears. Its sickly white eyes glared above the waterline. Teeth as long and sharp as a dirk stuck out of its upper jaw complemented by a long row of sharp spines that went down the length of the creature's backbone atop it's flat, eel-like tail.

Gliding along the surface of the water with ease, the creature made for Dinendale, who was desperately trying to run through the clay riverbed to shore. The group screamed and yelled at him to hurry, and Jesnake loosed an arrow at the beast, hoping to scare it away. The arrow struck the beast on the side of the body and glanced off like a pebble hitting a steel shield.

"Come on, Din!" Robert yelled, and the elf pushed on as fast as he could. But suddenly Dinendale stopped short in the water. By the look of panic etched into his face, Paige could tell his foot was stuck. She bolted to the gear stretcher and yanked her own bow out of it's housing, fumbling with the string in panic. But she was too late. The creature reached her trapped friend and reared its massive head out of the water. It bared its fangs and rose, dripping, out of the blue water to strike at his helpless victim. Jesnake loosed another arrow at the beast's exposed underbelly, and this time the arrow stuck. The beast cried out in pain, the sound resembling someone dragging their nails down a slab of slate. Those on shore all covered their ears and cried out in agony as the sound drove through their ears.

The beast lunged, mouth open to bite at the elf. As it struck at Dinendale, he was frantically trying to draw his dirk from it's scabbard. Then, in a great splash, the serpent drug itself and Dinendale down into the murky blue depths.

"Dinendale!" Paige screamed. The men started rushing to the river, and then stopped and watched the churning water. They cried out for their friend, and looked frantically into the blue darkness for some trace of him. The river frothed with the thrashing of the beast. The earsplitting shrieks of the animal pierced the silence so fiercely that they drove Jesnake to his knees in pain. The waves crashed, river water shooting high into the air, and all the while, the fight slowly moved downstream.

"It's dragging him to deeper water!" Duelmaster cried out. "Everyone shoot!"

"No! We might hit Dinendale!" Robert yelled.

The loudest scream from the beast yet sent all of them to their knees. The sound gave Paige a headache, the likes of which she'd not experienced since waking in Hanburg's village, cutting through her brain like a hot knife. Then, quite suddenly, it all stopped; the noise, the trashing, the headache. All was silent. Each one got up off the ground and looked at the river apprehensively.

The water lay still, save some bubbles rising to the surface. It was as still as it had been an hour ago. They all held their breath. The blue water began to turn dark, and blood branched out with wispy fingers and stained the beautiful water as it flowed downstream with the current.

"NO!" Robert screamed. He began running to the bank, but Woodcarver grabbed him and held him back.

"Let me go, you pixie!" he screamed.

"Don't be a fool. He's gone. You can't help him now!"

"This is all your fault! You brought us this way. You led us right to this thing!"

"I had no idea such a beast-" Woodcarver tried to say.

Robert interrupted, "I don't care what you knew! I'm getting him back dead or alive!" Robert tried to barge past him, but the magician threw him to the ground.

"You listen here you rash, arrogant unthinking excuse for a warrior!" he yelled back.

Robert glared at him, and then threw a fist into the sand.

"GAHHHHHH!" he shouted, his hoarse roar cutting through the air with an anguishing roar. But as soon as he'd released the initial outburst, his shoulders began to shake with tears that would not be restrained. Paige felt the tears well up in her own eyes until they spilled over like waterfalls running down her fair cheeks. She sank to her knees and looked down at the grassy bank. Tears fell silently to the earth as she began to choke on sobs that left her throat feeling hoarse and thick while her heartbeat drummed in her temples.

Thu-Thump. Thu-Thump.

"Hey! You stupid dwarf, get back here!" she heard Woodcarver shout angrily. She heard the splash of someone jumping into the water, and her head snapped up just in time to see Broadside in the river, armor and all, paddling like a drowning puppy. He was struggling to swim to the spot that the fighting beast and elf had gone down. As soon as he thrashed about enough to reach it, he took a deep breath, and then plunged himself beard first into the blue water.

Thu-Thump. Thu-Thump.

"Are you daft!?" Woodcarver yelled. For a moment, there was nothing. No bubbles or ripples gave any clue to the dwarf's position. Moments began to drag on, as agony gripped the group when the dwarf failed to make it to the surface.

Thu-Thump. Thu-Thump.

It felt like someone had taken a battering ram straight to the gut and then stuffed her mouth with sour sawdust.

Thu-Thump. Thu-Thump.

The bubbles and froth swirled around atop the water like ghosts slipping down stream and out of sight.

Thu-Thump. Thu-Thump.

A splash downstream caused them all to start. They leapt up as one and sprinted downstream where emerged a soaked and heaving dwarf, dragging the limp body of an elf towards the shore through the bushes. Robert and Duelmaster ran into the shallows and grabbed the two drenched members of the Brotherhood, pulling them to the shore. Broadside was gasping and gulping for air, laying out on the soft, sandy bank, his round belly heaving with every breath. Robert dragged Dinendale's still form next to the dwarf.

"He's not breathing! Dinendale!" Robert shouted, shaking him hard. "Dinendale! Wake up!"

"Woodcarver do something!" Paige shouted. "Use your magic!"

"Move!" Woodcarver yelled. "Princess, hold his head up!"

Paige dropped to her knees beside Dinendale and took her friend's head in her hands, gazing at the elf's ashen face. Dinendale's lips were blue, his eyes closed, his chest still and unbreathing. Woodcarver took out a hunting knife and slit through the elf's shirt. Dinendale's body was the color of the sky on a rainy day save for large gashes and holes where the river serpent had bitten him repeatedly. Dark blood seeped from the wounds.

"Hold him still," Woodcarver barked. She froze, willing her shaking hands to stop moving. The wizard placed a gloved hand at the base of the elf's breast bone. He counted to three, then quickly pushed, counted to three again, and pushed again. He repeated this four times.

"*Whyeghlah*," Woodcarver whispered, and hit the elf a final time. Paige translated him to have said breathe, and she bit her lip.

"It's not working," Woodcarver said, brow furrowed.

Paige's heart leapt into her throat. "Try again!"

"If it were going to work it would have worked!" snapped Woodcarver. "He's not responding, but I don't know why."

Paige didn't even hesitate. Her mind rushed back to her mother's many lessons in the garden terrace about healing and she moved into action. She shoved Woodcarver to the side and positioned herself next to Dinendale's neck and shoulders. Placing the heel of one hand over the center of the elf's chest, Paige thrust her other hand on top and gripped her own hand tight. She locked her elbows to straighten her arms and threw her whole body into a compression, trying to get the elf's chest to move.

She did this ten times before dropping her ear to the elf's lips. No air. He still wasn't breathing. She placed a clammy palm on his forehead and tilted his head back on her lap, trying to get the airways open. Still nothing. She took in a deep breath and pinched the elf's nostril closed, placed her lips on his, and breathed out slow and steady, trying to force something other than sickly blue water into Dinendale's lungs.

Still nothing.

She tried again and again, but with no different result. Panic gripped her even harder as she tried for a third time, reverting back to compressions when breathing did not work. She thrusted her clenched fists into his sternum until she could move no more. Tears salted her dry lips, and she collapsed onto his chest.

No shrieking creatures. No bickering Brotherhood. There were only silent tears falling on Dinendale's once-warm skin.

"Did you see that?" Broadsides whispered.

"What?" Jesnake asked.

"His face moved! Or twitched. Or something." Broadsides matted hair dripped down his armor as he squatted closer to his fallen comrade.

"Your eyes are playing tricks on you," Duelmaster said.

"Seeing what you want to see," Robert said. "You were brave little guy, but it wasn't enough."

"No, this isn't how this is supposed to happen," Paige snapped. She pinched the elfs nose again and once again went to breath her breath into his lungs, nearly slamming her fists into his chest as hot tears stung and blinded her eyes anew.

"Paige," Robert said, putting a hand on her shoulder. She pumped again teeth squeaking inside her head she was clenching her jaw so tight.

"Paige!" Robert said more firmly his hand now clamped onto her shoulder. "Enough!"

Suddenly Dinendale coughed. River water poured out of his mouth, mixed with blood. He took several ragged breaths and a few deep-chest coughs, and then opened his eyes. Paige felt the thumping in her ears subside and she grabbed the elf by the shoulder and pulled him up. Dinendale gasped and rolled onto his side vomiting more murky water and bile as he heaved for air.

"Don't you ever scare me like that again!" Robert shouted, taking the cork out of his wineskin and handing it to his friend. Dinendale took a swig and sputtered again, wiping his mouth with the back of his drenched sleeve. He looked up at Paige with his soft brown eyes and a half hearted smile.

"Hey," he said weakly.

"Hey, yourself," she said, this time tears of joy raining down her cheeks.

He struggled to sit up.

"Rest," Woodcarver commanded, keeping him from rising with a gloved hand. "Just lie still for now."

"I'm fine," Dinendale mumbled. "Not half as bad a scrape as getting this princess out of trouble."

"You stupid, stone-eared, *moronic*, deaf, half-drowned..." Jesnake cried. He stood over Dinendale, eyes blazing. "If you had listened to me, you wouldn't be in this state!"

Dinendale looked up at his kinsman.

"It's nice to see you too, Jesnake," he muttered.

The men snickered.

"You're welcome," grumbled a soaking but bright-eyed dwarf. Paige stood up, then knelt to the dwarf's height, and gave him a big, tight hug. She didn't care if it embarrassed him. She was just thankful both of them were safe. She let go, and he looked down at his feet, trying to hide the hot, red blush spreading across his face. The men all laughed, and Twostaves slapped a fist on the little man's back, nearly knocking him off his feet.

"I owe you one, friend," Dinendale murmured to the brave little dwarf. "You saved my life."

"No problem," Broadside growled, looking like a drenched cat.

"You didn't kiss me, right?" Dinendale asked the dwarf.

Paige could hear Duelmaster barely contain a burst of laughter as it came out through his nose like a horse snorting.

"I will do a lot of things for you, Dinendale," the dwarf heaved, shaking his black beard free of water like a dog. "But I would sooner shove my face in a Hippophant's dung heap then put my lips on yours."

"It was the princess," Woodcarver offered, and Paige felt her cheeks flush. "You were unresponsive to any magic, and she jumped in and saved you."

Dinendale looked up at her, a new gleam of surprise and admiration reflecting off his brown eyes. "Well, then it appears I am also in your debt, princess."

"Think nothing of it," Paige said, trying to combat the heat rising from her neck, threatening to stain her cheeks. "I would have done it for anyone."

"Oooh, *ouch*. Must not have been that great of a kiss!" Duelmaster jabbed.

"It wasn't a kiss. It was... oh forget it," Paige snapped, stomping up to her feet.

"Easy, princess. We didn't mean anything by it," Twostaves assured.

Paige rolled her eyes.

"Well then, seeing as we're all back in decent spirits, I feel I owe all of you an apology," said Dinendale, wincing as Woodcarver bound up one of his many wounds with a strip of cloth from his satchel. "I was too proud to trust Jesnake. I was so focused on my own drive that I didn't heed the signs, nor my friend's advice." He paused, breath a little shaky. "Can... can you forgive me Jey?"

"It's already forgiven," Jesnake mumbled.

"I'll have to think about it," said Duelmaster, pretending to ponder.

Twostaves, who was standing beside him, cuffed him in the back of the head. "That's not funny," he said in a deep, un-jovial tone.

"Stinkbug, it was only a joke!" the dryad said, rubbing the bump on his head.

Dinendale tried a laugh that became a deep, throaty cough spitting up blood. "Oh wow, that... that isn't good," Dinendale chuckled morosely.

"We need to tend to him," Woodcarver urged. "Otherwise, we revived him only to die of blood loss."

"Can't you heal all this?" Paige asked.

Woodcarver shook his head. "If he didn't respond to a simple breathing spell, he's not going to take any healing spells, either. We'll just have to bind the wounds and hope he can gather enough strength to move by tomorrow."

"You...could just leave me here," Dinendale said quietly.

Paige looked at him sharply. "That's not an option," she snapped. "Get that idea out of your head this instant, because it isn't happening."

"I'm just saying," Dinendale muttered but Twostaves cut him off.

"I'll carry you if I have to," the giant said. "Or we'll build you a stretcher. Were not going to just let you lay here in the middle of the Wild with winter fast approaching."

"Here, here," Dulemaster concurred. "There's nothing for it, Din. You're stuck with us!"

Woodcarver, Robert, and Jesnake volunteered to stay by his side the whole night while the others took turns sleeping, although Dinendale insisted it was completely unnecessary. Paige sat beside him, determined to stay awake through the night with him, but wound up falling asleep at some point in the blackest part of the night.

When she awoke, she was leaning with her head against the elf's shoulder.

"How did you sleep?" he asked.

"Aw, acorns," she muttered, undoing the braid out of her hair and holding the leather cord in her mouth.

"I know my shoulder can't be that comfortable," he chuckled.

Paige shrugged, and tied a braid into her hair binding it with the cord.

"Your hair looks beautiful," he commented.

Paige felt the back of her neck feel uncomfortably hot and prickly, like a bad sunburn had sprung up even in the early overcast gloom of a mountain morning, and she tried to stifle the smile that wanted to tug the corners of her lips.

"Thanks," she said dumbly, mentally kicking herself. Thanks. What kind of response was that?

"Are we ready to go?" he asked, standing uneasily.

"We are!" Broadside shouted out. Paige grabbed the elf's shaky arm as he staggered several steps

"But it looks as if you might need a little help," she said, gesturing to Twostaves. The giant grinned at Dinendale and patted his broad back. Dinendale looked puzzled for a moment, then realization dawned in his eyes.

"No. I don't need to be carried like a child," he started to protest, and then saw the look Paige was giving him. He stopped himself mid-sentence, mouth still opened in protest. "Okay, then," he said, smiling weakly. "Twostaves, break out the saddle."

CHAPTER 15

RAVEN-HEADS

*P*aige scrambled up a boulder as fast as she could, trying to keep her moccasins from sliding on the moss. The sun was out today for a change, unlike the last three since they had left the river. Dinendale was walking now with the help of a crutch Woodcarver had whittled out of a tree branch for him, and they were all in much higher spirits the further into the Raychels they traveled. Everyone could feel that they were closing in on their destination.

"I can't wait till we get to go downhill for a change," Broadside huffed as he crawled his way up several boulders ahead of Paige. She stifled a giggle when the sight of him struggling to clamber up the rocks reminded her of a toddler trying to climb stairs on all fours.

"Well, since our journey has been mostly uphill and our luck downhill," Duelmaster chirped, "perhaps when we start going downhill our luck will go up?"

"I don't think that's how that works," Robert held out a hand to Paige, helping her up the next boulder. She took it graciously.

"Hey Duely," Twostaves said, "how about a couple riddles? Or jokes? Might help the time pass faster."

The rest of the company groaned, but Duelmaster's face lit up in eager anticipation.

"Very well," he said, cracking his knuckles and choosing a punch line.

"Twostaves," Robert hissed through clenched teeth, "I am going to hit you so hard, it will make your breakfast come back up and slap you in the face."

"Did he have milk for breakfast?" Duelmaster asked.

"No, just a brick loaf," the dwarf said.

"That's a relief," Duelmaster said, wiping his brow with his hand. "If Robert did hit him with dairy in his stomach, it could have been an udder disaster!"

The group groaned, with the exception of the giant, who appeared to find this to be the funniest thing since court jesters.

"Sweet sassafras, what I wouldn't give for a glass of fresh, chilled milk right about now," grumbled Broadside. "Or a nice wedge of sharp cheese on toast!"

"Oh me, oh my, I could go for a biscuit with tartberry jam," Twostaves moaned, licking his lips.

"No use dreaming about that which we haven't got," Robert scolded. "You'll only get yourself hungrier and we're almost out of Impasca meat as it is."

It was true. Even with cutting back rations significantly, a troop of eight people was a lot of mouths to feed, and game had become more scarce the further into the Raychels they got. Yet the men always made sure Paige ate first and would refuse nourishment until she had finished her entire allotted portion.

She had grown very fond of each of them, although she'd never admit that to Broadside or Twostaves. They all treated her as if she were The Queen of Eirensgarth instead of the orphaned chieftain's daughter she was. They all did their best to see that she was taken care of, and the fact that they were helping her at all was still unbelievable. She wouldn't have traded these friends for a regiment of soldiers.

When they came to the crest of a small ridge, Woodcarver said, "Let's take a rest. We can spare an hour or so since we made good time yesterday."

No one objected as they all dropped their packs and lay about on the pine needle carpet of the forest floor. All except Dinendale, who said he prefered to keep his limbs stretched out.

"I'll go down the gully to that other small ridge," he said, pointing to the next ridge. "Can't see anything past the trees on it. Might give me a peek at what we're up against till sundown."

"But if anyone needs a rest it's you!" Paige insisted.

The elf shrugged. "I'm sure if I need to I can stop between here and there princess. I might even make it to the top before you all have finished your little kip."

Paige opened her mouth to protest again, but Duelmaster reached out and touched her arm.

"It's fine Din, we'll catch up with you," he said with a soft smile.

The elf nodded and hobbled off on his makeshift crutch, the soft thudding of his boots muffled by the pine needles as he made his way down the gully.

"He has to be more careful," Paige insisted, watching the tall elf hobble down the steep ravine. "He'll drive himself straight into the ground if he keeps this up."

"You'll be hard pressed to stop him, I'm afraid," Duelmaster said, pulling out a thin strip of jerky and ripping it off with his teeth. "He's stubborn, he is. Getting him to quit when his mind is on something is like trying to pull a boulder up that mountain with a sled of rabbits."

"Has he always been like that?" Paige asked.

Duelmaster grimaced. "In a way. He didn't used to have this much of a hero complex, though."

Paige thought for a moment. "What changed?"

The crew sat in silence, no one moving to answer her question. She scanned their somber expressions and looked back to Duelmaster.

"Duely, what happened?" she asked again. The dryad's normally chipper, sparkling eyes were filled with an unspoken pain. Paige had never seen this side of Duelmaster, and she felt an ache of empathy poke at a lump in her throat as she swallowed.

"She might as well know," Robert said, laying his head back onto his pack and closing his eyes.

Duelmaster shrugged, taking another ripped morsel from his jerky strip. "There used to be seven of us," he said softly. "We lost one about two years ago."

"What was his name?" Paige asked.

Duelmaster smiled a sad, somber smirk. "Elathia."

"But that's a-"

"Aye, a girls name," chuckled Duelmaster. "Guess it's fortunate for her she was a girl, otherwise it would have been rough life."

Paige let that information sink in while Duelmaster continued his story.

"Din used to be quite the joker actually, believe it or not," Duelmaster laughed. "And Elathia was one of the best archers I've ever known. She gave Jesnake a run for his money a couple times. The two of them had come north seeking adventure. Somehow we all accidentally wound up friends and banded together. Our goal was to do what we could to help the frontier settlements keep their freedom as the Shahir's armies pushed west."

"Were they close? Din and Elathia?"

"Oh, they did everything together, those two. Grew up together, you know. She had these eyes: soft, dark brown, almost sable. They were so big and beautiful that they could persuade you to do something you didn't want to do, like gut her deer for her or weed the herbs."

Duelmaster smiled as images of past moments flashed through his mind. "One day, Elethia volunteered to take hunting duty for one of us. When she didn't return by nightfall, we went out looking for her. We all figured she must have bagged a heavy one or else gotten lost somehow. Turns out it was neither; we found her broken bow in a trampled area of the forest. Thought it might have been a stampede or a wolf pack, but we found a dead Shauden soldier off the path with one of her arrows in his gullet. Never went down without a fight, that girl." His voice trailed off before continuing. "We followed that path and found a small outpost several leagues away. We tried our best to plan an effective strategy to infiltrate the small outpost but we took too long trying to lay plans and even as we conspired to break her out, she was taken to the encampment where Aschin was being built."

Paige felt her brain begin to connect the dots, and she felt her mouth go dry.

"And he went after her?"

"He did, and the fool got himself caught," Robert said, his voice low and quiet. "They beat him and put him to work, but not before they hung Elethia and tossed her in the rubbish burn pile. He spent six months in those labor camps cutting stone."

Duelmaster's voice broke as he tried to compose himself, that same haunting horror Paige knew all too well flooding his expression.

She placed a hand on his shoulder reassuringly. "I'm so sorry," she stammered. "I shouldn't have been nosey. It was not my place to pry-"

"No," Duelmaster cut her short. "It's quite alright. You might as well know. As for Din, he still feels the pain of those memories. He bears the guilt of her death every day he opens his eyes."

Paige started to say, "But why does he feel...?" Then she stopped short as she processed Duelmaster's words. They registered in her mind like a nail being driven through her skull. She felt her heart sink. "She went hunting for him, didn't she." Paige's words were a statement more than a question. She glanced back at Dinendale, who was now at the bottom of the gully and had started climbing the other side.

"He'd sprained his ankle in a fight," Duelmaster grunted. "So she swapped days with him. That's why he won't quit now. He figures any moment he allows weakness to keep him from moving forward, it's a moment he can't be saving someone else."

"I had no idea," she said, watching the recovering cripple hobble and hop his way up the incline on the opposite side.

"That's why he changed his mind about your sister that night at the willow," Dulemaster said, pulling off his boots and stretching his toes inside his wool stockings. "We all know your desire to save her and the fate she faces if we don't. But he knows, better than any of us."

Paige turned back and smiled at the dryad whose crooked grin was back, making his eyes shine. He laid back on his pack and crossed his arms dramatically behind his head.

"Now if the lady doth not protest too much, methinks I'll be snagging that kip we spoke of earlier," the duelist laughed, winking at Paige before closing both eyes and settling in for a quick nap. Within moments he was snoring along with Twostaves and Broadside. Robert lay motionless, but not snoring, so it was hard for Paige to tell if he was sleeping. Jenake dozed in and out while sharpening his throwing knives once more, occasionally testing the edge on his arm hair. The only one who remained vigilant was Woodcarver, who stood atop a boulder watching Dinendale ascend the next ridge with great interest. He glanced down at Paige who looked away quickly to avoid awkwardly meeting his gaze. The magician stepped off the rock and sat on her other side.

"May I just say that I know your mother and father would be so proud of you, Alwasu," he said, sincerity etched into every word.

"Thank you," she said. "Still doesn't change the fact they are gone."

"I know. For what it's worth, I know the feeling of losing your parents to those in the pursuit of power. And while the pain will always be there, I can promise you it will ease."

"Is that another story we have to bank for a better time?" Paige asked, her voice dripping with sarcasm.

The ageless wizard chuckled. "I know that isn't ideal, but as cliche as it may sound," he lightly laughed again.

"Don't you dare say," Paige countered.

Woodcarver said, "You'll understand when you're older."

Paige rolled her eyes, and Woodcarver chuckled as he stood and gazed out at Dinendale once more.

"He is getting stronger," the magician commented. "He's nearly at the top already."

"Why do you think your magic couldn't help him?" Paige asked.

Woodcarver got a curious look on his face. "You know I've been wandering this world for longer than any of these fellows have been alive, and yet I have never seen anything like it. Sometime I want to do a little more studying as to why that is, but obviously our current situation doesn't exactly warrant..." Woodcarver's words immediately drowned in a loud sound. A blast of a horn echoed across the gorge, and the Brotherhood's sleeping members all woke. Paige leapt to her feet. They gazed across the gorge to see Dinendale blowing on his hunting horn and gesturing wildly to them, hopping up and down as much as he could, and waving his arms like a madman between horn blasts.

"What is that fool going on about?" Robert rolled to his feet with a variety of grunts, mumbled curses, and heaving sounds. They soon gathered about Woodcarver and Paige, gazing at the elf who looked absolutely ridiculous.

"Maybe he's bleeding out," said the sleepy giant as he threw his pack and targe on his back.

"Whatever it is, we'd best be getting over there as quickly as we can." Woodcarver tossed his satchel back over his shoulder. "Let's go."

It took them about a third of the time it had taken Dinendale to cross the gorge and reach the peak. He was still waving them over urgently when they arrived near the top of the ridge.

"Confound it all elf, what is going on!?" demanded Woodcarver.

"Come and see, I promise it will be worth a shortened naptime," Dinendale urged, hobbling ahead of them to the top of the ridge. They crawled over the last few boulders and came out on a small, rocky precipice that opened up from the treeline overlooking the ridge. This provided a clear view of the rest of the Reychel's, the long, spine-like crags jutting north to south like a child's line drawing of a river. Many were already topped with small amounts of snow on the taller peaks, their white caps glistening in the sunset.

"Look there!" he said pointing to the sky, the fast sinking sun making its way to the eastern horizon.

Paige squinted. "What is it?" she asked.

"Can you not see it?" Dinendale asked.

She looked harder, then noticed far to the north and heading east, there was a hazy patch of sky that was more greyish-black than the pink and oranges that surrounded it.

"Why, it's smoke!" Broadside exclaimed.

"A fire?" Twostaves asked.

Robert rolled his eyes. "Yes, moron. Where else are you going to get smoke from?"

Dinendale gazed at the smoke. "Not just one fire."

Paige's heart leaped. There were only two explanations for many fires in the same area: an army camp, or a city.

"Aschin!" cheered Broadside

The men gave a whoop and holler of triumph.

"We're not quite out of the mountains yet," cautioned Woodcarver. "But yes. That is where Aschin lies."

"How far?" asked Paige.

"I'd say about forty miles as the crow flies," Jesnake surmised, narrowing his eyes as he judged the distance.

"Obviously arrival there depends on how many times we have to take switchbacks around mountains," Woodcarver urged. "We are close enough to now be back on our guard. We'll have to scout ahead to make sure the way is clear of vermin wearing helmets and carrying swords."

"I agree," Dinendale added. "We'd best keep our noise to a minimum as well from now on."

Jesnake stepped forward, knocking an arrow on his string.

"That inncludes hunting horns, Din," he chuckled, jogging forward with no more pitter patter than a squirrel. It did not take long for him to be out of their sight. They shuffled through the trees, down the slope, to the wide valley this hill and the ridge adjacent made between them. They snuck through what was left of the scant pines, like shadows and specters of the thinning forest. The trees gave way to moss-covered stone mounds offering only ferns and lichen for cover. The company moved in columns of two: Dinendale and Paige at the front, Duelmaster and Robert behind them, Twostaves and Broadside after them, and Woodcarver taking the lone position in the vanguard.

They walked like this for nearly an hour when they heard a low whistle in front of them mimicking a bird call. They all stopped, listening. It came again, only closer now. Soon, Jesnake came sprinting up the mountain slope as quickly and as quietly as possible.

"What?" hissed Dinendale to his comrade.

"Men," the elf whispered. "Five soldiers and a wagon carrying supplies. Hundred yards straight ahead."

"Probably foragers, my guess," Woodcarver muttered.

"Detour?" Dinendale asked.

Robert shook his head, eyes gleaming with anticipation. "I say we take em. We need the re-supply."

"We shouldn't risk it," Jesnake said quietly.

"I'm with Robert. We need the supplies," Duelmaster drew his rapier. "I say we at least have a look."

"Agreed," Dinendale said. Paige felt excitement, mixed with worry, well up in her as she glanced at Dinendale's bandages.

"I'm not sure. With Din's condition, that puts us at only seven on five, and I've never tested my metal in a battle not brought on by desperation and running," she pulled her hairpin from its braided home. "And I really think Dinendale should not be fighting in his current condition. At least not yet."

"She has a point," Broadside added. Dinendale looked disgusted.

"Who are you both? My mother?" He pulled himself up to his feet and drew his sword.

"You still need a crutch, I'd say," Paige started to argue, but Dinendale dropped the crude crutch and brought his sword down on it. The resounding 'twack' echoed through the woods and down into the basin.

"Shhh!" Jesnake glared at his fellow elf. "You idiot! This is no time for dramatic effect!"

"Oh shut up, Mother Hen," Dinendale winked. "Let's go check it out."

Jesnake led them quietly, glancing around himself to be sure they were safe. Within moments, Paige could hear the rumble of a wagon up ahead and a small, crude path came into view at the basin of the valley. The group dispersed along the lane, hiding in the bushes and behind rocks on the high ground, looking down at the foraging party. Paige dove for cover and found herself next to Duelmaster lying atop a boulder overlooking the wagon. He poked his eyes and nose over the edge to peer down at their foes.

It was a small wagon. Paige saw two giant horses with shaggy manes and socks of white hair overtop chestnut coats. A fat man with an oily mop of crow black hair and a clean, sunburned face, drove onward. He sang an off-key lullaby in some desert gypsy language. The five Shauden soldiers that accompanied him seemed to be quite annoyed with the man's endeavors to entertain them.

"Light guard," observed Duelmaster. "It must be headed to an outpost near here."

Paige nodded. The soldiers were slight infantry, carrying only swords and moon-shaped shields. The armor afforded them were mere metal helms poking out from underneath yellow turbans and breastplates lying over their white robes.

She looked back at Duelmaster, but to her shock the dryad was no longer lying at her side. He stood atop the outcropping of rock. She felt her heart race as he winked at her, then took a single step forward, dropping directly into the pathway of the cart. Landing on his feet and crossing his arms, a mischievous look glared in his merry eyes. The Shauds shouted out in astonishment, and quickly drew their swords.

"Gentlemen! Gentlemen! There is no need for that!" Dulemaster called out. "Just asking you to allow a poor fellow a drink of water!"

"Get out of the way, Wildlander!" snapped one of the soldiers.

"Eh, I've been called worse!" the dryad tucked his long hair behind his roundly tapered ears. The soldier in charge pointed and shouted.

"An elf! Get him!"

A young soldier rushed the dryad. Duelmaster merely sidestepped, stuck his foot out, and using the soldier's forward momentum flipped the man onto his back with one sweep of his arm. The wind ripped out of the man as he landed with a heavy thud.

"Oh, now, that wasn't very nice, was it?" Duelmaster cooed like a mother scolding a child. "You shouldn't call people names. An *elf*? My good sir, perhaps you need your eyes checked."

The man attempted a swipe at Duelmaster's feet but found that his limbs were immobilized by brown snake-like entities winding their way up his legs and arms from the earth.

"What the?" he started.

Duelmaster only smiled, and placed his boot over the man's mouth. "Now, now, no swearing! There are ladies present," he said. He turned to the woods were Paige felt her cheeks flushing red with adrenaline. Duelmaster looked towards her hiding spot and pretended to call from a long ways off.

"Not you m'lady, of course!" he called out. "I meant these pretty little girls down here dressed up like soldiers!" he pointed to the remaining guards.

"Witchcraft!" one of the humans screamed in terror.

Duelmaster made a disgusted face as the men raised their weapons in fear. "Hardly. I never touch the stuff! But I guess you wouldn't know the difference anyways. They don't teach that at state-run schools, I imagine."

The Shauds had had enough of this magic-wielding nutcase mocking them. They rushed him with a cry, and the dryad spread his arms wide, beckoning them come. One by one, large brown, eel-like entities popped up out of the ground like salmon breaking the surface of a stream and grabbed the men by the ankles and legs, wrapping up their bodies and pinning them to the earth. Soon, the only one not encircled by these strange things was the wagon driver, who was as white as a bleached sheet of vellum.

"Roots, gentlemen! A simple Creator-given talent!" Duelmaster laughed, pointing his finger in the air like a scholar. "They are most handy when rude men try and attack you and call you names like elf! The sheer audacity, I say! Now in the spirit of recompense and developing goodwill between his Royal Highness and ourselves, we, the Brotherhood must insist that you relinquish the wagon and supplies."

The driver immediately threw his hands up, one comically clutching a round silver flask. By the way he swayed, back and forth, off balance even in a sitting position, Paige could guess what was inside, or at least what had been.

"It's all yours. I never liked this job anyways," the fat man whined in a high-pitched voice that sounded like a pig.

"Thank you, my good man!" Duelmaster said with a dramatic bow. He approached the wagon and the trembling driver.

"So," the dryad asked casually. "What all have ye got?"

"Pots, pans, weapons, food, clothing for the people living in the outpost, spices, armor, um, tools, cloth and um, um, gold," he said in a rush of words. "You can have it all. Just don't hurt me. You can have any...."

He began to blubber, when a sharp, earsplitting crack resounded in the air. Duelmaster drew both his swords and crouched, eyes darting around and looking for the source of the sound.

"Oh," the driver stammered, staring down at a hole that had appeared in his breast. Blood began to pump out of it, soaking his white shirt and spreading through the fabric like a crimson waterfall. He let out a raspy grunt and fell backwards into the wagon, stone dead.

Paige had no time to react. Arrows began to 'zing' from the trees on the other side of the ravine. They struck the defenseless men that were still held down by the roots Duelmaster summoned from in the earth. They cried out in anguish till all of them were dead. Duelmaster felt stunned, and he looked around wildly. Paige burst out of hiding followed by the other members of the Brotherhood. She saw several carrying bows. Angrily, she scanned each face, till she came to Robert. She remembered his contempt for the Boggartrolls and saw the same contempt etched into his face as he stared at the bodies of the murdered soldiers.

"Why?" she shouted. "They were unarmed! Defenseless!"

Robert darkened with rage.

"Listen, princess," he said in vehement anger. "I had twenty arrows in my quiver this morning, and there are twenty arrows in it now!"

"Then, who?!" she screamed, pounding her knuckles against his chest. She was about to do it again, when Dinendale grabbed her wrist. She tried to yank it free, but the elf's grip was firm.

"The shots came from the other side of the gorge. We were all on this side," he said forcefully.

"So sorry to interrupt," slithered a dark, deep voice from the other side of the valley. Paige whirled around.

A man in a rust-colored cloak faced them, arrow drawn and pointed at Paige. Dinendale stepped in front of her at the same time Robert did. The archer was only a few inches taller than Paige herself, putting him about the same height as Robert. What could be seen of his face under his hood showed a scruffy, unkempt red beard and square jawline. He had a saber attached to his belt and wore a pair of old, scuffed up, worn-out boots.

"That's my kill," he said in a deep menacing tone. "Thanks to you, my tree hugging friend, my job is a whole lot easier. I thought I might actually have to fight those men for this haul."

He cocked his head at Paige, who peered around Robert and Dinendale at him. His yellow teeth grinned at her and gave her a sick feeling in the back of her stomach.

"And look at that, you brought me some female company to boot. What say ye, lass? Fancy being my dinner guest tonight?"

"Pig," she sneered, spitting on the ground in blatant disdain.

His smile only widened. "I do like me a fighter. Excuse my excitement, lady. We don't get many women folk out here, you understand?"

He winked at her and Paige felt her skin crawl. Robert's whole head was turning red with rage as he gripped his spear, end pointed at the archer defensively.

"Who are you?" growled Twostaves, thudding his massive staff against the ground.

"Not that you'll live long enough to remember," the stranger replied with a smirk, "but my name is Hranger. And you're in my mountains."

"Put that bow down, sir," Woodcarver said in a calm yet evenly forceful tone.

The archer chuckled. "Or what, mister? You'll swat me with that staff of yours? Ten gold pieces says I drop you before your heel could hit the ground on your first step towards me."

"Sorry to point out the obvious, laddie, but there are eight of us and only one of you. You don't know who you're dealing with," Broadside said, trying to give a brave laugh. The laugh froze on his lips as the stranger let out a low chuckle that made Paige's skin crawl.

"No, my fat little dwarf. It is you that don't know whom you're dealing with."

The stranger let a shrill whistle out of the side of his mouth and seven bowmen in capes identical to the leader rose from the bushes just a little ways away, arrows trained on the Brotherhood.

"Kill the others," he said with the voice of a viper, "But the girl is mine."

"Over my... cold... dead... body," Dinendale said in a slow, dark tone.

"Oh, I wouldn't have it any other way, elf!"

Dinendale shoved Paige towards the wagon. She hit the dirt rolling, leaping to her feet behind the horse cart, grinding her heels into the dirt for traction.

"*Klaíomh*!" She shouted, the magic hairpin leaping to life in a flash of blue sparks. Clutching her sword, she scanned the situation, gauging her next move. She saw blood on Robert's sleeve and felt an invisible hand seize her throat, but she felt a wave of relief to see Hrangar's arrow had merely grazed him. Twostaves held only one staff, having exchanged the other for his spiked targe. The shield housed two arrows he'd caught defending himself and Broadside. The Brotherhood dove through the air, rolling for cover, as they tried to escape the bandits' arrows.

The frightened horses screamed and took off, pulling away Paige's only cover. She leapt towards the side of the moving cart and grasped the wall with her free hand, lifting her feet to hang like a carnival monkey as the wagon lurched down the trail.

"*Gailogth*!" Woodcarver waved his staff in a wide, sweeping motion. The dust on the ground kicked up with a strong gust appearing from nowhere. The bandits slipped off their feet, crashing to the ground. This gave the Brotherhood just enough time to close the gap between them and their assailants, forcing all to abandon their bows for hand-to-hand combat.

Paige leapt off the cart, able to flank the bandits from their left. The numbers were even, and Paige knew her man; she picked a skinny twig of a human to her left. The bandits held hand-made swords and maces. The skinny lad fumbled for a saber at his side. He drew it just as Paige reached him.

"Ahhhg!" she screamed as she struck as fast and as furiously as she could with Klaíomh. All the pain, all the anger she'd held inside for the last month let loose in one furious burst, her sword flying in a flurry of strokes. She drove him back into the woodline where he gave ground to her blows with increasing speed. As fast as she fought, the boy backed up, scrambling on the inclining ground. Paige noticed the weakness and screamed as she began the hardest assault yet. With powerful swings, she brought the sword from over her head descending on the young man with all the might her small body could muster.

The boy blocked three of these bows feebly before his sword snapped in half with a sharp ping. He fell onto his back, scooting on his thin palms to get away. She closed in on him, and pointed the sword into the skin at the base of his throat.

"Go on, give me a reason to end you, boy!" she yelled. Eyes wide with panic, the lad fumbled to pull something from his belt. She had no idea what it was. It looked like a crossbow, but it had no bow or bolt. He yanked it out of his belt and pointed to her heart.

Something flashed past her ear. The lad's head snapped back, one of Jesnake's throwing knives lodged in his forehead. He didn't even make a sound as his body flopped backwards into the dirt. She stared in shock for an instant then whirled around.

Twostaves fended off a large man, who was not nearly as timid a fighter as Paige's opponent had been. The giant feigned a stumble and the man took the bait. He swiped, which Twostaves nimbly side stepped, especially considering his size. In that same motion, he back-armed the sharp point of the targe spike straight into the man's back.

Duelmaster did wonders with a single rapier, having thrown the other to Dinendale as the battle began. The dryad fought his man with lighting speed, dispatching him with a series of quick stabs to the chest like a wasp.

The others were also prevailing in their matches. Broadside ran right underneath one large man's legs, turned round, and sunk his short sword into the fellow's hamstring. Robert was winning a battle with his spear, and almost had the man backed into a mound of stones. Dinendale, though not moving about nearly as fast as he normally would, had managed to nick his assailant's arm and then grab his sword hand, pulling him in as if to embrace him. He then slammed the rapier hilt into the bandit's face so hard the man's nose broke. Jesnake had also dropped his own man with a throwing knife, and then had thrown one to help Paige.

Click.

The sound came from behind Paige. She turned her head. Hranger stood pointing another bowless crossbow at her, except this one was longer and required the use both hands. He pulled a piece of metal back, which made a second clicking sound. The metal looked like the head of a snake, and in its jaws was what looked like a piece of flint.

"Paige!" she heard someone scream as she was thrown to the ground.

CHAPTER 16

INTO THE MAW

An explosion filled the air, and Paige saw smoke and fire erupt from the end of the weapon as Twostaves shoved her to the ground. Pain shot through her torso as she hit the ground, heard one of her ribs crack, and struck the rocky slope with her head. With a cry of agony, she staggered to her feet. She had to get up before the man came for her, despite how much it hurt.

Out of the corner of her eye, she saw Robert charging Hranger, at full speed, rage carved into his face. He roared as he hurled his spear at the man with enough force to send it through a stone wall. It impaled the man in the chest, going all the way through and protruding out his back and driving into the ground. It propped up the sputtering bandit as he coughed and choked on his own blood before expiring.

"Princess!" Broadside cried, rushing to her side at a full run. "Are you hurt?"

"My ribs," she said clutching her side. "I think one is broken. I-wait! Twostaves!" she cried. The giant was on the ground next to her struggling to sit up.

"My leg. It's in my leg," he grunted, his teeth clenched in pain. Blood poured from an open hole like the one that had sent the wagon driver to meet his Creator. It was high in the meaty part of the giant's thigh. Robert pulled off his robe and shoved it on the wound, applying pressure.

"Not laughing at the robe now, are you ya bellowing cow?" Robert smirked. Twostaves let out a laugh that quickly turned into gasps of pain as Robert pushed harder on the wound, trying to stem the bleeding.

"Can you heal it?" Robert asked Woodcarver.

The magician looked the wound over. "Aye, but we must get the lead out first."

"Lead?" Paige asked, worried and confused.

"I'd heard the Shahir's army had been outfitted with a new type of weapon, but I've never seen one for myself." Woodcarver grimaced as he inserted his knife tip into the wound. Twostaves howled in pain, slamming his fist into the dirt repeatedly.

"It's called an arquebus," muttered Dinendale. "And I have seen one before. It uses fire to hurl lead out of that tube faster than an arrow could ever hope to be."

"I didn't know! Twostaves, I'm so sorry!" she pleaded.

"Not... your fault," he said with gritted teeth. "Didn't... know... better."

Woodcarver twisted the point of the knife around. The squishing sound made Paige want to vomit. Twostaves' bellows of pain helped drown it out slightly though but offered no comfort.

"There," Woodcarver said relieved, producing a piece of lead the size of Paige's thumbnail. "Lucky for you, these bandits probably had no idea how to properly load one of these. You have a considerable amount of tissue keeping it from your main blood vessels."

"Now what's that supposed to mean?" the giant asked, a mockingly insulted expression plastered onto his round face.

"You'll figure it out," the magician said dryly. "Hold still."

A pale light began to shine under his palm. He pressed the glowing hand onto the hole, and Twostaves let out a cry of pain. Woodcarver pressed firmly for several seconds, then released. The hole was gone, save for a small red scar in the shape of a ring.

"It will be tender for a few days, so be careful."

Twostaves stood up and tested his weight on the leg. He nodded and looked up at the magician.

"I'm much obliged, master magician."

"It's nothing," the wizard waved off, turning to Paige. "And now for you, princess. Lay down on your back if you please."

Paige did as he instructed, tenderly touching her ribs and wincing as a sliver of pain spread across her side. He pressed several spots on her waist and rib cage, asking for her to rate the pain.

"The good news is they aren't broken, just bruised."

"Well, that information certainly makes it hurt less," she muttered.

"Hold still." He pulled out a small bottle from his satchel, pouring an ointment on his palm. He gestured for her to lift her shirt up. She hesitated, feeling slightly awkward and uncomfortable. But, knowing they didn't have time to waste, she obliged the magician; he was a healer and apparently old enough to be her father if not her grandfather. The other boys turned around to lend her a bit of privacy, and Woodcarver quickly massaged the ointment into her ribs. It hurt for the first few moments but the pain began to ebb away slowly once the ointment was administered.

"Better?" Woodcarver asked.

"Much," she replied.

"Splendid. Now what?" Duelmaster asked. "I hate to duel and dash, but we have to get to the city, and soon. These missing soldiers will cause a ruckus, surely."

"Aye," Dinendale agreed. "Let's have a look at that what spoils are left."

After taking the weapons off the men, Shaud and bandit alike, they dragged them off the path and near a large boulder. Most of them were easily disposed of, except for the poor driver, who needed to be hauled by four of the lads. They threw the bodies into a shallow ditch, tossing stones and branches over top to keep them hidden in case anyone passed.

Jesnake had calmed the terrified horses, which were a pair of beautiful chestnut mares with feathery trimmed manes and tails. He murmured soothing elvish words to them until they settled down enough for the group to be able to get in the wagon. Robert threw the tarp off the top of the goods piled in the back and began dumping the contents to be sorted.

It was a well-stocked supply wagon, even if it was just a foraging party headed for a tiny outpost. The weapons were mostly the standard army-issue scimitars. Dinendale readily took one he judged to be of decent quality, talking about missing the feel of a broadsword in his hands. Nevertheless he swung the curved blade around easily and resolved to make it work for the time being. The clothing was varied in size and, oddly enough, contained several dresses probably meant for a commander's wife. Aside from the fresh salted pork, cabbages, and other assorted food provisions, nothing else appealed to anyone. Pots and pans would do them no good. Duelmaster did find a small sack in the back that he wanted, but he wouldn't explain why.

"Okay, now what's the plan?" Duelmaster asked, tying his prize to his backpack. Dinendale paused, studying the wagon and its remaining contents.

"Jesnake, cut the horses loose. We can't take the wagon into Aschin. It will be recognized."

"They'll just run back to their stables," he cautioned, unhitching one horse from the cart. Dinendale frowned.

"Well, the only other options are leave them tied up to the wolves, or ride them," he said. "And I'm not sure if we have the capacity to keep them, do you?"

"I can think of worse hurdles ahead of us," Jesnake replied bluntly.

"Agreed. We don't know anything about Olivian's situation as it stands. Fine, we keep the horses. Now, onto the more immediate issue, namely figuring out how to break the princess out of an impregnable fortress."

"Oh, is that all?" Twostaves laughed, picking up one of the Shauden dresses and examining it curiously.

"Here is what I propose," Woodcarver tossed out. "We go into the city and find out all we can, then use that information to formulate our escape plan."

"That may be all well and good," Jesnake said. "But how do we get this information without arousing suspicion? Some of us would stand out like a sore thumb in human cities."

"Disguises for those of us that can pull them off," Dinendale asserted, nodding to the chests of clothing in the wagon. He jumped up into the creaky wooden contraption and began to pull out articles of clothing, tossing them to his friends.

"Congrats, Duelmaster," he said, tossing the dryad the white tunic and helmet of a Shauden soldier. "You've just been conscripted into his Majesty's army."

The dryad wrinkled his face in disgust, holding the attire at arm's length.

"Robert, a rich merchant I think," Dinendale said, tossing Robert a bright red tunic and maroon cloak. A yellow scarf accompanied these to be tied into a turban.

"Really?" Robert said dryly. He eyed Dinendale's choice skeptically.

"I think it'll look good on you," Paige encouraged.

Robert scoffed. "Oh, please. I will own this role," he bragged.

"Ah, what have we here? A captain's uniform? Woodcarver, could you make use of this?" Dinendale asked tossing a golden gilded helmet to the wizard.

"This will be useful in getting information about the palace itself," Woodcarver asserted. "One of you can be my escort. I'll write us up some false Letters of Mark to help us sell our story."

"I'll volunteer for that," Duelmaster said, raising his hand like a schoolboy in class.

"Din, look," Robert said, holding up a hooded black robe. "One of these guys must have been a Raider. There's a whole kit in this satchel."

"What's a raider?" Paige asked.

Dinendale tossed a black, hooded robe to Jesnake, along with a long pole studded with brass tacks and a curved scimitar from the pile. "The Raiders are an elite group of rangers that fight for the Shahir's army. They're independent and travel as they please, for the most part."

"No one will want to tangle with a Raider, not even the high-up officers." Jesnake took long length of lack cloth and wound himself a turban low enough to cover his ears. "The Raiders have a strong reputation for cruelty."

"Well, when the only man you answer to is a ruthless tyrant, you tend to take more... aggressive liberties with the lives of those that stand in your way," Woodcarver said.

"I can go as a peasant," Dinendale said, "and Paige, you go with Robert." He tossed her a dress of red, yellow and black material meant for the commander's wife.

"What am I supposed to do?" she asked.

Dinendale shrugged. "I don't know. I guess you get to be 'his lady' or something."

"No!" Paige cried in protest. She looked over to Robert who was grinning ear to ear.

"Well, you can't exactly pass as a soldier, can you? And you wouldn't be able to pull off a child," Dinendale jumped off the wagon.

"Ugh, fine!" she gave a sharp glance to Robert. "But what about my hair?"

This was a reasonable cause to worry. As a race, the Shauds were known for their dark features, including dark black hair. Robert could hide his blond hair under a turban, but hers was a different matter altogether.

"*Drahgir ye loughnen beh,*" Woodcarver said, placing a gentle hand on her head. Paige felt a tingling at the base of her skull, and reached up to scratch an itch on her scalp. One by one, a grin or astonished look spread across her friends' faces.

"What is it? Woodcarver, what are you...?" Paige started, and then she grabbed her braid and pulled it over her shoulder.

Her hair, which had been the same beautiful gold as her mother's, was turning black like fire burning along a piece of birch bark. She untied the cord holding the braid in place, letting her long locks fall down on her shoulders like a flaxen waterfall as the black coloring ran down the length hair. Soon, not a blonde plat was left on her head, replaced by a mop of silky raven locks as dark as any Shaud.

"How did you?" she started, but was so astonished, she couldn't finish.

Woodcarver just smiled. "Don't worry. It's not permanent. It will return to its normal color if you wash it with water infused with pine bark."

"Wait, Woodcarver," Jensake said, his head popping up over the back of one of the large horses. "Will that spell work on any hair?"

Woodcarver was thoughtful for a moment.

"I can honestly say I've never tried," he said, approaching the horses slowly. "But there's only one way to find out."

He slowly stroked the larger of the two creatures on the mane, clicking his tongue softly. The gentle draft horse nuzzled him.

"*Drahgir ye loughnen beh*," he whispered again, and within half a moment, the horses mane began to bleed from white to black just as Paige's hair had done moments before. Within a few seconds, the white mane, star, and socks of the beast were all black as a raven. Dinendale and Duelmaster clapped in appreciative applause.

"Well done! Another!" Duelmaster laughed. Within a few more moments, both horses stood shoulder to shoulder, black as night and bearing no recognizable features.

"That should make things considerably easier," Jesnake said. "A nifty trick indeed."

It took a little time to get all the extra gear cinched up, but they managed to throw it on the backs of the horses within an hour and began making their way towards Aschin. They took a route off the narrow path, just in case more soldiers were trailing them. The night grew cold and dark, but they kept up a hurried pace, adrenaline giving their tired feet a much needed boost of raw energy.

When the moons were almost to the zenith of their celestial dance, they took a sharp turn and began climbing what Paige hoped would be the last ridge of mountains. Twostaves offered her one of his arms for support as they began zigzagging the steep switchbacks leading up to the crest. This side of the valley was significantly rockier than the other side, with far fewer trees and vegetation to grasp onto, so they took their time with the horses at a slow and steady plodding as they continued higher and higher once more.

"Thank you," she said appreciatively to the giant.

He smiled awkwardly. "I must say, that hair is going to take some getting used to!" he chuckled. "Threw me off for a moment!"

"Well, I'm sorry it's so off putting," she laughed, hopping past craggy rocks that resembled bison in shape.

"Oh no, my dear it isn't that," he took her hand and picked her entire body up like a rag doll. He then carried her over a fallen log blocking the narrow pathway. "It actually looks quite natural on you."

"Probably because Papa had dark hair. I always favored him in appearance," she said softly.

"I never got to meet your papa," Twostaves said, compassion lacing his words. "But I'm sure he was a fine man."

"The finest," she said simply. "He was the kindest, most warm and loving man I've ever known."

The giant chuckled. "My father was like that, too. Never turned down a stranger he could offer hospitality to, my pops."

A sad, somber expression replaced his default jovial nature for a moment as he plodded ahead. Paige recalled the story Duelmaster had told her about the giant's troubled and tragic past. As annoying as his endless laughter and argumentative nature could be, she knew he too had suffered just as much loss and hurt as she herself had.

"Well, I've been told he was the finest of giants," she assured, patting his arm. "I'm sure he would be right proud to see the warrior you've become."

"Pops? Oh no, princess. He was literally and figuratively the biggest pacifist you'd ever meet," Twostaves laughed. "Ten and a half feet tall my pops, loved hugs more than halberds. This second staff on my back is his. He used it for walking with his hounds back on the estate. I suppose I have sullied its purpose in my quest for justice. But I hope he would understand."

"I'm sure he would," Paige assured. She smiled at him encouragingly once more as she hopped up a few more boulders.

"Princess!" Robert called from up ahead. He had just crested another hill, beckoning her to hurry. She quickened her pace, ignoring the throbbing in her side from her still mending ribcage.

"What is it?" she asked, reaching his side. He motioned for her to be quiet and took her by the hand. She followed him through some heavy pine brush as he shoved the branches aside with his spear. The moonlight shone in wisps through the scant trees, making everything appear bluish in tint as they jogged their way across the crest of the mountain. Soon the brush thinned out even more until they came out of the woods and onto a rocky cliff. Jesnake alighted onto a boulder and squatted, pointing a slender finger to the horizon across a large, stoney valley.

A mass of craggy, bleak, grey mountains outlined the near twilight sky, reaching to the heavens like tips of a line of spears. Clouds hung low over cliffs, threatening rain from a heavy, foggy blanket of mist. In the middle of the valley, hardly a day's walk away, lay a large city as grey as the cliffs surrounding it. It was bigger than any village Paige had ever seen, with somber looking slate buildings surrounding a massive fortress that was carved into the mountain. Three walls surrounded the town, dividing it into separate sections, like tiers on a cake.

The keep lay in the center of the third wall, backed right up into the mountainside. Its onion dome raised high above the town like an all-seeing eye, keeping tabs on the comings and goings of its inhabitants. Flying proudly from the pinnacle of this dome flapped a white standard, with a coiled golden serpent at the center, it's swallowtail shape flapping in the breeze, crimson tassels fringing the entire banner. Paige felt a chill go down her spine.

"Well princess," Robert whispered in her tapered ears. "Welcome to Aschin."

The fire crackled, casting flickering shadows across the faces of each member of the Brotherhood. Most of them stared into the flames, deep in thought. Paige, however, couldn't keep her crystal blue eyes off the dimly lit city to the northeast. It looked to be about as cheerful as a haunted tomb. Somewhere, beyond those solid granite walls, her sister dwelt in a dirty, rotting dungeon. She felt both sick with dread and a thrill of exhilaration burrowed in soul knowing she was within a day's journey of Olivian. Even if that journey was through several stone walls, gates, countless guards and myriad passageways.

They had marched along the ridge towards the city for a few more hours that night till they'd stumbled upon a cave large enough to shield themselves and the horses from prying eyes in the valley. It also helped to block the harsh wind that had kicked up as the night wore on. They now all huddled about the small fire chewing on what was left of the Impasca jerky, which wasn't much. Paige felt her stomach growl. She squirmed, uncomfortable, and took a swig from her wineskin, hoping the water might quiet her abdomen.

"Princess, I've been meaning to suggest something to you, and now this close to the army I feel it necessary to bring to your attention," Woodcarver sat beside her and pulled a small rolled up cloth from his satchel.

"What is it?" she asked, eyeing the little parcel. He unwrapped it carefully, taking his time with each of the folds so as not to spill it's contents.

"I've been thinking about what to do with the page, since we can hardly risk it being found or captured," he said. "So, if you will allow me, I'd like to sew it into your moccasin."

"Into my moccasin? Can you even do that?" she asked skeptically.

He nodded his head slightly. "I believe I can. If I'm right, the spell protecting the page acts more like a healing spell than anything. If we were to try and cut it, the pieces would just mend themselves back together, but if we simply sew it, the bond will become tight and should allow us to hide it while not having to entrust it to a hiding place."

"But if I'm captured," she said, "Isn't my boot the first place they'll look?"

"Perhaps, but if it's part of the boot," Woodcarver explained, "I think we've more a chance of it going unnoticed, should the worst happen."

Paige thought for a moment, then yanked off her moccasin and handed it, and the page, to Woodcarver. He selected a needle from his precious sewing kit and quickly threaded what Paige assumed was dried animal sinew. He picked the pair up and walked over to his own bedroll, rummaging around in his pack before sitting back down cross legged to begin sewing.

"So once more, just so we're on the same page," Duelmaster said, shifting to a more comfortable position, "What is our plan tomorrow?"

"We'll split up and go into the city at different times during the day," Dinendale said, poking the fading fire back to life. "We need to skirt the entire grid and get every detail of the layout we can. We'll meet back half an hour before sunset."

The men grunted in agreement. The plan was simple enough.

"What about after? Assuming all goes well?" Woodcarver asked.

Robert looked up sharply.

"There is no assuming," Dinendale insisted.

Woodcarver held up a hand in apology. "Very well. When we are done, what then?"

"We come back and, with the information we glean, formulate a plan. Then we act on it as quickly as possible," he tossed one more log onto the fire. Dinendale looked each of them in the eye during the moment of silence that followed. "If we do this," he said, "we won't just be a bunch of miscreants in the Wild to the Shahir or his sons. We will have faces to them, and they will hunt us like animals."

There was a slight pause as the gravity overwhelmed them. Up till now, they had been of little concern to the Empire. But once they freed Olivian and made off with the page from the Book of Death, there would be a price on their heads forever. The Wild might never be safe for them again.

"I am prepared to take that risk," Dinendale continued. "But I don't want anyone else to have to."

"Oh, please," Robert cut him off, jumping to his feet. "We all knew the risk when we first set out from the willow tree."

"He's right, Din," Twostaves said, uncharacteristically somber. "It's a little late to turn around now."

"You'll have to dig me a hole and plant me if you plan on leaving me out of the fun," Duelmaster chuckled, crossing his arms and leaning against a large boulder.

"Besides," Woodcarver added, "If we're doing it right, they won't know what faces to pin this on, will they?"

"Agreed," Dinendale said, a slight, smug smile playing at his lips. "We'll then... let's play 'dress up.'"

"No, I'm not going to hold your hand!" Paige spat indignantly as she and Robert walked towards the huge gates of the stone fortress city of Aschin. Robert looked at her, wiggled his eyebrows and grinned. It looked so odd to see him in Shauden clothes and a turban.

"Oh, come now, my dear," he trilled. "Over the honeymoon phase already?"

She glared at him under dark lashes. He only widened his smile.

"Sell it, Paige. It's all about selling it."

"Moron," she hissed, slipping her slender fingers through his.

He chuckled. "There's a good lass, obeying your husband like a good woman!" he laughed. The chuckling ended abruptly when several joints in his hand popped.

"Oh come on, Paige. It was just a joke. Blimey, you have sharp nails!"

"And don't you forget it, husband dear," she growled. Paige wore the dress from the supply wagon and felt no envy for the woman that would have worn it if it had made it to the outpost. A mostly black garment, the sleeves and bodice were made of yellow satin and trimmed with red embroidery. The skirt was full length, and would typically have ended at a lady's ankles, but it was a bit big for Paige's smaller frame, so it dragged along the hard packed earth like a wedding dress train. The bodice was stuffy and restricting; a living nightmare to a girl born and raised free in forests, a place where a man's shirt was just as good for a lady as it was a man should she decide to wear it. There was enough material in this dress to make a tent, she was sure.

The only upside was that there was plenty of room to hide the several daggers she'd procured from the wagon yesterday. One was lashed to each leg with a leather cord just above the knee, and her antler-handled hunting dagger lay under the front apron of her dress. This, in addition to her hairpin in her tied up bun, was comforting psychologically to her. Yet these weapons did nothing to ease the pressure on her middle, thanks to the contraption Woodcarver called a "stay." She wondered how on Eirensgarth woman wore these things daily. It was a webbing of linen and cane that was supposed to make rich women look thinner in the middle and wider in the hips and chest. Aside from agitating her healing ribs, all it was doing for Paige was making her waist hurt and keeping her breath short.

She had protested this entire outfit heavily as the boys all started dressing in their own disguises. Sadly, there was nothing to do but clench her fists and change into the dress; Dinendale was right that she wasn't young enough to pass for a boy, and any other disguise would have aroused curious eyes in a place they needed to stay invisible. Still, that did not mean she would go quietly.

"Honestly, how do these women even function?" she'd hiked up the several layers of petticoats and aprons surrounding her hips so she could tug on her moccasins, the left of which, thanks to Woodcarver, now held the page stitched seamlessly into the calf portion of the footwear. The boys had chuckled mirthlessly.

"I'm afraid you'll find human women in the east are not afforded the same kind of leeway the women in the Wild are," Jesnake had said, clipping his black robe over his shoulders with a silver brooch. "Anything less than what you're wearing would be seen as improper."

In the end, each of their costumes turn out quite well, all things considered. As long as Dinendale let his dark hair hang over his pointed ears, and Jesnake kept his hood up, no one could see the points in their ears. Paige had been worried about this too, since she'd already seen how easily those in the outside world noticed her tapered ears, even if they were significantly less defined than the pure-blood elves in their posse. Woodcarver had alleviated this concern by offering to do her hair up. The princess had been skeptical of this idea, but once she allowed the magician access to her dark locks, she'd been surprised at how apt he was in hair styling.

"I had two sisters," he explained, finishing off her bun with a tight tying of cord and inserting the magic hairpin-sword into the side. He'd left just enough hair to pull down on either side of her face, just covering the tops of her ears. The men all nodded and murmured approval. Duelmaster even clapped. The dryad's own hair was shaggy enough to cover the half-moon shaped taper in his own ears, and the beard he'd developed over the last few weeks rounded off his square features just enough to make him look fully human, albeit a shaggy mess of one.

Those who were infiltrating the city had hiked through the early morning and on into the greyish dawn till they were hidden just beyond the city's outskirts in a clump of scraggy fir trees; Twostaves and Broadside, who would stick out like sore thumbs in the city, had opted to stay behind in the cave to ensure their gear and armor would be unmolested. Though remote and gloomy, there appeared to be no lack of activity coming in and out of the city, which would actually be a help to them. At least that's what Woodcarver explained to them.

"With more people going in and out, there will be less of a chance being noticed as strangers," he said, eyeing the road coming from the south of the valley as well as the one coming from the north.

"That road looks new," Duelmaster said, pointing to the northbound road.

"They must have cut a new one north to Franghal," Woodcarver muttered. "Poor miners. No wonder the Shahir found your village, princess. With an operation like this and the Wild at the back door, it was only a matter of time."

"We should try to circle about and go in from different directions if we can," Dinendale said. "Jesnake, you and I should come from the north, the rest can come from the south."

Duelmaster and Woodcarver left first into the city, the magician sitting nobly atop one of the horses while the dryad marched smartly along beside. Despite the fact that the uniforms they wore were of their enemies, they wore them with a sense of honor and dignity you would expect from a soldier of any country. About half an hour later, Dinendale went in, dressed as a peasant with an old sack of rags slung over his shoulder. Paige was impressed with his ability to act the part. Luckily he still had the bruising from his bout with a river serpent to pass as a beaten servant. Paige wasn't sure he needed to do that, but Robert had been more than willing to oblige. Jesnake left an hour after Dinendale, dressed in the imposing Raider's garb. He wore the sword on his belt, and carried the imposing staff in his hand as he mounted the second horse and circled about to make an entrance from the northbound road.

"Be sure you do the same. Wouldn't do for a bunch of people to see you just pop out of the bushes," advised the elf before spurring the horse into a trot away from the grove of trees and towards the northern edge of the valley. Robert and Paige waited another three quarters of an hour before heading off through the thin trees towards the south to meet up at the road and begin their journey into the city.

"It's no wonder men think women need saving every minute of every day," Paige pulled her skirts free of a felled pine log she'd attempted to jump over as they made their way east to the road.

"Well as I recall, you have needed saving on more than one occasion," Robert teased. "And you managed that while in pants, sweetheart!"

Paige shot him a nasty look. He smiled an impish grin as he offered a hand for her to jump over another felled log. She begrudgingly obliged him, not wanting to risk falling face-first in the rocky soil and giving him an excuse to plaster on that smug look he reserved for such occasions.

"So maybe we should get our backstory straight," Robert offered as she hopped over the log. "Might help us keep our characters believable, in case we get questioned."

"Makes sense."

"Alright. There's a small province in the Shahir's kingdom to the southeast called Behlore. We live there on a small plantation."

"Alright. Why are we in Aschin?"

"We're meeting some business contacts to discuss a contract for a caravan coming from Franghal."

"Fine. How did we meet?"

"We've been married for...oh, say four years? Arranged of course, by my parents."

"That would explain why we aren't a very happy couple," she chuckled mirthlessly, tearing her petticoat away from a snagging branch that lay prostrate on the ground.

"Are we not, dearie? And here I thought we were doing so splendidly," Robert said, feigning hurt. They both laughed as they stumbled out of the trees and onto the side of the road. Luckily, there were no people on this bend in the road, so it was easy to turn north and double back towards the city. Paige felt relieved that they wouldn't have to explain to any curious onlookers or suspicious guards that two decently well-off Shauds were suddenly appearing out of the woods.

"So how many kids do you want?" Robert asked as they walked towards the city.

"One, a lovely little boy we will spoil to death and shall grow up to be an absolute brat," Paige laughed.

"Best to hope he doesn't get his mother's temperament," Robert quipped.

She slugged him playfully on the shoulder. "Hey, I can be a dear when I want to be. I just don't see the point with you," she laughed.

"I rest my case," Robert said, rubbing his arm but smiling. "Though I would have expected better of a chieftain's daughter. And after all the trouble I went through saving your hide!"

They walked in silence for a few moments, every step bringing Paige closer and closer to Aschin. Her hands felt clammy and her heartbeat rose; it felt like a colony of bats was thrashing about in the pit of her stomach.

This was it.

This was the moment she'd been looking forward to for weeks now, and now that it was here, she was having a hard time keeping her hands from shaking.

"So, what's next?" Robert asked.

Robert stooped to pick up a stone, skipping it along the roadway as they rounded a bend in the path. The road was curvier and more winding here than it was close to the city, and though Paige could see the smoke, she could not actually see Aschin through the sparse, tall pines.

"How do you mean?" Paige turned to look Robert in the eyes.

"I'm mean after all this. After we save Olivian. What's next? For you, that is."

Paige pondered the question a moment. She would be lying if she'd said she hadn't spent a great deal of time thinking about that question. She honestly hadn't come up with a good answer to it. The Wild had been all she'd ever known, and Kapernaum the only place she'd ever truly called home. But going back was no longer an option. Her village lay in ashes, and what was left of her friends and tribe had scattered to the wind or had been sold off like cattle.

"I don't know," she said truthfully. "Obviously I'd want to eventually settle down, though I've no idea where or if that would ever happen."

"You really think you could go back to living a quiet life after all this?" he laughed, gesturing around them. "You don't want to sleep out on the cold ground in the harsh elements for the rest of your life?"

Paige laughed. "As much fun as freezing my toes off every night has been, I would love to live in a house again."

"A three-story treehouse, I imagine?"

"Actually, I've always fancied living in a home build on solid ground. Seems like it could be fun."

"Haha, better atop the ground than under it. My croft does its job well, but I hear there are some underground homes that are more like nasty, dirty, wet, holes filled with worms and an oozy smell."

"Well, I havn't had much experience with them aside from my brief stay at your home, but I'm sure I'd be much happier above the ground."

"Well, for what it's worth," Robert kicked another stone as they rounded another bend in the road, "I would love it if you all stayed with us. You are as much part of the Brotherhood as anyone. And we'd love it if you stuck around."

"Thanks, Robert. That means a lot."

"Don't mention it. I just thought I'd tell y-" He was cut short as they rounded the last bend in the road. Paige felt her heart stop as she found herself standing face to face with the great fortress of Aschin.

The giant stone city was even more imposing up close. Paige could see the thick outer stone wall fronted by a deep, black chasm acting as a dry moat. How deep it was, Paige had no way of knowing, but judging by the inky blackness, she was willing to wager a fall into it would be deadly. The outer wall rose three stories high with a space wide enough for two soldiers to walk abreast on the top. Turrets for archers were placed one hundred feet apart, each crowned with the banner of the royal family. The gates of the city stood at least twenty feet tall and were made with thick, pinewood boards. Each board was bound with solid, wrought-iron bands and studded nails.

The two walked boldly, hand in hand, towards the gates to the fortress. Its single entrance on the outer wall was a hulking mass of carved stone with a thick, wide drawbridge crossing the deeply-chasmed gouge in the earth. Paige would never admit it to him, but the feeling of Robert's warm, strong, hand helped settle her nerves.

Several guards dressed in full armor stood at the gate, and Paige tried to swallow the lump forming in her throat. The sight of the same soldiers that had massacred her people filled her with rage and fear. A few of them eyed her with piercing gazes under their turbaned helmets. She squeezed Robert's hand reassuringly, and he leaned over to whisper in her ear.

"Don't worry. I will protect you."

"Likewise," she said, taking a deep breath.

They passed through the gates with no incident, and she sighed in relief. Robert smiled at her. She tried to give half a smile back, but it came out like more of a grimace with her stomach still doing somersaults. The view before her beyond the first wall did nothing to abate her body's internal acrobatics.

Before her stretched out a city with streets lined by countless stone and brick structures. Men and a surprising number of women walked to and from these buildings like termites in a rotting oak log. Tents and booths clogged the streets and alleyways, their owners hawking wares and goods in an accent that was thick and unrecognizable to her ear. She gazed around at the bustling city with wide eyes, never having seen so many people in one place before. She felt frightened and lost in the confines of this city; growing up free in the Wild had made her enjoy the wide open spaces. Now she felt trapped, cramped, and confined.

"I've never," she started to say, but was jostled in the arm by a man with a donkey muttering under his breath as he passed.

"Don't look too shocked, remember you're supposed to have grown up around these kinds of sights. I'd heard stories about the mott and bailey at Aschin from traders, but I always assumed they had to be exaggerating," Robert whispered. "And that keep! This prince Feridar may be relatively young, but you have to hand it to the man. He is impressively cunning."

"What is a mott?"

"It's the courtyard and village surrounding the castle," Robert interrupted her question, his gaze sweeping the battlements.

The keep could more accurately have been called a palace. Raised on a small hill overlooking the mott and bailey, the keep had been built into the mountainside itself, protecting it from behind with the deep mountains of the east. The palace itself was hewn out of solid granite, the rock color varying from charcoal black to the cold grey of wet ash in a fire pit. It was at least four stories high with its massive grey onion dome glaring down on them imposingly.

Protecting the keep, within the city's main wall and dry moat, were two smaller walls separating them from the palace, each having its own set of guard towers and gates. The towers were all connected by a series of stone archways and bridges, reminding her of a colder version of Kapernaum's bridged system. On the north end of the city, to their left, she could see the giant aqueduct pouring a waterfall down into the city. Between themselves and that aqueduct sat a smaller, shorter, wall with a tiny gatehouse big enough to hold four or five soldiers.

Robert whistled.

"This place is designed beautifully. They could shut the outer gates and be on lockdown for months if they had an enemy brave enough to lay siege. That aqueduct is a feat in and of itself!"

"Let's hope they focused so much on keeping out armies that they won't be looking for a couple misfits," she breathed, trying to calm her nerves.

"Looks like they've done their best to section off the city within the walls. I'll bet that gatehouse is to keep just anyone from accessing the cistern. Markets must all be separated from high-risk areas."

"To think, pumping all that water in and then keeping people from it," she muttered.

"Well, best crack on then," Robert said, squeezing her hand in reassurance. They turned to the right and walked away from the inner wall and gatehouse into the busy marketplace with quick steps. Paige tried to ignore the filth and mud that they sloshed through to get to the vendors.

The marketplace was more to the left than in the city plan. It reminded her of a dirtier, less colorful version of Kapernaum's market. Tattered banners of shops and the occasional hitching post lined the streets and byways. Troughs with brackish liquid sloshing out gave a rank stench to the air.

There were a few buildings that seemed to be dedicated shops, most notably a tavern and what appeared to be a gambling establishment crowded with lewd, loitering drunkards seeking female companionship. The scent was enough to make Paige's meager meal of dried Impasca strips crawl up the sides of her stomach. At least if she hurled, it wouldn't diminish the property appraisal for any of these establishments.

The first vendor they passed sat under a homespun tent, selling what looked to be baskets made of weeds. He was a short, round man with a wart placed on the end of a crooked, broken, nose. He boasted squinty, piggish eyes that were constantly darting down to Paige and Robert's money satchels, like a dog awaiting a scrap of fat from the table.

"Ah, my lord," he said in an accent as thick as fresh cream. "You seek a basket to please the beautiful mistress, yes? I have the finest baskets in Aschin, made of the bulrushes that grow along the Great River, yes I do. What can I interest you with?"

"Good merchant," Robert said, mimicking the accent by rolling his r's like the basket weaver. "What a stock you have. Tell me, of what use would one of your baskets be to me?"

"Ah, my lord has a keen buyer's eye, yes you do. May I say that these baskets are fine for carrying goods and keeping household items in order, yes they are. What seek you, my lord?"

"A small basket, for my lovely wife to place her toiletries," Robert said, winking at Paige. "She must keep all those pretty paints in order you know! She does tend to love the rouge a little too much."

She definitely needed no rouge at that moment to make her cheeks red. He would pay. Oh, how he would pay, when they were done.

"Ah, I have just the thing, yes I do," the merchant babbled, pulling out a small woven box that looked about as dry and cracked as his parched lips. Paige looked at it in disgust. What a worthless piece of junk.

"Hmm," Robert mumbled with a little disapproval. "Maybe something else."

"Oh, I see. Not quite right. Let me find the perfect one, yes?" He dug under the table through more baskets.

"Business must be booming with all the soldiers," Robert looked out at the street. "Seem to be a great deal more of them here now than last time I took a trip here. Is there an enemy of the Empire about?"

"Actually," the merchant slurred, "there was a revolt, yes there was. In the forest to the west. Our soldiers came out, they did, and quelled the bloody rebellion, yes."

"Bloody revolt, indeed!" said a merchant who sold fishing hooks and trinkets at the booth next door. "I heard they slaughtered many of our men, and had an army of wild savages from the forests ready to attack our helpless settlements!"

"But, it's all better now. Prince Feridar, may he rule long and happily, returned two weeks ago with the prisoners, he did. Slaves they are now, yes. Sent them all up to Franghal to work as punishment for their insurrection!"

The man popped his head up from under the table and produced another basket that looked no different from the one he'd just shown them.

"Never mind," Robert said with an airy wave of his hand. Paige thought he played the belligerent, wealthy, dorbel quite well. It took all her control not to lash out at the news. Insurrection? Murdering villages? She hadn't even known this world existed when the Shauds attacked, and this man seemed to think Prince Feridar's massacres had saved them all from death at the hands of bloodthirsty savages. If only they knew. Robert took one look at her face before grabbing her arm and steering her away.

"You're going to have to do better than that, Paige," he cautioned, his voice stern in her ear. "You look like you want to jump across the table and choke that man out."

"But he said..."

"I know what he said," Robert cut her off. "But if you want to get your sister out of enemy hands you are going to have to start thinking like them. That man believes what he is told because that is all he is told. Propaganda and fear-mongering are tools those with dark intentions use to blind otherwise decent people."

"Fine," she said, trying to compose herself. "I'll try better."

"That's my girl," Robert said, patting her cheek. She smiled forcefully and firmly removed his hand from her face.

"You touch me like that one more time, and I don't care who's watching. I will drop you like a sack of grain. Do you understand?" Paige hissed through her teeth.

"Noted," Robert laughed, clearly unperturbed.

They spent the rest of the afternoon stopping by countless shops, asking about the recent affairs, and gathering information about the palace and city itself. Paige was impressed with how well Robert asked innocent questions that led to such detailed and useful information.

The late afternoon sky grew darker as the sun began to dip beyond the western mountains they had crossed in past days. The smoky haze that lingered all day began to descend upon the valley like a demonic spirit creeping out of the darkness. Paige felt fatigue pulling at her as the light faded. Her muscles were cramped, and her waist ached from wearing the stays. This bloody contraption lifted her chest and made breathing a chore of short breaths.

"Can we leave now?" Paige felt her head ache from the strain of the stays. It wasn't that she wasn't motivated to get to Olivian, but she wouldn't be able to play her role convincingly if she fainted from lack of oxygen or stumbled in shoes she should supposedly be accustomed to wearing.

Robert leaned in towards her sun-kissed cheeks.

"Not quite, my dear. One more vender," he said.

"Robert," she whispered through gritted teeth. "I don't know how much longer I can last in this thing. You said that six vendors ago."

Compassion flickered in his crystal blue eyes, but he shook his head.

"I know. Let's finish this and we'll head back. One more for Olivian?" He kept his voice at a whisper.

Paige took as deep a breath as she could as Robert led on. The booth where they stopped was an open-air farriers forge, with a gigantic beast of a man working to beat life into a glowing piece of black iron. The metal cried out in pain as the hammer struck it over and over, the sharp ping sound reverberating through the mucky streets. The man's skin was as black as polished ebony, like Papa's old friend Xandla. Two other men sharpened blades of short swords on round grinding wheels; one man spun the wheel with a crank, while the other carefully worked the blade against against the stone, sparks shooting out and dancing upon the ground. None of the men looked up when Robert stopped at the edge of the short brick wall surrounding the lot.

"Evening," Robert said. The two apprentices grunted, but the big man with the hammer looked up. He scowled, but didn't stop his work as he addressed them.

"What do you want?" he barked gruffly. Robert was taken aback by the man's direct nature, but he kept his smile plastered to his face as he continued his query.

"I uh-," Robert stumbled, trying to come up with a different approach. "Beg pardon, sir? Are you the proprietor?"

"Come again?" the smithy barked.

"The owner, I mean. Do you own this shop?"

"What kind of stupid question is that?" the man spat, beating the hammer to the pulse of his words. "Of course I own this shop. Or at least I'm supposed to."

He threw the hammer onto the dusty earth that looked blue in the lasting twilight. He plunged the glowing iron into the bucket of oil at the foot of his anvil with enough force to skewer a wild boar. It spewed and sizzled as he swished it around to chase the sparks till they were all out. He quickly returned it to the small forge made of stone in the back of the shop and glared at the couple.

"That bottom-dwelling, inbred Prince Feridar has every free smith working like a slave. As if he didn't have enough swords, now he wants new ones. Rather than pay us a fair wage, he threatens us with prison if we do not deliver. And all this after being made to make new chains for the dungeons."

"Must have been quite a number of chains for all those prisoners the army just brought in. Must be a full jail."

"The dungeon was already full. Those slaves went straight to Franghal, say for one. The prince's personal pet. Some woman."

"Was she blond?" Paige blurted out. Robert gave her a sharp glance. "I mean, the barbarian woman? I hear they have hair colored like flax?"

"I don't know, I was just forced to make the chains," the smithy spat. "And if you don't mind I've got more work yet to be finished today."

"Terribly sorry, you have my sympathy."

"I don't need your Raven Head sympathy, your pity is as cheap as the dirt on my shoes. It's the outcasts and immigrants like me that make up for your cursed king's campaigns," the man glared at the fire as he pulled out the hot iron. "I spit on the day he came here, may he rot in his stone palace."

"Words like that could get you killed, Idech," a low voice slithered from around the corner of the back wall.

Paige felt her skin crawl as she saw a soldier slip out of the building's shadow. He was a well-built man, with a gleaming officer's sword at his side, partially tucked into a crimson sash. His narrow eyes and high cheekbones granted him a sinister appearance. The blacksmith spat into the dirt defiantly.

"A thousand apologies, friends," the soldier hissed with a serpentine smile. "It appears my friend Idech has had a long day. I'm sorry, but he can take no commissions at present. Any arms to be had belong to the army, by order of that, oh what was it you called him, Idech? Bottom-dwelling inbreed?"

"Bold words when you are the only ones with the means to enforce them," the smith spat, looking hard at his anvil. The soldier chuckled, walking over and placing a hand on the smith's shoulder, gripping it tightly.

"Something like that," he said quietly.

Without warning, the soldier pulled a dagger from under his cloak and drove it into the black man's neck with an enormous amount of force. Paige screamed as the smith sank to the floor, grasping for the knife and gurgling for air that could not enter his flooding lungs. The soldier didn't even blink, merely pulling the knife out and wiping the blood off his blade with the sash at his waist. The smith sputtered, twitched, then ceased to thrash, his eyes open wide and lifeless. The shock of the immediate brutality made Paige weak in the knees. She clutched Robert's arm for support. He was tense, his hand fingering the scimitar at his waist.

"It's damnable shame, treason," he said, as calm and guiltless as if he had just picked a flower in a meadow even with a man lying lifeless at his boots. "Idech here seemed to think free speech came without a price. Should have kept his mouth shut."

Robert took a step back.

"I believe we'll be on our way now," he said with measured words.

"Easy there merchant. You are free to go, assuming you give up your sister."

Paige's grip tightened on Robert's arm. She could have sworn she felt heat pulse through his clothes.

"This is my wife, and you will have no such thing," Robert hissed through clenched teeth. The man chuckled.

"First off, neither of you wear an armband, so even if she isn't your sister, she is not yours. Secondly, I wasn't asking."

Without warning six other soldiers jumped out of the dark alleys on either side of the booth and pounced onto Robert. Two of the men ripped Paige away from Robert while the others knocked the fellow on his back. Paige screamed. A nearby soldier clamped a hand over her mouth. She struggled as hard as she could, kicking and thrashing, biting even though the man's leather glove kept her from being able to do much damage. The other troops were beating and kicking Robert, who was shouting and shoving at the soldiers as hard as he could. Paige's heart raced with terror.

"Take her away," the leader hissed, and the soldiers began to drag her down the alley. The leader looked around to be sure no one was following them. Paige tried screaming, but they just slapped her in the face, not even bothering to cover her mouth. Who would help her?

"Quickly," he hissed. "To the barracks."

They made their way down another ally and were heading for the street on the other side when a black cloaked figure leapt from the house rooftop above, landing in their path nimbly like a cat, standing slowly. He was tall, thin, and held a staff with a hooked blade on the top.

Jesnake. She bit her tongue so as not to give him away.

The elf flung the hood off his head and glared at the men with slanted eyes like a wolf's that reflected the white moonlight. Paige could feel the hatred and hostility emanating from him like heat waves off a hot stone.

"Raider!" one of the soldiers gasped in apprehension. Jesnake took a defensive stance, the bladed staff pointing wickedly at the men.

"Get out of the way, Raider. We have no beef with you!" another soldier shouted.

Jesnake glared. "Where are you taking that girl?"

"None of your business. Just having a bit of fun," one responded.

"It doesn't look like the lady is having fun."

"Enough. Just kill him if he won't move. No one is going to miss a Raider this far west," the leader snapped. Three of the guards rushed the elf, leaving one to hold Paige immobile.

The men who charged Jesnake showed immediate skill. They attacked in a V-shaped formation, two advancing first with the other running close behind. They had drawn scimitars raised above their turbaned heads with no fear of the dark warrior before them.

The first tried to attack Jesnake on his left. Jesnake swung the bottom end of the studded staff upwards, catching the falling blade before it descended upon his head. He twisted the staff around faster than a diving eagle, hitting the second attacker in the stomach, knocking him backwards. The elf planted the butt of the staff in the dirt and, grabbing it with both hands, propelled both legs into the third man. The tough soles of his boots slammed into the Shaud's face, the force lifting the man off his feet and throwing him to the ground.

Jesnake landed nimbly as he completed the full circle swing, sending the hooked blade end of the staff into the first soldier who was trying to jump him from the side. It sank through his chain mail shirt like a garden rake through a ripe squash. The soldier didn't make a sound as he slumped to the muddy ground.

The second and third attackers approached more readily, the second looking a bit green from the blow to the stomach while the third boasted a crimson line of blood trickling from a thin cut on his upper lip.

"Last chance, Raider. Get out of the way," the leader said from behind, grabbing Paige himself. "You might scare others into doing as you wish, but no one will avenge you when I kill you out here."

The soldier holding Paige shoved her to the ground and joined his comrades, bringing their ranks to three once more.

She tried to scramble up, but the leader placed a cold, sharp sword blade to her throat and kept her on her back in the dirt, heart racing.

Jesnake tossed the staff up and caught it like a javelin.

"As long as the Creator gives me breath," he said in a low voice, " you will go no further with that woman."

"Better begin a prayer to that god of yours," the leader roared, and the three charged him once more.

Jesnake waited until they were within a few feet of him, then he cocked his arm back like a crossbow, throwing the staff with all his might. It left his hand like a bolt of lightning forking across a dark sky, nailing one soldier in the face, laying him low. Equally as fast, the elf drew the curved sword at his side and slashed upwards with the same movement at the next attacker. The Shaud caught the slash with his sword and parried, catching Jesnake on the arm. Paige heard the fabric rip and winced as she imagined the blood that was most certainly pouring down his arm. Jesnake didn't let out so much as a whimper. He grabbed the man's arm and pulled, driving his assailants' body into the ready blade of his curved sword. He let the screaming guard fall, the weapon still lodged in his body, and whirled to face the third assailant.

This Shaud charged with a roar, and at the last possible moment Jesnake sidestepped a stab that would have ended his life. He twisted his body so the guard ran past him. The elf quickly laced his long arms around the soldier's neck, cutting off the air flow and grasping his fist to hold the choke. The man struggled, fighting to get free. He dropped the sword and grabbed Jesnake's arm, trying to pry it from his neck. He tried to breathe, and his eyes rolled backwards. Then he sank to his knees and fell over face-first onto the dirt. Jesnake rose from the ground and faced the now lone leader.

"Don't move!" the leader hissed, pressing the sword's edge harder against Paige's neck. "I'll bleed her out, don't think I...."

The cold steel against her neck suddenly disappeared and she whirled around to see the man gasping for air as a dark, angry figure clutched at his throat from behind.

"Princess!" Jesnake shouted, lunging to her side. He shielded her eyes. "Don't look. You don't need to see this."

But he couldn't shield her ears from the gasping sound followed by a loud CRACK as the Shaud's neck snapped. The soldier's body thudded hard on the stoney ground without another sound, save the clank of rock striking metal armor.

Paige shoved herself free of the elf's protective embrace. Robert stood over the soldier, heaving. Paige ran to him and threw her arms around him, tears of fear and relief silently sliding down her cheeks.

"I'm sorry," he pleaded, hugging her back. "I'm so sorry. We should have left. I'm so-"

"I hear soldiers," Jesnake urged, ushering the two back out of the alleyway. Paige heard the clatter of armor and men calling out to each other quizzically.

"Let's get out of here before they shut the gates for the night," Jesnake said, taking off down the alley. "We need to make it back to camp s quickly as possible."

"You idiot!" Dinendale burst at Robert's conclusion of their story. The three had arrived at camp a few hours later.

"It's not his fault," Jesnake winced as Woodcarver bandaged the wound on his arm.

"The initial encounter, no," Dinendale spat. "But when six soldiers die in a garrison, that's a red alert to everyone in the city!"

"What would you have me do?" Robert shouted. "They saw us and knew our faces!"

"I know that!" Dinendale shouted back. "But now they'll be looking for us. They will have shut down the city, and you know the prince will hear of it. He's no fool. He'll put two and two together!"

"You'd rather I'd have left her to those men?" Robert roared back. "So they could do to her what they did to Elethia?!"

Dinendale's face contorted into a nasty, wicked glare. "How dare you." The cold whisper sent chills through everyone in camp.

"No, how dare you, Dinendale," Robert spat back. "I did what I had to do to protect someone I care about, and for you to scream at me because I couldn't stick to 'the plan' doesn't change anything."

"ENOUGH!" Duelmaster leapt off his perch against the cave wall, his face etched in a glare Paige had never seen before on his cheerful face. He stormed over to the arguing warriors, his face red with rage. "You're both acting like children. Din, we can't do anything about it now. So let's crack on and get a new plan together so we can bust out the princess who isn't currently rotting in a jail cell. Eöl, you have no right to use that against a friend, do you understand me? Elethia was a friend to all of us. You can't blame Dinendale for what happened to her. None of us got to her in time, including you!"

Both Dinendale and Robert stood there, stunned at the dryad's outburst, both at a sudden loss for words.

"Now both of you shut up, sit down, and let's move on!" the tree spirit snapped, immediately dropping to the ground in front of the fire, legs crossed. The two glared at each other a moment longer, then followed Duelmaster's example and sat down. There was a moment of silence as everyone calmed down, then Twostaves spoke first.

"How did you end up in the ally, Jesnake?" the giant queried.

Jesnake took a swig of water from a wineskin and wiped his mouth on his non-bandaged arm. "Luck or higher intervention, take your pick. Entering the city was a breeze. The soldiers were scared as rabbits in a hunt. I was able to walk past any post without being bothered, so I went into the officer's encampment to see what information I could glean. They take their residence within the second wall, on the southern side of the city."

"And?" Robert prodded. "What did you find out?"

"The soldiers here are all the way from the capital of the empire. Not many knew why, but one plastered lieutenant told me they were, in fact, the regiment that had attacked the princess's village. They wiped out several other tribes along the way."

"Barbarians!" Twostaves, mashed his fist into his other hand with frustration and anger.

"So I visited several inns that the higher-ups frequent. There I heard several men at a corner table talking about some secret operation. The more I listened, the more I realized there was some sort of plot going on."

"A plot?" Dinendale's head snapped up.

"Aye. When one of them went outside for some air, I pretended to be in on the secret, and he was so afraid of being confronted by a Raider that he told me he wasn't the one in charge. He gave me a location I could find a brigadier general, but I got turned around, and to my shame, slightly lost. I tried climbing a building and looking for him, and that's when I heard Paige scream."

"I can't thank you enough," Paige said softly.

Jesnake smiled. "Let's call it an even score," he said. "I couldn't have done it if I'd fallen off the cliff."

"Fortunate indeed," Dinendale said emotionless. "But Jesnake, this plot?"

Jesnake's somber expression did not sit will with Paige. "Well, judging by what I heard at the table, I think we have a real problem. They know about Paige, and they know about the scroll. I think they know we're coming."

Dinendale spat into the dirt.

"News must have reached them faster than we could take the path over the Raychels."

"We still have some advantage of surprise," Jesnake shrugged. "They don't know when or how we are coming. For all they know, we're still trying to sneak past the outposts on the normal route from the Wild."

"True," Dinendale said thoughtfully. "Woodcarver, why don't you fill them in on what you and Duely found?"

The magician looked up from where he was sharpening one of the blades in his gloves. "Duelmaster and I entered the city with little difficulty, much like Jesnake. I managed to get into the barracks, on the very south side of the first wall, past the marketplace. It's the sickest, vilest place I've ever had to walk through, and I've been around a long time. Men laying in drunken filth, no regards for moral standards of any kind, and blatant disregard for any authority. The only reason those men follow orders is fear of the savage punishments those above them will inflict. We were, however, able to glean that at least two of the regiments stationed there were at Kapernaum. Many had prizes from their plunder, and it took all my power to keep Duelmaster from cutting them into bits and pieces as they showed off their spoils."

"A person's scalp is not something to be happy about," Duelmaster said. Paige shuddered in horror realizing that those scalps could have been her people's. Xandla? Matildra? That sweet merchant who had sold her the necklace she now wore around her neck? A hatred welled up inside her like a tea kettle coming to a boil.

"One crucial piece of information is how stupid these soldiers are, especially at night. After just a few drinks, these men are as chaotic as cats going around for a mouse. I've noticed that drinking is quite the prevailing pastime. When not stabbing blacksmiths and making off with young ladies, that is. They also take forever to get in rank, judging from the drills we saw. I've seen young lads gather for their parents faster than these men can line up for their commanders." Woodcarver stated.

"But there are over three hundred soldiers in that camp. One division of three that had originally set out from the capitol at Telesan. There is no chance for any of us if they are called to arms while sober," Duelmaster watched as the group nodded in agreement.

"There is a window of time when they're changing the guard, and it seems that the later the hour, the longer the gap," Robert added. "From what a rabbit hauker told us, it takes fifteen minutes for the turret guards to change at midnight. He swore it was true because it happens every night when he goes outside the city gates to snatch rabbits in the valley, and the noise they make scares off the rabbits. Hurts his business, so he had no problem venting his frustration to us when we asked if we could help him in any way."

"Then I think I know how we get in," Dinendale said. They all looked at him expectantly. He took a second to collect all his thoughts, then picked a stick off the ground and drew a diagram of the city's layout on the dusty cave floor.

"This is the outer wall," he said, drawing a square into the dirt with the stick. "Here is the keep and its wall, then the second inner wall that divides the city from the barracks. The dungeon is in the back of the palace, carved right into the mountainside."

"It may be easy to go through the first two walls," Robert commented, "but the palace will be better guarded, especially now. I doubt that even we could get by without an incident."

"Incidents are our specialty," Broadside teased.

"There is another way," Dinendale said. "I found it on my own search. Look here. See this turret attached to the palace itself?" He pointed to the westernmost turret nearest the mountain backdrop. "The aqueduct funnels water over the first wall and into a giant cistern here on the outside of the first interior wall. Now there is a grate that lets the water through the wall. Then it flows in a deep moat straight into the palace itself. All these towers are heavily guarded, but the channel flowing into the palace is not."

"Which means we have an unguarded entrance into the fortress," Twostaves said.

"Well," Broadside said. "All we'll have to do is get over the outer wall, hop into the cistern, claw our way under the second wall, then swim straight into the palace. All during the time it takes for the guard to change. Seems easy enough."

"It's definitely not going to be easy," Dinendale smirked. "But it's the only option, shy of knocking on the front door, that I see."

"Well, we could give that a try, too," Twostaves laughed, slapping Dinendale good-naturedly on the back. Dinendale screamed in pain, his agonizing wrenching threw him face first on the cave floor, clawing at the dirt. The rest of them rushed to his side, but Woodcarver held them back.

"Don't," Woodcarver said, holding Broadside back as the dwarf made a lunge for his fallen friend.

"Let me go. Dinendale, what's wrong?" he demanded.

"Stay back!" Woodcarver pulled the heavy little creature back. "Don't touch him."

Dinendale's cloak slipped off one of the elf's shoulders as he heaved for a few seconds and slowly sat up. Paige gasped in horror to see his dirty peasant's shirt covered in blotchy patches of dark, wet blood. He turned to face them, trying to hide his back.

"Dinendale," Woodcarver said quietly. "Show us your back."

The elf didn't move. He just stared at the dirt floor.

"Now, Dinendale," Twostaves demanded. The elf looked up with sad, angry eyes, and slowly turned and lifted the back of his shirt. The group gasped in alarm.

"Dinendale," Paige gasped. "What have they done to you?"

CHAPTER 17

THE WOLF
& THE BOBCAT

*D*inendale's back was a webbed mess of bloodied stripes, each as long as Paige's forearm. The wounds oozed dark liquid like wine being squeezed from wild grapes. While probably not life-threatening by themselves, the risk of inflammation and putrefaction was real with a mess this horrific.

"Dinendale," Paige demanded again. "What happened?"

"They whipped me, obviously," he laughed in pain, voiced laced with agitation.

"Calm down Din. I'm just trying to help," Paige snapped.

He rolled his eyes and sighed, wincing as the cold night air stung the cuts.

"Why?" Twostaves asked. The elf let out a menacing chuckle.

"Because they could," he mocked. "I was walking in the street."

"People don't get flogged for walking down the street, Din," Duelmaster said, suspicion in his voice. "Not even in Aschin."

Dinendale paused for a moment, resting his hand against his thigh, his knuckles popping as he clenched his fist in an attempt to reign in his emotions. "It doesn't matter."

"It does matter," Jesnake said, sliding next to his comrade and examining the mess of stripes. "These kind of wounds don't just happen."

"They were hitting a little girl. You happy?" Dinendale snapped.

"Oh, no problem having an altercation with a guard who definitely could have pegged you as an elf if he'd inspected you close enough, but I'm the one that drew too much attention to myself," Robert snapped.

Dinendale glared at him, then sighed. "I know. I'm sorry," Dinendale rubbed the bridge of his nose as his shoulders drooped in silent defeat. Robert grunted and Broadside threw some more scratchy scrub brush onto the fire.

"When will you learn you can't always be the hero? You're not immortal," Broadside shouted as he hopped up and slowly walked around the small fire.

"What is that supposed to mean?" the elf demanded.

"You throw yourself in front of any danger you face as if you can defeat it all," the dwarf scolded. "But you can't. One day, you'll find a soldier, or serpent, or even a dragon that is bigger than you. Then what?"

"It's only a few stripes!" Dinendale said indignantly. "They'll heal, eventually."

"Eventually?" Paige barked.

Din looked surprised but not affronted by her outburst. "That is how wounds tend to heal."

"We don't have time for eventually," Jesnake insisted.

"Can't you do anything for him?" Paige asked, whirling to look at Woodcarver.

"It wouldn't do any good," Dinendale muttered.

"I agree," Woodcarver said glaring at the elf. "But my question is why? What makes you immune to my magic?"

Dinendale was silent for a moment, but Woodcarver stared him down, his clear eyes probing for an answer. After a moment or two, Dinendale looked over at the magician and shrugged.

"It won't work because I've had the Aondraíoch curse put on me."

Woodcarver vented an exasperated grunt as his eyes flashed in anger and annoyance. Duelmaster and Jesnake had shocked looks on their faces, while Paige and the others were oblivious to what the Aondraíoch Curse was.

"Cursed? Is it bad?" Broadside's worried expression was pronounced by a quivering lip.

"Well, I think the term 'curse' is hardly ever used in a good way," muttered Robert.

"It's not a curse if you chose it," Dinendale said defensively.

Woodcarver laughed sharply. "Oh, is that what happened? How great of a fool are you, Dinendale? I thought you would have had more sense than that."

"It's not," Dinendale started, but Jesnake cut him off.

"Why didn't you tell any of us?" He shoved a finger at his friend. "This isn't something you just keep from your brothers, Dinendale!"

"Will someone please explain to me what in the name of moons the Aondraíoch curse is?" Twostaves bellowed.

"It's curse put on a magical person," Woodcarver spat, disgusted. "It renders the recipient unable to use the Mist even if he's of the bloodline."

"It takes a very powerful wizard or magician to perform it, and once cast, it cannot be undone," Duelmaster hopped off his rock perch. "Which begs the question, Dinendale, how and more importantly why?"

"Because what it also does is keep the person from being affected by other attack spells or magic," Dinendale shouted. "I gave mine up because it's one more thing I don't have to worry about."

"Even still, to keep that from us? It was this 'I can do it on my own, I can handle it all myself' attitude that has already caused so many of our problems," Jesnake quipped.

"I'm strong enough," Dinendale spat, drawing away from Jesnake, "and frankly I don't need your permission to do with my life what I see fit."

"You're not as strong as you think, Dinendale," Duelmaster said, his voice low and quiet.

"I can take care of myself!" Dinendale yelled, his temper flaring.

"Oh that raw back clearly says 'I can take care of myself' right? Then why do you need us, huh?" Robert shook his fist at the elf. Dinendale was taken aback. Robert smirked. "Because you can't do it by yourself. You have one of the strongest wills and bodies I know. But you need to quit thinking you can do it yourself, you selfish twunt."

There was a long pause, and Dinendale glared at Robert with an intensity that could have melted wrought iron. Robert merely returned the gaze. A terrible amount of tension throbbed through the cave.

"I don't need to rationalize my decision to you any more than I have to apologize to you for saving that child," Dinendale glared.

"You're missing the point," Jesnake retorted. "No one here is saying saving a child is a bad thing, but this mess on your back? This was not the way to go about it. There are people there who could recognize you!"

"Well, whatever. We can't change any of that now," Paige said, pulling a roll of bandages out of her pack. "All we can do is move forward. Sit down Din. Woodcarver? Help me dress these."

The magician was still furious at Dinendale's revelation but did not argue with Paige. He knelt next to her as Din sat on his knees with his bloody, raw stripes turned towards them. They worked on his back carefully, putting on ointment from a bottle Woodcarver kept tucked in his boot. He explained it was a natural remedy to help keep swelling down, so it should work on Dinendale without any issues. To aid in the numbing process, he mixed the powder with some of the wine they'd taken off the Shaud's cart.

"I'm sad I cannot heal these, Dinendale," the wizard said, still angry but taking deep breaths. "But you brought that on yourself."

"I will sleep in the bed I made. I have no regrets."

"You say that now. I can get these to stop bleeding," Woodcarver said. "But you have to be careful with them."

The wizard applied the salve gently to the elf's shredded back. Paige helped mix the foul smelling paste of pine needles, lichen and wine as the magician applied it to each stripe. Dinendale whimpered once but kept silent beyond that. Once Woodcarver had applied enough salve, they carefully wrapped the elf's bare torso in clean linen cloth so he could put on his old shirt.

"No infection will set in, at least," Woodcarver sighed, still visibly irritated. "Rest now. You'll need as much strength saved as you can muster."

Dinendale didn't move. He just laid there, motionless in the dull euphoria that follows great pain. Paige sat for a moment before she stood and followed Woodcarver out of the cave into the dark night air. She took her cloak and threw it about her shoulders as she stepped out into the open.

Taivian and Suntra shone brightly overhead casting pale white light through a cloudless sky as they chased each other across the heavens. The air turned Paige's breaths into waltzing wisps of fog that danced ever higher till they disappeared into the breeze. Woodcarver faced the two moons as that same steady breeze ruffled his forest green cloak.

"Why are you so angry with him?" Paige demanded.

The magician sighed. "Angry? No dear one, not angry. Frustrated, but it's not my curse to bear nor my choice. Does little good to be angry over someone else's mistakes."

"But why is what he did a mistake?"

Woodcarver ran a gloved hand through his hair before raising his hood to keep warm. He held out his palm and mumbled something Paige couldn't hear. Little wisps of white smoke appeared with blue sparks, taking the shape of a galloping horse that ran circles around the magician's hand and arm.

"It was a gift," he said. "It is always a gift. No matter what people say about bloodlines, and heritage, and all that rubbish, to be blessed with such power is a privilege. The Creator gives some people the ability, just as he gives others a beautiful voice, or an eye to see the raw beauty of a summer sunset and turn it into a painting," he explained.

Paige wrinkled her brow. "And you think he squandered it?"

"If you had a beautiful voice, or an ability to paint the most lifelike portraits ever created, would it not be a waste to cut out your voice box or break your own fingers?" he asked.

Paige shrugged.

"I just hate to see people throw away a gift others would kill, indeed have killed, to possess."

"But there are evil people who use magic as well, and now he cannot be touched by that, correct?"

"That is the one benefit, which I dare say is the only reason I can nearly understand his thought process. But magic is just like any other gift. It can be used for evil or good and is only as strong as the person who wields it."

"So then why doesn't the Creator take it away from those who use it for evil?" Paige asked.

Woodcarver looked at her sorrowfully. "If you sing for evil purposes or paint evil pictures, will he take it from you? No. He gives us the gifts. We choose what to do with them. There's a lot of evil in this land, but there is also much good. It is up to us to take the tools and use them to do good, and not ill."

"Still, I think I'd prefer he just get rid of the ill altogether. Can't be much of a Creator if he allows his creation to be infected," she said. A note of bitterness held her tone.

"No?"

"Can he though? What kind of being creates something, then just sits back and watches the world tear itself apart?"

"And you think He's done that? That you've been abandoned on this journey?"

"Well He sure didn't see fit to keep the Shahir at bay."

"No, perhaps not. But then again," the magician said. "It's awful good luck for you to have run into the Brotherhood if He does in fact just sit back and watch."

"Still." Paige saw his point but continued to feel hurt, angry, and bitter. "Sure would save us a lot of trouble if He'd keep the bad from happening. It isn't fair that bad things happen to good people." She felt all the loss of her mother and father. Of the life she once enjoyed so carelessly. She thought of Olivian, closer now but still in danger. Her throat grew a lump and burned around it. Some Creator to turn her life upside down over the choices of an evil empire.

"Princess," the wizard said, his eyes warm with understanding. He took her by the shoulders reassuringly. "I have lived in this world a long time, and I have come to realize one thing to be true. The Creator allows suffering for a reason, even to good people."

"What possibly could be a good reason to let so much pain and hurt affect those He's supposed to love?" Paige felt the hot tears in her eyes. The magician smiled softly, his wise eyes filled with compassion. He pulled her into a strong, warm hug. She wasn't expecting the gesture, but returned the embrace, grateful.

"Because if we never suffered in this world, then we would never want to leave."

Paige nodded. The pain of loss stung her heart, but she couldn't deny the wisdom of his words. It's exactly the kind of thing Papa would have said. She looked up at Woodcarver and tried to smile past the lump in her throat.

"We should get some sleep," the magician said, turning towards the cave. "It will be a long day of resting and preparing for the coming storm."

They entered the cave to find the others making up their bedrolls for the night. Since Robert had told them his story and the intelligence they had collected regarding troop numbers and housing arrangements, Woodcarver and Duelmaster were filling them in on the infrastructure they'd seen.

"The aqueduct drops past the second wall and into a cistern. They use a floodgate apparatus to control the flow into the city," Duelmaster was saying. "From that cistern, it flows under the wall and to the main city providing water for everyone that isn't housed in the barracks, which rest inside the secondary wall outside the actual wall surrounding the keep."

"And you think we could get under the wall through that waterway?" Dinendale asked.

"Not unless we had someone already inside the barracks," Woodcarver said, laying down on his bedroll. "There's a manual floodgate down there as well. Best as I can tell it's usually unguarded but once it's shut there's no opening it from that side."

"And the possibility of getting someone inside the barracks early before the gates close?"

"They'd probably be caught," Duelmaster yawned, stretching out on his own bedroll. "They drill all about the grounds all day long, so hiding for the amount of time it would take to ensure being behind the gate when it closes would prove difficult. I'm not sure it would work out."

"But under that floodgate would be the perfect way into that second level, no doubt," Jesnake surmised, fingers laced as he stared up at the cave ceiling in concentration.

"We'll sleep on it and formulate a plan tomorrow," Robert grunted. "Can't do any proper thinking this late with the mind so jumbled."

Paige yawned and agreed, resting her head on her pack and closing her eyes to the world to escape it for a few hours.

She'd no idea how long she'd been asleep when a stirring noise in the cave awoke her. She rolled over and looked into the darkness to see the source of the commotion, squinting into the black air around her. It was Dinendale; he'd staggered up and was heading out the mouth of the cave. She silently rolled to her feet and followed him into the chilly night air, her wool cloak and blanket pulled snugly about her neck.

The elf stood out a ways on a rocky outcropping facing the city. He stared at the fortress, as if glaring would make it crumble at his feet. Her stealth evaporated as her foot crunched on tiny stones. Dinendale flinched at the noise and looked around till they locked eyes.

"Why are you still up?" he asked in a quiet tone.

She deftly joined him on the rocky outcropping. "Why are you?" she retorted.

"Can't sleep."

"Why not?"

"Well, I'm normally a back sleeper," he chuckled.

Paige didn't find it amusing.

The elf cleared his throat uncomfortably. "Because I've been an idiot. I've let you all down, and I've failed at every turn."

"Dramatic much, Mr. Troubador?" she rolled her eyes. "You know that's not true."

"It is!" he spat. "The whole time. I was selfish and almost didn't come at all. Then I chose the wrong path to come, and we were nearly imprisoned for who knows how long. I refused to trust the word of my closest friend when he told me the river was a bad place to cross. It was my idea to go into the city the way we did, nearly killing three of you. And now apparently my choice to relinquish my magic is also a character flaw."

"Well, even that's not such an exhaustive list," she countered.

"Oh no. The list goes on," the elf laughed bitterly. "I let a friend die because I was too lazy to push myself to work through a little discomfort. And I escaped slavery all by myself, but that's it. I didn't even try to take anyone with me. And now this entire trip has been one nightmare after another that I've been the cause for! Did I leave anything else out?"

"How about the fact that everything has still worked out despite all that?" she offered.

He sighed. "It was still my fault," he muttered.

"Oh, come on Dinendale, get over yourself," she snapped. "Robert never should have said the things he did. You're a good leader, even if you can't see it."

The elf looked at the ground for a long moment, refusing to meet her gaze.

"They're right, you know."

"About what?"

"About being stubborn."

"You mean your hero complex?"

The elf snorted.

"Call it what you want, that is what it is, Din. So let's get down to it. Why are you like that? Why do you want to throw yourself into danger?" she asked.

He turned his head back to the city.

"Is it because of Elethia?" she asked.

His shoulders tensed.

"She meant a lot to you, didn't she?" she spoke more softly this time, sitting on a boulder and propping her knees under her chin.

"She was my best friend."

"How did you meet?"

A faint flicker of a melancholy smile twitched at the elf's lips.

"We grew up together in the Faun Forest. When we heard about the Empire growing in the east, we decided to leave our home and help those who couldn't help themselves."

"One day, after we had formed the Brotherhood, she took my place hunting after I'd sprained my ankle. It was a stupid stunt-gone-wrong and I piddled around till she announced she'd swap with me and left. I should have been with her. But instead I leaned back in a hammock and let her go alone. What kind of a friend does that? I mean, *gierah*!" Dinendale swore, clenching his fists so tight his palms blanched. "When she didn't come back, we searched for hours. But they'd taken her."

"And you went after her?"

"I thought I could break her out on my own," Dinendale rubbed the bridge of his nose. "I thought we had spent too long planning and debating about a strategy, so I left and didn't tell the lads I was leaving. They caught me stealing into the barracks and dragged me to Prince Feridar. They had already tortured Elethia, and the prince was going to make an example of any elf he could get his hands on."

"Did he give you this?" Paige asked, gently reaching out and brushing the elf's hair away from his face. Her fingertips touching Dinendale's scar and he nodded.

"He did. And then he... he hung her body from the walls."

"Why on earth would he just kill her like that!?"

"Same reason most men would. They hate elves about as much as elves hate men."

"I didn't realize...."

"That's because you grew up in the Wild. Out here a Raven-head would sooner kill an elf as look at him. Or her."

A single tear slid down Dinendale's cheek, twinkling silver in the moonlight. He took a deep shuddering breath.

"Ever since then, I've been throwing myself at anything I can, as if it would ease my pain to defeat the obstacles. Or maybe I simply had a wish to die. Either way it has put everyone I care about in danger. It's my curse. More a curse than not having any magic left."

There was a long pause as Paige tried to think of something to say, but she had no words. The silence sat between them as the chilled wind swept locks of hair around Paige's face. As he looked toward the ground, Paige decided perhaps the best thing she could do for this hurting creature was just to listen.

"Tell me more about her?"

Dinendale turned, looking surprised.

"What?"

"Elethia. Tell me about her. She obviously meant a lot to you."

Dinendale looked up at Taivian and Suntra, taking a deep, long breath in through his nose.

"She was as wild as the sunset. Never content staying in one place, always wanted to see what was beyond the horizon."

"Sounds like you," Paige said, shifting so her legs could hang off the boulder.

"Aye. Two apples off the same branch. She always dreamt of following the Great River to the Sea. I've had that dream since I was a lad. We'd made a pact to do it as soon as the Empire had ceased its tyranny and our idealism had been satiated. But that never happened."

"Well, maybe someday you'll get to do that in her honor."

"Maybe so," he said softly. He straightened up a little and cleared his throat. "And what about Olivian? Is she like you?"

Paige laughed. "Not really," she answered. "Olivian has the curiosity of a turnip when it comes to adventures. I was the wild one at home. Always wanting to go with Papa on his escapades."

"I could definitely see that," Dinendale chuckled.

Paige shrugged. "Funny. Growing up I always wondered what lay beyond the Wild. Thought I might like to see what was out there someday. Just never thought it would be like this. Now all I want is to be back in Kapernaum."

"Home is a funny thing like that."

"Will you go back to your home ever do you think?"

Dinendale shrugged. "My father and I didn't part on the best of terms," he explained. "And to go back without Elethia there, I doubt I could handle it."

"I'd give anything to see my home one more time," Paige said, knocking her heel against the boulder in no particular rhythm. "My father too."

There was a long pause as the pair looked out into the dark horizon.

"Well, one day you will have to show me," she slid off the rock to face him. "I've never seen a city of elves."

"It would be my honor to show you one."

He looked at her, but the brown eyes she gazed into were not the same ones she'd seen that first night at the willow tree. They had lost the anger and haunted expression. Now, even though they were still haunted by sadness, they held a light she'd never seen before: hope. She couldn't think of what to say next. And she realized in that instant she didn't have to say anything.

"If we, by some miracle get through this plan alive, I will take you," he laughed.

She smiled. "I would like that very much."

Then, without warning, the elf reached out and wrapped his strong arms around her and held her close. She was taken aback for a moment, her heart thundering in her ears, but quickly returned the hug. The elf sucked in a breath sharply, and she instantly remembered his tender back. She felt her cheeks flush even more as she tried to release him.

"Oh, I'm sorry! I'm so sorry!" she stammered, but he didn't let her go. Instead he looked down at her and smiled.

"I'm sure I can muscle my way through a simple hug, princess. I'd better be able to or I'm in deep trouble come tomorrow."

As gently as she could possibly be, Paige returned the hug. They stood together for a long moment, Dinendale's warm body felt so safe and protective. She smiled in his embrace. As much as she hated the circumstances, she was glad to have found friends like Dinendale and the others.

"If it makes you feel better, I don't think I could feel any safer than I do with you and the others."

"Oh?"

"Yeah. The Shahir can keep his army. I'd rather have the Brotherhood."

"Oh, I don't know about that. An army could come in handy right about now."

They both laughed and Dinendale lightly scratched Paige's back. She felt like a jar of moths had been emptied into her gut, and the tapered tips of her ears tingled as they turned a shade of pink.

"Well, I'd better get back to bed," she said, breaking from their embrace. "Goodnight Din."

She turned to enter the cave again but he caught her arm.

"Princess?"

She turned and looked back at him, her heart still fluttering.

"Yes?"

"We will get your sister out. If I make and keep one promise to you, let it be that."

"I know we will. I have complete faith in you," she replied with a smile.

"Ah, it feels so good to be back in these!" Broadside bellowed, now in his mail and armor. Paige agreed, tying her moccasins tight. The men had woken up the next morning with an air of confidence they hadn't had in awhile, undaunted by the painful reality that the soldiers were on high alert. They changed their clothes and burned the costumes they'd worn the day before. With festive cheer they watched the flames lick at the colorful fabrics.

"Yes, it does," Robert agreed, running his finger across the edge of his spear head, testing its sharpness. "Now we just need to whip his Royal Heartlessness into the grave he's dug himself."

"Looks like a storm's threatening. Might cause an issue," Twostaves commented, looking out of the cave's mouth at the low rolling black clouds overhead.

"If that's our biggest problem today, I can live with it," Paige said, taking some wine and scrubbing her hair to remove the last of the black coloring. Her now wet, tassled blond hair lay across her shoulders like stringy pasta.

"I don't know. I kind of liked you as a Raven-head," Robert chuckled.

She reached over and socked him in the arm but flashed him a smile as she did so.

"Nah, Shauden doesn't suit your sunny disposition m'lady," Duelmaster laughed as he checked the edge on his rapiers for what must have been the one hundredth time.

Jesnake chuckled, checking the fletching on all the arrows the group had left.

"Well, assuming the rain isn't our biggest problem tonight," Twostaves stomped his way back into the cave, "can you use that nifty magic to help protect us from injury, Woodcarver?"

"You see things shallowly, master giant," the magician replied. "I can heal and cast spells, it's true. But I can't keep people from dying or stop them from making foolish moves in a battle. Magic is just a tool, like a bow or a sword. It can't be used to interfere with what is to be. The only one who can do that is the Creator."

"So why can you use spells on people at all then?" Robert countered.

"I can help to heal a wound or use it to fight an opponent, but I cannot change someone's fate. In theory, one could heal a mortal wound or cast a shield against someone, but magic comes at a price. Every spell I cast and incantation I mutter takes energy from my body to complete. If someone were to breach the limitations of his body, he could end up dead."

"He's right," Jesnake commented, checking the shaft of an arrow. "So since we can't use it to make you impenetrable, try your best not to get shot."

Even with the anticipation building and pumping through their veins, it was not hard for any of them to fall asleep that afternoon. Paige dozed in and out of consciousness for several hours till eventually Robert shook her awake. She jumped with a start and clocked him hard in the nose. He swore, and jumped back, rubbing his throbbing schnoz.

"Well good morning to you too, Sunshine," he grimaced.

"I'd say I was sorry," she yawned. "But I'm not."

The princess rose out of bed feeling drugged and groggy. The men were all in a similar state of undead unrest as they stood around the small campfire, rubbing their arms and legs into semi-warmth. Dinendale stood across the fire tying on his leather vambraces.

"Well, friends," Dinendale spoke loud enough to gather their attention. "This is it. We all know what's expected, and I have absolute faith in each of you. A princess's life hangs in the balance tonight. In the event something goes wrong, know that I count it an honor to have served by your side in every battle we've faced."

"Well, don't be so chipper with the trumpet call, Dinendale," Duelmaster chuckled. They all grunted somberly in amusement.

Dinendale smiled and shook his head, resting his hands on his sword belt.

"So, do we even have a plan?" Broadside asked.

The others laughed.

"I've been thinking about all the information collected yesterday, and I think I have an idea that just might work," Dinendale said.

"Care to share?" Jesnake asked.

The dark elf grinned at the Western elf. "Depends," he teased. "How do you feel about crawling through another water trough?"

"As long as there are no millstones on the other end, I think I can handle it," Jesnake said, twanging his bow like a lute.

"Alright, then," Dinendale said, "I'll explain on the way. Now that we've got the darkness to cover us, the hourglass has been tipped."

CHAPTER 18

BEYOND THE GATES

$\mathscr{P}$aige leaned on the stone archway holding up the gigantic aqueduct, the thunder and vibrating pillars humming as the water rushed through it high above on its course into the city. The cold granite did little to soothe her hot neck and flighty stomach that churned like a barge's wake. Robert was next to her, and Twostaves beside him. She reached up and touched her hairpin reassuringly. Yes, the sword was there. In addition to that, the bow Broadside had lent her snuggly rested against her back. The quiver of arrows lay lashed to her belt for easy access. The coil of rope draped across her shoulder and midsection like a nobleman's sash.

Paige stared at the fortress, a series of stone blocks mounted over three stories high on the opposite side of the chasm. It was darker than midnight. She gulped as she ran her fingers across the crevasses between the stones comprising the aqueduct's pillars. They'd come this far together, but now it was up to her to climb a wet, slippery, stone structure a hundred paces high.

Right.

She took a deep breath to calm her nerves. She looked at Robert. "Ready?" she asked.

"Whenever you are," he offered, extending her a hand. She took a moment to pick up a decent-sized stone and slip it into her pocket.

"Well, wish me luck," she said. She nodded to the giant, pulling her scarf up above her mouth as a makeshift mask. Twostaves squatted next to the pillar, offering her his back. Paige took one more breath then slammed her foot into Robert's laced fingers, jumping to the giant's back and standing atop his shoulders. He leaned against the column, trying to stand on his tiptoes to give Paige as much height as possible as she prepared to climb the damp stone.

Each of the stone blocks were about three feet high and four to five feet long. She grabbed hold of the crevices and stretched for the next hand hold. She climbed slowly at first, taking her time as she inched her way further from the ground.

Luckily there was not much lichen or moss growing on the aqueduct, but the dribbling of water from above did make several of the blocks harder to grasp with her toes or finger tips. Paige held no fear of heights growing up among the treetops, but the near death experience on Craymoghr Cliff was now branded into her memory. The thought of that moment felt like a boat sinking in the pit of her stomach. Paige could feel gravity's pull on her strengthen with every stone she climbed.

The shrill blast of a horn startled her. Changing of the guard wasn't expected this soon. Paige struggled to keep her balance amidst the eerie sound. Her heart skipped a beat as she clung to the stone. She couldn't fall now. Just because they almost fell before didn't mean that she couldn't climb. She wanted to be confident but she felt as small as a cricket staring up at this enormous wall. Paige whimpered as the blast of sound died away. She gripped the cracks in the wall with the pads of her fingers till she mustered her poise. She forced air in and out of her lungs.

"Careful!" Twostaves hissed in the darkness. It took her a few more moments to literally and figuratively get a grip on the situation. Slowly, she began to ascend again.

Inch by inch she crawled up the top of the pillar, passing the archway, to the lip of the trough that plunged water into the city. She crawled within reach of the battlements, her fingers so sore they felt as if they might fall off. She reached the lip of the water trough, gripped the edge of the stone, and hauled herself over the top.

Having not been able to see the top of the aqueduct from below, Paige had no idea what to expect once she made it up there. Turns out there wasn't much room to maneuver on the lip, as it was barely as wide as a man. Paige was thankful for the low hanging clouds that kept the bright moonlight from making her visible to the guard towers along the city's first wall. Her biggest concern right now was the trembling current. Paige was sure the stone under the surface would be slick as glass.

But she could not go back now. In order to give the others access past the second tier of fortifications, Paige, Robert and Twostaves would have to get beyond it to open their makeshift back door. Glancing at the guardhouses of Aschin's outer wall and assuring herself all was quiet, she slipped the rope from off her shoulder and tied it around a makeshift iron hook she'd made back at the cave.

Carefully, she found a crack in the mortar and fished her hook into it. Deftly, she pulled the rock out of her pocket and used it as a hammer to hit the hook into the stone crevice. The sharp plunking sound echoed in her ears, and she had to convince herself not to stop and get it all done quickly, like ripping off a bandage, otherwise the prolonged noise might attract attention. Inch by inch, she seated the hook into the crevice until there was nothing left for her to hit. She prayed that it would be strong enough to hold Twostaves, and then tossed the remainder of the rope to the ground.

She saw the slack in the line tighten. Finally a tuft of black hair popped up and the giant crawled over the side and splashed into the running water, keeping his head down.

"Nicely done, princess," Twostaves congratulated. "Gods above, this is some fast moving water!"

"It is, so keep your head down and hold on tight!" she hissed. The rope went taut again and she gasped. Finally Robert's sandy hair popped above the rim.

"Not bad. I've never seen someone catch themselves from falling so gracefully," Robert nodded to her. "I've also never seen anyone cry at the blow of a horn."

Paige smacked him on his left cheek. He was in the act of aiming a strike back when Twostaves caught his hand.

"Shut up!" he pointed to the tower closest to them. They followed his gloved finger and saw a lone soldier on the tower's balcony. He held a bow with a nocked arrow while gazing about the wall in his white turban and spiked helmet. Paige was afraid he'd look down and see them. She waited with baited breath. She watched. In a moment, the man instead returned to the shelter of the tower's guard house. A rumble of thunder sounded off in the distance as three collective sets of lungs let out a shaky breath.

"That was close," Robert hissed.

"Way too close," Twostaves whispered. Paige tugged on the rope to release it from the plaster but it didn't move. She tried again, thrashing the rope in all directions, but to no avail.

"Um, guys? This rope isn't coming with us. Not with the hook, anyway."

"Well at least we know we wouldn't have fallen," Twostaves offered.

"Yes, but how are we going to get down now?" She felt the panic in her voice.

"We could dive into the cistern?" Twostaves offered.

Robert shook his head. "We've no idea how deep it is. We could break our necks, legs, or both."

"Well, there was a regulator, right? Some sort of contraption to help regulate the water's flow? They have to be able to get up to it somehow. Maybe there are some stairs? Or a ladder?" Paige said.

"Cut the rope, just in case," Robert whispered.

Paige knotted and yanked her hairpin out, gripping Klaíomh tightly, its tiny silver rose buds giving her wet hands the grip they needed.

"Twostaves, I need your shadow," Paige hissed. The giant slid around behind her, blocking her from potential prying eyes that might take note of a flock of blue sparks.

"Klaíomh."

The blade leapt from the pin in a shower of blue sparks dancing atop of the water, disappearing as they rushed downstream. She sawed through the wet rope, glancing over her shoulder to ensure no guards were peeking out of the tower again. After cutting the rope, she coiled it, returned Klaíomh to its hairpin form, and nodded to Robert.

"Right then. We wait for the next changing of the guard and then we move," he said, throwing the hood of his robe up. "After that, the real work begins."

Minutes dragged by as they sat in waist-high water waiting for the next horn to blow. Paige clenched her jaw to keep her teeth from chattering, glancing up at the moons to gauge time. Twostaves held in a couple alarming sneezes as he lay on his back in the water to hide his height as best he could. Occasionally a swell washed over his face and caused him to sputter, but to the giant's credit, he kept his boisterous tone low.

Finally, the horn blast echoed through the city. Paige jumped into action knowing their time was short. The later the change, the longer the gap got, but they still needed to hasten. As soon as the horn died away, Paige, Robert, and Twostaves crawled forward through the water in a single file line. As they neared the wall, they heard soldiers calling out orders, their voices muffled by the stone walls. Paige felt herself slip once or twice, but Robert grabbed her jerkin and kept her from sliding further towards the end of the aqueduct.

"Keep going. We're almost past the first wall!" Twostaves urged, risking a peek over the edge of the trough. Paige scurried along, her hands numb with the cold. The stones beneath the water were smooth and slick, and she feared pushing herself too fast would cause her to slip. Luckily the rushing water covered their own splashing noises which helped them considerably.

As soon as they could, the three passed over the wall of the city. Paige felt her heart give a great leap. Only one more wall stood between where they were and where they needed to be.

Her heart raced, longing to see Olivian. They pushed onward, the city below sprawling out to the west and south.

The next wall was thinner with fewer guard towers, the nearest of which lay far from the aqueduct. Hopefully they would not be seen. They kept inching their way along till they saw the end of the aqueduct. They stopped abruptly to observe the water cascading downwards to the cistern far below.

"There's the floodgate," Robert pointed ahead. The iron doors were opened wide, allowing the water to flow unimpaired to the ground. Paige could see a wooden windlass attached to the doors on the left side of the aqueduct. It stood on a small stone platform that had stairs leading down to the ground below. Robert sighed a huge breath of relief.

"Oh good, stairs. I was afraid we'd have to..."

He stopped abruptly as his hand slipped, pushing him forward and bumping into Paige. On the slick stone, Paige immediately lost her fragile grip and felt herself sliding towards the end of the aqueduct. Water rushed forward with them in a tempestuous current. She gasped and spun around, clawing for a grip on anything she could reach. Her pruny hands wouldn't latch onto anything as the water dragged her towards the edge.

"Paige!" Robert leapt after her, but slipped on the same slick surface and rolled towards the edge of the aqueduct at an alarming rate. Paige could hear the rush of the water over the edge of the stone, feel the icy tendrils grabbing hold of her and dragging her to that same doom. She gritted her teeth, wondering if the cistern would be deep enough to catch her fall a hundred feet down.

Suddenly a great creaking sound echoed in Paige's head. Just as she was about to slide over the edge of the aqueduct, the two iron doors swung inwards and stopped halfway shut. Paige kicked her feet out, catching the doors and straddling the opening while laying on her back. Water blasted past and poured over her to its natural pathway. She yanked her head out to take a deep breath as Robert bumped into her from behind. She pushed with her legs, trying to keep them both from popping through the narrow opening of the gates. The doors kept closing. Paige felt a strong hand grab her by the collar and pull her back and raise her up over the side of the aqueduct.

She gulped the air back into her lungs and whirled around. Twostaves, drenched as a cat on bath-day, had each of them grabbed by the collar and had hauled them onto the little platform where the windlass sat. One of the giant's quarterstaves sat lodged in the mechanism.

"Thanks, Twostaves," Paige coughed. She felt a momentary panic set in again as she whipped her hand up to her braid to make sure the hairpin was still there. It was. She felt the fear melt away slightly as she swallowed hard.

"Don't mention it," the giant said. "Now, come on. We're too exposed. We need to get down to the ground!"

The marble steps leading down the aqueduct were steep, and Paige had a hard time keeping her footing as they began the rapid descent. Twostaves yanked the staff out of the mechanism, and the gates creaked back open, allowing the waterfall to commence at full trust. The tiny, zigzagged, stone steps felt like they continued forever.

"Aw, snapdragons," Robert muttered as they rounded a course of steps halfway down the aqueduct. The stairs ended abruptly at the next run of steps, leaving a fifty foot drop to the grass below. A ladder lay propped up on the wall beside the cistern, clearly the easiest way to deter unauthorized people from accessing the water controls. Aside from the ladder, there was only a storage awning touching the pillar of the stairs below them.

"Too far to jump," Twostaves whispered. "We'll have to use the rope."

"But we haven't a hook. How will we secure it?"

Twostaves glanced back up the stairway, a thoughtful expression on his large brow.

"We could wedge something in the small nook where the stairs change directions."

"I don't think a knot would hold any one of us, let alone all three of us," Paige looked at the ground pulling the rope off her belt.

"Is there a loose stone we could lash it to? Maybe an old nail in the stonework?" Robert asked, looking around.

Twostaves paused for a moment then grabbed the rope out of her hands and lashed a knot in the middle of his father's staff. Paige grabbed his hand.

"Twostaves, no!"

"Sticks are replaceable, I'll get another," he assured, climbing up to the last bend in the stairs. He dropped the staff in such way that it straddled the last step of the previous run of stairs and the first step of the series they were on, the rope dropping straight down to the ground.

"You're sure it's secure enough?" Robert asked skeptically.

Twostaves shrugged. "Only one way to know for sure!" He let out a light laugh and grasped the rope. Then without giving them any more time to protest, he leapt off the side. The rope snapped tight as his weight pulled against the mighty staff, but it stayed true as he repelled down the rest of the the stone stairway. As soon as he touched the ground, Paige looked at Robert, shrugged, and followed suit.

When her feet touched the soft green grass grown in the barracks for the horses and soldiers to march on, she glanced up to see Robert making his descent. The heavy fellow was about half way down when the three heard a *creeeeaaaaak*. At that precise moment, the rope went slack in Robert's hand.

"Oh," he said as his body froze in mid-air for an instant before he plummeted to the ground. Robert crashed into the corner of the awning before barrelling into an array of large pots. Paige winced as she heard the shattering of now broken pottery he'd landed on. Fear stabbed the bottom of her stomach at the sound of the commotion suddenly piercing through the night's silence.

Paige held her breath as she heard shouting from the guard towers. Twostaves pulled her into the shadow cast by the aqueduct's arch. Torches and soldiers' heads appeared atop the barracks wall from the guardhouse on their left; they searched the training ground and cistern below them. Twostaves cupped a hand around his mouth and let out a yowl, mimicking a cat. Paige let her breath out as she saw the guards shrugging in confusion and dismissal.

As soon as the soldiers were back in the towers, Paige scampered over to the mess of torn canvas, broken wood, and pottery. Robert moaned as she reached him, and she crouched low beside the tangled mess.

"Are you okay?" she asked in a hushed whisper. He slowly sat up, staring at his feet. In answer to her question, he pulled the end of the rope out from under himself and let the broken piece of oak dangle in the air.

"Secure? Right," he huffed. "Last time I take that giant's word for it."

"Well, it did hold him, so I'm not sure what that says about you," she smiled, taking hold of Robert's forearm and hauling him to his feet. Twostaves jogged over as quietly as he could, still producing a thudding vibration in the earth below Paige's feet.

"If you two are set, we have some work to do," Twostaves said. "Let's pray Duelmaster plays his part well."

Duelmaster's good-natured demeanor was completely suppressed under a cloak of cold, clammy fear. He breathed in through his nose and out through his mouth, reminding himself to channel that fear into being cautious and attentive to his surroundings.

At present, he was positioned outside the small gatehouse and wall between the battlements of the outer fortifications and the wall separating the barracks from the rest of the city. He wore the black robe Jesnake had used last night but he kept the hood off so it looked like a normal peasant's cloak. Instead, he wore a wide-brimmed felt hat over his shaggy brown hair and sat in the driver's seat of a cart they had "commandeered" an hour or so ago. He'd waited till they were well into the night to put his part of the plan into action, after the second blast for the changing of the guard had echoed across the city.

"Ok. Deep breath. It's not like the lives of all of your best friends rest on your ability to play your part. Nothing to fret about," he assured himself. He picked up the slack in the reins and urged the horses onward.

A company of six soldiers manned the gate, though none of them stood there now. Instead, they enjoyed the warmth of the small guardhouse and, by the sound of it, also enjoyed several mugs of warmed ale. Duelmaster screwed up his nose in disgust. Even with extra guards on watch this night, they were still some of the most undisciplined ruffians he'd ever seen. No disciplined army would allow its pickets to touch a drop of alcohol, but he was glad this one did. It made their evening much easier. Feridar had not met a foe who could best him in battle, and so the outpost became lax in military protocol. Duelmaster said a silent prayer of thanks that this cocky attitude mixed with mulled ale might be the key to the Brotherhood pulling off this rescue.

The dryad drove the cart up to the old wrought-iron gate with a click of his tongue, keeping his hooded head low and out of the torchlight. A lone soldier, a low ranking officer by the looks of his turban, stumbled out of the lit doorway and slammed it behind him. He dragged himself up to the cart, leaning heavily on a spear as if it were a crutch.

"Ho there! Just where do you think your going?" he slurred, grabbing hold of the front wheels. Duelmaster could smell the yeast on his breath, so he spoke slowly.

"Good evening, sergeant," he said, noting the circlet of gold around the man's bare forearm. "I've fodder for the prince's steeds."

"Delivering in the middle of the night?" the soldier said. His bloodshot eyes blinked excessively as he scowled at the cloaked dryad.

"Well, I know it's a bit late. Been some trouble on the roads, you know, what with those bloody highwaymen. But the master won't care about that. He'd likely beat me if he found out I waited till tomorrow to deliver."

"Not my problem," the man spat. Duelmaster pulled out a wineskin and shook it in the air for the Shaud to see.

"I'll make it worth your while," the dryad said. The soldier stared greedily at the wineskin, then glared again.

"I've half a mind to search your cart," he slurred, jabbing an armored finger at the pile of hay.

"I'd wager you do," Duelmaster grabbed a coin purse from under his robe. "So to hurry this along, and I can sweeten the deal."

The soldier blinked again as the bag of coins fell at his feet. Duelmaster held his breath, and extended the wine skin, glancing nervously at the closed guardhouse door.

"There will be more where that came from, I assure you, sir," Duelmaster said.

The officer waited a moment, then took the wineskin and scooped up the coin purse.

"I want you out of here within an hour. Got it?"

"Naturally, sergeant."

The officer opened the gate, and Duelmaster quickly drove through to the other side. He heard the man uncork the wine and take a long swig. He waited a moment, then heard the man spew the liquid from his mouth with a disgusted retching sound.

"What kind of bitter garbage is this?" He threw the wineskin onto the dirt.

"Oh, blast!" Duelmaster slapped his forehead in exasperation. "I must have given you the one I laced with that stupid sleeping powder."

The soldier opened his mouth to say something, but then slumped into the cold muddy roadway. Jesnake was right behind him, a large rock in his hand.

"Good call," Duelmaster said. "I wasn't sure if the potion would take effect soon enough to do any good."

The elf nodded, reaching down and grabbing the spear off the ground. He quickly padded over to the guardhouse door and used it to deadbolt it in place so those inside wouldn't be able to get out, even if they were sober enough to stand up straight.

"Let's move," the western elf whispered, knocking on the side of the cart twice. Broadside popped out of the hay, coughing through the mist of dust. He rolled out of the back of the hay wagon and landed on his back.

"Oh, good heavens," he heaved.

Jesnake shushed him with a wave of his hand. "Help me drag him over off by the guardhouse," the elf commanded.

The dwarf obliged, leaning the man against the side of the small hut, arranging the wineskin in his hand to make it look like he'd merely slumped over and passed out. They both clambered back into the cart and Duelmaster urged them onward. He looked around wearily, but there wasn't a sound to be heard, save for the wind that blew through the small peach trees scattered about. Duelmaster loved peach trees; they reminded him of the maiden dryads back home that lived in them. Those maids were considered by most of the dryad race to be the softest and most beautiful of their kind. But Duelmaster could tell these trees were the trees of men. They had no spirit in them, and his heart ached to know why.

He took a deep breath and quietly drove the wagon down the east side of the inner wall towards the mighty aqueduct. He had one more role to play tonight, possibly the most dangerous. He was the distraction.

They wheeled the cart to the eastern side of the palace and backed up into the shadow of the outer wall. He stopped the cart and took a deep breath. Scanning over the quiet courtyard, Duelmaster satisfied himself that no one was around. He softly caressed the side of the cart.

Tap, tap, tap-tap.

Instantly, the bottom of the cart fell open. Dinendale, Broadside, and Jesnake rolled to the shadowy packed earth. All three had drawn bows, and looked around in a triangle formation, covering all their sides.

"Ah-CHOO!"

"Broadside!" Dinendale snapped.

"I'm sorry," the dwarf wheezed out a whisper. "Hay fever is terrible on dwarfs. I can't help it."

"We need to get to the cistern," Dinendale urged. "You think you can handle the water Broadside?"

"Handled that serpent in the water just fine, if you'll recall." The dwarf's face was still noticeably pale even in the patchy moonlight. A toll of thunder rolled through the valley, echoing off the stone structures of Aschin. The group made their way to the huge stone pool that lay against the secondary battlements. The wall for the cistern sat as tall as Broadside with several clay pipes running along the wall to the rest of the city.

"Okay, this is where we should find the floodgate," Woodcarver said. "But since it's under water I've no idea if the others have gotten to open it yet."

"Here's a bright idea, morons," a voice spat in the dark. "Why not ask?"

The group tensed, looking at the stone wall where the voice originated.

"Robert? Is that you?" Jesnake called in a hushed tone.

"No, string bean," the voice muttered sarcastically. "This is the captain of the guard."

"Don't do that!" Jesnake heaved, releasing the tension on his string. "I could have shot you!"

"Seeing as there is a four foot stone wall between us," Robert commented, "I count that as highly unlikely."

"Perhaps next time, I'll do it just to prove you wrong," the elf hissed.

"Enough already," Dinendale snapped. "We don't have forever. Tie up the horses, Duelmaster."

"Over here," Robert's voice instructed. "By the cistern wall, there's a small hole."

Dinendale and Duelmaster saw the small passage through the wall. The dryad smashed his face up against it and could see Robert's eyes on the other end.

"Gotta have a way to communicate to the men running the cistern floodgates, I imagine," Robert explained.

Duelmaster nodded. "You can open it from that side?"

"I think it is open as far as it will go. Twostaves is holding it just to be sure," Robert offered.

"We'll be there shortly," Duelmaster said, swinging his leg over the short wall. From their vantage point it was impossible to tell how deep the cistern was, but they had no other options. The dryad took in a huge gulp of air and slipped down into the icy water.

The cistern was murky, but Duelmaster could still make out the shape of a large set of iron doors at the bottom which lay open outwards into the basin. The collection tank was a lot larger than he had originally thought, dipping down at least three fathoms. He could feel the slight current the distribution pipes were causing but easily swam to the bottom and made his way past the iron doors. Within a minute, his head rose from the water on the other side where Robert stood with an outstretched had to haul him up over the lip of the cistern. The dryad shook himself like a soaked dog, drenching Robert.

"Thanks," Robert growled as he wrung out his tunic. "Not sure why you dried off, though. We're just going to get wet again."

"And miss that precious look on your face? In your dreams," Duelmaster countered.

Shortly after, Broadside bobbed out of the cistern like a cork, sputtering and making an obscene amount of racket. After him came Jesnake, Woodcarver, and Dinendale.

"I'm so glad I'm going with you, Duely," the dwarf sputtered as he positioned his helmet on top of his soggy head. "I'd rather face a hundred soldiers than swim another cistern."

"Be careful what you wish for, Master Dwarf," Woodcarver flexed his gloved hand.

The five waded through the man-made stream to a grate that flowed under the final wall through the rusty iron grate.

Twostaves and Robert stomped against it together until it bent and crumpled like a spider on a candle flame.

"Alright, everyone ready? Duelmaster?" Robert dusted off his hands.

Duelmaster looked at Twostaves and Broadside, his two compatriots for the next phase of the plan. The giant and the dwarf nodded, and the dryad drew his rapiers from their home on his back.

"Well, boys, I believe there are some stables and gates that need visiting," he said nodding his head southward towards where the rowhouses and barracks lay. The others agreed.

"Try not to cause any mischief, alright?" Paige urged.

Duelmaster smirked. There was no sense making a promise he had no intention of keeping.

"You're sure they can handle the rest of the plan?" Paige asked Dinendale as they watched the dryad, the dwarf, and the giant slip into the darkness.

"We don't have another option. I'm sure they'll do fine." The elf began to slide forward in the trough of water. He poked his head through the hole in the grate to see the palace.

"Oh, thank the Creator. The trough runs straight into the palace," Dinendale sighed. "At last some good luck for a change."

"Don't get too comfortable. We don't know what that channel leads to. Could be a storehouse or even the keep's garrison," Woodcarver cautioned. Jesnake murmured an agreement, stowing his bow and drawing to knives from his belt.

Dinendale sat like a child going down a hill in a sled and then propelled himself to the the other side of the wall. Paige followed suit, the water shooting her forward faster than she'd anticipated. She sped along the trough like a bolt from a crossbow. Her feet hit Dinendale's back as they propelled across the courtyard, and she bit her lip as she saw him flinch from the impact. Through blurry, water sprayed eyes, Paige saw a couple guards standing at the palace's front staircase. She bit her lip, praying that they wouldn't turn the wrong direction and see them scurrying into the drain like a pack of sewer rats.

"Duck!" Dinendale hissed. Paige dropped onto her back just in time to miss the stone archway leading into the palace wall. The channel immediately dipped to a steep angle, and the pair of them shot into a dark black abyss. Paige's heart leapt into her throat. She landed with a splash into a basin that was hip deep. Paige scrambled to her feet to keep her quiver and sword out of the water as she stepped over the edge of the basin. Feeling her way down to the floor, she crouched on the cold damp stone. She blinked to adjust her eyes, leery for any threat that might jump out at them in the darkness.

There was no sound in the emptiness, save for the dripping of water. Dinendale crawled out of the basin. Robert,

Jesnake and Woodcarver slid in right behind them, trying to keep their splashing to a minimum. Woodcarver muttered some elvish words in the darkness and a small green glow sprang to light in his fist. The green lumination emanated from the stone he held in his hand dimly lighting the room in a cool, soft glow.

"Are you ok? Your back-" Paige whispered, but Dinendale hissed for her to be silent. The space where they landed appeared to be a large kitchen under the mof the castle, large enough to have at least fifty workers running around with ease. The chamber was strewn with small kilns, ovens, tubs of dirty dishes and counters of carved black marble. The basin was the primary water source in the room, with several steps leading up from the floor. At the far end was a large, carved door without a latch, allowing the servants and slaves to enter and exit with full hands.

"Best be quiet," Robert smirked. "No telling who might be sleeping down here."

They crept across the room to the door like a den of panthers trying to take down a buffalo. Robert cracked open the door and looked into the hall, insuring a clear pathway. He poked his head back in, looking at the others with concern and said, "There's no one in the hallway, but we have a problem."

"What?" the other four demanded in unison.

"Does anyone know which way the prison is?"

"Into the mountain," Woodcarver responded.

"Yeah, but the hall splits three different ways, all into the mountain," Robert said. "Which fork do we take?"

There was a pause as the other four poked their heads out to examine the situation. Sure enough, the stone hallway split into three halls illuminated by the faint light. One branch went to the right, the other to the left, and one straight into the mountain.

"Oh, dear," Woodcarver said softly.

"What should we do?" Jesnake asked.

"Split up," Dinendale said.

"I thought you knew the layout?" Woodcarver snapped.

Dinendale glared at him. "I was here when they laid the foundation. That's all. We knew there might be a problem once we got inside. I'm as blind down here as you are."

"Then splitting up is the only option we have," Robert said. "We can do two pairs and one of us will have to go alone."

"I'll go alone," Jenake volunteered. "I'll be a lot quieter by myself if I don't have to worry about who's with me."

"Fine, Jesnake take the center. Robert and I will take the left," Dinendale said.

"I'm not leaving the princess," Robert argued.

"She'll be safer with me," Woodcarver countered.

Dinendale looked at Paige. "What do you think?" he asked.

Paige glanced down the dark hallways. "I think we don't have time to squabble over picking teams. I just want to find Olivian," she said. "I'll go with Robert. You stay close to Woodcarver. There. Everyone happy?"

Woodcarver took the stone in his hand and forced it into three pieces, passing a piece to Jesnake and another to Paige.

"Let's make a plan to meet back here within the hour. Leave your stone in the water basin to let everyone know you made it back and made it out if you get the princess before the other groups make it out."

"Sounds good to me. Jenake be careful on your own," Robert moved through the door. Dinendale and Woodcarver took the left, Jesnake took the middle, and Robert and Paige went right.

"Be careful, princess," Dinendale whispered as they parted ways, and Paige nodded at him. She drew her bow and followed Robert into the tunnel and descended into the mountain.

"I count three guards," Broadside whispered, pulling his head back from around a pillar.

"There's probably more," Duelmaster hissed. "There were six at the gate guarding the cistern, no way they would leave the barracks guarded with fewer men, right?"

"I'm not sure if the three of us could take out six men, let alone more," Twostaves said from behind the next pillar. The trio had skirted around to the south barrack where they now waited in anticipation for their jail-busting compatriots.

"Well, we can't exactly drag Olivian through the cistern," Broadside whispered. "She'll be in no shape to swim as far as we know. Remember what Din looked like when he came back?"

"It may require a theatrical performance," the wood sprite laughed, smugly. "But it will be a show for the ages, I guarantee it!"

"Well, as soon as the guard changes, I'd say let them have it," Broadside hissed. "They should be changing soon anyways."

They sat in the dirt twiddling their thumbs until finally the horns sounded. Duelmaster peeked his nose around the pillar and watched the guardhouse eagerly. Four men waddled out of the structure while another set staggered into the box, ridiculously out of form. Duelmaster felt a grin slide across his rugged face.

"Well fellas, four men it is then."

"You ready?" Twostaves asked.

"Give it a minute," Broadside urged. "Let them settle in and get real tired."

They counted off the moments till the evening's stillness could be trimmed as easily as a candle wick. Duelmaster took a deep breath and shook out his limbs, sheathing his rapiers temporarily.

"Here's to hoping this actually works," the dryad said, drawing a bottle from inside his cloak. He splashed the remains of a foul smelling ail on his face and swished some of the brew in his mouth, nearly gagging at the flavor.

"How do people drink this stuff? The taste alone...."

"Duely, focus!" the little dwarf waved his arms around frantically.

The dryad nodded. "Right," he heaved, taking a slight bow to his brothers. "It has been an honor serving with you all."

"Just make it back to us in one piece, aye?" Twostaves clasped the dryad's shoulder. Duelmaster's eyes twinkled as his signature grin tugged at the corner of his mouth. He staggered towards the door of the palace gates. He swayed, even though it was unnatural for him to be off balance. He got within four paces of the barred wood doors, then sang an old ballad completely off key.

> *"Come lads, have a drink,*
> *And dance atop benches,*
> *Ignore soldiers and King,*
> *And their foully stenches!"*

He gave the bottle in his hand a swig and hurled it at the barracks door. It splintered glass as it crashed. Duelmaster continued his shouting monotone.

> *"Give to me a broken spoon,*
> *And a shield of ham shank,*
> *I'll whip the whole Shaud army,*
> *And cook them in my cake!"*

Two guards hustled out, quickly putting their helmets on. They ran at what they perceived to be a drunken man with raised spears and annoyed expressions.

"How in the name of Shah did you get inside the gate?" one of them shook his fist.

Duelmaster looked at them with rolling eyes, pasting on a goofy smile. "Hey! You're soldiers!" he said, stumbling into one of them. "I like soldiers! We're gonna be great friends, you and I!"

The soldier shook him off quickly. Duelmaster stumbled to the ground and lay on his back, looking at the Shauds with the goofy smile still plastered on his face.

"How did you get in here?" the first guard repeated angrily, thrusting a spearhead at the stumbling dryad.

"Relax, Hadarack," the fatter guard yawned. "He's just a drunk, probably stumbled in before the gates were shut."

Duelmaster sneaked a look past the two guards and saw the other two huddled in the gatehouse. A large hulking black mass moved in the shadows to his right, and one of the soldiers turned. Knowing Twostaves would be impossible to miss, the dryad acted fast to snag the guards attention back.

"She LEFT ME," he wailed, suddenly changing from the happy drunk to the sobbing sot. He fell to his knees and held his arms out as if looking for a comforting embrace. "She LEFT me, OH! How did I not see it coming?"

"Shut up!" the man kicked Duelmaster in the foot. "Shut up!"

"Oh, WHY? He was a banana merchant! What did I say? Was I not a-peal-ing enough?" Duelmaster continued to wail.

"Oh, let him sit and sob." The fat guard lit a rolled tobacco leaf with a match. "The sorry drunk isn't in shape to hurt anyone, even if he was inclined to."

But before Duelmaster could stop him, Twostaves was sneaking up behind the unsuspecting smoker. The thin guard turned.

"Intruders!" the man yelled. "We have a..."

Duelmaster kicked out his foot with a snap, connecting with the back of the man's leg. The soldier's legs buckled, and he crashed to his knees. The fat guard whirled around facing a hulking Twostaves.

Duelmaster heard shouts behind him, "*Gradhrahal!*" He immediately complied with the order and ducked his head to the left as a small bolt whizzed inches over his head. Although it was no time for contemplation, Duelmaster couldn't help but think about how horribly the dwarves, as a race, slaughtered the elvish language. Geyahal, or " Look out" was such a simple word, yet the dwarf continued to butcher it with his nasty guttural sounds.

The shaft of the arrow sunk deep into the fat man's tunic, making a clinking sound as it sank through the chain mail. The man cried out as he crashed to the ground. The first guard struggled back to his feet and drew his curved scimitar. With a resonating grinding sound, the steel scraped against its steel scabbard. Two more guards ran out of the guardhouse.

"Help! Forghadra hal addi!" he shouted in Shaudar, the ancient language of the Shauds. Duelmaster leapt up and pulled out his knife, his face bereft of its grin.

The first soldier rushed him with a shout. Duelmaster cried out as the scimitar sliced through his robe and cut deep into his right arm. The dryad stumbled back, hot blood pumping dark green from the open gash. The Shaud drove his free hand into Duelmaster's stomach with a sickening thud. The dryad hit the earth with a crunch, gasping to reclaim the wind that had been ripped from his lungs when the metal gauntleted fist connected with his leather jerkin.

Thinking quickly, Duelmaster reached into his belt and felt the small sack he'd taken from the supply wagon two days prior. He ripped the drawstring open and flung the black powder contents into the face of the oncoming attacker.

The powder flew into the man's face, and he cried out as the sulfur burned his eyes. Duelmaster kicked him back to the ground. The guard scrambled in the dust around the dead Shaud; he staggered to his feet, and charged the dryad in a blind rage.

Duelmaster leapt to meet the soldier, driving a still smouldering tobacco wad into the man's face. The powder residue ignited like a vat of whale oil. The man screamed in pain as fire engulfed his head and helm. He dropped his sword, smashing his hands against his face to put out the smouldering flames. Wasting no time, Duelmaster drove the man into the courtyard steps and beat his helmet into the stone until his body stilled.

"Awe, acorns," Duelmaster cursed, hearing the shouting of men echoing across the green.

"We need to get out of here," Broadside snapped, running up behind the bloody dryad. The trio looked up to see guards on all the surrounding battlements rousing out of guard houses. Noise blended with shouts and glances into the barracks and parade field.

"They're waking the whole bloody garrison," Broadside snapped.

Twostaves dropped the Shaud he'd just finished choking to the point of unconsciousness. "We have to do something," worry etched his every word. "We've lost the element of surprise."

"Aye, but perhaps we can let the others keep theirs intact," Duelmaster said, blowing a strand of hair out of his eyes. It stuck to his cheek which was sticky with his own blood. The dryad quickly ripped the hem of his shirt and used his teeth to tie a makeshift bandage around his arm.

"What are you suggesting?" Twostaves asked.

"We need to draw the guard out from the palace," the dryad said, looking at several soldiers with torches in hand hurrying to the steps on both walls, descending like ants upon a carcass.

"Ah, time to whip up a few tricks, you think?" The dwarf's eyes glinted.

"It's never not a time to whip up tricks Broadside," Duelmaster chuckled. "Twostaves, think you can get these gates to stay open?"

"Is a dragon's fanny-" Twostaves began.

"Not the time!" Broadside shouted.

The giant nodded. "The gate will be open. No worries. You two get to work with those tricks. I'll make sure the escape route is open."

"Great. Duely, to the stables?" Broadside asked.

"Aye. I hope Dinendale knows what he's doing," the dryad said, tossing aside his cloak and drawing his rapiers. "Otherwise this is going to be a much longer night than I wanted it to be."

Paige and Robert quietly inched down the corridor. Only a few torches remained lit in the long halls; the only other light was the dull green shine from the stone Woodcarver had given them. Thick oak doors were spaced every so often along the passageway, each bearing a gold plaque with writing Paige couldn't read.

"What are they? Cells?" Paige asked, hopeful. Robert shook his head, taking a torch from a peg in the wall.

"Hardly. They're rooms of state. That one says *Map Room* and that one says *Archives*." He stopped at a turn in the hallway, and peeked around the corner.

"There's a stairway," he said beckoning to Paige to follow. "Stay close. It's a horrible choke point."

They walked around the corner to the stone stairway, with Robert's spear shining in the green light as it led the way. The crude stairs looked to be newly constructed granite, spiraling up several stories. The steps were wide enough for four men to walk abreast of each other. Paige and Robert moved quietly, their leather clad feet padding softly on the stone steps.

"You really think the dungeon is up a flight of stares?" Paige asked.

"Well, it's carved into the mountain," Robert replied. "I just have no idea where in the mountain the door might be. For all we know it could be at the top floor of the palace."

"What do we do if she's not up here?" Paige asked.

"We'll meet up with the others. We're not leaving here without her." He suddenly turned to her.

"Paige, just in case we don't get through this," he stammered. "I need you to know something."

Paige felt a slight ache in the pit of her stomach. "Don't talk like that. We're going to be just fine."

"I know, but on the off chance something were to happen... that is to say... I want you to know..."

Whatever he was trying to say, he couldn't seem to find the words. Paige felt the ache in her stomach grow. She felt as if she'd swallowed something so sour that it was putting her entire body on edge.

"Spill it Robert," Paige hissed. "We don't have all night."

He closed his eyes and nodded.

"I just want you to know I consider you the best friend I've had in a long time, and I care a lot about you...."

"Robert!"

Eöl's cheeks flushed. "No, princess, please let me finish."

"No, idiot," Paige said, pointing up.

Robert turned to see the light of a torch descending down the staircase. Robert shoved the green stone onto the stairs, both hands gripping his spear. The light approached, and they could hear nasal, fast-paced chatter. Robert threw up his hood as a lone man rounded the stairwell.

"And just who does he think he is! Am I supposed to make him a papaya salad in the middle of the night? I mean do I look like a chef? Yet he says 'Marco! Fetch me a salad,' as if I were his slave. No sir. I prefer the term 'bonded for the foreseeable lifetime,'" the man mumbled. He was of a dark skin, with long black hair and big bulging eyes. He wore a shockingly bright coat with every color of the rainbow and a cylindrical hat of the same material. He was skinny as a yew sapling; he held a candle in one hand and an empty plate in the other.

Paige's heart thundered in her ears. This was it. They were going to be found out. She gripped the hairpin till her knuckles popped.

Robert wasted no time. He jumped up the stairwell and threw his weight into the slender slave who landed flat on his backside.

"Hey now!" the man pouted. "Watch where you're going!"

"What are you doing up at this hour wandering the hallway?" Robert barked authoritatively. The man looked puzzled as he pulled himself up.

"He wants a pomegranate salad for a tummy ache. 'Go fetch a salad Marco,' he says, and then throws a chair at me. A chair! Why not? That's what normal people do right? Try and high-five the servants in the face with a chair? Well, I'll take my own sweet time making his salad and hope he gets indigestion. Where am I even supposed to find a papaya out here? We live in a glorified cave in the middle of nowhere just before winter!"

"Oh shut up will you!" Robert growled. The man looked him up and down and then past him to Paige, and his expression changed.

"Wait, who are-" he started to say, but Robert threw his hand against the man's thin chest and shoved him against the turret wall. He pulled back a heavy fist and slammed it into the servant's pointed jaw so hard, the man spun round a full turn before crumpling to the ground, snuffed out like the candle he dropped.

"That was way too close," Robert said with a shaky breath, picking up the green stone out of his pocket. He grabbed a handkerchief and shoved it into the man's mouth, taking his woven belt off his thin waist and tying his spindly hands behind his back.

"Tell me about it. Let's go check out the top of the stairs before he wakes up," Paige urged. They climbed up the stairs, taking them two at a time.

The top landing opened to a long hallway curving sharply to the left. They rounded the corner to see another hall lined by lit torches and a single door at the end. The gigantic slabs of iron-studded wood was inlaid with the gold engraving of a snake. Elegant silver lettering scrolled around the frame, glittering in the torchlight. They approached it apprehensively.

"I... I don't think this is the dungeon," Paige said with a sinking feeling in her gut.

"Hey, Paige?" Robert asked quietly. "Did that nutcase say who he was getting a salad for?"

"No, but you know what I think?"

"What?"

"I think we need to leave right now," Paige said, backing up towards the stairs.

"I agree. Let's go," Robert said, following suit.

Just as they turned their backs, the door opened, slamming against the wall. Wind howled through the corridor, filling the hallway. Torches extinguished. Paige blinked in the dim hallway, her bow drawn and ready for action.

It was deathly still for a moment till a crawling chuckle echoed in the stone hallway. It sent a chill down Paige's spine and made her heart freeze within her bosom. A shadowy figure slithered into the edge of the green light, a pair of cruel eyes catching just enough glint to shine like sharpened obsidian.

"Oh, but I have been waiting so long for you to stop by, my friends!"

The sinister voice chuckled as its owner stepped into the light. Paige felt her grip tighten on the bow as she pulled it back to her cheek at full draw. She saw the golden intertwined snake-crown resting atop the young man's head. He smiled in the magical stone's light as he stared them down. His eyes glinted with the same intense hatred Paige remembered the night he'd taken everything from her.

"The prince!" she whispered.

CHAPTER 19

BLACKEST OF PRISONS

*D*inendale felt a bead of sweat forming on his upper lip. His hands shook slightly. The fewer numbers were a risk, and he wasn't happy about that. It also increased the odds that they would be discovered. When he escaped Aschin before, this building had only been about half constructed. Now he felt as if a tomb had swallowed him. Try as he might, he couldn't push out the nagging fear that, if this rescue went south, he could once again become a slave in this forsaken place. He ground his teeth thinking about it and just decided he'd have to trust the others to keep out of sight.

They wound through the hallway, going deeper and deeper into the mountainside. The dim green light provided an eerie glow on the walls. It shadowed every crack and crevice in the stone, every splinter in the creaky joists spanning the ceiling.

"Do you think this is the right tunnel?" Dinendale asked the wizard. A huge iron door stood around the next bend. It was thick, with a single-barred window revealing torch light from the room within.

"I'd wager a guess," Woodcarver whispered as he quietly approached the window. He peered in, and a moment later, looked at Dinendale.

"Dungeon," he whispered.

"Guards?" Dinendale asked.

"One jailer. Sleeping. Could be more down the other corridors."

"All this and it comes down to one jailer?"

"I don't like it. It's almost too easy."

"What should we do?" Dinendale queried.

"Oh, I don't know, get the bloody princess?" Woodcarver whispered, bending down to the cast iron lock. He paused for a moment.

"Poor choice of words. I apologize."

"Do you have a spell that could open this?" Dinendale asked.

Woodcarver sniffed. "You can't solve every problem with a wand and a spell, Dinendale. Or did you not keep your magic long enough to learn that?"

"You're really going to talk about this now?" Dinendale glared at Woodcarver for a long uncomfortable moment.

The magician rolled his eyes and pulled a small set of lockpicks from his belt. He placed them into the oversized keyhole, twisting it gently. Following several attempts, the lock clicked open. They slipped in, careful not to let the damp, hinges squeak.

The jailer passed gas in his snore-laden sleep, and Dinendale felt himself gag. The man was a gristly fellow, thin as a stalk of corn. A several-day old beard adorned his grimy face, and he breathed through greyish teeth. An empty liquor bottle leaned against his bare torso. His skin was covered in smudges, greasy dirt, and twisted tattoos. He rested with his chair propped against the left entrance where he sat snoring as comfortably as a babe in a cradle.

Dinendale and Woodcarver entered under the arched roof. A cave spread forward as long as they could see, splitting into a T-shaped hall at the end. Thick oak doors covered cells on each side of the cave dotted with small, barred windows that allowed the prisoners to see into the hallway. Dinendale heaved at the stench filling the air. He knew the scent of death and imagined it clawing at his chest. The walls of this wretched place may have gotten taller since he was last here, but that smell hadn't changed a bit.

Dinendale knelt next to the jailer, looking for the man's keys. He saw them attached to the man's belt by a thin iron hoop. Though he did not count, the ring held at least several dozen. He began to reach for them, when the man snorted and his eyes flickered open. The elf held absolutely still, while the drunk's bloodshot eyes tried to focus on him. Then the jailer's eyes squinted at Woodcarver. The drunken man almost gathered enough of his wits to see them, but his head slumped back to his boney bosom with a snort and a shuffle.

Dinendale breathed a sigh and took the keys.

"We should dispatch him," Woodcarver hissed.

Din's eyes snapped over to the magician in disbelief. "Kill him?"

"We can hardly risk him waking and sounding the alarm."

"We're not going to stab an unarmed man in his sleep," Dinendale snapped. The jailer let out another loud snore and both warriors tensed.

"Don't be a fool," Woodcarver whispered again, squeezing his fist and releasing one of the blades out of his gloves.

"Don't be like one of them," Dinendale snapped back. Woodcarver glared at the elf for a moment, then shrugged.

"Fine. It's your hide. Let's find her and get out as quick as we can," Woodcarver urged softly. Dinendale nodded, then walked down the corridor; the elf looked in the left side, the wizard on the right. The first few cells were empty, but the farther ones were all filled. The pitiful sight of emaciated men, chained to the solid stone walls made Dinendale shudder. The prisoners slept, not noticing their seeking eyes. The duo gazed with increasing anger at these poor souls locked in the cells. Occasionally, the inmates moaned or squirmed in their sleep.

At the end of the row of prisoners, Dinendale stopped abruptly. The inmate in the third cell from the split-hallway caught his attention.

"Woodcarver!" Dinendale hissed. The magician immediately stopped and came to his side.

In the cell lay the shape of a female figure. She was thin and frail, dressed in rags. Her ankles and wrists were red and chaffed with the thrall rings that encircled them. She had ratted long hair, and her body was as thin as a dessert tree in a draught.

"Princess?" Dinendale hissed. There was no answer. The figure was still, unmoving. Dinendale searched the keychain till he found the skeleton key in the center; the one key that could open all the cells, and he inserted it into the lock.

The door swung open on well-oiled hinges, and the two warriors entered quickly. Woodcarver bent down to the motionless form and took a finger below the woman's neck. He looked up and his eyes held a sadness that made Dinendale's heart skip.

"No," Dinendale whispered. "No, not..."

"Dead," Woodcarver finished. "Her body is stone cold. She's been gone at least a day."

"No," Dinendale hissed through clenched teeth, turning his back to the wizard. He knew he couldn't cry out aloud because of the jailer, so he pounded his fist over and over again into the solid rock, making a dull, thudding noise with the soft part of his hand.

"No, no, *NO*," he hissed. "Not again." Dinendale slumped onto the ground by Olivian's lifeless figure. He cradled her head in his hands for a long moment.

"It wasn't your fault," Woodcarver consoled.

Dinendale lifted bloodshot eyes to behold the magician.

"Olivian is *dead*. I made a promise to save her. What am I going to tell Paige?"

"You tell her the truth. You can't fix everything, Dinendale." Woodcarver placed his hand on Dinendale's shoulder.

"We could have been here sooner!" he spat. "I promised."

"Promises mean nothing if they aren't in your power to guarantee."

"But I *failed* her." Hot, angry tears poured down his cheekbones. "I failed Paige."

"Shut up," Woodcarver thrust a hand over the elf's mouth to cease his self-loathing. "Don't talk to me about failing. I failed her father. I wasn't there for him. But you don't see me blubbering on about it do you? Only thing to do is to get her body and get out of here."

"I don't-"

"Shhh. Did you hear that?" Woodcarver hissed.

"Hear what?" the elf asked.

"Listen," the man hushed. Dinendale was quiet but heard nothing at first. But then heard the faintest wisp of a whisper from outside the cold stone room. It was soft, but not inaudible. The sound then broke into hushed sobs, and Dinendale backed out of the cell. They were coming from two cells down, the chambers they hadn't yet searched.

Dinendale looked into the cell, and found the source of the noise. It was a young lady, dressed in rags that would have been white at one time. She peered out through dirty, matted hair.

The girl looked up and saw Dinendale in the moonlight. He stared, her red-rimmed eyes bloodshot with sobbing and fear. Her cheekbones stood out on her thin face, and dark circles ran under her eyes. The same blue crystal eyes Dinendale had seen many times before, only not on her.

"Just kill me!" she sobbed. "Please, I can't take it anymore. I would rather be dead than endure another single night in this pit."

"What is your name, girl?" Dinendale hurriedly found the skeleton key.

"Why would any of you care? You animals are all the same. Now just get it over with," she nearly screamed.

"Shut her up!" Woodcarver hissed.

"But what is your name?" Dinendale whispered.

"Olivian."

Dinendale looked at Woodcarver in disbelief. Had he heard her correctly? This couldn't be.

"*Meya Cara, nofayne en emategh,*" Dinendale whispered.

574

I am a friend, not an enemy.

The girl's head snapped up. She looked at the elf with a dawning realization.

"Are you... are you here to take me to heaven?" She whispered.

"No, Princess. Not yet. My name is Dinendale, and we're here to rescue you."

She stared in wild disbelief, then her eyes rolled back in their sockets, and she slumped to the floor. Dinendale shoved the key into the lock and wiggled it, but the lock did not open.

"What's wrong? This is supposed to open every door," Dinendale snapped.

"It must need a different key," Woodcarver cursed tartly.

"Which one?" Dinendale said, looking through the plethora of keys on the ring and finding nothing.

"This one?" a voice growled from behind. The duo spun around to see the jailer, standing with a drawn scimitar in his right hand and a cast iron key in his left.

Dinendale immediately drew his sword while Woodcarver backed up to the wall. The jailer stood tall. His muscles swelled as he grinned, showing off more gold teeth than Dinendale had fingers.

"Going somewhere, gents? Trying to make off with my prized pigeon?" His voice was deep like a roll of thunder, and he jingled the lone key in a mocking manner.

"Smart for a human," Dinendale said, his brown eyes narrowed to mere slits. "You had a special lock made."

"What can I say? My lord is a brilliant man." The jailer spat, chewed tar raining down on the stone floor. He tucked the key ring on his belt and held the scimitar with both hands.

"Get the princess out of here," Dinendale whispered behind to Woodcarver. Out of the corner of his eye he saw the wizard nod in acknowledgement.

"How fortunate for me. Now I can give my lord two more bodies this morning," the soldier sneered. Dinendale gripped his sword with both hands, ready for battle.

"If you want us, come and get us, Raven-head," he called.

The the jailer rushed toward them. Dinendale ground his left boot into the floor for traction. The jailer charged like a lion leaping at a gazelle. But this particular gazelle was actually a panther, and Dinendale bared his teeth, ready to battle.

The clash of steel resounded in the dim light. Sparks flew as the blades connected and slid on impact. A series of harsh blows and attacks followed, the jailer hacking like a madman as the elf met each blow with parries. Dinendale blocked overhead, then thrust outwards at the mans stomach. He missed.

Dinendale blocked as the jailer slid his blade down to the elf's hand guard. It glanced off the hilt and cut Din's upper arm through the leather vambrace. Dinendale cried out in pain, but managed to block the next blow as they circled in the hallway.

"I'm cutting you up into ribbons for jerky, you elfin scum!" the man shouted. Dinendale felt his strength leaving him. His body wouldn't handle the fight much longer with so many wounds already endured through the journey. He felt the hot blood dripping down his arm and off his elbow. The weariness and pain made it nearly impossible to do much more than parry. There had to be another way.

The jailer stabbed with the scimitar blade wrenching Dinendale's sword free. The metal clanked on the ground out of reach. The Shaud kicked the elf in the stomach so hard, Dinendale flew through the door of an empty cell and felt his shoulder dislocate as he slammed into the solid wood.

"Goodnight, elf." The jailer picked up Dinendale's sword and backed him farther into the cell. The man raised his own sword to stab the defenceless elf in the heart.

Dinendale's eyes caught a movement behind the man and gave the jailer a mirthless smile. "Say goodnight yourself," he said.

The jailer laughed. Abruptly the laugh turned to gutteral coughs as two thin blades flashed through his bosom. They disappeared just as quick with a sickening shlick. The jailer gave a creaking gasp and fell face first to the stone floor, lifeless as the granite he landed upon.

Woodcarver stood behind the now lifeless corpse with two bloodstained saber blades protruding from his gloves. He was breathing hard, looking at the Shaud's motionless body. Dinendale stood up, wiping the sweat and blood off his face.

"Say hello to Locamnen for me," Dinendale spat at the body, wrenching his shoulder back into place. He looked up at Woodcarver. "I told you to get her out of here!"

"He had the key, remember?" Woodcarver chuckled.

Dinendale rolled his eyes.

"In that case, help a few moments sooner might have been nice, old one!"

"You seemed to be handling it, but I figured it would do neither I nor the princess good to see you dead," the magician said.

Dinendale nodded. "You're right. Olivian needs to get out of here," he said, glancing at the cell. A burst of Woodcarver's obnoxious laughter caught him off guard.

"What?" Dinendale demanded.

"Oh, no. I meant the other princess. You'd be no good to Paige dead, now would you?"

Dinendale scoffed as he bent down to the jailer's body and took the key from his belt. It entered the lock smoothly, attesting to it's newness. Feridar obviously protected his prizes.

Woodcarver picked the locks of Olivian's chains. Then the magician checked her over for any major, immediate injuries and broken bones. While the magician did that, Dinendale tore a bit of his sleeve and bound the wound on his arm.

"You're no good to carry anything with your arm like that. I'll get her out," Woodcarver said. "Duelmaster and those two asinine dunces will be needing all the help they can get, I suspect. You go get the others, and try not to get into any fights, you're in no condition and I can't heal you."

"You shouldn't take her without backup," Dinendale pushed, pulling the knot of the bandage tight with his teeth. "I'll go with you."

"I'll be fine," Woodcarver said. "You'll slow me down faster than you will the others."

Dinendale bit his lip as Woodcarver picked up the frail princess. He took a long look at the poor girl, and brushed back the matted hair from out of her face. Even in her frail state, she was one of the most beautiful creatures he'd ever seen.

"Take care of her," Dinendale said, and the wizard nodded.

"Sirs?"

The two looked to the left and noticed that several of the other prisoners had come to the barred windows of their cells. One in particular addressed them with smokey, hollow eyes.

"Please help us," he begged, his eyes welled up with tears that streamed into his white beard. "Please!"

Dinendale worked his jaw in frustration. They didn't have time for this, yet they could not just leave these men to their cruel doom.

"What is your name, friend?" Dinendale approached the cell.

"Hamish the Cooper, sir," he said.

"Why are you in here, Hamish the Cooper?" Dinendale searched the man's haggard face.

"Stole a loaf of bread," Hamish stared at the the floor, refusing to look the elf in the eyes. "To feed my sweet Eufrasia. We were starving."

Dinendale scanned the man's face for any sign of deception but saw only sincerity. He quickly inserted the skeleton key on the jailer's key ring and opened the door. It swung out with a loud creaking noise that echoed down the chamber. Several other prisoners sleepily poked their noses through their windows.

"I have little time, so pay attention," the elf hissed. "This is a Skeleton key. Free yourself and anyone of the others. Do you know how to escape this wretched place?"

"I've been planning an escape from here for weeks. I think we can manage."

"How will you get out?"

"We'll go through the ash shuttle on the south side of the palace," he said, quite confident. "I know the guardhouse on that side is hardly ever attentive."

"There's an ash shuttle?" Dinendale felt the interest burning in his chest. Hamish nodded, rubbing his chafed wrists where the shackles had held him captive.

"That may be a better option then," Dinendale said. "Hamish, could you get this man and this woman out that way?"

"It would be my honor sir," the cooper saluted smartly.

"Are you sure it will be a better way?" Woodcarver asked, skeptical. "We have no reconnaissance that way."

"I assure you, it's there, sir. My little Eufrasia collects the ash to make soap to sell at the market. There's a small servant's door leading into the Barracks that comes out right by the stables."

"How many guards?"

"One, two at the most. They guard on the outside so they can monitor the horses as well."

"Can you handle two guards?" Dinendale asked.

Woodcarver's indignant expression was all Dinendale needed.

"Right. Cooper? Get those you can out and head that way. Best of luck to you. Woodcarver, I'll go grab the others and we'll meet you at the rendezvous point."

"Thank you, sir," the human blubbered, tears of joy overtaking him. "I'll never forget this debt."

"Be safe," the elf admonished.

The magician slung the unconscious princess over his shoulder as gently as he could and nodded.

Dinendale dashed through the door of the prison, jogging back to the fork in the hallways. He took a glance in the kitchen to be sure there weren't any glowing stones left behind. Then he took the center of the three hallways intent on catching up with Jesnake. This one took a flight of stairs even deeper into the palace spiralling downward into the bowels of the mountain.

When the staircase ended, Dinendale came to another long, curved, hallway. He could hear sounds of metallic clanking and low booms from around the corner. He cautiously entered the void, sword drawn and ready when a body hurled past him and shoved him into the wall.

"Shhhh!" Jesnake hissed, putting a finger to his lips. "Did you find her?"

"Aye!" Dinendale said. Jesnake grabbed his arm and hauled the dark elf back to the stairs.

"What's around the corner?"

"Hell," Jesnake snapped. "We have to get out!"

"Agreed!"

"No, I mean we need to get out now!" Jesnake said in short gasps. "They know we're here!"

"What?" Dinendale ran to keep up as they dashed up the stairway. "Jey, what's happened?"

"That's the foundry and the torture chamber," Jesnake spat, jabbing his finger down the hallway. "I watched them for about two minutes, when a man burst through a door on the opposite side from where I was. He yelled for the men to wake the palace garrison. They know we're here."

Dinendale ran up the flight of stairs, a feeling of sinking dread overtaking his stomach.

"Paige and Robert!" he pumped his legs up the stairs.

"Where were they?" Jesnake huffed up the flight of steps behind Dinendale.

"Third hallway," Dinendale heaved. "I haven't seen them yet and they aren't back outside!"

They dashed out to the main hall, and flew up the third flight of stairs. Emerging into the hallway, they abruptly halted.

Three bodies lay in the dimly lit passage. Two were dressed in mail and wore disheveled turbans, so Dinendale knew they were guards. But when he saw the third, Dinendale felt his heart stop.

"Robert?" he shouted, running to his comrade. Blood covered his friend's body as he lay on the ground. Dinendale immediately felt for a pulse. A faint heartbeat was still there.

"Eöl," Dinendale demanded. His voice shook with worry and rage. "Can you hear me? What happened?"

"You should see the other guy," Robert sputtered, blood splattering his robes as he spoke.

"Creator have mercy," Dinendale spat out the prayer. "Where are you hit?"

"Side," Robert grimaced. "A knife. I can feel it. Missed my stomach but it's... not exactly... ideally located."

Dinendale looked at his friend's brown robe soaked with blood. He found the Shauden knife just above Robert's kidney. Jesnake quickly notched an arrow, aiming it at the door emblazoned with a golden serpent, standing guard.

"Hold still," Dinendale grabbed the hilt.

Robert grabbed his wrist before he could remove the blade. "NO!" he bellowed. "Leave it. I'll bleed out faster if you pull it out, moron. Go!"

"I'm not going to-"

"Dinendale," Robert gasped for air. "He... took... *her*."

Dinendale felt his veins turn to ice. Blood drained from his head. The room around him spun.

"He took her through those doors," Robert heaved. "You have to stop him."

"Jesnake, get Robert out of here."

Dinendale flew through the hallway to the golden serpent door.

"Din!" Robert called out. Dinendale halted for moment.

Robert gulped, then coughed. A sliver of blood came out the corner of his mouth. "You kill that son of a pixie," he spat. "For me. For her. She's... she..." Robert didn't have the energy to finish his thought. He slumped back, gasping again for breath.

Dinendale nodded furiously. Hot, angry, tears glazed over his view as he realized this could be the last time he ever saw his friend.

"Din," Jesnake called out, tossing something from a body of a Shaud. It was a small hand cannon, much like the ones they'd encountered in the forest just days ago.

"One shot. Make it count." Jesnake grabbed hold of Robert and dragged him back to the stairs.

"There's an ash shuttle on the south side of the palace," Dinendale said as he tucked the hand cannon into the back of his belt. "You might have better luck that way."

"I'll find it," Jesnake assured, hauling Robert up to his feet. "Alright, Eöl. Let's get you out of here. Din? Be careful."

Turning to the giant door, Dinendale drew his scimitar, a dangerous glare glinting in his eye. He took a long deep breath and yanked the door open.

He rushed into what looked like a throne room. The carved furniture and rich tapestries emblazoned every inch of the round chamber. A large oak dining table graced the left wall with a series of immaculately carved chairs with soft, blue cushions. But it was the four heavily armed men who stood in a semicircle in front of him that Dinendale took note of first: the prince's personal guard. Unlike normal soldiers, these men wore crimson garb to stand apart from white linen of the army. Two men held curved scimitars identical to Dinendale's while another held a heavy battle axe. The last man held a nasty looking hand-and-a-half sword, also known as a bastard, that very well could have been as tall as the man himself.

They rushed him all at once. Din snapped his gaze around the room and saw an oil lamp on a small writing desk to his right. He switched sword hands and snagged the melon sized object in his right, hurtling it into the oncoming attackers.

The ceramic lamp hit the floor with a crash, and the oil flew, catching fire in multiple directions. The guards avoided the flames as they rushed forward, but it gave Dinendale the split-second distraction he needed. The elf leapt onto the desk, grabbing one of the tapestries and yanking it off its hanging strings. He tossed it over the closest guard like a tablecloth.

Dinendale leapt up, landing on the entangled soldier's shoulders, driving him to the ground beneath the temporary woven confinement. He thrust his scimitar straight down on the guard as he landed feeling the blade connect with soft tissue.

He whirled around to duck an attack made by the man with the bastard. He caught the back swing on his sword, deflecting it and following up with a kick to further unbalance the attacker. Din caught the arm of the stumbling soldier and used the weight of his own heavy sword to drive the tip into the marble floor.

Using his momentum, Dinendale finished his attack with several vicious blows to the jawbone fueled by unstoppable rage. As he pummeled the man's face, he grabbed the bastard and wrenched it out of the man's grasp. Driving the hilt into the soldier's nose, he dropped the Shaud like a sack of lead. Then he prepared to meet the other two.

Before the second human hit the ground, Dinendale hacked furiously at the other swordsman, trying to keep moving so the axe-wielding Shaud couldn't join his comrade in a double-teamed effort. The skill of this swordsman was excellent, but when Dinendale feigned a limp, the Shaud took the bait. Dinendale spun at just the right time and brought the bastard down as hard as he could into the man's exposed side. The Shaud heaved as the blade hacked through a chink in his armor and into his ribcage.

The final soldier attacked, swinging the mighty axe with broad sweeps meant for cleaving holes in the ranks of enemy lines. This Shaud was as big as a mountain bear and roared like one, too. He had an ugly, pudgy, pock-marked face, with bellowing jowls. Dinendale knew if he was even slightly nicked by that whirling broad-head, he would find his lower limbs severed from his body.

He backed up a few steps to the throne, which was made of solid granite. He ducked behind it as the human juggernaut attacked. The axe head connected with the back of the stone throne, shattering into a myriad of pieces and scattering them in all directions. Dinendale dodged a large marble chunk, slid on the slippery stone floor and jumped down to the court floor. The roaring giant advanced on him like a bull charging a lamb.

Dinendale saw a door on the other end, and bolted for it. He looked for anything that could give him advantage over his adversary. His battle with the jailer and now three more guards had exhausted him, and he was willing to take any advantage he could get his hands on.

Suddenly, things came to a head rather rapidly; Din tripped on a loose rug and went flying towards the door. He landed with a gasp, his breath sucked out of his body like a blacksmith at his bellows. Dinendale's borrowed sword ejected from his hand and clattered down on the stone floor. He rolled over onto his back, gasping for air. The Shaud ran at him with his axe raised high, preparing to let it cleave his enemy in twain.

As the Shaud reeled his axe to crush the elf, Dinendale remembered something he had learned by watching Paige fight: the downfall of every man.

He threw the heel of his boot at the man and caught the Shaud right in the fork of his legs.

The man's eyes seemed to pop out of his face when Dinendale's kick and his own inertia connected and registered as pain in his brain. He dropped the axe in mid-swing and toppled to the ground with a thud. He made a high pitched squeal that was so unlike the roar that he blasted from his lungs at the beginning of the fight.

Without wasting time, Dinendale jumped up and kicked the axe out of the man's reach. He knelt at the dropped soldier, drawing his dagger to the man's throat.

"Where is she?" he said in a menacing tone. The man looked at Dinendale, gave a smug grin, and then winced in pain.

"You'll never get out of here alive," he said through gritted teeth. "You and your barbarian princess will fall at the wrath of Prince Feridar."

"I'll take my chances. Now tell me. Where did he take her?" Dinendale moved the dagger closer to the man's throat.

"You have no idea what you're dealing with," the man said, wincing as Dinendale glided through outer layer of flesh with the tip of the dagger. A small trickle of blood ran down the man's neck and onto the floor.

"WHERE IS SHE?" Dinendale barked, sliding the knife just enough to draw another stream of blood. The man's face contorted in pain.

Dinendale saw fear and defeat flash on the man's eyes.

"He's taken her to the roof," he said, "he's ending this little game once and for all."

The soldier shut his eyes tight. It took Dinendale a moment to realize that the man was waiting for him to kill him. It was what he would expect, being a soldier of the Shahir.

"I'm not going to kill you," he said, withdrawing the knife blade.

The man looked surprised, then disgusted. "Coward," he spat wearing a confused expression.

Dinendale shook his head. "No. It's called honor." A solid punch to the man's jaw sent him unconscious. Dinendale stood and shook the pain out of his punching hand. His ears tuned to indiscriminate yelling of men in the hallway he had just come from. Reinforcements were on their way. He ran to the door and opened it a crack.

Immediately, a hail of arrows thudded into the wooden door frame. Dinendale slammed the door shut as fast as he could. He drew the bolt across the door, but knew that it wouldn't hold them off long. He grabbed the battle axe off the floor and sunk it into the wooden barricade, letting the axehead cut into the frame as well. It was by no means permanent, but would seal it for the time being. He flipped the heavy oak table and shoved it in front of the barricaded door.

Dinendale bolted to the other door, grabbing the bastard off the floor and a torch off the wall. He flung open the door to reveal a narrow passageway. The hall ran a hundred paces and turned to a staircase that branched off. He took the stairs two at a time, he felt the burn of his thigh muscles as he burst into the cold night air on the roof.

The elf stood on the roof of the palace with the large onion shaped dome in its center. A short battlement with staggered crenels surrounded the edge of the roof with four staircases continuing up to form minarets on each corner of the keep. Dinendale ran from the back corner tower towards the front of the keep. He frantically searched for any sign of Paige. As he circled the dome, something thrashing in the darkness caught his eye, and Dinendale felt time stand still.

Paige was struggling desperately for breath, clawing for life on the stone. A tall, broad-shouldered man was kicking her in the ribs repeatedly as she lay on her side. She cried out in agony as his boot caught her in the side so hard Dinendale could feel the thud of the blow through the soles of his feet. On each side of the man stood two armed guards holding shields and torches.

The man shoved Paige onto her back and leapt upon her like a jaguar, a long, thin dagger in his hand. Dinendale saw him cut the lacing on Paige's jerkin and rip the side open. Paige flailed, but the attacker backhanded her hard across the face. Stunned, she couldn't struggle as the man ripped the jerken off the rest of the way leaving her vunerable. Muffled screams escaped Paige's lips as her attacker held her down.

Dinendale felt his voice welling up inside him like a gale across the great plains as Paige's assailant turned and looked at him.

"Feridar!"

CHAPTER 20

ESCAPE

D inendale's heartbeat pounded in his ears. His fingers gripped the bastard so hard his knuckles popped. Like a boulder of obsidian smashing into a mountainside, it felt like his soul shattered into a million pieces. He raised the torch high in his shaking hand and charged towards Paige and Feridar.

Hurling through the darkness, the elf flew towards them like an arrow in the sky. The two guards standing by dropped their torches and drew their scimitars. They held up round, spike-adorned shields in defiance, but Dinendale was having none of it. His lungs roared with a mighty battle cry. He threw his torch to the ground and brought his sword to the ready.

Dinendale leapt into the air with his heavy sword lifted high and brought it down on the shield of the leftmost opponent. The blow knocked the soldier backwards enough to lose his footing. Dinendale swung the sword around but the soldier caught the blade with his shield a second time. The deafening clang reverberated across the rooftop like a gong, knocking Dinendale back a few paces.

The other guard attacked twice in quick succession. Barely recovering, Dinendale blocked the man's blows in quick succession. The strikes descended heavily upon him, but he met them with attacks of his own. A heavy slash downward was followed by an uppercut that tickled Dinendale's chin. The dark elf twisted, withdrawing from the third slash. He let out another yell as he attacked the man with a series of ferocious blows: left, right, left, left, under, and thrust home.

Dinendale could feel the blade separate the links of mail and cut through to the man's beating heart. The Shaud made a sputtering noise as he crumpled to the floor like a spider on a candle flame, sliding off Dinendale's blade.

The first attacker rushed at Dinendale. Moving out of the way, Dinendale let him come, sliding his right foot back a bit for traction. As the man rushed and slashed, Dinendale caught the blow with his vambrace. He felt the sharp pain as the thrust splintered one of the bones in his forearm. In turn, he grabbed the man's sword arm and wrenched it forward, throwing the Shaud off balance. The man staggered forward, stumbling on top of his own shield with a mighty crash. As he struggled to get to his feet, Dinendale yanked his helmet towards the sky, then repeatedly slammed his fist into the Shaud's face till his body went limp.

Dinendale panted for breath as he whirled round and looked at the prince. He felt his heart skip a beat. Feridar had ripped Paige's armor off, leaving her in only a bloody, ripped up shirt. The prince now stood at the edge of the palace grasping Paige's throat as he leaned her out over the battlements. The only thing keeping her from falling was the fact that she had her toes still holding onto the edge of the building. Sweat and splattered blood rolled down Dinendale's forehead as he took a step closer, his dark eyes filling with moonlight.

"Such *savagery*," the prince haughtily sneered, looking genuinely impressed. "I've never encountered one of your kind in The Wild before, but I must say, the stories do not disappoint."

"I'd give you one to tell your children," Dinendale shouted, taking another step forward, "but you won't be around long enough to have any."

"Such adorable threats, I must say," Feridar grinned.

Dinendale took another step, but the prince wagged the finger of his free hand at him.

"Not so fast, vermin," the prince hissed. He shook Paige's body enough that the stone beneath her feet crumbled. She screamed. Dinendale watched as she struggled to keep a foothold on the embrasure. He halted, the icy fist of fear wrapping itself around his stomach.

"Easy now," the elf hissed, holding out a hand. "Don't do anything rash."

"Oh, you mean like breaking into the strongest fortress on the frontier? Tell me, elf, how is 'not doing anything rash' working out for you?"

Dinendale lowered his sword slightly, feeling a strong combination of panic and rage burn inside his chest.

"Let her go," the elf said firmly. "And let's settle this like warriors."

"You think I have anything to prove to you, Wildlander?" Feridar laughed cruelly. "Everything you see, everything you passed through to get here was built by me. We stand now on the grounds of my achievement. A duel of honor? I think not."

"I wouldn't expect a man who hangs elvish women from his balcony to have any honor to duel over."

A flicker of recognition danced across Feridar's face, and he grinned.

"Wait. You're *that* elf? Well, isn't this a coincidence. Seems like I've got another one of your tarts out on a limb. You really are bad at this whole rescuing thing, aren't you?"

"I made it to you, didn't I?" Dinendale said evenly, grinding his teeth. He suddenly had a thought strike him like a bolt of lighting. It was a long shot, but it was the only one he had at the moment. "You won't hurt her. Not while I have what you've been looking for."

Feridar threw his head back and laughed.

"And what on earth could you have that I want?"

"Perhaps a different sort of page?" Dinendale kept his voice even despite the lie. Paige's eyes darted to her own feet where the leather was still stitched, undiscovered by the prince, then back up to Dinendale.

"Oh, I take it you mean the page that bastard stole from my father?" Feridar chuckled, carelessly.

Dinendale felt bewilderment set in but it didn't take the steel out of his voice. "Are you saying you don't want it?"

"Oh, I'm not too worried about it," Feridar laughed cruelly, reaching into the pocket of his robes. The action cause his grip on Paige to shift. She whimpered, stiffening her legs to get a better hold on the still crumbling stone.

"I would be," Dinendale reached into his satchel and pulled out his polishing cloth. The prince looked taken aback, but laughed again.

"You still think this is all about the page?" Feridar snickered as he held out his free hand. Out of his fist dropped a thin silver chain on which dangled a key. Dinendale recognized the key Paige had been wearing since the day he met her.

"A key?" the elf laughed, trying to hide his confusion.

"Yes, you inbred imbecile." Feridar rolled his eyes. "Do you think it's been the page I've been after all this time? That scrap is merely a tool that will allow me to unlock the power contained within this."

"But you can't use it without the Book of the Dead," Dinendale guessed. "So hand her over and I'll give you the page."

"Dinendale, no!" Paige heaved through the prince's grip.

"You can't bargain with this Halfbreed Idiot," Feridar smiled. "I've already got what I need from her. Anything else I take from her will just be," he turned to look at Paige, "sugar atop the cake."

Dinendale felt his flesh crawl and his blood pressure rise. His grip on the bastard tightened and the leather grip squeaked under the pressure.

"Oh, he did not like that, did he?" Feridar shouted, looking back at Paige with smouldering eyes. "If only he knew."

"If you harm her, I swear to the Creator, I will-" Dinendale snapped.

"You'll *what* exactly?" Feridar shouted. "*Kill* me? Like you did last time? Oh, that's right. You slipped away like a coward after I stretched your poor little lady!"

"Dinendale, don't worry about me. Just shoot this bastard!" Paige shouted as hard as she could through the choke hold.

"My, what a foul little mouth," Feridar shouted, yanking Paige so hard her feet slipped free and she was suddenly dangling above the ground. The prince winced as her full weight pulled against his arm, but held tight.

"I'd teach her a lesson, like I did your last little girl," Feridar hissed, turning to look at Dinendale with a cruel, mirthless smile. "But I don't think I have time to do it properly. Not like last time. Shame, too. She went over the balcony before she could tell you all about it, elf."

Dinendale's blood ran ice cold.

Feridar chortled and inhaled deeply. "Besides, the last one smelled better. Like a batch of fresh peaches."

Dinendale's world suddenly grew numb, and he felt his knees buckle.

"Oh, well," Feridar grunted. "Could have been fun."

With that, he released his grip on Paige's throat and threw her over the edge. Paige screamed as she slipped from view. Dinendale felt claws of anguish rip through the shattered remains of his heart.

"No!" The elf grabbed his sword with both hands and rushed forward. The prince drew his scimitar and ran to meet Dinendale. The elf swung the hand-and-a-half sword with all his might at Feridar's head. Sparks flew as the prince drove his own sword into the oncoming blade and deflected it easily to the left. The Shaud took his other hand and slashed at the elf with his dagger. Dinendale felt the blade cut through his jerkin's shoulder as if it were made of butter. The elf shouted in both rage and pain whirling to face his assailant.

Feridar charged him again, with more grace and skill than that of his soldiers. He came wearily, crouched like a viper deciding where to strike. Hatred blended with an evil madness glinted in his coal black eyes. The prince sprung forward like a cobra, the clash of steel resounding in the night air as Dinendale's blade met the blow.

Feridar swept down at Dinendale's legs with his scimitar, then slashed high at the elf's face with the dagger. Dinendale's head surged with adrenalin. His body shook in panic and fear, distracting his focus. He jabbed at the prince's neck, but the stab was easily deflected. Feridar followed up with a sweeping strike of his own. The scimitar and bastard sparked and clanged in the night air as the two warriors fought ferociously back and forth. Dinendale slashed across the man's chest and caught the loose folds of the prince's garment. Dinendale could hear the rip of the cloth. The prince backed up and spat, heaving.

"Is that all you've got?" Feridar hissed.

"You talk too much," the elf spat, rushing the man again.

Their blades met in a frenzy of furious hacking and slashing, more primal than calculated. Dinendale ran to keep speed with the agile prince. He was weary and bleeding in the shoulder. Though rage coursed through his veins, the fights of the last few hours had sapped him of his strength. He felt his stamina waning. The prince forced him backwards, away from the dome, and closer to the slotted battlements of the palace. Dinendale slashed low, and the prince flipped backwards, landing on his feet like a cat. Feridar rushed again, driving Dinendale's sword down towards the flat, granite, roof of the palace. Dinendale felt the prince's fist against his jaw, and sparks flashed before his vision as he stumbled backwards.

"You can't beat me, you pathetic excuse for a sentient being," the prince heaved. "You thought you could save her? Be the hero?"

Dinendale rose slowly, shaking, blood spilling from his mouth. "I don't have to be a hero anymore," he hissed, hot tears stinging his cut cheeks. "Tonight, I just have to be an avenger."

The elf grabbed the cleaning cloth out of his belt and threw it at the prince. It landed in a crumpled pile at Feridar's feet, it's naked, blank surface staring the heir to the throne in the face. Feridar's expression contorted in hatred as his eyes bored into Dinendale.

"Where is it?" he screamed. Dinendale coughed more blood out of his mouth as he chuckled.

"It won't matter to you," the elf heaved, spitting once more. "You're not getting off this roof alive."

And then he lunged.

The prince blocked by bringing the sword down on Dinendale's right arm as hard as he could. The elf felt the blade deeply in his flesh as Feridar kept pushing. Hot blood spurted down his arm. Blinding pain from the already splintered bone caused the elf's vision to almost completely black out. He shoved the Shauden prince to the ground and the two grappled for their lives, each trying to get on top of the other to deliver the choke. Dinendale started with an advantage, but the prince quickly punched him in his wounded arm, causing Dinendale to scream out in pain.

From there it didn't take much for the prince to overpower the dark elf, his strong, tawny brown hands wrapped around Dinendale's pale throat. Dinendale gasped for breath, but the prince was crushing his windpipe. He could feel his brain firing off sparks as they were starved of the sweet nectar of air. Dinendale let fly a punch that caught Feridar on the side of the head. Angered, Feridar hissed words that were unintelligible to the elf. Dinendale felt a sudden, burning pain on his throat, like a hot iron searing his flesh. The elf screamed as Feridar let out a wicked chortle.

"Absolutely pathetic," the prince spat. "You thought to stand up against the might of the Shahir alone? You and your kind shall be wiped from this land, till not even the memory of you taints the rule of civilization and power."

Dinendale saw big dark spots as he clawed for air. Just when he was about to slip into the black recesses of unconsciousness, the prince's hands released. Dinendale ripped a breath into his chest with a gutteral gasp and a cough. He sat bolt upright and felt his aching heart leap.

It was Paige.

Holding onto Feridar, she screamed through gritted teeth. Her hands pulled a choke hold around his neck. Feridar flailed and punched. He hit her in the eye, and she reeled back onto the roof. He jumped to his feet and grabbed her by the hair, throwing her backwards.

"You're a lot harder to kill than your father was!" Feridar marched up to the fallen princess.

Paige rolled and stopped against the battlement, staggering to rise as the prince marched over to her.

"Tell that rogue and your mother I said hello," he snapped, raising his sword to deal one last blow.

"Klaíomh!"

Paige leapt to her feet, her hairpin clutched in her fist as blue sparks shot forth and bounced on the stone around her feet. The saber elongated just in time for her to reach up and deflect the blow, spinning around Feridar and taking a jab at his thigh. The prince was taken off guard as Klaíomh sank deep into the muscle tissue.

Feridar howled in agony then whirled on the princess dealing a series of fierce blows with his dagger and scimitar. Dinendale leapt up and grabbed his own sword, joining Paige in the heated engagement.

Back and forth they sparred the Prince to the edge of the battlements. When Dinendale went low, Paige swiped high. But Feridar took no more hits. The man had trained in the art of war since he was a child. Though he winced in pain and was clearly winded, neither the elf nor the princess could get in with a solid strike.

Dinendale struggled for life. His wound poured radiant blood to the ground around them. Breathing could only keep him alive for so long. He heaved and swung, but Feridar drove his blade into the stone and kicked him hard in the chest. Dinendale found himself floating off the ground before landing on his back. He felt something hard dig into his spine but scrambled up.

Feridar caught Paige's blade between his own and hurled Klaíomh to the side. He shoved her backwards into the parapet wall poising his dagger to strike.

Dinendale leapt to his feet. "FERIDAR!"

The man glanced over his shoulder just as Dinendale yanked the tiny hand cannon out of his belt. The elf smiled, then pulled the trigger.

The ball whizzed past the prince harmlessly, connecting with the stone parapet far beyond the palace battlements. The prince laughed uncontrollably, white teeth flashing as a lightning strike lit the sky.

"You know, you should really get up with the times if you plan on...."

The laughter stopped.

A blade sliced through the prince's chest, blue sparks dancing all around his bosom. His expression went completely blank then was slowly replaced by a white, sickening look of shock as he saw the enchanted elven sword protruding from his chest.

"That is for my parents," Paige whispered, ice layering her frosty words.

Feridar gasped, blood sputtering from his mouth. Paige ripped the blade from his back with a sickening suction sound as Klaíomh freed itself from it's fleshy sheath. Feridar let out a single croak, glaring ahead at Dinendale before his eyes went dim. He fell backwards onto the cold stone roof of Aschin's fortress, coughing and wheezing through his final breaths until he ceased to breathe all together, lying still in death's icy clutches.

"Paige," Dinendale limped over to the her as fast as he could, his sword clattering onto the stone. Paige sat up, wincing.

"I'm alright," she assured, sitting up slowly. "He did a number on my ribs earlier. I think he bruised that one again, if it's not broken."

"How are you alive? I was so sure," he gasped, his bloodied hand holding her cheek. Paige held up Klaíomh and returned it to its original form.

"I managed to jam it into a crevice like you did back at Craymoghr Cliff."

"Thank the Creator," Din gasped, grabbing her and pulling her into an embrace. She returned the gesture quickly, then pulled away urgently.

"Olivian?" she asked, fear etched into her face.

"If Woodcarver made it out, she is safe," Dinendale said.

"We need to get out of here, now. Can you walk?"

"Yes," Dinendale nodded.

"But first things first." The princess crawled over to Feridar's lifeless body and stuffed her hand in his bloodied robe. She pulled out her chain that held the mysterious key and returned it to her neck. "Let's get out of here."

"If we can make it down one flight of stairs, there's an ash chute we can take." Dinendale urged as they limped as fast as they could to the turret.

"Quick, go!" he heaved, and they descended the steps.

"Wait," Paige whispered not two steps down. They both saw a light coming up the stairs and heard shouting of men.

They dashed back out into the cold night air. Dinendale slammed the door shut and drove the bastard into the hinge to block it shut.

"That won't hold long," he looked around frantically. Suddenly he heard a loud, shrill whistle that he instantaneously recognized as Duelmaster's.

"Come on!" the elf shouted, grabbing her hand as they ran for the edge of the palace.

"What are you doing?" she cried.

"We have to jump."

"Are you out of your mind?"

"Trust me," he called back and then whistled a reply into the night air.

"Jump!" he leapt over the battlement into the cold night air. Without a second thought, Paige followed suit and threw her body over the west edge of the palace.

Paige held her eyes shut tightly. For a moment, it felt as if time slowed down as she hovered in the cold grey sky of the pre-dawn. Then things sped rapidly as her body plummeted towards the ground. She suppressed a scream as they pitched into the night.

Then, quite violently, she hit a pile of moldy hay. She let out the scream she'd been holding in as she landed on her cracked ribs. Her head hit the edge of a wooden wagon as the vehicle lurched forward. She struggled up in the hay and shoved her body out of the pile, sputtering. Paige glanced wildly around to see Duelmaster in the driver's seat urging the horses give it all they had.

"Hello, princess," the dryad called over his shoulder. "Have a pleasant evening in the castle?"

"What on earth?" she screamed, wincing at the stabbing pain in her side.

"I'm fine. Thanks for asking," Dinendale called out to Duelmaster, trying to hold an old sack to his arm to slow the blood loss.

"Well, I think the prince wanted you both to stay for dessert," Duelmaster jabbed his thumb behind them. She looked and saw guards pouring out of the palace like termites on an upturned mound. "Or maybe that's because Broadside and I lit their bunker on fire. Who knows? It's hard to keep track of who's mad and why."

"I told you we should have used more powder," a gruff voice said, buried in the straw mound.

"Oh, shut up Broadside. Hold on," the dryad shouted back, and they made a sharp turn to the right. Paige felt her stomach lurch as the two outside wheels left the ground.

"Ho," Duelmaster called. Paige heard the creaking of the gates as the shouting intensified.

"Twostaves," Dinendale called as they burst through the gates. Paige saw a huge shape leap off of the rising gate, blotting out the stars for a few moments. With a crash, the giant landed in the back of the wagon with them.

"Nice to have you drop by," Duelmaster said, snapping the reins again for more speed. The crew took off through the barracks towards the second gate.

"Get off me you lumpy lard ridden," Broadside hollered.

"Oh, do shut up." Twostaves shoved a fist into the hay as the dwarf yelped.

"Where is Olivian?" Paige asked.

"We got Woodcarver a couple horses. He took Olivian, and Robert managed to climb up on the other one somehow. They rode out at a solid gallop while we were delaying the guards at the barracks," Dulemaster shouted.

"They passed the gate from the stables about ten minutes ago," Twostaves confirmed. "After that, I've no idea how they fared."

A thud of arrows hit the wooden wagon. "Stay down," Dinendale shouted. The giant threw himself over the princess, and she heard a grunt of pain as a bolt thudded through the armor in his back.

They raced through the streets, and the archers were soon out of range. Twostaves got off of her and grunted as he snapped the shaft of the arrow lodged under his shoulder plate. They heard the warning horn blast from the palace. The horn to wake the whole army in the city. The city they now raced through.

"Horseman," Dinendale shouted. Paige turned and saw a lone rider galloping low over the saddle of a blood-red colt.

"Jesnake," she cried.

"Get on. It will lighten the load," he shouted. Dinendale stood up and leapt onto the horse. He nearly slipped off the saddle, but Jesnake grabbed his arm and hauled him up back up, which wrenched a cry of pain from the dark elf. Paige noticed a slight shift in the speed of the cart, but then she heard something that made her heart stop.

Boom. Boom. Boom.

There were war drums beating all across the city. Outposts lit up. Towers came alive with staggering soldiers rushing to arms. The commotion of the palace had spread. Officers shouting orders attempted to resolve the widespread confusion and chaos. All around them, men stumbled out of tents in various states of undress, grasping for swords and shouting out commands.

Boom. Boom. Boom.

"The gate!" Paige pointed forward at their last obstacle. The main gate and the bridge across the gorge loomed before them. The bridge was jerking its way up as several guards twisted the giant windlass near the gates effectively sealing them inside the city. Paige felt her throat tighten. They were going to be trapped. Paige felt her heart sink as they came ever closer to the bridge.

Boom. Boom. Boom.

"Go on." Duelmaster shouted. "Get ahead!"

"We're not going to make that!!" Twostaves shouted.

"We have to try!" Paige shouted.

Boom. Boom. Boom.

Jesnake pressed his steed on harder, and they inched slowly ahead of the wagon. The bridge was only a bowshot ahead of them. Paige saw the blood mare gallop forward with a burst of speed, closing the gap for the jump. Several guards stepped out with raised spears, but Jesnake let go of the reins and fired several arrows in quick succession, wounding two of the men and killing a third. The horse clacked up the inclined bridge and leapt beyond the edge of the gorge.

"Hold on," Duelmaster shouted.

Paige grabbed the side of the wagon and held her breath. Quite suddenly, she heard a sickening snap as the back wheel crunched and shot off the wagon. Paige cried out as her cracked rib slammed into the jolting cart. She heard the dryad curse.

"Princess!" Twostaves cried out. "Move to the far left front of the cart."

Paige did as he said as the giant moved forward. The grinding axle lifted with the shift of weight but tottered dangerously on the brink of falling over. The bridge neared, and Paige shut her eyes tightly. She felt Twostaves wrap himself around her.

"I've always wanted to do this," Duelmaster screamed as they hit the bridge.

Paige felt the change of incline. The wagon seemed to go limp. It tottered in the air as they launched into the night, the horses screaming in fear and protest as the wagon sailed through the black void. It lasted only a few heartbeats, but each heartbeat dragged on for an hour in her mind. The wagon jolted as it crashed onto the other side of the stone chasm.

Twostaves held on tightly to protect Paige. The impact sent tsunamis of pain through her body, and she screamed. Hot tears ran down her face. The wagon rattled on as she bit her lip. They continued for what felt like an eternity until the wagon abruptly stopped.

"Twostaves, there's a spare wheel lashed to the bottom of the wagon," Duelmaster instructed. The giant and dwarf popped out of the hay and went to work while Duelmaster bandaged Paige's wounds.

"Thank you." She held his eyes. "I can't believe we got through that."

"Aye, I told you we'd get her out." He placed the bandages back in his pack and hopped into the driver's seat. "But we're not out of it yet. Hold on tight. We've still got a little lather left to work out of these steeds."

They continued down the road away from the castle at a steady trot turning along the northward road as fast as the horses could muster. Their mouths were frothing from the mad dash.

Paige was sweating from head to toe, so the cool night breeze was welcome as it washed over her. She breathed it in as if she could never get enough to wash out the stench of that accursed place.

"Are you okay?" Duelmaster asked.

Paige winced, but nodded. "What now?" she asked.

"We need to put miles between us and that city," Broadside muttered.

She heard a horse trotting from in front of them, and soon Jesnake and Dinendale were back by the wagon's side.

"Paige," Dinendale said as he jumped into the cart. "Are you alright?"

"I just asked that. You're such a copycat," Duelmaster pouted.

Dinendale ignored him, looking into Paige's eyes with worry carved in every feature on his face.

"I'm fine. How is your arm?"

"It will mend," he said, shrugging it off. "To be honest, my throat is what hurts most."

Paige looked up at the elf's sturdy neck and saw a raw, red patch right under Dinendale's jaw. It was a large blister with a squiggle shape branded beneath it. The brand reminded her of coils of rope or maybe a snake.

"Come on," Jesnake said, clicking his weary horse on. "The others will have made it to the rendezvous point by now."

"Aye!" Duelmaster called out, clicking his tongue and coaxing the horses. "Oh, I know girls. Daddy is asking a lot of you tonight. But if you can get me a little way farther, I'll let you free to run where you please for the rest of your lives."

"Will the mounted soldiers pursue us?" Paige asked.

Broadside laughed. "I imagine they will once they can catch their horses."

The jolt of the wagon tossed Paige against Dinendale, and he caught her in his arms. Paige didn't pull away, and he didn't let go. She looked into his deep brown eyes and let a hint of a smile tug at her lips. He smiled back, and she wearily rested her head against his chest. She let out a tired sigh.

"Din?"

He looked down at her, holding her softly in his embrace. Her heart fluttered for a moment.

"Yes, princess?" he asked.

She inhaled then said, "Thank you."

He smiled at her, his smooth, white teeth gleaming in the faint light. It felt good to see him smile again. It made her suddenly have a harder time breathing. Though she wanted to blame that on her ribs, she thought it might be some other reason.

"No trouble at all," Broadside grunted in the moonlight, but Paige didn't care. Right now, she felt a feeling she hadn't felt in months.

She felt safe.

Paige's eyes ached as they fluttered open in the early morning light. She thought she was still asleep and dreaming, but the pain when she moved told her she wasn't. Dreams didn't have real pain. She found herself inside a small tent made out of blankets, the pinkish grey light from outside streaming in through the greyish material.

The princess was wrapped in an identical blanket to the ones constructing the tent. She vaguely remembered having Woodcarver ease her wounds at some point after the jarring ride finally came to an end. She checked her side. It didn't hurt nearly as much as before, and she could feel the soft leaves of some healing plant under the bandage.

The full weight of what they had accomplished hit her and she staggered to her feet in earnest. Stumbling out of the tent and into the misty dawn, she clutched her blanket around her as her lungs sucked in clear, frosty air.

The Brotherhood were camped in a small meadow nestled between two large mountain peaks. They were still in a gloomy, misty area of the range, but they had made it far enough away from Aschin that the grass was vaguely green even well into the cold season. Paige wasn't sure how long they had continued on, but it had been well into the pre-dawn light before they had stopped.

"Princess," Woodcarver called out, breaking away from the fire where the Brotherhood sat in a huddle. "How are you feeling?"

"Where is she?" Paige demanded, ignoring Woodcarver's question and craning her neck around his tall frame to look past him. He smiled at her and gestured to the left where a small shelter had been constructed out of thick evergreen boughs.

She walked over to the shelter, the tall wizard guiding her by the arm like a gentle grandfather. Woodcarver motioned for her to enter as they reached the door, so she stooped low under the small opening.

Olivian lay on a pile of gear and blankets that kept her off the cold, wet, ground. Her thin frame looked as if it might disintegrate at Paige's lightest touch. The princess's hollow cheekbones stood out on her thin face, casting dark shadows under her once vibrant eyes.

Paige noticed that under her sister's fluttering eyelid, her left eye was now an opaque, milky white with a spiderweb of scar tissue that made her left side look like it was glaring. Her skin glowed a ghastly white, but her hair had been gently washed and combed as rudely as one could comb another's hair. She was wrapped in what appeared to be Jesnake's cloak since her own garments had been shredded to ribbons in the prison.

"Ala?" the older sister said feebly, weakly raising her head a bit to see. Paige gulped, emotion clogging her throat. "Is... is that you?"

"I'm here, Liv," she managed to say, her voice choking back tears.

"Am I?" Olivian asked. "Or am I just dreaming?"

"It's real," Paige assured her with a smile. "You're safe."

"Oh," Olivian's eyes fluttered closed again.

Paige knelt down next to her sister and picked up Olivian's hand. Warm tears that could no longer be dammed, trailed down her cheeks and cascaded to her hands. It was all Paige could do not to throw her arms around her sister and crush her in a huge hug. Olivian's body was icy cold and thin, but Paige prayed a hard, earnest prayer to the Creator thanking him that it had a pulse.

They sat there for a long time, not speaking.

After a while, Paige finally whispered, "What happened to you?"

Olivian's eyes snapped open, looking angry and fearful at the same time.

"When they attacked," she breathed, "they took me and several others in the midst of the... massacre. A poor little girl tried to curtsey to me... so the Prince found out I was father's."

"So they made you a hostage?" Paige asked.

Olivian nodded. "He took us on a forced march to Aschin. He drove us hard, never resting. Many of our captured people died along that road. If the trail did not kill them, the Shauds would. A few of them purposely dropped just to end the suffering. I had to watch all this chained up in a cart like an animal."

"When we reached the city, the prince had what was left of our captured people sold off, except for me. I was put in that cell. For the first few days, I wasn't bad off. Then the prince began to interrogate me about father and you, things about leather scrolls, and keys, and things I had no understanding of in the slightest. When I couldn't tell him what he wanted to hear, he became... *so* angry."

"My living conditions became worse, and then he began torturing me with no mercy. He kept demanding where this scroll was. I tried to tell him I didn't know what he was talking about, so he began to torment me with even more intensity. After he gave me... this," she said, motioning to her scars and now blind eye, "he gave me only enough food and water to keep me alive. He said he'd heard about you from some soldiers and figured you'd come for me. Once he knew you were coming..." Olivian halted, shuddering.

"Liv?" Paige asked, her own voice trembling.

"He... he..." Olivian tried to get out, but she began sobbing uncontrollably.

Paige threw her arms around her sister, sobbing with her. "It's okay Liv," she cooed, stroking her sisters nearly white hair. "He's gone. He can't hurt us anymore."

"I know," Olivian choked. "I never thought I'd see you again. The men told me you were dead. They told me I would die in that prison."

"But you didn't," Paige said. "You are safe now."

"It's all thanks to you and those strangers out there," Olivian said, sucking in a deep breath.

"They are my best friends," Paige said. "They all are so sweet and respectful. I am beyond fortunate to have them on my side."

"Especially that elf," Olivian said smiling through the tears. "Last night I don't think he ever left your side."

"Oh," was all Paige could say feeling the tips of her pointed ears flushing with embarrassment.

"The large one, too," Olivian said. "The one with the robe and the spear."

"Robert?"

"He wouldn't shut up about you."

"They're both just... friends," Paige insisted, blushing. She didn't really want to think about any of that at the moment.

"Well, you've turned into quite the little social butterfly while I was away," Olivian chuckled, laying her head back and closing her eyes as she drew in a shaky breath.

"Get some rest," Paige insisted. Olivian sighed and Paige patted her hand comfortingly before exiting. When she walked out, she nearly ran into Dinendale. He looked at her quizzically, his brown eyes probing her.

"You okay?" he asked.

She nodded her head.

"Are you sure?" he asked, searching her face.

"Should I not be?"

"Well," he chuckled, "you're nervous."

"What makes you think-"

"Princess, those tapered ears of yours may be the elf in you," he smiled. "But when they turn pink like that, that's the human in you, and they are as red as a poppy flower right now."

Paige looked up at him. He was looking at her, his eyes soft. Her heartbeat quickened. She felt uncomfortably warm, yet it was still chilly enough to see her own breath coming out in short bursts. Was she coming down with a fever?

"Fine," she said, and then mentally slapped herself. Fine? What kind of response was that? She sounded like an idiot, and why was it so hard to breathe?

"Listen," he said, stepping closer. "I need to ask you something."

"Yes?" she said, suddenly completely breathless.

"You and I," he said, "are the only two that know about the key."

She felt her pulse slow a bit, the weird excitement drifting away as if on a light breeze.

"Oh," was all she said.

He looked around, then continued. "I think we should keep it that way," he said. "The less that know it's the key they are after, the better."

"Not even the others?" she asked.

The elf shook his head. "They can't know or else it's one more thing they'd have to lie about if captured, and I'd rather them not have to carry that burden."

"I still don't understand what is so important about it," she said, rubbing her forehead.

"Neither do I," he said. "But we need to find out."

"So much blood for a single piece of leather and a tiny trinket," she muttered. He looked like he was about to say something else, but Woodcarver walked up at that moment.

"How is she, really?" Paige asked the magician.

"She'll be okay," he said. "She just needs rest."

"She has a strong will," Dinendale said. "A hard head as well. Remind you of anyone, Woodcarver?"

Paige punched the elf. He laughed, rubbing his shoulder and trying to hide the wince.

"At any rate, Dinendale, I need to discuss something with you. Paige, tend after your sister, won't you? And be sure to take care of those ribs. I only have so much salve, you know."

"I can do that," Paige nodded, feeling her side through the baggy shirt she wore. It felt nice to not have to wear any armor.

"You needed to speak?" Dinendale asked the magician.

"Yes, lend me your ear for a moment?"

The two walked off and began talking in hushed tones, and Paige left them to their conversation. She sought out Broadside who was boiling up a couple wild onions and potatoes he'd scrounged around the stony earth for supper. They weren't very good, but she did eat a small amount just to keep her strength up.

"Well princess, now that we've rescued the damsel," Broadside laughed, taking a bite of the mashed mush. "What do you want to do now?"

"I honestly haven't given it much thought," Paige admitted. "First things first, Olivian needs to be strong enough to travel."

"Of course," the dwarf stuck his pudgy hand into the pot and ate a fistfull of the gruel. Paige felt her stomach roll but laughed at the ridiculous nature of the short creature she'd learned to accept as a friend.

"Well, whatever you decide, know I'm in. You do pick some of the dandiest adventures."

"I appreciate that, Broadside," Paige laughed, standing and excusing herself while he began to lick the little pot clean with his fat, purple tongue.

She sat next to Olivian all through that night, wiping a damp cloth across the head of her sister who slept peacefully. She hummed the elvish lullaby their mother had sung so many times in their childhood. She was so relieved to have her sister back, and to have the boys to call family now. This meant, for the first time since that dreadful night so many weeks ago, she finally had a place where she belonged. She thought about what Broadside had said, mulling over several scenarios in her head as what she should do once Olivian was well. Would they stay with the Brotherhood? What did the fellows want to do next? They couldn't very well go back to Kapernaum. What was the next move?

"How is she?" Dinendale stooped to enter the shelter.

"Better," Paige shook herself from her thoughts. "She just needs some time."

"I see," he said.

Paige looked at the elf. He seemed a little more tense than normal. He was pressing a cloth into the burn mark on his throat. "How are you?" she asked.

"Fine," he said quickly. "Why do you ask?"

"You're uptight," she said.

He eased up a bit. "Hardly, it's just this burn is giving me grief. It's in an unfortunate location," he said, trying to wave it off, but Paige could hear the lie in his tone.

"I know you better than that, Din," she said.

"Maybe," he forced a smile. There was a moment of silence between them before he spoke again. "I just wanted to thank you," he said.

She looked at him quizzically. "For what?"

"I was hurting," he said. "I was a hateful creature a few months ago, so full of bitterness. Then you came along. You've done us all so much good, Paige. We had forgotten how to believe in ourselves till you came into our world. Into my world."

"I did nothing except supply a tragedy," she drug the cool cloth across Olivian's forehead again.

The elf shook his head, his black hair dancing. "No. It was so much more than that."

"Well, then you're welcome, I guess," she said quietly.

Dinendale smiled. "I just wanted to say that in case I never got the chance to later," he said. He sad down beside her, the warmth of his body a welcome reprieve from the chilly air. Paige felt something like a moth fluttering inside her chest. She sighed distractedly as Dinendale took an extra blanket and unfolded it in his lap, spreading it out and offering half to Paige.

"You don't have to stay up with me, you know?" Paige said, her voice uncharacteristically breathless.

"I know," Dinendale said. His face wore a distracted, almost distressed gaze. "I want to."

Paige felt her ears getting warm. Her heartbeat hammered in her ears as she reached out and took the elf's hand. It was rough and calloused, with strong fingers and bony knuckles scraped and bruised from fighting. The elf flinched slightly, but relaxed and let his fingers intertwine with hers.

"I, too, have to thank you," she said softly. "Without you, I'd be dead. And so would she."

Paige took her free hand and applied another warm cloth to Olivian's forhead. Dinendale squeezed her hand and a slow, low warmth spread from the back of her heart and across her chest.

"I need you to remember something, alright?" The elf said, taking his free hand and turning Paige's chin to face him. She gulped unconsciously and felt the inside of her mouth go dry.

"What?"

"No matter where you are, no matter how many miles lie between us, I will always be here for you when you need me. I will have your back when you stand your ground, and I will protect you with my life when you can't stand any longer. You...you are my best friend, Paige Alwasu of Alataria. And I need you to remember that."

This time it was her turn to squeeze his hand. Unsure what to do next, she cautiously leaned her weary head against his chest. He was warm and solid, just as he'd always been. The elf buried his nose in her hair and inhaled softly. Paige felt like her skin was absolutely glowing.

"And one more thing?" he whispered.

"Mhm?"

"You could use a bath."

"Well, you are no batch of roses yourself, mister," she chuckled.

He snickered. Paige could feel his chest vibrating under his coarse shirt.

"Fair point," he replied.

Paige smiled, feeling her eyes grow heavy. She yawned quietly as Dinendale grazed his thumb over her knuckles.

"I'll watch Olivian, if you need to get some rest."

"I don't need long," Paige yawned again. "Maybe just a few minutes?"

"Go for it," the elf whispered. Paige smiled again and nuzzled her head into Dinendale's chest as she pulled the blanket further up her body and made herself more comfortable. It wasn't long till she drifted off to sleep to the even rising and falling of the dark elf's chest.

"Dinendale!"

The shout startled Paige out of her sleep. She looked about bewildered, alone under a blanket beside her sister's bed. Olivian moaned and sat up weakly.

The makeshift blanket door to the lean-to was thrown back to reveal blinding sunlight. Paige blinked as Broadside jumped inside.

"Is Dinendale here?" he asked, out of breath.

"He... he was in here when I fell asleep last night," Paige said, puzzled.

"He's gone!" the dwarf said.

Paige rolled her eyes.

"He's probably out hunting," she said. "Probably didn't want mushy potatoes and bitter onions for breakfast."

"With his blankets, gear, and the red colt we took from the castle?" Jesnake asked, stepping in behind the dwarf. Paige got to her feet.

"You're kidding. He wouldn't just up and leave." A nervous laugh escaped her lips. The eyes of the elf and dwarf held no mirth. They were deadly serious, Broadside wringing his hands like a worried mother. All three of them exited the lean-to together in a bustle.

"He's gone," Robert said, walking up to them, a scowl on his face. "I'm not finding any tracks either."

"That doesn't make any sense," Paige said. "He wouldn't just go without telling anyone."

"Actually, that's exactly something he would do," Jesnake muttered.

"Someone has to know where he went!" Broadside said. "We need to find him."

"Someone does," the western elf said.

"Who?" Paige demanded. Duelmaster and Twostaves walked up.

"Woodcarver," Duelmaster finished for Jesnake. "He's gone, too."

"We need to find them," Broadside insisted. The poor fellow was wracked with grief.

"Maybe he doesn't want us to find him," Robert said. "No trail means he didn't want to be followed."

"But why?" Paige demanded in shock. He'd just left. He hadn't even said goodbye.

"Who knows?" Twostaves asked. "But I know he wouldn't just leave us for no reason."

"He has to be here somewhere," Broadside said. "He has to be!"

"Well, he's not!" Robert snapped. The force of the yelling sent Broadside back a few feet in surprise. Robert clenched his jaw, and looked away, focusing on a far-off peak to cool himself down.

"Paige," Robert said evenly. "Where is the page?"

"It's in my moccasin," she said confused.

"Is it?"

Paige felt a sinking feeling in her soul as she ripped off the moccasin and drew her knife, her fingers fumbling numbly as her hands shook with emotion. She angrily cut the leather Woodcarver had sewn into her footwear away from the moccasin and held it up.

It was blank. Woodcarver had never sewn the actual page into her moccasin.

"What?" Paige shouted. "What is this?"

"Either Woodcarver has betrayed us, or they left together. Either way they have the page from the Book of Death. Doubtless, if they are together and not one hunting the other, they are off to try and unlock its secrets," Duelmaster muttered.

"But where? How? And why not tell us?" Paige demanded, her mind scrambling for a rational explanation.

"Well, isn't it obvious? I don't think we're supposed to know, seeing as he's abandoned us," Robert spat.

"No. He... no!" Paige shouted. With that, she took off, running into the tree line near the creek. She felt angry, hurt, and scared. He'd just left. No explanations; no goodbyes. She stood by the creek, her fists in tight balls at her sides, her knuckles white and popping with the grip. She sank to her knees, looking into her reflection in the bubbling brook. She sat like that for a long while, her head was spinning so fast she didn't even hear the soft footsteps behind her.

"A rose for the lady?" Duelmaster pulled a flower from the bank. Paige shook her head angrily. The dryad sighed, playing with the little flower.

"He didn't leave just to leave, ya know?" he offered.

"Doesn't change the fact that he just... just... ugh." Paige punched her reflection in the stream. She felt the sting on one of her knuckles as the blow skinned the boney nubs on her fist. Duelmaster was quiet for a moment before chuckling.

"He'll come back."

"You don't know that," she said, not looking at him.

"Yes, I do," the Dryad said.

"How?"

"Because," the dryad said, smiling, "you're here."

"Didn't stop him from leaving though," Paige said.

"Sure, but that doesn't mean he didn't fall under your spell."

"You're delusional."

"Most of the time, yes," Duelmaster smiled. "But I think I know him well enough to say without a doubt that he cares for you."

"Then why did he just... leave?" she demanded.

The dryad shrugged. "Who knows? But I promise you what I do know is he'll be back. Just wait and see. If there's one thing you can count on, it's that Dinendale will always come back."

Paige felt slightly reassured even in her anger, but she stood up wiping her hands on her shirt. Duelmaster smiled, and Paige wrapped her arms around him in a tight hug. The dryad didn't even seem surprised as he squeezed her right back.

"Ow!"

"Oh, sorry m'lady," the dryad said, breaking off a tiny branch that had poked her in the head from his beard. "I haven't had a chance to shave yet."

"Well, aside from that, now what?" she asked, releasing him from the hug and jerking her chin towards the camp. "We can't stay here for long."

"Winter is coming," Duelmaster agreed. "We'll need to find a place to lay low for the season."

"Then what after that?"

"Well, I'm not quite sure, my lady," Duelmaster said, a twinkle in his eye. "We kind of always play it by ear. But you know? I think that's the adventure of it all. I hear there may be a few other places that need emancipating now that I think about it!"

He held out his arm like a princely escort, and Paige smiled, taking it.

"Shall we, princess?"

Paige nodded. And with that, arm in arm, the two returned to camp, ready to face their next grand adventure.

For there is always another one right around the next corner, if you know where to look.

THE END...

Acknowledgments

Thank you to all the members of my Brotherhood, for all the memories and heartache, good times and bad, I'd trade every page of this book for one more day like the ones we had.

To my Alpha and Betas, for all your feedback and encouragement:
Paul and Shanna-Kaye Fancher - Drake Pledger
Marissa Grammoll - Karin Salisbury - Author Kim Gibson
Author Christy Miller

Thank you to all the Kickstarter backers without whom this project never would have taken off:
Alayna Dudock - Amanda Belcher - Amy Bardwell - Amy Daniels - Anthony Hamilton - Bill Nimchuk - Brian D Lambert - Brian James Sipe - Caleb Tolbert - Cameron Piner - Charles Davis - Cody - Corrine S Garrison - Deanna Young - Debra Thomas - Derek - Dylan Edward Culver - Emerson Kasak - Esa Eriksson - Fallon Leigh Smith - Fermin Serena Hortas - Fiona - Gerald P. McDaniel - Ginny Jordan - Hannah Heppenstall - Holly Graf - Ian - Isaac Kennedy - James H. Murphy Jr. - Jen - Jennifer Nicklyn - Jennifer Priester - Jennifer Pyle - Jessica Sindeldecker - Jhannah de Castro - Joel Raulerson - Jonette Carlson - Jordan Lewis - Joshua C. Chadd - Joshua Gramoll - Joshua Tolbert - Josiah Teel - Kate C. - Kenneth Ost - Knights of the Pen Productions - LAURENCON - Liz Steinworth - Lloyd T-Taylor - Madison West - Marie - Marie Schatzman - Mary Therese Ward - Marye Dedmon - Matrix Melinda Dixon - Melinda Stanley - Mikel Carr - Mirranda Prowell - Nash-Cytex - Nathan Lee - Nelots - Nicholas - Olivia - Orlando C. Jaime - Pat H - Pyxis Gate Library - Rebecca Blackwelder - Rob Henschen - Rob Speer - Ryan Shutt - SF Gavin - Shayla Jordan - Shelly Leonard - Skywings14 - Stef Joseph-Kruyswijk - Steven Fadule - Sue Tolbert - Terra Danielle - The Creative Fund - Thomas Pape - Tiona Wade - Yousef

And All Our Anonymous Kickstarter Donors

Guest 104774134 - Guest 1218906450 - Guest 1320847658 - Guest 1327640176 - Guest 1399908007 - Guest 1430961563 - Guest 1541038289 - Guest 2043842909 - Guest 254097540 - Guest 263058489 - Guest 301286079 - Guest 393969326 - Guest 430487372 - Guest 469162557 - Guest 630819149 - Guest 649954216 - Guest 652671415 - Guest 69580432 - Guest 699407399 - Guest 942794827 - Guest 972126988

About the Author

Philip Smith was born in Fairfax County, Virigina. From a young age he enjoyed drawing and writing stories. When he turned fifteen, he grabbed a piece of copy paper, folded it in half, and wrote the first words of what would become the book you just finished reading. He continued to work on it for over twelve years and finally published it in early 2019.

Philip lives in the hollers of Kentucky, writing his next adventure as he continues to build his homestead.

Meanwhile, in the Heart of the Ohlmar Mountains...

"Are you sure you don't want to ride for a bit?" Dinendale asked the magician.

Woodcarver shook his head, his long stride keeping up easily with the young rust-colored horse.

Dinendale shrugged.

"I want to enjoy my legs while I still have the ability to walk," Woodcarver smirked, his staff crunching in the rocky earth of the mountain they were skirting around as they headed south. Dinendale looked up at the bleak sky. Only another month and these dreary mountains would be covered in a thick blanket of snow. He thought back to his friends in the valley, wondering if he had made the right choice.

"Son of Aedard, you are doing the right thing," the magician said, not even having to look at the elf to know the conflict that raged within him.

"Couldn't we have at least told them? Told Paige?"

"You know we couldn't."

Dinendale scowled. He knew the magician was right, but it did not lessen the ache in his heart at having to leave so quickly and not have the chance to say goodbye, or to explain.

Dinendale touched the still tender burn mark on his throat. It lay right atop the jugular vein, a vein Dinendale knew all too well from his years hunting and fighting.

"And you're sure we can't just cut it out?"

"Not unless you want to bleed to death."

"I still don't understand how it could work. I have the Aondraíoch curse. It's supposed to keep magic from being able to affect me, isn't it?"

"It is, but a Branding Spell doesn't work like that. Aondraíoch Curses only work by blocking magic from directly affecting your body. So you cannot have your life-force leached from you through magic, which is also why healing spells won't affect you. But someone could still use magic to throw you against a wall, or as in your case, brand you so they can find you if they have the object that marked you."

"And none of this was worth sharing earlier?"

"You're the one who had the curse put on you. I figured you'd know it's limitations before making such a rash decision."

Dinendale glared at the magician but kept his mouth shut. He didn't think a person of Woodcarver's power to have the perspective on magic that Dinendale did. But he knew the man was right; he should have paid more attention before he'd had the curse put on him all those years ago.

"But what's done is done," Woodcarver said. "And the sooner we get to Karadúr, the sooner we can try and find a solution."

"You really think the dwarves will be able to help?"

"I don't know. But we have to try. They may not have many Mages left. But the ones they do have are very powerful, and they may be the only ones capable of concealing both of us from the Shahir."

Dinendale glared at Woodcarver.

"Don't think I've forgiven you for failing to tell me about that part of your plan."

Woodcarver pulled Paige's leather scroll out from his cloak and pointed it in the air for emphasis.

"My deception was necessary, and if you understood half of the importance of this page or the sacrifice spilt to retrieve it, you wouldn't judge me so harshly, elf."

"No deception was necessary. All those men were never anything shy of honest with you. And Paige? She trusted you."

"I do not need a lecture from you, Dinendale. There are more things at stake here than anyone's opinion of my moral character."

"It's not about an opinion. It's about honor," snapped the dark elf. The magician whirled around to face Dinendale and thrust his palm outwards.

"*Thryvyne!*"

Dinendale felt himself punched by an invisible force and felt his body thrown from the saddle and dropped violently to the ground. He scrambled up and drew his sword, but the magician shouted another ancient word and Dinendale felt his hand sear as the iron became too hot to hold. He dropped it with a shout, but before he could rush the man, Woodcarver thrust his hand out, and Dinendale felt his body picked up into the air and slammed into the trunk of a large beech tree. The magician held him there, the elf's arms trapped at his side under coils of invisible rope.

"Now as long as you're just hanging up there, pay attention," Woodcarver snapped. "Honor has nothing to do with this. This is about keeping them safe and keeping this out of the hands of a deranged madman. He will stop at nothing to get this back, and he will kill anyone who stands in his way. The Shahir is obsessed, and he will not quit so long as life is in his body. He will hunt you like an animal as he has hunted me like an animal. Trust me, that is not where you want to be, and it sure as the moons isn't the kind of danger you want to put Paige in. Or am I wrong?"

The magician was shouting by now, his clear eyes flashing. He released Dinendale who fell the the ground with a thud. The elf moaned as his still battered body received the concussive force with a less than stellar landing. The magician crouched down next to him and looked Din square in the eye.

"I know, Dinendale. I know because he killed my Alwasu forty-two years ago."

"What?"

"Aye," Woodcarver said, his tone now a mere somber whisper as he grabbed the elf firmly by the shoulders and pulled him to his feet. "And that is why we must protect them. Once the Shahir sees what Prince Feridar saw in his last moments, he will not hesitate to use her against you and vise versa. She has enough of a burden to bear as it stands."

"What burden? Is she still in danger?"

"Because of who she is she will always be in danger," Woodcarver said, pulling Din up to his feet. "And so it is our job to make sure we do everything we can to keep him away from her."

Dinendale was quiet for a moment before he shook himself free of the magician's grasp and brushed the dirt off his cloak and sleeves.

"Fine. But we'll come back as soon as it is safe?"

"Well, we're not going to abandon family," Woodcarver assured. "But first we have to get your new... condition addressed."

Dinendale mounted the horse one again.

"Fine. Let's hope your plan works."

"I'd trust these doctors and mages with my life," Woodcarver assured him. "And if there's one thing I can say for certain about dwarves, they are problem solvers."

Dinendale will return

in

The Crypt

Book Two in The Eirensgarth Saga

www.ingramcontent.com/pod-product-compliance
Lightning Source LLC
Chambersburg PA
CBHW030838030726
47495CB00005B/1274